I CURSE YOU. . . .

Pointing a shaking finger, Grizelle screamed, "I curse you, Mairi of Shiels and Traquair, and all the daughters of your line. For your treachery the Maxwell women will never rest. Cursed to pay for your deed, their sleep will be haunted by the dead until they die of foul and tragic means. Only when Scotland's Stone of Destiny is found will the curse be lifted."

" 'Tis your own flesh and blood you condemn," cried Mairi.

An angry murmuring swelled through the crowd.

Robert the Bruce held up his hand. There was silence. "Bring out the stones," he ordered, confident Mairi would confess once she saw the instrument of her death.

"No," gasped David. "I won't allow it."

"Restrain him," ordered the Bruce.

Two soldiers stepped forward and gripped David's arms. His face haunted, he began to struggle. "Robert, I beg of you. Do not do this," he shouted, twisting against the arms that held him like bands of steel. "Please." Panic caused his voice to crack. "Spare my wife."

Mairi was pale as a ghost but her back was straight, and her eyes, gray and icy as a mountain tarn, stared at the man who would be king.

"Your end is near, Mairi," Robert said. "Speak now or stand before your God with a lie on your lips."

The flashing scorn in her eyes withered him. He could scarcely form the words. "Kill her. . . ."

The Family Lines

MAIRI MAXWELL OF SHIELS (1271–1298)

Parents: Patrick Maxwell and Jane Sutherland. Married David Murray in 1296. Gave birth to his son, James, 1297. In 1293 gave birth to a daughter, Margaret Plantagenet, by Edward I of England.

DAVID MURRAY (1267–1314)

Parents: Murdoch and Grizelle Murray. Married Mairi Maxwell in 1296. Had one son, James, 1297.

JEANNE MAXWELL (1488–1513)

Parents: Donald Maxwell and Flora MacDonald. Married John Maxwell in 1509. Gave birth to twins, Andrew and Isobel, 1510.

JOHN MAXWELL (1482–1513)

Parents: Andrew Maxwell (mother unknown). Married Jeanne Maxwell in 1509. Had two children, twins, Andrew and Isobel, 1509.

KATRINE MURRAY (1726–1746)

Parents: George Murray and Janet Douglas. Married Richard Wolfe in 1745. Gave birth to Alasdair, 1746.

RICHARD WOLFE (1715–1765)

Parents: Susan Maxwell and Alasdair Wolfe. Married Katrine Murray in 1745. Had one child, Alasdair, born 1746.

CHRISTINA MURRAY (1956–   )

Parents: Donald Murray and Susan Maxwell.

IAN DOUGLAS (1958–   )

Parents: Evan Douglas and Kerry Maxwell.

JEANETTE BAKER

LEGACY

POCKET BOOKS
New York   London   Toronto   Sydney   Tokyo   Singapore

This book is a work of fiction. Names, characters, places and incidents are products of the author's imagination or are used fictitiously. Any resemblance to actual events or locales or persons, living or dead, is entirely coincidental.

An *Original* Publication of POCKET BOOKS

POCKET BOOKS, a division of Simon & Schuster Inc.
1230 Avenue of the Americas, New York, NY 10020

ISBN: 0-671-53674-5

First Pocket Books printing September 1996

10 9 8 7 6 5 4 3 2 1

POCKET and colophon are registered trademarks of Simon & Schuster Inc.

Cover art by Mitzura Salgian

Printed in the U.S.A.

This book is dedicated
to the memory of my father,
a very special man and a gifted storyteller,
who taught me to understand the power
of the written word.

ACKNOWLEDGMENTS

It is with heartfelt appreciation that I thank Patricia Perry and Jean Stewart for their unfaltering faith, their insightful suggestions and, most of all, their friendship and love. Without them, this book would never have gone beyond a character and an idea.

I would also like to thank my editor, Kate Collins, who from the beginning recognized the potential in this story and worked to make it even stronger. Her encouragement continues to inspire me.

AUTHOR'S NOTE

Traquair House does exist and is still inhabited by the Maxwell Stuarts. The geographic location of the house, the descriptions and significance of the rooms are all historically accurate. Mairi of Shiels and her descendents are pure fabrication.

For story purposes, I have condensed Scottish history and changed the ages of several of the characters. Edward Longshank, Hammer of the Scots, was born in 1239. He would have been fifty-nine years old at the time this story begins. I chose to make him closer to Mairi's age. Eleanor of Castile was twelve years old when she left Spain to become Queen of England. The marriage remained unconsummated for several years. Eleanor bore Edward four sons, three of whom died in infancy.

In Scotland, there is a legend, maintained by more than a few, that the stone which currently sits under the Coronation Chair at Westminster Abbey is a fraud. Loyal Scots believe that while Edward was en route to Moot Hill to claim the real stone, monks learned of his coming and replaced the stone with another.

❦ PROLOGUE ❦

Moot Hill, Scotland
1298

"Hurry." Mairi's voice broke the hush of moonless darkness. "We must be back at Traquair before morning."

In silence the two men hoisted the large irregular stone into the cart and tied it down with rope. Then they settled the other, nearly identical stone in its place on Moot Hill.

Mairi could barely make out the burly, black-clothed figures through the dense fog. When at last she saw one of the men jump into the cart and take up the reins, she breathed a sigh of relief. It was nearly done.

"'Tis finished." The voice at her elbow startled her. She turned to her loyal retainer. A look of worry marred Peter's usually cheerful expression and not without cause.

He would return to Scone Castle at dawn when crofts and villages stirred with the first light of a new day. Wearing the livery of the Maxwells, he would lift the counterfeit stone from its resting place, put it on a cart, and, in full view of curious eyes, carry it through Dollar and Stirling, past Edinburgh and Linlithgow, across the moors and through the borders until he reached the gates of Traquair House. He would answer questions along the way. No one would doubt that Scotland's Stone of Destiny had been taken to the stronghold of the Maxwells.

With a smile that lit her entire face, Mairi raised her hand in farewell.

"Take care, m'lady," Peter warned. "Keep to the woods. There are brigands on the roads."

Her journey back to Traquair was made without incident. It took three men to drag the stone up the narrow stairs and

1

then down the long, twisting tunnel into the burial crypt. When they were finished sealing the door, Mairi handed each of them a pouch containing five gold coins. "Godspeed," she whispered in a choked voice. "Perhaps, if the Bruce is victorious, we shall meet again."

The men looked at one another and shifted uncomfortably. "Dinna' fash yoursel', m'lady," the oldest spoke gruffly. "There is no' for us here. Wales is no' such a bad place." He grinned. "The gold will help."

Mairi nodded and stepped aside. "Godspeed and stay out of sight."

Night had already fallen by the time Peter reached Traquair House. Again it took three men to carry the boulder through the entry into the small hall. Mairi covered it with a cloth and left the room, locking the door behind her.

She held out her hand to her henchman. "I am in your debt, Peter. You have served me well. How can I ever thank you?"

"Bless you, m'lady. What you do is for Scotland. 'Tis I who should thank you."

She pressed a pouch of gold coins into his hand. "Make haste. Send word when you reach Wales."

He nodded and would have said more, but the tight look of pain on her face stopped him. "Farewell, lass," he said softly. "May we meet again in heaven."

Peter had served the Maxwells for as long as she could remember. She turned away, unable to watch him walk through the hall and out the door. All that was left was to wait for Edward.

He would come. She knew it as surely as she knew the familiar sound of her child's cry. After five long years, she would once again look upon his face. Only this time it would be different. It would not be her lover's face that she saw. It would be the face of Scotland's enemy, her enemy. There would be no tenderness in his expression, his mouth would not curve with laughter, and his eyes, those incredible eyes that could glow with warmth and passion, would be the cold, ice-flecked blue of the North Sea.

Mairi shivered. She was afraid. He had threatened to kill her if she married David. There was no one to prevent him from doing so. Her husband was an outlaw, hiding in the Highlands with Robert the Bruce.

Edward had bided his time and waited for such a moment, waited for David to choose sides, knowing as surely as a hawk knows the lee of the wind that he could have chosen no other way. Even were David here at Traquair, there was nothing he could do. Once Edward issued a command, it was executed.

The royal herald had come two days before to the very gates of Traquair House, proclaiming that the king would ride into Scotland with an army of men to take up Scotland's Coronation Stone, the Stone of Destiny, and bear it into England as a reminder that Edward Plantagenet was king of all Britain.

It was not the words themselves that drove a wedge of ice into Mairi's heart, but the handwritten message that followed, sealed with the royal crest and written in the bold, flowing script she remembered so well. *"Lest you believe I have forgotten, know that I have not. We will meet again Mairi Maxwell of Shiels."*

She did not really believe he would kill her. He was not a man to vent his wrath on women and children. No, Edward would not harm her by taking her life. He would take his vengeance in another way, a way so purposeful, so calculating, so impossible to withstand, that her immortal soul would be forever jeopardized. And then, to assure that David would not avenge his wife's honor, he would take her child.

David Murray's son would be a powerful hostage in Edward's fight against Robert the Bruce. Mairi prepared herself for the greatest deception of her life, knowing that the man she would face was a master of the art.

For days she waited, her nerves frayed and stretched to the breaking point. At meals she forced food past her unwilling lips, knowing that without sustenance the weakness she carried with her from childhood would prevent her from feeding her son. At night she lay in her bed, staring at the ceiling until her exhausted body, crying out for rest, wiped all conscious thought from her mind. She was up before dawn, listening for the sound of armored horsemen at the Bear Gates.

They came at nightfall. Mairi was in the nursery, watching the rise and fall of her son's small chest as he settled into sleep. His eyes were closed, and she smiled in appreciation at the long black lashes and wispy new hair growing in above his forehead. He was David's son, but no one with eyes could deny his Maxwell strain. Mairi smoothed the soft down on his head. The heir she had borne David Murray was extraordinary. That, at least, she had given him. If only for this child and nothing else, her blood would be well spent.

The boy was beautiful in the flame-lit wild way of his mother's people. Black lashes rested like half-moons against his cheeks, and beneath his shuttered lids were eyes the same startling gray as Mairi's own. They were Maxwell eyes inherited from his Celtic ancestors. Dark skinned and fine boned, that mysterious, warlike race had long ago marched into the mists of time, leaving their legacy in every man, woman, and child in Britain. Some, like Mairi, had the high cheekbones, square jaws, and sharply chiseled features. Others had small frames and pale olive skin. But they all shared the eyes, those eyes that smiled back at her from the face of her babe.

Mairi smoothed his blanket with a trembling hand. Dear God, how could she do it? How could she not? For the babe and for Scotland, she must go through with it. She must battle a legend using only words. God help her if she failed.

❈ 1 ❈

Innerleithen, Scotland
1993

I had never heard of Traquair House until the spring of my thirty-eighth year. Looking back with the clarity hindsight so often brings, I now realize my oversight had more to do with fate than timing. For an ordinary tourist, the lapse wouldn't have been unusual. But I was Christina Murray. By no stretch of the imagination could I be considered an ordinary tourist.

For nearly eight hundred years the hills surrounding the Innerleithen Valley have shielded Traquair House from the world. Fifty minutes from Edinburgh, off Highway 709, between Selkirk and Peebles, the turn is easy to miss. Most travelers, intent on reaching the sites of the capital, pass by the poorly marked detour with barely a second glance. For me, there is no such excuse. For me, to have missed Traquair House borders on the absurd.

For fifteen years Gaelic antiquity has consumed my life. Even now, in moments of depression, when I seriously entertain the notion of giving it all up and opening a gourmet coffeehouse or a used bookstore, I have only to close my eyes and relive that first semester at the University of Edinburgh.

I was nineteen years old, a student in the foreign exchange program on my way to visit Holyrood House, when I stopped in at the museum on the Royal Mile. It was such a small out-of-the-way place, I didn't expect to find anything important. But Scotland, I was to learn, is filled with surprises.

Reverently I ran my hands over the protective glass containing the Scots' Covenant where the bold scrolling signatures of Montrose and Argyll leaped out at me from the aging parchment. A sword from Philiphaugh stood propped against the wall, and a well-leafed prayerbook said to have been used by John Knox sat forgotten on a corner bookshelf.

Farther down the street, in the graveyard of Saint Giles Cathedral, I traced fifteenth-century death masks with trembling fingers and watched angry clouds gather above my head. For the first time I knew what it was to taste rain on the wind, to see the Grampians, gateway to the Highlands, and, in the distance, the clear light-struck waters of the Firth of Forth pooling silver blue into Leith Harbor. My eyes burned from holding back tears. The cobblestoned streets of Edinburgh welcomed me as if I had come home for the first time after a long and empty journey.

That was the beginning. After that first trip, I returned to Scotland once a year. My knowledge of British landmarks became second to none. I learned to navigate every twisting country road between Stonehenge and Dunnet Mead better than I could the streets where I was born, and my driving time from Heathrow to Edinburgh, at night without street-lights, was clocked at just under six hours.

Now, after twelve years of teaching at Boston College and five more of coursework, I was ready to begin my dissertation. My academic reputation was at its peak and my personal life just beginning to rebound from its downward spiral when Ellen Maxwell's letter arrived. The incredible realization that, in all my years of research, I'd never even heard of Scotland's oldest manor house made her invitation appealing. Someone like myself did not just overlook an eight-hundred-year-old manor house.

From the moment I climbed the gravel path to the top of the hill and looked down on Traquair House, it became my obsession. If any of it had happened differently, if the plane ticket from Ellen Maxwell's solicitor had come at another time, if Stephen and I hadn't gone through with the divorce, if I'd taken the grant or answered the summer school advertisement, the whole confusing tangle of the Maxwell–Murrays and the Stone of Scone might have remained unsolved for all eternity.

My introduction to Traquair bordered on the macabre. After a brief word of welcome, a servant ushered me up the stairs to an enormous bedroom and then disappeared. It was my first and only meeting with Lady Ellen Maxwell.

She lay still as death, stretched out under the sheets of an enormous four-poster. I moved closer to the bed, prepared for the worst. It wouldn't be the first time I had seen a corpse. There is something about the absence of life that can't be mistaken. It's the fundamental missing piece, that mysterious primal core of the human condition that no scientific laboratory or skilled mortician can successfully reproduce. The nuns at Mount Holyoake would have labeled it a spirit or, better yet, a soul. *Life force* is the best I could come up with. Looking down into Ellen Maxwell's face, I knew she wasn't there yet.

Beside the bed, IVs attached to tubes led to her frail wrists. A pitcher with a glass straw sat on the nightstand near a bouquet of sage and purple heather. It had all the elements of a hospital room except for the smell. It didn't smell like a sickroom. This room smelled of pine and spice and the moors near Jedburgh. Who was Ellen Maxwell and why had she summoned me, so peremptorily, to her sickbed?

I frowned and felt the skin between my eyebrows fold into accordian pleats. Consciously, I relaxed, forcing the muscles back into smoothness. Lately, since the divorce, I'd become critical of my appearance. There was nothing more damaging to a woman approaching middle age than frown lines.

The sound of soft breathing reclaimed my attention. I stared down at her face. Despite her age, vestiges of beauty still showed in her features. Her skin was smooth and paper thin. The veins in her temples stood out like blue lines against a white road map. Her hands were immaculate and surprisingly youthful, with long, thin fingers and raised oval nails. Patrician hands.

Somehow I knew that those hands had never felt the sting of cleanser against an open cut. They had never wielded a broom, scoured a pot, scrubbed a floor, or pushed a vacuum. Looking down at that haughty, aristocratic face, I felt a flash of resentment and was instantly ashamed. The poor woman was bedridden and old, and despite the fact that she had money, no one, no matter how indigent, would willingly exchange places with her.

The nurse entered the room, smiled at me, and leaned over the bed. "Lady Maxwell," she said in the precise, clipped tone of London's Mayfair district, "Miss Murray is here all the way from America to see you. Don't be stubborn now. She's been traveling a long time."

Like birds' wings, Ellen Maxwell's eyelashes fluttered against her cheeks. With great effort, the lids lifted, and eyes, foggy from their drug-induced sleep, stared up at me. Several minutes passed as she struggled to focus.

"She'll be fine now," the nurse said. "You may speak to her if you like. Only her body is paralyzed. Her mind is sharp as a tack." She nodded and patted my shoulder before leaving the room.

Ellen's dark eyes, now lucid with intelligence, moved over my face, carefully analyzing each feature. It wasn't a comfortable sensation. Never before or since have I been so calculatingly scrutinized. Feeling somewhat self-conscious, I stared out the window, allowing the old woman to look her fill. I was about to speak when the atmosphere in the room changed. Something was wrong, terribly wrong. Perplexed, I looked down at the aged face and felt the smile freeze on my lips.

Ellen Maxwell was terrified. There could be no mistake. Her body was rigid, her hands curled into claws. Every muscle in her too-thin face was strained by a hideous contortion. Her forehead was knotted, her nostrils flared. Her lips were pulled back, exposing teeth clenched in a feral grimace. Violent tremors rocked her frame, and her breath came in harsh, laboring gasps. A wrenching moan escaped from deep within her chest, a sound so primitive and gutteral, so completely filled with despair, that it shattered what was left of my fragile control. I knew with terrifying certainty that Ellen Maxwell's agony had everything to do with me.

"What is it?" I managed to whisper, bending over the bed. "What's wrong?"

The anguished eyes fixed on my face pleaded for mercy. I backed away and then turned and ran to the door, throwing it open. "Help!" I shouted down the empty hallway. Where was the nurse? Why had she left us alone? The inevitable tears I had never been able to control welled up in my eyes and spilled down my cheeks. "Someone please help me," I begged.

Behind me, a door opened. The nurse's sturdy, white-clad figure crossed the threshold where I stood and walked quickly to the bed. She placed expert fingers on the sick woman's wrist and then against her throat. Frowning, she leaned her head against those lips still frozen in their snarling grimace. Finally she stood, shook her head, and pulled the sheet over Ellen Maxwell's head. "Poor dear," she said softly. "The strain was too much for her. We've been expecting this for quite a while. I'm sure the diagnosis will be heart attack."

"Do you mean she's dead?" My voice cracked. "Just like that?" Visions of Hollywood emergency room scenes and frenzied doctors shouting for digitalis, while heart monitors bleeped their reassuring vertical lines, signaling the victim's return to life, flashed through my mind.

"I'm afraid so, miss," the nurse said regretfully. "It was only a matter of time. She didn't want to be kept on with life support. It was her last wish that she meet you before she died."

"But why? I didn't even know her."

"I couldn't say. Perhaps your questions will be answered by her solicitor."

Desperate for fresh air, I found my way down the stairs, past a maze of rooms, to the front door. A soft Scot's brogue stopped me.

"Can I help you find anything, miss?"

My hands wouldn't stop shaking. I recognized the stone-faced maid who'd ushered me inside when I'd first arrived. I considered telling her about Lady Maxwell but decided against it. It certainly wasn't a stranger's place to break the news of an employer's death. "I needed some air and thought I'd take a walk," I answered instead.

"I don't blame you. The weather is lovely. Why don't you take the path toward the Bear Gates. It's a charming walk, and maybe you'll find a docent who can give you a tour."

"A docent?"

"Traquair House must make a living, Miss Murray.

There's a small restaurant and gift shop around the corner. In the summer, the company rooms are open all week for tourists." She looked at me strangely. "Have you never been to Scotland before, miss?"

"Many times," I replied. "I can't imagine how I could have missed Traquair House."

"Perhaps it was meant to be."

"What do you mean?"

"We Scots believe in *the sight*. Some things are best left to the hand of fate."

I almost smiled, then thought better of it. "If I meet anyone, who shall I say sent me?" I asked instead.

"Kate, miss."

"I'd be grateful if you would point me in the direction of the Bear Gates, Kate."

"Just walk the path, and you'll find them. Enjoy your day, Miss Murray."

I stared at her back as she walked away. For an instant, she'd reminded me of someone, but I couldn't recall who it was.

The late afternoon sun warmed my head and calmed my frayed nerves. Drawing a deep, cleansing breath, I walked up the hill to the end of the gravel path. From there I turned back to look at the house. Never, in all my travels through Scotland, had I seen anything quite like Traquair House. It was as if time had rolled back, and I, Christina Murray, an unwelcome stranger, had intruded on the ancient fief of Maxwell.

The grounds were steeped in a halo of welcoming light. Four stories high with a gabled roof and rounded towers, Traquair looked more like a large manor house than a fortress. I knew from reading the brochures Ellen had sent that the original structure dated back over eight hundred years when Alexander I signed a charter in the common room and that the modern wings weren't completed until 1680.

In times of peace, Traquair had been a pleasure ground for royalty, in war, a place of refuge for Catholic priests. The lairds of Traquair had remained loyal to Mary, Queen of Scots, and the Jacobite cause without counting their personal cost. Imprisoned, fined, and banished for their beliefs, their home still stood, a sentinel to a nobler, more gallant age.

Something moved on one side of the far tower. A workman climbed down the scaffolding and disappeared behind the house. So much for romanticizing. In spite of all my efforts to the contrary, practicality had its own insidious way of invading my fantasies. Living in a home over eight hundred years old had some disadvantages after all. Traquair's repair bills were probably stupendous.

It was obvious that the house had been well maintained. Stucco covered the original stone and mortar, but the dozens of rectangular, small-paned windows looked like the real thing. The grounds were exquisite with acres of manicured green lawns reaching past the gates to a forest of pine and black oak. A maze with shrubbery over twelve feet high grew in the back garden, and everywhere I looked squirrels and cotton-tailed rabbits stared at me from a healthy margin of safety.

Traquair House had been home to the Maxwells since the beginning of Scottish history. Once again I marveled at how I could have bypassed such a wonderful relic from the past. A simple diversion of ten miles on the way to Edinburgh would have brought me directly to the front gates.

My nose felt numb. Grateful for my wool pants and lined jacket, I slipped my hands into my pockets and increased my pace. Scotland was always cold. While the rest of the world celebrated the advent of summer, the first green shoots of spring were barely visible in glens north of the Firth of Forth. Even here in the borders where the temperature was ten degrees warmer, winds blew with the promise of snow and ice-covered lochs showed no inclination to thaw.

With my shoulders hunched and my head buried in the collar of my jacket, I would have walked right past the gates if Ian Douglas's voice hadn't stopped me.

Years later, I would recall the timing of that moment with pristine clarity. I would remember the crisp air and the leaden late-afternoon sky. I would smell the clean scent of pine, taste snow on the wind, and see stalks of gorse, golden and russet, growing wild beyond the tilled fields of Traquair. I would speculate on the odds of our meeting at all. What would have happened to the two of us if I'd explored the garden maze or the brewhouse instead of the gates? What if I'd taken a wrong turn or walked in the opposite direction?

I always shudder with grateful relief that none of those things happened. One small moment in time had determined my destiny. Or had it? Was it really such a coincidence or had fate woven its tapestry, capturing Ian and me with silken fingers, forever entwining our lives in the mystery of the stone?

"Hello, there." Firm hands gripped my shoulders. "At that pace you'll miss the gates altogether."

I blinked and then stared. Could this apparition possibly be real? He came from nowhere, a man legends are made of. He was dark from the sun, with dramatic bone structure, a high-bridged curving nose and piercing blue eyes. Thick, sun-streaked hair fell across his forehead. The look on his face was flattering. I'm not the kind of woman men follow with their eyes, or anything else for that matter. I'm attractive enough, I suppose, slim and tall with a talent for wearing whatever is currently in style. I've got thick hair and good bones and teeth, a blend, someone once said, between wholesome and elegant. But I'd been told more than once there's a reserve about me, an old-world standoffishness, that puts men off. It had certainly put one off, even after fifteen years of marriage. I swallowed the lump in my throat that thinking of Stephen never failed to bring up.

"That is what you came to see, isn't it, the Bear Gates?" He smiled and dropped his hands to his sides. Tiny lines around his eyes and mouth deepened.

I swallowed. "Yes, it is. I mean, they are." I laughed, flustered by an unfamiliar awkwardness. He laughed with me, amused by my obvious embarrassment. He was older than I first thought, somewhere in his midthirties, a man with a sense of humor, a man comfortable with himself and with women.

"I can't place your accent," he said. "You're not English?"

"American."

He looked thoughtfully at me. "You don't sound like an American."

"I'm from Boston. We speak a different sort of English in eastern Massachusetts."

"Perhaps that explains it." His eyes moved over my hair and face. "You don't look like an American and you certainly don't act like one either."

Startled, I said the first thing that popped into my mind. "That makes two of us."

The flicker of interest in his blue eyes increased. "How so?"

"You're not like any Scot I've ever met," I explained slowly. "They're usually much more reserved."

He laughed. "Touché. Let me redeem myself. My name is Ian Douglas, and I live nearby. Do you know the story of the Bear Gates?"

"Not yet."

He reached out and pulled me down on the grass so that we sat facing the gates. "Traquair is the oldest inhabited house in Scotland," he began. "The Maxwell Stuarts were cousins of the royal Stuarts, and even though the families didn't visit regularly, the familial bonds remained strong. During the Jacobite rebellion, Bonnie Prince Charlie stayed at Traquair. There are some who believe that he planned his strategy here with the earl." His speech was very clear, the brogue nearly unrecognizable. "When he rode out of the gates for Drumossie Moor in 1746, and news of the defeat filtered back, the old earl closed the gates and vowed never to open them until a Stuart king sat on the throne of Scotland once again. They remain closed to this day. The family, out of respect for the earl's wishes, installed another entrance, which you probably entered when you arrived."

"How tragic." Blinking back tears, I stared at the ferocious twin statues positioned on the pilings. "All this time to live on false hopes."

"You are a romantic, aren't you?" he teased. "I'm quite sure Ellen Maxwell doesn't hope for anything of the sort. She's English to the core."

Of course he couldn't know the woman was dead. "Do you know Lady Maxwell?" I asked.

"Everyone knows her, although she's been bedridden for a number of years now." He stood and extended his hand to pull me up.

"Have you seen everything you wanted to see?" he asked. I nodded.

"If you're agreeable, I'll walk you to your car. Peebles is only about five kilometers from here. I'd like to buy you tea."

"I don't have a car. Lady Maxwell's driver picked me up from the airport."

The blue eyes narrowed. "Who are you?"

"Christina Murray."

"Ah, of course. I should have known." His mouth twisted up at the corner.

"Excuse me?"

"I thought you were a tourist." The warmth had left his voice. "And to think I was telling you the legend of the gates."

The cold was painful. It was definitely affecting my hearing. "I came to Traquair because it's the one place in Scotland I've never seen," I offered. "Ellen Maxwell sent me an airline ticket."

He stared at me as if he were trying to remember something important. I knew he hadn't listened to a word of what I said.

"I know we've never met before, but there is something familiar about you," he said slowly. "One doesn't often see hair so black paired with those eyes. I just can't place where I've seen your face."

My bones ached, and I couldn't feel my hands. It was time for a bold step, even if it was out of character. "If you don't mind," I said politely, "I'd really like to get out of the cold. It's freezing out here, and tea sounds wonderful."

He smiled, and I forgot to breathe. The pain of my divorce was very far away. "Have you tasted raspberry scones, Miss Murray?"

An hour later he watched as I worked my way through my third buttery scone piled high with cream and raspberry jam. The waitress paused by our table. "Anything else today?"

Ian shook his head and grinned. "Not for me, thanks."

He motioned toward my plate. "The lady might like something else. She has an unusually healthy appetite."

I could feel the heat rise in my cheeks. I hadn't eaten since breakfast.

"Do you always eat as if there were no tomorrow?" he teased.

"I was hungry."

"To say the least." He laughed. "I would never have believed it if I hadn't watched you fill that plate twice. You might have warned me before I offered to pay."

At a loss for words, I wiped my mouth and crumbled the napkin on my plate. "Thank you for the tea," I managed. "Everything was delicious." I leaned forward, chin in my hand, and took a deep breath. If I didn't ask, I'd never know. "Will you please explain to me why you were surprised when I told you my name?"

He studied me carefully. "You mean you really don't know?" he asked at last.

"No."

"It appears, Miss Murray, that the late Lord Maxwell left Traquair House to you."

I felt cold all over again as if I had never eaten the sweet desserts nor drunk copious amounts of sustaining tea. "You must be mistaken," I whispered. "I don't even know the Maxwells."

"That's a bit unusual, isn't it, considering your background?"

"What do you know about me?"

Ian frowned. "Ellen Maxwell hasn't been an invalid forever. Once she was an active woman with friends throughout the entire valley. Everyone knew her quite well. When the terms of her husband's will were revealed, she was curious enough about you to do some investigating of her own. After all, it's a bit unusual for a man to leave everything to a child he's never seen. People gossip."

Suddenly I realized what he was implying. I was furious. My voice sounded thin and tight. "I'd like to go home now."

"Back to Traquair or to Boston?"

Without a word, I walked out of the restaurant. Ian caught up with me near the car. He turned me around to face him. "I'm sorry, Christina. I didn't mean to offend you. Of course, none of this is your fault."

I pulled away, opened the door, and climbed inside the car.

We were nearly at the gates of Traquair when I couldn't stand it any longer. Of course, I believed the whole thing was a misunderstanding that could be chalked up to a case of mistaken identity, but it wasn't in my nature to speculate when I could know for sure. "Where do you fit into this, Ian? Is it just my imagination, or does the idea of someone inheriting Traquair bother you more than it should?"

A thin, white line appeared around his mouth. "Don't be ridiculous. It's nothing to me who inherits Traquair House."

"Are you sure?"

He sighed and pulled up to the gate. It was after dark, and the gas lanterns guarding the entrance to Traquair flickered wildly inside their shades. "You are persistent, aren't you?"

Embarrassed, I stared out of the window. "I beg your pardon. I didn't mean to pry. It's none of my business."

Ian frowned and reached out to touch my shoulder. Something changed his mind. When I looked again, both hands were on the steering wheel, and he was staring at me with a curious expression on his face. "I wonder why I seem to be spending most of my time apologizing to you when I'd much rather be doing something else."

"What's that?" I whispered at the same time his mouth closed over mine. I'm ashamed to say that the details of that first kiss dissolved, lost forever, in a wave of pure sensation. My only clear recollections are the incredible warmth of his lips, the feel of soft wool under my hands, and the clean, waxy smell of soap that I was to associate with him from that moment on. But it was enough. Enough to know I had never, in all my thirty-seven years, experienced anything like it. After a long time, he lifted his head.

"Do you believe in déjà vu?" he asked.

"No," I lied. "Tell me why you don't want me at Traquair House."

His fingers were warm against my neck. "It isn't like that at all. In fact, it has nothing to do with you. I'm an agricultural engineer, Christina. The improvements in farming over the last ten years have been phenomenal. If I appear a bit resentful, it's only because my ancestors, unlike the earls of Traquair, didn't take advantage of new methods and machinery. I hope you appreciate what you've been given."

"Are you having financial difficulties, Ian?"

He stared down at me, an expression of exasperation and amusement on his face. "You do get right to the heart of the matter. Didn't your mother tell you never to ask a person's age, his politics, or the extent of his bank account?"

He had the bluest eyes I'd ever seen, and I was behaving completely unlike myself. "I'm an American," I told him. "My mother gave up on me long ago. Have you considered a loan?"

"I have," he replied. "The bank wants my land as collateral. I'm not ready to take that risk yet." He smiled his bone-weakening smile. "You have an unusual effect on me, Christina Murray. I don't believe I've shared this much with a stranger in a very long time."

I felt the color rise to my cheeks and was grateful for the darkness. "How old are you?" I asked abruptly.

He grinned. "Thirty-five and Church of Scotland. How old are you?"

"Thirty-seven and Catholic." I didn't bother to explain that my membership in the Roman Catholic Church had lapsed years ago.

"The Murrays have always been Catholic," he murmured and leaned toward me again.

I pulled away. "You haven't asked the most important question of all."

"What might that be?"

"Aren't you curious as to whether or not I'm married? Most women my age are, and I am wearing a ring." I held out my hand displaying the delicate gold band engraved with the Murray crest. It was an unusual piece of jewelry. He couldn't have missed it.

The silence between us lasted for a long time. I was uncomfortable and then embarrassed. We'd shared nothing more than raspberry scones and one incredible kiss. I stared at his chest, his mouth, at the sharp line of his cheek, the blade of his nose, the pulse beating in the hollow of his throat, everywhere but into his eyes.

Under his breath, I heard him curse softly in Gaelic. Startled, I looked up, meeting his gaze. He laughed, cupped my cheek, and uttered the short, unbelievable words. "You're not married, Christina, but it wouldn't have made any difference if you were."

The tension inside the compact was thick and cloying. I needed air immediately. Fumbling with the handle, I opened the door and jumped out. By the time Ian walked around the car, I was composed again.

"Have Americans introduced a new fashion or is it my company you're in such a hurry to leave?" His face was expressionless, his eyes veiled against me. My teasing companion of the gates was again a remote stranger.

"Neither," I answered. "It's just very late. I went for a short walk hours ago. They must be wondering where I am."

"Ellen isn't in any condition to wonder about anyone."

I considered not telling him at all and then changed my mind. He would know soon enough anyway. "Ellen Maxwell died this afternoon. I'm sorry."

"I see." There was no mistaking the coldness of his voice. "May I offer you my congratulations, Miss Murray. You are a very wealthy woman." With a brief smile he turned away.

"Ian?" I couldn't stop myself.

He turned, an impatient look on his face.

"I suppose I'll see you at the funeral."

"Of course." He stayed where he was, waiting for something I couldn't begin to imagine.

I rang the doorbell. Unexpectedly, tears gathered in my throat. Horrified that I would lose control before someone opened the door, I turned away. *Let him think I'm rude,* I thought, pressing my fingers against my eyelids to staunch the inevitable flow. Better that than the alternative.

"Christina." He was directly behind me, his voice warm and compassionate, the friend of the gates once again. "Pay no attention to me. I'll see you at the funeral."

I didn't turn around, and he didn't touch me. The car

door slammed, and the engine roared. Kate opened the door and stared at me curiously. Then she looked at the taillights disappearing down the road and smiled. On my way to my room, I didn't stop to consider, after everything I'd experienced that day, how odd it was that Traquair felt much more like home than any other I'd ever known.

❊2❊

I wrinkled my nose, deliberately sealing off my nasal passages. The church was musty, smelling of damp and mold and the subtle odor of decaying flesh entombed deep within ancient stone walls.

Wiping clammy palms on my skirt, I concentrated on the curved arches and stained glass windows of the Maxwell family chapel. Even after all these years and countless visits in the name of research to mausoleums and family vaults, I could never quite acclimate myself to the stench of death. It seemed to me that I could feel the essence of those who died. They haunted me with their images, touching my skin with bloodless fingers, pulling at my hair and clothing with pale, insistent hands.

Like an old enemy, the panic inside my chest lifted its head. Balling my fists, I focused on the words of the liturgy. It was an Anglican service, enough like those of my childhood to sound familiar. Throughout history, the Maxwells had stubbornly refused to renounce their Catholicism. But Ellen had been a staunch Episcopalian. Since her husband's death twenty years before, only the rites of the Church of England were practiced in the small Maxwell chapel.

It was jammed to full capacity with mourners lining the walls of the inner sanctuary as well as the stone steps outside. I experienced a flicker of guilt. There were so many without seats. Who was I, a stranger, to take up an entire pew when so many of Ellen's friends and acquaintances stood outside? I looked around uncertainly. Why had no one entered the pew where I sat? I turned and looked directly behind me, surprising a whispering couple into instant silence. The woman blushed scarlet.

I turned back to face the altar and saw him from the corner of my eye. Ian sat three rows back. I hadn't seen nor heard from him since Ellen's death three days before. Attached to his side, her arm through his, sat a woman whose face could be on a magazine cover. Much as I would have liked another look, I didn't have the nerve to turn around again. Embarrassed, I bent my head and closed my eyes, pretending to pray, thankful that I was in the front and no one could see the flaming color rising in my cheeks. It had never occurred to me to ask if *he* was married. So much for fantasies.

The priest had finished the eulogy. Rows of mourners stood and slowly inched toward the open coffin to pay their last respects to the lady of Traquair. The only exit was through the entrance to the chapel or out the doors on either side of the coffin. My palms were clammy with a cold that had nothing to do with the weather.

Clutching my purse, I slipped out of the pew and stood in the line of mourners, resolving to forego the distasteful and, in my mind, pagan practice of viewing the dead and escape through the door. The woman in front of me wept into her handkerchief, soaking it completely. Fidgeting with the clasp of my purse, I managed to open it. Locating a packet of tissue, I offered it to her. She clutched my arm and thanked me with a watery "Bless you, my dear." With her arm holding me captive and her solid body wedged between Ellen's coffin and the first row of seats, I was caught. There was no help for it but to stare down at the woman who had taken one look at my face and died.

I'd expected Ellen Maxwell to look peaceful. But she didn't. She looked angry. I couldn't know it at the time, but the mortician had arranged her features as he remembered them from life, haughty and incensed. Looking down at that cold, sour face, I could only believe she wore that expression for me. Lady Maxwell wanted to send the unmistakable message that, despite her husband's last will and testament, she held me in contempt. An American woman from Boston was no fit heiress for the ancient seat of the Maxwells. Why, then, had she invited me? There was a hint of something else in the frozen mask of her face. Something even the skilled fingers of the mortician couldn't eliminate. Something dark and terrifying that I wanted no part of.

"Please," I whispered to the woman on my arm. "Let me by." She stared blankly. "I'm not feeling well." By now, I was desperate. "I need air." Had Ellen's eyes flickered or was it a trick of the candles? The room swayed. There was a whisper of cloth sliding against polished wood. A hand gripped my shoulder. Then the floor rushed up to meet my head, and everything went black.

Cool sheets, smooth from wear and washing, soothed the back of my neck. Strands of hair released from the French twist I had worn to the funeral lay splayed across the pillow under my cheek. Quiet, careful voices whispered just out of hearing. I felt weak. My eyelids were heavy, too heavy to lift.

"Are there any medical problems that you know of?" A stranger's voice asked the question as firm, competent hands checked my pulse.

"None that Lady Maxwell ever mentioned." I'd heard that voice somewhere before. "I'll check the file." The door opened and closed.

"What about you?" the first voice asked someone else. "Have you any information that might help me?"

"For Christ's sake, John," an exasperated voice answered. "I'm not involved in this. Why would I have any knowledge of Christina Murray's medical history? She fainted in church. That's all there is to it. Maybe she forgot to eat breakfast. Or maybe she doesn't like looking at dead people."

I couldn't help smiling. There was no doubt as to whom that voice belonged to.

"Take it easy, Ian. I'm only an overworked physician trying to get some answers. If you don't know the woman, that's all you need to say. I believe I know what her problem is anyway."

"I didn't mean that I don't know her," a more subdued Ian corrected him. "We just never got around to discussing whether or not she had a medical condition."

"I can imagine." The doctor chuckled.

I decided that this man was worth seeing. With enormous effort I opened my eyes and focused on the scene at the foot of my bed.

"What do you mean by that?" Ian demanded. He was leaning against the mantel, his arms folded forbiddingly against his chest.

A slender man with prematurely gray hair pulled something out of his bag. It was a syringe. "Come now, Ian," he said. "A woman who looks like that, the right age, with the right background. If it weren't for the conference in Edinburgh, I would have met her plane myself."

Ian braced himself on the desktop. "I hadn't realized you were taking notes, John. Just exactly what is it about her background that appeals to you?"

"Don't tell me you haven't been listening to Ellen for all these years?"

"As a matter of fact, I haven't," Ian replied. "Other than the fact that Christina is from Boston, university educated, and stands to inherit Traquair, I know next to nothing about her." He eyed the needle suspiciously. "What is that you're giving her?"

"Insulin. She's very pale, and her skin is cold and clammy. The blue around her lips indicates diabetes."

Thank God he had figured it out, and I didn't have to say anything. I doubted that I could have anyway. Seconds later I felt the reassuring sting of the needle in my left thigh. Almost immediately I felt my body normalize. When I spoke, my voice was surprisingly strong. "Thank you, Doctor. Your diagnosis was correct. I'm a diabetic."

Showing remarkable calm at my unexpectedly conscious condition, he asked, "Do you have medication with you, Miss Murray?"

"Yes, it's in the top drawer of the dressing table."

"You gave us quite a scare, young lady. I presume you have a good explanation for not having anything with you that identifies your condition?"

I rearranged the pillows behind my head and sat up. "I had an insulin injection before breakfast. Something else must have triggered my reaction." I smiled at him, and the worried look around his eyes eased. He was a good-looking man, about Ian's age, with spaniellike brown eyes and a friendly face. I decided to ask the question that had been hovering on my lips ever since I'd regained consciousness. "You never answered Ian's question, Doctor. What exactly do you know about my background?"

I had no mercy despite the red tide sweeping across his face.

"I beg your pardon, Miss Murray." The man was truly beside himself. "It was unpardonable of me to exchange idle gossip over a patient this way."

"Apology accepted." He really was sweet, but I had to know. "Will you tell me?"

Ian grinned. "You aren't getting out of here scot-free, my friend. Tell the lady and then leave us alone."

The doctor cleared his throat and looked down at his feet. "Only that your degree is in Celtic history. You read and write Gaelic as well as a Highlander. Your parents retired and moved to California. You married early and were recently divorced." He hesitated.

"Anything else?"

"You have no children."

"Is that all?"

He looked up, startled. "Yes. Of course."

I couldn't decide if he was telling the truth. He looked so honest, and yet I knew, through painful personal experience, that the best liars were masters of the art. They had the ability to look a person straight in the eye and protest their innocence with the blood of their victims still warm on their hands.

"It doesn't matter," I said quickly. Ellen Maxwell had probably told everyone anyway. "I'll fill you in on the rest, although I can't imagine why anyone would be interested. I'm an only child, and I can't have children." I took a deep breath and bit my lip, bracing myself for the familiar recurring pain. If I hurried through it fast enough, this time I might avoid the embarrassing tears that welled up at the most inappropriate times. "My husband left me for someone younger and more fertile, at which time I took back my maiden name. I'm the last of a long line of Murrays."

"I'm terribly sorry, Miss Murray," the doctor mumbled. From the red staining his cheeks, I could tell he hadn't recovered from his own embarrassment.

"Thank you." I smiled generously. "I'm over it now. Really I am."

"Why did you say that?" Ian asked abruptly. There was a strange expression on his face.

"What?"

"That you were the last of the Murrays?"

"Because it's true. Why do you ask?"

"It's odd, that's all. People don't use that expression any more. You're the expert in Gaelic history. Do you know anything about the Murrays?"

"Of course."

"Tell me everything you know."

"Good God, Ian," the doctor protested. "The woman just fell to the floor in insulin shock. Is this necessary?"

Ian ran impatient hands through his sun-streaked hair. "Not really. We can discuss this later if you're tired."

He was probably the best-looking man I'd ever seen, and I felt like a washed-out disaster. It was suddenly terribly important to find out if he was attached. "I'd be very happy to," I said. "Can you come back later?"

He smiled, and once again I felt a definite shortness of breath. "Will you have dinner with me this evening?" he asked.

"Yes."

"I'll come for you at seven. Everything closes up early."

"I'll be ready."

The phone jingled in the hallway. I tensed, waiting for the second ring. It didn't come. There was a knock at the door, and the maid poked her head inside, not at all bothered that I was half dressed. Formality, I found, was not a major concern at Traquair House.

"Phone call from America for you, Miss Murray. It's your mother, returning your call."

Knotting my robe around my waist, I walked into the hallway and picked up the phone. "Mom? How are you?"

"Just fine, dear. Is everything all right?" Across ten thousand miles her crisp, no-nonsense voice greeted me over the telephone wire.

"Of course." I didn't ordinarily confide in my mother, but something made me tell her. "I've only been here two days, and I already have a date."

There was silence on the line. "Don't you think you're rushing it?" she finally said. "It's awfully soon after the divorce."

When would that word *divorce* no longer bring a painful tightness into my throat? I struggled to answer my mother. "Please try and understand, Mom. I know it's only been legal for three months, but I've been separated for over a year. Stephen's already remarried."

"Is that what you called about?" Ever-practical Susan Murray didn't believe in wasting money.

"Actually, I called to speak to Dad."

She laughed. "Of course you did. I'll put him on." It was no secret that I had always preferred my father's conversation to almost anyone's, including Mother's. I was definitely a daddy's girl. Fortunately, I'd been blessed with a mother secure enough not to resent it.

My childhood had been unique to say the least. Born nine months after my parents' wedding day, I adjusted quickly to the fact that life with a couple barely out of their teens wasn't going to parallel the lives of my childhood friends. There were no scheduled bath or bedtimes at the Murray house. My mother's idea of healthful cuisine was a can of fruit cocktail poured over cottage cheese. Exercise and water cured all illnesses. I was eight years old before I saw the inside of a dentist's office and that was only because I had fallen on the cement and knocked out a tooth.

It was a delightful childhood, free of all expectations and most restrictions. Nothing was censured. I had grown up on Shakespeare, D. H. Lawrence, and William Faulkner. Before the age of twelve I'd read *The Virgin and the Gypsy,*

Lady Chatterly's Lover, and *A Streetcar Named Desire* with full awareness of their contents. Sometimes I wondered if my unconventional roots and impossible expectations weren't the cause of major problems in my marriage.

"Hi, hon. How are you?" My father's familiar voice, soft on *r*'s, interrupted my thoughts. I loved that voice, and so did everyone who listened to it. Donald Murray was a slightly famous trial lawyer. Or at least he had been before he retired. In his last twenty years of practice, he hadn't lost a case. I still maintain, as I always have, that his enormous success lay in the exceptional quality of his voice. It was low and clearly pitched, every syllable enunciated, a New Englander's voice, informal, thick with vowels and bare of consonants. That voice never let me down.

"It appears that I'm due to inherit an eight-hundred-year-old house," I told him.

He laughed. "Is it still standing?"

"I'm serious. And yes, it is still standing. It's really more of a mansion than a regular home. Have you ever heard of Traquair House?"

There was silence at the end of the line.

"Dad? Can you hear me?"

"I'm here, Chris. Tell me more about Traquair House."

"I don't know anything yet. The lawyers will be here tomorrow. Do me a favor. See if you can locate any information on entailed estates and rights of survivorship. I'd like to know what I'm up against here. And if you can find out anything about our family tree, I'd appreciate it."

"I'll do that. Be careful, Chris."

It wasn't until I'd hung up the phone that I realized he hadn't said that to me in years.

The car that Ian parked at the entrance to Traquair that evening was not the small compact that we had ridden in before. It was a lovely old Jaguar sedan of deep forest green with leather seats. The camel sports jacket and wool trousers he wore confirmed what I'd already assumed. Dinner in Scotland, even in the small town of Innerleithen, was a dress-up affair. I was grateful that I'd thought to include in my travel wardrobe a form-fitting dress of fine wool with a vee neck. I'd been told the deep cherry color with its white border was flattering to my hair and eyes. The look on Ian Douglas's face when I came down the stairs was worth every minute of the time I'd spent in preparation.

"You look lovely, Miss Murray."

His old-world formality was endearing, but I was ready to do away with it. The man had kissed me, for heaven's sake. "Please call me Christina."

"All right, Christina. We've reservations for seven-thirty."

We were the only ones patronizing the restaurant that evening. The conversation remained light as the proprietor ushered us into what looked like a formal drawing room where large comfortable chairs were arranged around the fireplace. Ian ordered a drink while I looked over the menu.

"I recommend the salmon," he said, a hint of laughter in his voice. "There is enough of it to satisfy even your appetite."

"Well then," I replied, determined to remain as cool as possible, "I'll take it."

"Two poached salmon dinners with dill sauce, Angus. Have you any *criachan* today?" Ian asked the waiter.

"Kirstie was here first thing in the morning making it, sir. It's the best of the lot, if I do say so myself."

"We'll have some of that as well. Miss Murray loves sweets."

"What makes you say that?" I asked.

"Three raspberry scones gave me a small hint."

Heat rose in my cheeks.

"Surely you know I'm teasing, Christina?" His eyes were clear and contrite. "I admire the fact that you don't pick at your food. There isn't anything more aggravating than buying an expensive meal for a woman, only to have her eat two bites and push it away."

It was obvious that he spoke from experience. "I'll try not to disappoint you," I said.

His gaze swept over my figure, lingering on the long expanse of crossed legs visible below my skirt. "I don't think that's possible," he said dryly, swallowing a healthy portion of his drink.

"Actually I'm not supposed to have sweets," I reminded him. "I'm a diabetic. The raspberry scones were a rare treat."

He looked startled. "Good God! I never even connected it. Why on earth did you eat them?"

I laughed. "I'm only human and I love sugar. When I indulge, I pay for it. Fortunately I'm not tempted often or easily."

I leaned my head back against the chair and closed my eyes. The room was lovely. The warmth of the fire and the intimate flickering lights wove their spell. I felt mellow and slightly drowsy, otherwise, I would never have said what I did. "I'd like to think you invited me here tonight because you were bowled over by my charms. But I don't really believe that."

He looked at me curiously. "Why not? You're not exactly the type a man would overlook in a crowd."

Again, I could feel the color in my cheeks. "Thank you," I murmured, clearly uncomfortable with the way the conversation had turned. "I wasn't begging for compliments."

"I know. That makes you even more appealing." He studied me thoughtfully. "What was your husband like?"

"I beg your pardon?" Whatever I had expected of the evening, it certainly wasn't this.

"He must have been the worst kind of fool to make a woman like you unaware of her appeal."

My stomach knotted in that twisting, painful way it always did when I thought of Stephen. I couldn't discuss him. Not yet. "He wasn't a fool," I said quickly. "We just wanted different things. What about you?" I remembered the beauty seated beside him in church. "Are you married?"

He grinned, and the pain in my stomach disappeared. "Shame on you, Christina. Would I be here if I were?"

"I hope not," I answered, "but I don't really know you."

"That can be remedied. In answer to your question, no, I'm not married. I came close once, but it didn't work out."

"What happened?" The minute I asked the question I wished it back. "I'm sorry. Please don't feel you have to answer that."

"I don't mind at all," he assured me. "I took her to

America with me while I earned my degree at Cornell. She refused to come back."

"Why didn't you stay?"

He shrugged, a beautiful fluid lifting of his shoulders. "This is my home. I've spent my entire life preparing to take over the land. I can't imagine living anywhere else."

I agreed with him. "Scotland is a wonderful place to raise children. Much better, I think, than America."

"Thank God children were never an issue."

"Do you dislike children, Ian?"

"Not at all," he replied promptly. "But I do believe that every child deserves two devoted parents. I deplore the current trend of selfishness that puts children's needs last in a relationship."

He spoke with such feeling. I wondered if it came from personal experience. Curiosity prevailed. "You can't actually believe that people should endure a miserable existence for the sake of their children?"

"Of course not." He set his empty glass on the table. "But people's definitions of miserable are varied. Most of the time, problems can be worked out with a bit of effort. There are few things important enough to break up a marriage."

What about infertility, I wanted to cry out. *What if a man wants children so desperately that nothing else will satisfy him, not even the woman he promised to love, honor, and cherish fifteen years before.* Of course I didn't say it. It was ridiculous to even think it. No one would believe me. This was the twentieth century. A woman's worth was no longer measured by the number of children she brought into the world. Or was it?

I closed my eyes and remembered the hands. I could still feel those hands, sterile, competent, cold, sure, precise, sliding across my skin, probing, prodding, inspecting every inch of flesh, examining over, under, inside, the tests inconclusive and never ending, until that night when I couldn't tell my husband's hands from the hands of the hundred specialists I'd seen, and the very thought of exploring fingers inching their way across my body was like the exploding pain of brilliant light against eyes that had been too long in dark places. I simply couldn't bear it, and in the end it cost me my life as I'd planned it.

Deliberately, with great effort, I pushed the memories aside and opened my eyes. Ian was staring at me again. Why did I feel as if he knew exactly what I was thinking?

Just then, the proprietor walked through the door to the dining room. "Please follow me," he said. "Dinner will be served shortly."

Over a bottle of wine and the best salmon I'd ever tasted, Ian brought up the real subject of our dinner conversation. "What do you know about your family history, Christina?"

"If you mean my personal family line, not much. But I know a great deal about the Murrays."

"Did you know that the widow of the last Murray of Bothwell married the third earl of Douglas?"

Pausing, with my fork halfway to my mouth, I stared at him. Ian was a Douglas and I, a Murray. "Are you telling me we're related?"

He laughed. "In a manner of speaking. I don't believe we're close enough to worry about genetic defects in our children."

Even before he saw the stricken expression on my face, he realized what he'd done. "I'm terribly sorry," he said, horror at his faux pas evident on his face.

"It doesn't matter any more," I assured him and quickly changed the subject. "My family is descended from the Atholl Murrays. George Murray, leader of the Jacobite troops at Culloden, is my direct ancestor."

"A good man," Ian acknowledged, cutting off another piece of salmon. "When you made that comment this afternoon, I remembered something."

Somehow I knew this was it, the reason we were here, eating salmon and drinking wine in this lovely restaurant, cloaking our true intentions in the mantle of polite conversation. "What comment?" I asked, although I knew exactly what he was about to say.

He repeated my words exactly as I had said them. *"I'm the last of the Murrays."* He was silent for a moment, allowing me the full impact of the words before he continued. "When I first saw you, I thought you reminded me of someone." His voice was quiet and reflective with the familiar lilting cadence of a born storyteller. Intrigued, as usual, with any tidbit describing the ancient lore of Scotland, I hung on every word.

"During the 1700s, before Culloden, Janet Douglas married George Murray. For some reason, neither the Douglases nor the Murrays approved of the union. I believe it had to do with an ancient curse. Her diary is in the family archives at Traquair House. Apparently she came back to Traquair after the Battle of Culloden Moor to collect her daughter's belongings. She must have left it there. It was found, surprisingly intact, in a remote guest room. When it became obvious that Janet was pregnant, the families put aside their objections and the wedding was hastily arranged. A son was born six months after. Later, they had a daughter named Katrine. According to Janet's diary, Katrine grew up and fell in love with an Englishman, the infamous Sir Richard Wolfe, on the eve of Culloden. She died tragically, fulfilling the prophecy. Nothing in her mother's diary explains the nature of the curse, but apparently Katrine's death didn't surprise her."

The flickering candlelight made a circle of golden light in the bottom of my wineglass. Was it a trick of the flame or was Ian looking at me strangely? He had stopped talking long enough to refill his wineglass. "The reason I reacted so strongly to your words this afternoon," he continued, "is because Janet used almost the same ones in her diary. She wrote that her daughter was cursed because *Katrine was the last of the Murrays.*"

Reaching across the table, he lifted my chin and thoroughly scrutinized my face. "I have a portrait of Katrine Murray. It's only an oil painting, nothing like the accuracy of a photograph, of course. She's younger and her clothing and hair are different, but only a blind man could miss the resemblance. Gathering dust in my attic, Christina, is the picture of a woman who could be you."

3

I shivered and pulled the covers up to my neck. The cozy fire crackling in the fireplace wasn't enough to warm my entire room. Traquair had central heating, but the cost was too phenomenal to even think of turning it on in June. At least my feet weren't cold, thanks to the warming pans Kate had insisted on slipping between the sheets.

It was late, and I should have been tired. But I couldn't sleep. All I could think about was Katrine Murray. After dinner, I'd insisted on returning to Ian's home to view the infamous portrait. I suppose she might have appeared differently in the glaring brightness of electric light, but the attic had no electricity.

Softened by the flickering glow of candles, the hollows under her cheekbones deepened in purple shadow, Katrine Murray was beautiful. Her black hair was unpowdered and pulled off her face to surround her head in a cluster of curls, one lying temptingly against the swell of her white breast. Her bodice was very low and edged with lace in the fashion of the day. Wide skirts flared out from an amazingly tiny waist. Her nose was small and straight, her cheekbones pronounced, her mouth turned up in a tantalizing smile. But it was her eyes that held me. They were large and light, a clear lucid gray, framed with feathery black lashes.

They were my eyes and they looked out from my face. Or at least it had been my face twenty years ago. This girl from the past, at the height of her beauty, knew the full extent of her power. She had not yet experienced doubt or disillusionment or loss. Looking into the eyes of that undeniable ancestor whose genes had passed down two hundred years, through generations of Murrays, to show up in the face of an innocuous American, I felt a strong and inexplicable desire to weep.

Ian seemed to understand what I was feeling. He said very little on our way back to Traquair. I didn't mind that he didn't speak or that he didn't kiss me good night. All I could think of was getting my hands on Janet Douglas's diary.

Kate had left a pot of hot milk on my nightstand. It had a strange pleasant flavor, unlike anything I'd tasted before, something between cinnamon and sage. I drained the pot, turned out the light, and drifted into an unsettled sleep. At least I think it was sleep. There could be no other explanation for the events I experienced that night. I remember it began with the cold. Not the kind of clean cold that comes from being outside in the wind chill of January in Boston. This was a clammy cold. The kind that works its way deep inside aching bones.

I stood on a narrow, dangerous stairway in a chamber that I'd never seen before. The walls were granite and very close together, hewed unevenly by a negligent craftsman with crude tools. The dripping dampness increased my feeling of dread. I rubbed my arms, wondering why I had chosen to wear nothing more than a cotton nightgown with thin straps. The only light came from a glow farther ahead, down the stairs. Bracing myself with my hands on opposite sides of the wall, I carefully inched my way, one step at a time, toward the light.

I can't begin to describe the near misses on those slippery steps, the growing tension, the aching muscles in my shoulders and arms as I braced my body weight for what seemed like hours during that dark, twisted descent into the unknown. All I could do was follow the light. Instinctively, I knew wherever it led was my destination. There were moments when I looked up from the next treacherous step, when the stairwell straightened for a bit, that I thought I saw shadows and the fluttering of a dark cloth or it could have been a blanket.

Finally it was over. There were no more stairs. Turning sideways I managed to squeeze through a narrow opening and stepped into a cavelike room lit by foul-smelling torches mounted on the walls. I looked around. The hair on my neck lifted as I recognized where I was. The tiny altar with a statue of the Virgin Mary set above a large irregular stone, the flickering candles, the faint subtle hint of herbs, the square stones set inside the granite walls, and the death masks, peaceful and expressionless, etched into the granite. There could be no mistake. I had been led into a crypt, a family burial chamber. Goose bumps appeared on my arms and I panicked.

I can't explain my trauma regarding the whole idea of death. I have no idea how long I've felt this way or where it even began. I only know that for as long as I can remember I've lived with the recurring nightmare that walls are closing in on me. With every heartbeat, they move closer and closer until, with one last sobbing breath, one painful scrape of nails against stone, one horrified memory of light and life and effortless breath, I feel the unbearable pressure crushing my chest. Then I feel no more.

My heart slammed against my ribs. I slid to my knees, my hands shaking. I would have closed my eyes, but something stopped me. A movement in the darkness. The panic receded. I wasn't alone. A slender figure, shrouded in a dark, feminine cloak, the hood pulled up to shield her face, moved out of the shadows and faced me. She said nothing.

"Who are you?" I whispered. I couldn't be sure, the cloak hid so much, but there was something familiar about the way she moved. "Please, speak to me."

She moved aside and gestured toward the altar. I shook my head. "I don't understand."

With an impatient shrug of her shoulders she turned, walked to the altar, and placed both hands on the stone. I don't know how long I watched her standing, her face hidden, her hands on the pyrite-studded sandstone. I was no longer cold. The woman changed position. She knelt, pressing her lips against the stone. Then I saw it. Rays of light, warm and breathtakingly beautiful, dim at first and then growing steadily brighter, illuminated the rock. There was no window, no outside light, no artificial source. It came from inside the stone. In that piercing, crystal-bright moment, I realized what I was looking at. This was the Stone of Destiny, Scotland's Stone. The stone that was supposed to be sitting under England's Coronation Chair in Westminster Abbey. It had been there since the thirteenth century. But what was it doing here?

Forgetting my fear, I stood and walked toward the woman and the miracle of light. She stood and turned to meet me, dropping the cloak. I stopped, riveted to the freezing granite under my feet. Framed in long black hair, gray eyes stared back at me from a clear, finely featured face. It was my face and Katrine Murray's. No, definitely not Katrine's. This woman was older, closer to my own age than the lovely girl in the portrait. Her hair was braided with gold thread and hung, thick and black, past her knees. A twisted red girdle gathered the draping folds of her white dress around her hips, and the deep, square bodice showed a slender neck and sloping shoulders.

It wasn't her face that separated her from women like Katrine Murray and myself. It was her expression. This woman had known suffering. There was pain in the trembling lips and desperate lift of her chin. Pain and pride. But it was her eyes that revealed the depths of her despair. Those clear gray eyes were filled with a longing so complete, it consumed her. I knew without question that whatever trials I'd experienced in my life, they were nothing compared to the heartbreak this woman with her white gown and ravaged face carried with her.

Her features were so like my own it was like looking into a mirror, and yet she was nothing like me. This was a woman who would stop conversation when she entered a room. The smooth, graceful glide of her walk, the imperious wave of her hand, the richness of her hair, the passion brimming from her light-filled eyes. This woman had conquered fear. She stood before me with the bearing of a queen, straight backed, her head held high. Like Helen of Troy and Eleanor of Aquitaine, this was a woman who had it within her to change the course of history.

"Who are you?" I asked again, refusing to allow her identity to remain a mystery.

She tilted her head, as if considering my question. Then

she turned back to the stone, motioning me to join her. I hurried forward. We stood together, two women so alike and yet nothing alike. Together we knelt. Together we placed our hands on the stone.

The pulsing began in my fingers. Spreading like a wave, it moved to my temples, down to my throat and across my chest, until I could no longer separate it from the pounding of my heart. There was an explosion of light, a sensation of heat. The room rocked and then disappeared.

And then I was alone, standing at the Bear Gates of Traquair House in broad daylight. Horrified, I realized that I was still in my nightgown.

Even now, when I try to recall my experience, I find it difficult to explain with any clarity at all. There is nothing by which to compare it. It had the essence of a dream, but it was far more than that. I had full awareness of the events without the power to participate or influence their outcome. But I wasn't spared the ability to feel. I felt everything: the horror that surrounded me, the hot tears that blinded my eyes and burned my cheeks, the rage at my inability to alter the course of fate, the fierce pride that welled up inside of me when I realized who this woman was.

From early childhood, I have always been a dreamer, remembering events with a clairvoyance found only in those particularly susceptible to hypnotism. But never before had I experienced such total omniscience. I was everywhere, knowing all things, without the ability to interfere, like a novelist who has lost control of her book to Hollywood screenwriters. That must be why I heard the angry crowd advancing on Traquair House before anyone else was aware of it.

I could still see it in my mind just as it happened in my dream. The blood pooled out between the stone slabs into the courtyard, welling and eddying up to my knees, soaking my nightgown. A dark, ugly purple-red, it crept to the level of my neck, then my chin, and finally my lips until I was drowning in the warm animal smell and taste of it.

I will never forget the dark-eyed woman whose face looked frighteningly familiar. She cursed the women of the Maxwell line, damning them to tragic deaths and ghosts who walked in the night until the Stone of Destiny was restored to its rightful resting place.

Recalling the horrifying events never fails to make my skin crawl, but I can't help looking back and remembering every lifelike and terrifying detail. The events are clearly etched in my mind as was the knowledge that whatever Mairi of Shiels was, a traitor to Scotland she was not. But how could I, an insignificant American, prove her innocence and why, after seven hundred years, should it be so important that I do so?

❈4❈

With intense relief, I watched the first pale fingers of dawn streak the sky. Breakfast with Ellen Maxwell's solicitor was hours away. Pulling on a pair of gray leggings and a black, oversized sweatshirt, I tied my tennis shoes and started out in search of the family archives.

They weren't difficult to find. Traquair wasn't a castle with endless, twisting stairways and massive staterooms. It was a manor house, extremely large by American standards, but a house all the same. Common sense told me that the archives would be in the public rooms. Sure enough, that's where I found them, locked behind glass.

Disappointed, I turned back to my room and surprised a maid dusting the picture frames in the hallway. She smiled shyly and spoke. "We didn't realize you were such an early riser, Miss Murray. If you're hungry, the housekeeper will see to it that you have a bite of something before breakfast."

"Thank you," I replied gratefully. "I am hungry."

She nodded. "You'll find her in the kitchen."

The housekeeper turned out to be Kate. Again, I had the unsettling feeling that I'd seen her somewhere before, or at least someone very like her. Her figure was rounded, almost matronly, but her skin was smooth and unlined. She could have been anywhere between forty-five and sixty, although I guessed the former. She was the perfect age for a British housekeeper. I sat down at the table, chin in hand. "I didn't realize you were the housekeeper here at Traquair, Kate. Why is it that everyone calls you by your first name?"

She smiled. "We're not so formal here at Traquair as in some houses. My position is a hereditary one. My mother was the housekeeper at Traquair before she died, and my grandmother before her. I grew up here. Lady Maxwell began calling me Kate when I was a little girl. She couldn't quite get used to using a more formal address. Everyone just followed her lead." She opened the oven and peered inside. "The scones are almost done. Is there something you needed?"

"Something to eat," I replied. "Those look delicious. I don't think I can last until eight o'clock."

"Would you like some coffee or tea to go with them? I thought I'd have a cup myself."

"Tea please." I watched her measure the leaves into a delicate teapot. While they steeped, she set two cups and saucers, two spoons, and a pitcher of milk on the scrubbed oak table.

"Do you take lemon?"

"No, thank you. Just milk."

Kate nodded and poured a small amount of milk into each cup before adding the tea. "Shall I plan on breakfast this early every day?" she asked, tilting her head until it almost rested on her shoulder.

I couldn't help smiling. She looked like a small, inquisitive bird waiting expectantly for the next bread crumb. "I don't usually get up so early," I answered. "But I just couldn't sleep. Yesterday was quite a day."

"I can imagine." She blew on her tea before sipping it. "If Ian Douglas should ever take me to dinner, I don't believe I'd sleep either. Not that he would, of course," she said hurriedly. "We're not so relaxed about our class differences as they are in the bigger cities."

Not knowing quite how to reply, I changed the subject. "Would it be possible to look at Janet Murray's diary?"

She threw me a sharp, questioning look. "Why on earth would you want to look at that?"

I bit back the urge to tell her everything. Self-disclosure was a problem of mine. Stephen had reminded me of it often enough. Instead, I strived for the correct degree of calm professionalism, enough information not to be rude, but not so much as to be overly familiar. "I'm a historian," I explained. "An eighteenth-century diary of someone who might be my ancestor is something I can't ignore."

She stood without answering and pulled the scones from the oven. Dishing out two, she arranged them on a clean plate and set it before me. "I'll bring out the butter if you like, but I don't think you'll need it."

I bit into the hot, flaky bread and sighed. "Don't bother with the butter."

The uncertain look on her face vanished. She smiled and reached into the pocket of her apron. Handing me a large ring she pointed to the single skeleton key. "This one will open all the cases in the museum. The others are for doors and closets throughout the house. I'll show you where they fit if you like."

I hedged. "That may be a bit premature."

She shook her head. "I don't think so, Miss Murray. We've all known for a long time that you're to take Lady Maxwell's place. Traquair House and all that's in it is yours."

There was no appropriate answer to such a statement. If I stopped to think about it, the odds against something like this happening were as overwhelming as winning the lottery. I was sure there would be some catch that the Maxwell family lawyer would reveal soon enough.

I retraced my steps back to the museum and unlocked the glass case. My hand shook as I reached inside to take out the ancient leather-bound book. It fit comfortably in my hand. I looked at the sturdy spine and the careful stitching of the dark leather. It was beautifully preserved. I looked at my watch. It was later than I thought. There was just enough time to change before breakfast. The diary would have to wait.

Dressed in a straight, calf-length maroon skirt, gray blazer, and flat shoes, I made my way to the cheerful breakfast room on the eastern side of the house. Morning sunlight filtered through the sparkling windows and reflected off the silver-covered dishes on the sideboard. Mr. MacDougall, a small, friendly looking man with thick eyeglasses, was seated in a comfortable chair, reading the paper. He stood when I entered the room and pulled out a chair beside his own.

"Good morning, Miss Murray. I hope you slept well."

"Fine, thank you," I replied, reaching for the coffee pot. I saw no need to go into the details of my sleepless night. "I hope your drive was pleasant." The road from Edinburgh was virtually empty at this time of the morning, but the Scots were fond of polite formalities.

"Very nice, thank you. Your housekeeper has a lovely breakfast for us. If you don't mind, I'd like to eat first and then we can discuss Lady Maxwell's affairs in the library."

I was conscious of a flash of disappointment. If the man didn't want to talk during breakfast, why hadn't he eaten at home? If the rumors were true and I was the new mistress of Traquair House, a great many people worked for me, and Mr. MacDougall was one of them. Maybe he needed a gentle reminder. "There are a few things I'm curious about, Mr. MacDougall," I said, testing the waters. "It will give us something to talk about while we're eating."

"An excellent suggestion, Miss Murray," he replied. "May I interest you in some of this ham?"

"Please." I held out my plate, my mouth watering at the generous helpings of scrambled egg, ham, haggis, and stewed tomatoes he'd ladled out. The two buttery scones I'd eaten earlier seemed very far away.

"What is it you would like to know?" asked the man between mouthfuls.

"I've heard that Ellen Maxwell left the entire estate to me. Is that true?"

He nodded and swallowed, wiping his mouth with a linen napkin. "Quite true. Or rather, her husband did. Lady

Maxwell never owned Traquair House. For the last twenty years she has been a mere tenant."

So, it was true. Irrefutable. I still couldn't believe it. "Do you have any idea why he left it to me?"

"I can't answer that one," said Mr. MacDougall. "All I know is that my firm has handled the affairs of the Maxwells since long before I came aboard. Lord Maxwell had the papers drawn up once he found you." He tilted his head back and squinted at an imaginary calendar on the ceiling. "That would have been approximately thirty years ago. When he died, Lady Maxwell, unaware of the terms of the will, tried to sell Traquair. When she found that she couldn't, she asked us to provide her with information about you. She's kept track of your whereabouts since you were a little girl."

I felt the embarrassing color flood my face.

"Everything was very legal, of course," he hurried to assure me. "All that we knew was a matter of public record. Your academic awards, your parents, your course of study, your marriage and divorce." He looked at me over the rim of his glasses. "I want you to know I'm very sorry about that, Miss Murray. We've never attempted to interfere with you in any way. If you hadn't accepted Lady Maxwell's invitation to come to Scotland, that would have been the end of it. You would have been notified of your inheritance, that's all." He drained his coffee cup and placed it back in the saucer. "Still, it is interesting that you chose such an unusual course of study. Perhaps, subconsciously, you were preparing yourself for Traquair House."

I decided at that moment that I liked him. "You're a lawyer, Mr. MacDougall. I expected someone extremely logical and pragmatic. Don't tell me you believe in *the sight?*"

He smiled, a full smile that showed his bottom teeth and all of his gums. "Not at all, Miss Murray. What I am is a proper Calvinist. We believe that one's fate is inescapable."

The eighteenth-century library contained over three thousand books and all of them belonged to me. The priceless paintings, the elegant faded carpets, the tapestries, the cellars, the grounds and tearoom, the brewhouse, the gates, it was all mine. Along with enough money to keep anyone comfortable for a lifetime.

In a daze, I wandered through the house, coming upon a group of tourists led by a gray-haired woman in a service-able tweed suit. They were in the King's Room, staring at the bed said to have been used by Mary, Queen of Scots, when she visited Traquair. I was impatient for them to leave. Now that I knew the house belonged to me, I wanted to explore every corner, climb every step, run my fingers over every piece of wood, every painting, every lace curtain and embroidered tapestry, without interruption.

It was impossible, of course. Traquair was on the list of tours, and it was open to visitors until the last day of September. Only after that would it be mine without interruptions. Through all the gray, damp darkness of late fall and winter, I could roam the rooms in selfish privacy. The servants would be here and the craftspeople, but ultimately, I would be alone. Until then I would concentrate on solving the mystery of my connection to the Maxwells. There was also the diary and my uncanny likeness to Katrine Murray and the woman in my dream, Mairi of Shiels. I hurried to my room in search of the diary.

Now that my official status as the lady of Traquair had been confirmed beyond all doubt, I no longer felt like a guest. I decided to read Janet's diary in the library. Making my way down the long hallway, I entered the room, pulled a winged-back chair close to the peat fire, and opened the book.

Janet Murray's handwriting was lovely, clear, and consis-tent, with the letters artistically crafted in the style of the day. She was also amazingly articulate with the thoughtful analogies and colorful descriptions of a born writer. Once I acclimated myself to the ancient script and spelling, I was able to read with satisfactory fluency. Hours passed, but I never noticed. Kate came in to leave a pot of tea. It was delicious, sweet, flavored with honey and an unusual spice I couldn't place. I emptied two cups without realizing it.

Caught up in the richness of the words and the personal story of Janet's daughter, I didn't realize, until the names and events became familiar, that I was reading what would be a veritable treasure to any historian, a first-person account of the horrifying months leading up to the single most tragic event in the history of Scotland. The fact that it was undoubtedly written by my direct ancestor was staggering.

The dull headache that had bothered me since I sat down to read had increased in intensity. The pain was now severe. I lifted a hand to rub my aching temple and closed my eyes. A log snapped inside the fireplace, and a soft summer rain drummed against the windows. The day had been long and exciting, and I was in that state of numbness beyond tired. Resting my head against the back of the chair, I tried to open my eyes, but the lids were too heavy to lift. It didn't matter. The picture in my mind was as clear as a movie screen.

Edinburgh
May 3, 1745

The royal palace of Holyrood was alight with the blaze of ten thousand candles. At the other end of High Street, one mile from the primitive grandeur of Edinburgh Castle, the nobility of Scotland gathered in the sophisticated splendor of the reception room. The duke of Mansfield was there with his brother, George Murray of Atholl, Angus MacIan of Ardnamurchan, MacDonald of Lochaber, and Campbell of Inveraray.

Lord Richard Wolfe, heir to the earldom of Manchester and a major in the King's Regiment, rested his shoulders against the mantel and frowned into his champagne. It looked as if the entire cohort of Jacobite supporters was assembled under one roof.

Richard didn't believe for one moment that the rumored rebellion would come to pass. The Scots were absurdly sentimental, but they weren't fools. Even if Charles Stuart gathered a few French regiments and rallied the Highland clans, he would be no match for the might of the English militia. His mouth twisted in amusement. James Murray, Lord Mansfield of Scone, his friend and host, was as harmless as a lapdog and dangerously free with his information. What could have possessed the duke of Cumberland to send Richard on such a fruitless mission? The Scots were the same as they had always been: loquacious, argumentative, fiercely patriotic, and loyal to their 'King over the Water.' But that was the end of it. There would be no uprising.

Richard drained his glass and placed it on the mantel. The ball had just begun, and he was already bored. More than one young lady had been attracted to the lazy grace of his lean, wide-shouldered frame and the stern, austerely handsome features under his shockingly light, unpowdered hair. Not once was he tempted to respond. For the last nine of his thirty years, Lord Wolfe, heir to an immense fortune and ancient earldom, had dodged the determined efforts of matchmaking mamas. He would marry when he pleased and not before.

Consciously, with painstaking care, he made it his practice to seek out comfortable women, phlegmatic and slightly used, with opulent charms and habits. Richard had spent a lifetime observing the soul-wrenching arguments between his quick-witted, silver-tongued mother and equally verbal, fiercely political father. He wanted nothing to do with a woman who harbored a brain.

The future countess of Manchester would attend to her husband's needs, her children, and her household. She would be attractive enough, of course. Richard could not see himself married to an unattractive woman, but beauty, in itself, was not a requirement. If she had the other necessary qualifications, it would be enough. She would have no interest in the affairs of government, foreign politics, or the plight of England's working classes. She would be ignorant of the whereabouts of the library and leave his morning paper undisturbed. Until such a paragon could be found, he would remain a bachelor.

There was a commotion at the door. Richard couldn't see for the crowd surrounding the entrance. He watched James Murray excuse himself, leave his brother, and walk across the room. The gathering at the door opened to allow the duke into their ranks and then closed behind him. Several moments passed before he reappeared with a vision on his arm.

Richard ignored the young man walking beside them. He had eyes only for the woman. Unbelievably, James was leading her directly to where he stood.

Unconsciously, Richard straightened to his full height as James introduced them. "Lord Richard Wolfe, my niece, Katrine Murray, and her brother, Alasdair."

Dismissing the boy with a cool smile, Richard bent over the woman's hand and drawled in his best drawing room manner, "I'm overwhelmed, Mansfield. I had no idea that you had such a beautiful niece. This time I've fallen in love."

A frown marred the perfection of Lady Katrine Murray's clear forehead. "How fortunate for you," she murmured, lifting her hand to stifle a yawn. "I'm sure you'll be very happy."

Murray laughed and walked away. The lazy expression disappeared from Richard's face. His eyes narrowed as he assessed the beauty before him. It would be too much to hope that she was less intelligent than she seemed. "Why have I never seen you at Scone, my lady?" he asked politely.

"I usually visit in early spring," she answered, "but this year my mother needed me. Do you know my father?"

Richard nodded. "George Murray is respected in England as well as Scotland." His eyes lingered on her bare shoulders. "Perhaps your mother will spare you and those of us at Scone will have the pleasure of your company."

The young man at her side stiffened. "Katrine will stay at home with her family until——" He stopped abruptly.

"Until?" Richard's silky voice encouraged the boy to speak.

"Until June," Katrine broke in hurriedly, laying her hand over her brother's. "That is less than a month away. Can you wait that long, Major Wolfe, for the pleasure of my company?"

His lips twitched. "Somehow I'll manage."

She answered with a clear, musical laugh that would have broken a lesser man's heart. "I'm sure you will." Holding out her hand, she surprised him once again. "Will you dance, Major Wolfe?"

They came together in an intricate movement of the quadrille. "Katrine is an unusual name," he observed. "I've never heard it before."

"You are English," she said with the faintest curl of a lip. "My mother named me for a loch because I was born with kelpie eyes."

"What is a kelpie?" He cared nothing for the angry glare of her brother, watching from the side of the room.

"A water horse with the eyes of an elf." They moved apart, bowed, and curtseyed to the members of their set and came together again.

"I know nothing of kelpies, Lady Katrine, but I know something of lochs. They reflect the blue of the sky or the green of the land. Your eyes are neither. They are the color of water on glass."

"Are you taken with me, *Sassenach?*" she asked softly, drawing out the syllables of the hated name for Englishman.

His eyes moved to her mouth. She smelled like flowers. "Very." His whisper moved the hair at her temple. "But a Jacobite and a *Sassenach* would never do, would it, Lady Katrine?"

The violins stopped. She tilted her head to look into his eyes. "You know nothing of *kelpies,* but unless I am mistaken, you know enough Gaelic to understand what *Sassenach* means, do you not, Lord Wolfe?"

His eyes narrowed and moved over her face. With unusual perception, she had picked up on his mishap immediately. The minx was more than lovely with a wild Celtic kind of beauty not often found in the Lowland borders below the Grampians and never in England. Looking at her face sapped the breath from his lungs. He felt awkward, like an untried youth in the throes of his first crush. His heightened senses registered black hair and eyebrows, olive skin, and high cheekbones. But it was her eyes that held him. They were large and clear and brilliantly gray, as if a flame of pure silver burned eternally within her. So, this was George Murray's daughter.

Richard swallowed. "Christ," he muttered under his breath. "I don't need this. What's the matter with me?"

❄5❄

After a long absence, the heart-stopping beauty of Scone Castle, ancient seat of the Murrays, never failed to alter Katrine's breath. Through a forest of pine and black oak, on the banks of the silvery Tay, rolling green parklands stretched for nearly a mile around the castle. Geographically set in the center of the country, the granite turrets and proud battlements had witnessed much of Scotland's history.

Here Kenneth MacAlpin, King of Scots, brought the sacred Stone of Destiny to Moot Hill. On that same hill Constantine proclaimed that the laws of the Celtic Church be established. Here, MacBeth bled to death on the rush-strewn floor. Robert the Bruce, after slaying the Red Cummin, rode to Scone to be crowned by the bishop of Saint Andrews. David II, the first King of Scots to be annointed with sacred oil and the last monarch to be crowned in Scotland, was crowned here and King Charles II accepted his kingdom and sceptre on these very grounds.

Reining in her shaggy Highland mare, Katrine paused before the lichen-covered walls, gray in winter, brilliant red in autumn, and now green in celebration of spring. Breathing deeply several times, she waited for the coach to catch up with her. Even though Scone boasted many of the most modern amenities of the eighteenth century, the postern gate was not one of them. It would be the height of selfishness to ask the servants to raise the gates now and then once again when her mother's travel coach arrived. Although it was less than three full days from her home at Blair-Atholl, Lady Janet Murray refused to make the journey on horseback. Katrine chafed impatiently at the delay. Her mother was not a stern parent, but there were times when she would not be budged. Resigning herself to at least an hour's wait, Katrine was pleasantly surprised when she heard the sound of horses in the distance.

Reining in her mount, she waited for the familiar outline of the Murray coach with its driver and four horses to rise above the knoll. The two riders galloping toward her bore little resemblance to her mother's entourage. Within moments they reached her side.

James Murray, his musket across his saddle, triumphantly held up two pheasants. "You've arrived in good time, my dear. We shall eat well tonight. Where is your mother?"

"Still on her way, Uncle James." Katrine was very aware of the golden-haired gentleman by his side. "I didn't want to disturb the gatekeeper."

"Nonsense." James Murray flourished his birds. "I pay him, do I not? Raising the gates now and then relieves the boredom. Follow me," he cried, digging his knees into the belly of his mount.

Richard Wolfe maneuvered his horse next to Katrine's. "How do you do, Lady Murray?"

"Call me Katrine," she said quickly. "My mother is the one who answers to Lady Murray."

His sudden smile warmed her like a shaft of summer sunlight. "Very well, Katrine."

The sound of her name on his lips disconcerted her. The way he lingered over the syllables made it sound almost indecently personal. She was very conscious of her disheveled appearance and unconventional riding apparel. Laughing off her mother's suggestion that it was more suitable for a lady to ride sidesaddle, Katrine had pulled on her divided skirt and ridden astride. She was sure Richard Wolfe was too much of a gentleman to mention it, but she was equally sure he had noticed. She flushed and lifted her chin. What did it matter what he thought? He was, after all, only an

Englishman and she was Katrine Murray of Blair. Besides, Uncle James's reasons for inviting her to Scone did not include flirtation.

"You ride very well, Katrine." Richard's voice broke the silence. "Of course, 'tis easier to ride astride. I wonder how you would do in a lady's saddle."

She set her teeth. "Well enough."

"You must show me some day."

"With pleasure."

"Is tomorrow too soon?"

Katrine's eyes widened. "Are you always so persistent, Major Wolfe?"

"Only when I have so little time." He was every inch a Saxon with his golden hair pulled back neatly into a queue and those impossibly blue eyes. "Please say yes." The husky quality of his voice seduced her.

Their horses were very close. Katrine leaned forward and placed her hand in his. "I would be very pleased to go riding with you, Richard," she said.

Aware only of each other, neither of them heard the creaking wheels and rattling bridles that heralded the arrival of the Murray travel coach. And so it was that Janet Murray's first sight of Scone Palace in over a year included the never-to-be-forgotten image of a very tall, very fair young man pressing her daughter's hand to his lips.

"What do you know of this Englishman?" Janet asked her brother-in-law later that evening.

James looked over at the seating arrangement near the fire where the two young people were intent on their chess game. "He's a good man," he replied. "Now that his brother is dead, he will give up his commission. He stands to inherit the earldom of Manchester."

"I don't like the way he looks at Katrine."

James's bushy eyebrows drew together. "She could do much worse."

"We must know everything about the lineage of Katrine's husband, James. Too much of the English nobility carry royal blood. Nothing must be left to chance."

"If I recall correctly, you were not swayed by such an argument, Janet," he said dryly. "If you are referring to the infamous curse that no one has believed in for centuries, then a marriage between a Douglas and a Murray would have been the worst of all unions."

"All the more reason for us to take Katrine in hand." The knuckles showed white through her clasped hands. "You're wrong, James. You may not believe in the power of the curse and I know George does not, but neither of you are women. It does not affect you."

Her voice took on a low, eerie cadence, and James remembered another, older rumor of witchcraft in the Douglas line.

Janet nodded at her daughter. "You haven't had the nightmares as I have. Neither has Katrine."

"That's all right then," James said heartily, hoping to turn her from the subject. He had never been completely comfortable with his brother's wife. "She'll be spared, as are most women in the Murray line."

Janet shook her head. "You don't understand. The nightmares didn't come until I carried her in my womb. They were shadowy at first and not completely clear. Later they changed. It was almost as if I were there." Her face was pale, and she lifted shaking hands to her throat. "When Katrine was born, they stopped altogether."

James reached over and grasped her hand. "Have you told George of your fears?"

She nodded. "He laughs at my foolishness."

"Perhaps you are reading more into them than you should," he said soothingly. "You are only a Murray through marriage. Others must have seen what you have and lived out their lives without harm."

Her eyes were haunted. "You forget that I have Maxwell blood, the same as the Murrays. You have no daughters, m'lord. George and I have the only female child. *Katrine is the last daughter of our line.* Until my son marries and sires his own, Katrine is the one who will suffer."

James lifted his hand. "Stop, Janet. I'll not listen to another word. More than two hundred years have passed since our clan was under suspicion for witchcraft. Would you stir up ill feelings against us on the very eve when Scotland needs every loyal man?"

She sighed and gave up. "No. Of course not," she said.

He stood and offered her his hand. "I thought not. Shall we join the children?"

"Check. Your king is in danger, Katrine," Richard observed, moving his rook into a strategic position.

Katrine leaned forward, her chin resting on her palm, and assessed the position of her players. "I think not," she replied, capturing the rook with an unexpected move of her knight.

Richard Wolfe was an experienced chess player. He stared at the young woman beside him in surprise. "Where did you learn to play like that?"

"At the French court."

He frowned. "Who at the court of King Louis is so adept at chess?"

"Our prince," she said deliberately, turning the full force of her captivating gray eyes on him. "Charles Edward Stuart."

"I see." Richard was more than a little surprised. He had grown up with the belief that the Pretender could be no threat, not only because of his lack of support in England, but because of his character. The Chevalier and his son, Prince Charles, were said to be foppish in manner as well as unparalleled womanizers with lascivious tastes. It appeared that Richard's sources were in error. The man who taught Katrine Murray to play chess was a born tactician.

"Why do you stare at me?" she asked.

"I beg your pardon, but I find it strange that a young lady of your temperament would find suitable entertainment at the French court."

"Why is that?"

He leaned back and stretched his legs. Katrine was distracted by the firelight playing over his face and hair. Blond men didn't normally appeal to her. Fair hair and blue eyes seemed softer, less masculine, more suited to women and children. But there was nothing soft about this man. He was darkly tanned and his bright wheat-colored hair, massive shoulders, and deep blue eyes reminded her of the legends of Dalriada when the Vikings raided up and down

51

the coast of Scotland. Indeed, he looked more Viking than Saxon. A chill began at the base of her spine. Both were sworn enemies of the Scots. Katrine, always completely honest with herself, admitted that she was terribly attracted to him and that attraction was heightened by the differences between them.

"The French are cloying and extremely concerned with appearances," he said. "The men paint their faces and the women simper. You, Katrine Murray, are nothing like that. You say exactly what you think. And even if you didn't, your eyes would give you away."

She flushed and lifted her chin. "I find the French charming, and despite what you think of my temperament, I believe there were more than a few gentlemen at court who were sorry to see me leave."

"I'm sure of it," he replied dryly.

"I beg your pardon?"

"The Pretender's reputation with women precedes him, even to England."

Katrine leaned forward and spoke between clenched teeth. "He is not the Pretender. He is our prince. His father, King James, is the rightful ruler of England and Scotland."

Richard set his teeth. "King George is our rightful king, chosen by Parliament."

"Damn Parliament!" Katrine cursed in Gaelic. "It has no right to make such a choice. Kings are born, not made."

Richard's words were carefully controlled. "I disagree. A king is responsible to Parliament. He must rule properly. The Stuarts are greedy and self-serving. England does not want them back."

"She may have no choice." The words were out before she could call them back.

Richard's eyes narrowed, and the silky words carried their own hint of danger. "Really? How interesting. You must tell me more."

"What are the two of you discussing so seriously?" James Murray's voice interrupted them.

Katrine's cheeks burned. She lowered her eyes and bit her lip. She had no more self-control than a child. It would serve her right if Uncle James sent her home.

Richard's voice, laced with amusement, answered, "We

were deciding where to ride tomorrow and if we should
make it a picnic."

Katrine lifted disbelieving eyes to his face. He smiled and
stood. "'Tis late. I believe I'll retire. Shall we meet at seven,
Katrine?"

"Seven will be fine," she answered. "I'll inform the cook
that we'll take our luncheon with us. Good night, Major
Wolfe."

"Good night." He bowed over Lady Murray's hand, bid
his host a pleasant evening, and left the room.

Spring in the glens of Scotland wasn't really spring at all,
reflected Major Richard Wolfe as he looked up at the leaden
sky. He thought of his gracious home in central England.
The rose garden would be in bloom and the promise of
summer heat would encourage a round of picnics and
parties that would rival the famous watering holes of Bath
and Harrow.

He tightened his long, booted legs around the stout
middle of the shaggy Highland pony and looked at Katrine.
She had an excellent seat. Even in a sidesaddle on that
absurd mount the Scots referred to as a horse, she looked
beautiful and completely at home. Her riding habit, although of excellent cut and expensive material, showed
signs of wear. Her boots were scuffed, the heels run down,
but her back was straight and her hands were relaxed on the
reins. The clean loveliness of her face, unmarked by paint
and powder, threatened to take his breath away. If only she
were English or at least a member of a loyalist clan like the
Campbells. He grinned ruefully. If she were either of those
things, she would not be Katrine Murray.

"You are very quiet this morning," he said, urging his
horse to catch up with hers. "Have I done something to
offend you?"

She looked directly at him, her eyes moving over his face,
considering his question. "On the contrary," she said at
last. "You rescued me. If my uncle realized the extent of our
conversation, I would be posted back to Blair."

He did not pretend to misunderstand her. "In that case, I
am pleased to be of service."

His hair was the color of winter sunlight and his eyes were

deeply blue above the darker color of his coat. He smiled engagingly. She could have withstood his undeniable charm. After two seasons in Paris, Katrine had seen enough of charming men to last a lifetime. But his smile disarmed her. It was appealing and deeply personal and filled with such warmth that she couldn't look away. Instinctively she knew that she would never lie to this man. "Don't you want to know what Uncle James is so afraid I'll tell you?"

Richard was surprised. Whatever he had expected of Katrine Murray, it wasn't this. "Not yet," he said, his expression reflecting only polite interest. "First, I'd like to see something of the country."

Several hours later, they stopped to eat amidst the ruins of an ancient castle set high on the banks of the River Tay. The sun made a late-morning appearance, and the clear water of the richest salmon river in Britain reflected the brilliant blue of the sky. They dined on oatcakes, cheese, and cold chicken. When Katrine handed him a linen napkin filled with *criachan,* a sweetened mixture of oats, nuts, honey, and whiskey, he started to divide it in two.

"No." Her hand on his arm stopped him. "'Tis all for you."

He looked at her small waist and remembered the slim, long legs outlined in the breeches she had worn on her journey to Scone. Richard deplored the current fashion that demanded women be thin to the point of emaciation. "Your waistline won't be affected by a morsel this size, Katrine. Are you sure you won't share this with me?"

She laughed. "You're very flattering, but it isn't that. Sweets don't agree with me. It started when I was a child. The least bit of sugar makes me tired and anxious. If I have a great deal, I fall down in a faint." She shrugged her shoulders as if tired of the subject. "I don't think of it much. As long as I eat properly, I'm as healthy as a horse."

He had slipped the *criachan* back into the napkin and lay back on the blanket, his arms under his head. "I don't care a great deal for sweets myself," he said gently.

Katrine removed her jacket and lay back on her elbows beside him. Closing her eyes, she lifted her face to the sky, welcoming the kiss of the sun on her cheeks. The heat made her drowsy. She was content with the unexpected beauty of the day, the gentle lapping of the river, the drone of bees, the muffled nickering of the horses, and the golden-haired Englishman lying by her side. She was almost asleep when his voice startled her.

"What is James Murray keeping from me, Katrine?"

She wet her lips and turned to face him. It did not occur to her to tell him anything less than the truth. "He expects a French invasion. Charles Stuart will sail to Scotland with an army and challenge the elector."

Richard breathed a sigh of relief. "Is that all?"

"Isn't it enough?" Katrine asked indignantly. "If your King George were aware of such a plot, he would quake in his boots."

Richard studied her flushed passionate face and silently cursed Prince Charles Edward Stuart for the power he had over the Highlanders. If their bonny prince attempted to bring his foolish dreams to fruition, this girl and her family would be ruined, as would half the clans in Scotland. For some inexplicable reason, the thought incited Richard to a murderous rage.

"Scotland is a far different place than it was thirty years ago, Katrine. There are British forts, three hundred miles of road and over forty bridges to enable government troops to penetrate the mountains. Companies of your own Highlanders have been recruited to keep order."

"We will not be alone."

"Oh, but you will," he countered. "There are many who drink to 'the King over the Water,' but they will not risk their fortunes to help him. Charles will have no allies in England, and the French have already abandoned one such expedition. He will have to rely on the Highlands, and as you know, there are many who are not Jacobites."

"You know a great deal about us, m'lord," replied Katrine. "How is it that you are here, in Scotland, when your government surely needs you at home?"

He told her, knowing he should not admit it but realizing she probably knew already. James Murray was a shrewd politician. Most likely he had invited his lovely niece to Scone in the hopes of loosening the English major's tongue.

"Your uncle and my late brother became acquainted while they were both members of the House of Lords," he explained. "We have a slight family connection. Somewhere back in time I had a Maxwell ancestor as do the Murrays. When rumors of a Jacobite landing circulated through Parliament, I was the obvious choice to gauge the temperament here in Scotland. Your uncle appeared pleased when I suggested the visit."

"Is the situation what you thought it would be?"

"Yes."

Katrine turned to stare out at the river, her profile outlined by the stones of the ancient castle wall. "What will you tell them?"

"That your prince has enough support in Scotland to take the country," he said quietly. "I will propose that we allow him his kingdom. We can live as two countries, side by side, like the Scotland and England of old. But if he takes one step across the borders into England, he will be crushed."

Her fist clenched on the handle of her whip. Her eyes were large and brilliant, and she spoke fervently. "If only he will listen."

"Charles isn't the only one who will need convincing," said Richard. "England isn't likely to accept a Scottish secession without a fight."

He watched the thin, high-boned features tighten and marveled, once again, at the clear Celtic beauty of her face. Desire, primitive and demanding, consumed him. His eyes moved to her mouth, and his breathing altered.

"We should go," she whispered.

"Yes."

Neither of them moved.

"It would never do, *Sassenach.*" Her voice was unsteady.

"I know." Without warning, he reached out, his hands rough and insistent, and pulled her against him. For a timeless moment he stared down into her face, and then he set his mouth on hers.

Katrine did not once consider resistance nor did she think of her half-hearted promise made months before to Duncan Forbes, a strong-minded Scottish lord whom she had almost agreed to marry. Instead, her hands slid up to curl possessively around Richard's neck, and her lips parted. She felt the weight of his chest and the muscles of his legs pressing down on top of her.

With shaking fingers he loosened the buttons of her high-necked habit. His mouth moved from her lips to her throat. She moaned, and her head fell back, giving him greater access to her smooth olive skin. He lifted his head. "Katrine." His voice was hoarse. "Are you . . . Have you ever . . . ?"

"No."

With tremendous effort, he put her away from him and sat up, breathing heavily. Quickly, she buttoned her jacket.

"Why did you stop?" she asked when she trusted herself to speak once again.

"I should never have touched you," he reproached himself. "I never intended it." With his hand under her chin, he forced her to meet his gaze. "Why did you allow me?"

Her eyes were slate gray, the pupils large and dilated. "I wanted you," she said simply. "I've wanted you since the night we met at Holyrood House."

At that moment, Richard knew with a terrifying certainty that even if he lived a thousand lifetimes, he would never love anyone half as much as he loved Katrine Murray.

"Will you marry me, Katrine?"

Her eyes widened. "You can't possibly want to marry a Jacobite."

"I've never wanted anything more."

She shook her head. "I can't marry you, Richard. My father won't permit it."

"The devil take your father." He took her hands in his. "It is *your* answer I want."

The color darkened her cheeks, but she didn't look away. "Oh, yes." She laughed shakily. "I want to marry you very much indeed."

"You know nothing about me."

"On the contrary," she said. "I know a great deal." Closing her eyes, she recited his accomplishments from memory. "You are a Whig and a second son with an exemplary military record. Your older brother recently died, forcing you to give up your commission, which you are loathe to do. Drinking and dicing and playing the 'grand seigneur' doesn't suit you. You've the ear of your king as well as the prime minister, and when in England, you spend most of your time at your home in Manchester rather than your London townhouse. Your mother is renowned for her sharp tongue and remarkable ability to manage. Your father is dead, and your three younger sisters adore you." Her eyes opened, spilling light and warmth and something else that threatened to destroy his carefully reconstructed self-control. "But not nearly as much as I do."

Happiness surged through him, and he pulled her back into his arms. "I'll take care of your father, darling. Leave everything to me."

Traquair House

1993

"Miss Murray. Miss Murray." I could hear the insistent voice clearly. Fighting against it, I strained to recapture my dream. It was hazy but still faintly visible. "Miss Murray." This time the voice carried a note of panic, and sharp fingers pinched my shoulder. I opened my eyes.

"What is it, Kate?"

"It's after nine o'clock," she said accusingly. "You've slept away the entire day and missed dinner. Are you all right?"

"Of course. I must have been more tired than I thought." Kate still looked disapproving. "If it isn't too much trouble, I'd like something to eat."

She smiled and lost some of her anxious expression.

"There's lamb and potatoes, and I've made fresh biscuits. Will you take it downstairs or shall I bring up a tray?"

"I'll come down," I replied, looking around the darkened room. The fire had died to a few glowing embers, highlighting the old-fashioned chair and footstool, the picture of the ninth earl of Maxwell over the mantel, and the floor-to-ceiling shelves of musty leather-bound books. The more modern conveniences, the electric wiring, the heating pipes, the pillow-strewn sofa, and current world map, had blended into the night shadows. The library must have looked exactly this way to a weary Prince Charles in 1745 when he briefly occupied the upstairs bedroom.

For some reason I wanted no part of the room or its memories in the meager half-light of the hearth fire. It was ridiculous, but I couldn't deny it. I was afraid. Kate, with her pursed lips and no-nonsense attitude, was exactly what I needed. That and a hot meal washed down with a glass of authentic, Traquair-brewed ale.

"Have the Maxwells always occupied this house?" I asked as I followed the housekeeper down the stairs.

"As far back as I can remember." She flipped on the kitchen light and removed a covered plate from the oven. My stomach juices came alive. Tilting her head in that birdlike pose I was beginning to associate with her, she said, "Of course, the family intermarried with other clans. There's no telling how pure the bloodline really is. The person to ask is Mr. Ian Douglas. He knows more about the history of the borders than anyone I know."

"I'll do that," I said between bites of lamb.

Kate poured out a glass of ale and was about to slice a wedge of cream cake when she hesitated and put it back in the refrigerator. Instead, she reached for an apple and began to peel with an efficient, circular motion. "I'll have to get used to leaving out the sweets," she said. "The doctor told me about your condition." She looked at me curiously. "Have you always had it?"

"Ever since I was a child. It's not a problem, really," I assured her. "Don't deny yourself or anyone else their desserts. I'll manage."

She sat down across from me with a cup of tea and

changed the subject. "Mr. Douglas stopped by today. I went into the library and found you asleep. He thought it would be best if I didn't wake you."

"Thank you, Kate," I answered, surprised at the extent of my annoyance. "In the future, I'd prefer that you wake me."

"It's like that, is it?" Amusement colored her voice.

I could feel the betraying blush stain my cheeks. "I'm not sure what you mean," I lied. "The fact is, I have some questions I'd like to ask him. If he calls again, be sure to let me know."

"Why don't you call him? I'll ring his number for you."

Apparently the women's movement had infiltrated Scotland after all.

Kate reached for the phone.

"Not now," I said hastily. "It's late. Tomorrow would be better." I really did want to ask Ian about the past residents of Traquair House but not in front of Kate. I still wasn't sure what I thought of this woman or, more importantly, what she thought of me.

We had reached the end of our conversation at the same time I finished my meal. As if on cue, the phone rang. "Traquair," Kate said into the old-fashioned mouthpiece. "I'll see if she's available." She raised her eyebrows and held out the phone. "It's Mr. Douglas for you."

"Thank you, Kate," I said. "I'll take it upstairs."

Forcing myself to walk at a normal pace, I reached the upstairs hallway and picked up the phone. "I've got it," I said, waiting for the click at the other end. When it came, I breathed a sigh of relief. I'd never lived with anyone other than family since my undergraduate days in the dormitory. The lack of privacy was affecting my nerves. "Hello, Ian."

"How are you, Christina?"

"Fine, thank you."

"Did everything go as expected with the solicitor?"

His voice was low and unusually pleasant. It was one of the first things I'd noticed about him after his spectacular looks. "I knew what to expect if that's what you mean," I said. "It's still overwhelming to think of Traquair as mine."

"You'll get used to it."

Had I imagined it, or was there a trace of mockery in the

friendly words? I decided to ignore it. "I understand you're something of an expert on the history of this area."

He laughed. "In light of appearing immodest, I must say that whoever told you that is exaggerating."

"I'd like to know something about the previous owners of Traquair," I persisted. "Can you help me or should I go the university library in Edinburgh?"

"If you're really interested, I'll tell you all I know. After that we can drive up to the capital if you like and I'll introduce you to Professor MacCleod. He's the true expert on Scottish history. Perhaps you've heard of him?"

I couldn't help smiling. "I've known him for over ten years. He was the lecturer on Gaelic antiquities when I attended the University of Edinburgh. Somehow we never got around to discussing my family tree."

"That was before you inherited a Scottish antiquity. I'm sure he'll be thrilled to see you. We should call first and give him time to prepare."

There was silence on both ends of the line. Then we both spoke at once.

"Christina—"

"Ian—"

"I'm sorry," he said. "You go first."

Suddenly, I didn't want to be the one to speak. "No, you."

"All right," he said agreeably. "The reason I called was to ask if you'd like to go fishing."

I could feel my stomach heave. "I'm a terrible sailor," I confessed. "I get seasick."

His chuckle was pure magic. "You won't this time. I meant fly-fishing. You know, on the riverbank, for trout and salmon."

"I've never been."

"I'll show you. That is, if you'd like to learn."

"Yes, I would."

"Good. Sleep well. I'll pick you up tomorrow morning at five A.M. Good-bye, Christina."

I had never felt less like sleeping. My bed had been turned down and the fire banked. A bouquet of heather sat on the nightstand along with a mug of warm milk. It tasted of cinnamon. I drained the last drop, shrugged out of my clothes, and pulled on my nightgown. In less than five minutes I was asleep.

Five A.M. in the borders brings a soft blue dawn with the rays of a muted sun streaking the clouds pink and silver. I was wakened by a gentle hand shaking my shoulder and a cup of steaming coffee held under my nose. Kate was upholding her reputation for having *the sight*. There could be no other explanation for her knowing my plans. The phone had been silent all night after Ian's call, and even if he'd told her why he was phoning, she had no way of knowing that I'd agreed. After biting into one of her buttery, raisin-filled scones, her omniscience no longer bothered me. As long as she continued to create these mouth-watering confections, she could practice all the black magic that she pleased.

Less than an hour later Ian strode ahead of me, impervious to the cold. I shivered in the early chill and huddled deeper into my thick, Icelandic sweater, watching the morning sun pick out the lights in his hair, silhouetting his head in a halo of silver. The fluid movement of his bunched athlete's muscles under the navy sweater and worn jeans called to mind the piercing beauty of Shakespeare's words: "all my fortunes at thy feet I'll lay and follow thee, my lord, throughout the world." I knew the story of the Pied Piper and the danger of becoming too fascinated by the unknown, but that morning I would have followed him anywhere.

He carried two fishing poles, two pairs of rubber boots, and a tackle box. I carried our lunch basket, the contents created by the redoubtable Kate, and a blanket. If I had stopped to consider it, I might have wondered why my housekeeper was so persistent in encouraging my relationship with our attractive neighbor. She was behaving like a desperate Victorian mother trying to marry off her spinster daughter.

I followed Ian out into a clearing of such sheer beauty that words escaped me. I had to sit down. Taking deep, restoring breaths, I looked out from my seat on the bank, over the crystalline falls, to the mouth of Saint Mary's Loch. Never had I seen water so clear. The deep blue of the sky and the green of the trees was reflected like a mirror image from the glassy depths. At the bottom of the loch, stones, worn smooth from centuries of slow-moving currents, provided resting places for speckled trout and pink-skinned salmon. On the banks, purple heather and delicate blue gentians peeked out from sun-baked boulders. The air was scented with pine and sage and a strange, sharp odor that I'd never smelled before.

"Why aren't they afraid of us?" I asked, making eye contact with a large, spotted trout.

Ian knelt down, resting easily beside me. "This is private property. The fish have no fear of people because they rarely see them."

"I didn't realize Traquair had its own river."

He chewed on a piece of wild mustard. "This land isn't part of Traquair."

"But we're less than five miles from the house. Whose land is it?"

He grinned. "Mine. I told you we were neighbors."

"I had no idea our land was connected." Stretching out my legs, I leaned back on my hands and nodded toward the fishing poles laying in the grass. "You did say you would teach me to fly-fish, didn't you?"

I could feel the approval in his glance. "I said I would teach you to fish," he said softly. "Fly-fishing is another matter."

"Why is that?"

He released the catch on his tackle box and pulled out what looked like a brightly colored insect and a hook. Reaching for one of the poles, he tied the hook to the fishing line, knotted the pseudofly, and secured it to the hook. "Bait," he said, holding it out for my inspection.

I laughed. "You can't be serious?"

"The best trout bait in the world." He reached for my hand. "Come and see."

We climbed down to a grassy knoll near the shore. I pulled on the boots he handed me while he cast out into the water. The line tightened as the current took it. Within seconds, the pole bent nearly in two, and the line went taut. With a quick flip of his wrist, Ian jerked the pole back hard. "I've hooked up," he said. "Watch carefully."

With exquisite skill, he alternated between pulling back on the pole with one hand while he reeled in his catch with the other. Finally, I could see the head emerge from the water, followed by the entire body, a large brown and silver fish hanging slack on the hook. Again with the precision of a surgeon, he cut the line, hooked the trout to what looked like a rope, anchored it into the bank, and set the now limp body gently back into the icy loch.

Ian rinsed his hands, tied another lure to the line, and turned back to me. "Your turn," he said, holding out the pole.

I hesitated. "I've never done this before."

"There's no hurry. I'll show you." He stood behind me, his arms around my shoulders, his hands covering mine. Together, we cast out. I saw a flash of silver, and immediately the line went taut. "Can you feel it?" he asked excitedly. "You've hooked up."

Considering our proximity, I responded with remarkable calm. "What do I do now?"

"Pull hard to embed the hook and then let him take the line."

I leaned back against his chest, forgetting, for the moment, our intimate position. "Why not just pull him in?" I asked, thrilled at the idea of catching my first fish.

"The swim tires him out. That way he won't fight and break the line." His voice sounded strained. Caught up in the drama of the chase, I ignored it.

Sure enough, within moments, the pull lessened, and I was able to reel in my catch.

"Very nice," approved Ian as he inspected the medium-sized trout. "You're on your own." Handing me the clippers to finish the task, he turned and walked up the bank for his own pole and boots. Instead of returning to the banks of the loch, he walked to the falls, waded into the current, and took his position at the mouth of the small burn that fed into the larger body of water.

We fished all morning. To be completely truthful, Ian did most of the fishing while I watched in appreciative silence. Caught up in the precise art and studied grace of a master at his craft, I sat mesmerized by the magic of the quiet glen and the ceaseless flow of water over clean stones.

I drank in every movement of the tall blond man standing thigh-deep in the sun-drenched river. The play of muscle across his back, the dip of his shoulder, the swing of his cast, the impatient way he threw his hair back from his forehead, became as familiar to me as my own reflection staring up from the loch.

I don't have words to explain why the embarrassing tears sprang to my eyes every time I saw his arm lift, his wrist loosen and snap back, and the inevitable flash of twisting line as it skimmed across the water, dancing like a dragonfly in the sunlight. Time passed without notice. I sat for hours, content just to stare at the sky, the water, the trees, and a man whose smile made my blood run hot after such a long and lonely winter.

It wasn't until late afternoon that we ate Kate's sandwiches. The ice-cold ale followed by a thermos of hot coffee had an unusual effect on my nerves. I was relaxed but wide awake. The blood drummed loudly in my ears, and my inhibitions were so completely extinguished that it seemed the most natural thing in the world for Ian to lay back on the blanket and pull my head against his shoulder. I rested my hand on his chest and fitted my body against the length of his. His hand sifted through my hair. It moved to my neck and then my cheek. His eyes met mine, and the need reflected there shook me.

"Christina?" he breathed the timeless question.

I nodded. This time I was ready for the taste of his mouth, the hungry pressure of his lips, and the powerful surging flood of desire when he flicked his tongue against mine. We kissed for a long time, lips teasing, tongues tasting, breath mingling until, for both of us, it was too much and at the same time no longer enough.

There was no pulling away, no turning back. Again I was ready when his hands slid under my sweater and unhooked the clasp of my bra. The weight of my breasts fell into his hands. His thumbs rested on my skin, circling the sensitive peaks until they stood up, firm and erect through the sweater. Lowering his head, he took a stiffened nipple into his mouth and sucked gently, wetting the soft wool.

I ached for him. Throwing away years of inhibition, I reached out and stroked him through his jeans. "My God,

Christina," he groaned, pulling me tightly into the saddle of his hips. He was fully, powerfully erect. Carefully, working around the straining flesh, I unbuttoned the top two buttons of his fly. He stopped breathing as I maneuvered the rest free. The full length of him surged into my hand, and he pushed me back into the grass.

Those were the last details I remember along with the smell of cold air and clean wind, the taste of coffee and ale on a searching tongue, and the sweetness of hot, hard flesh pounding into mine, filling the aching emptiness with life and warmth and hope. We came together on the banks of Saint Mary's Loch in a flash of blinding need, hungry for the feel of urgent hands and naked skin and the ancient, primal splendor of dark blood calling for the culmination of a ritual older than time.

When it was over, I felt no awkwardness, no remorse or guilt, only a grateful relief that the long dry wait was finally over. It was as if we had done this a thousand times before and it was right. We dressed and lay down together once again, curled up like spoons in the blanket. I slept briefly and woke to the sound of his heartbeat against my cheek. His fingers were threaded in my hair.

"Was your husband's name David?" he asked casually.

I pulled away to look at his face, wincing as a few strands of hair came away in his hand. "No. Why do you ask?"

"You called me David just before you fell asleep."

"I don't know anyone by that name."

He gathered me close to his chest. "Perhaps I misunderstood."

David. The name was naggingly familiar. It was common enough for me to have heard it many times over the course of a lifetime, but it seemed more familiar than that. Suddenly, I remembered.

"Ian."

"Yes," he murmured sleepily.

"Tell me everything you know about the previous owners of Traquair House."

He chuckled. "We'd be here all night, Christina. Traquair is eight hundred years old."

"Did the Murrays ever live there?" I persisted.

He was silent for a long time. At last, he spoke. "The Maxwells have always held the title to Traquair, but during the course of its history, a number of marriages with Murrays took place as well as with other border families." His fingers caressing my head lulled me into a sense of complacency. "As you well know," he continued, "Scotland was more or less an isolated country for centuries. The nobility was limited to about two hundred families. Over an eight-century period, it would be very unusual to find a family that hasn't intermarried with every other clan in Scotland."

"That doesn't explain why Lord Maxwell left Traquair House to me."

"I'm sure he had good reason. The Maxwells had no children, and you're obviously related in some way."

I knew he would be skeptical, but I decided to tell him anyway. Sitting up, I turned to face him. He lay on his side, resting easily on one arm, his right eyebrow quirked askance at my serious expression.

"I read Janet Douglas's diary," I began.

"The whole thing?"

"No. Only the beginning where she explains how her daughter met Major Richard Wolfe. Then I fell asleep."

He grinned. "That boring, was it?"

"Not at all. I had the strangest dream, Ian. It was so real, as if I were watching a movie. There was a celebration at Holyrood House. Katrine was there and Richard Wolfe. I saw George and James Murray and Katrine's older brother, Alasdair. I could hear their conversations and read their thoughts. I've never experienced anything like it."

Was that tension I saw in Ian's expression? I couldn't tell, but his eyes were narrowed and he was suddenly very intent on what I was saying.

He sat up and took my hands. The blue eyes were very close. "It could have been the portrait, Christina. It isn't every day that one finds such an unusual likeness to an ancestor. You read the diary, and you know a great deal about Scotland's history. The names you mentioned are men famous for their roles at Culloden Moor. I don't think what you experienced has any special significance."

"There's something else," I said. I hadn't planned on telling him, but it was suddenly very important that I said it aloud. "The night you took me to dinner, I had another dream. It was terrifying. I wrote it all down just the way I saw it."

Some of the desperation I felt must have shown in my face because he smiled reassuringly. "Relax, darling," he said. "What exactly did you see?"

"A woman who looked like Katrine, only older. Her name was Mairi Maxwell."

This time I didn't imagine it. Ian's face paled under his tan. "That's impossible," he said flatly.

I shook my head. "She was Mairi Maxwell of Shiels, and she lived at the end of the thirteenth century. Her husband was David Murray. I believe Traquair House was another Murray family holding. Ian"—I gripped his hands tightly—"she was in the courtyard when Robert the Bruce came to accuse her of sedition, and she looked exactly like me." His expression hadn't changed. I could feel the panic rising in my throat.

"How could you possibly know that?" he whispered.

"It was all in my dream," I cried out in frustration. "There was more, much more. It had to do with the Coronation Stone, Scotland's Stone of Destiny."

He held his finger against my lips. "Stop, Christina. Let's take it slowly. What was your mother's maiden name?"

"Donnally."

"And her mother's?"

"Wilder. What has my mother got to do with anything?" I asked impatiently.

He looked down at his watch. "It's late. Let's gather our things and get back."

I looked at him, feeling the helplessness that relinquishing control brings. "Please don't do this to me," I whispered.

Dropping the blanket, he pulled me up into his arms. "I don't have any answers yet, darling. But I will. I promise you that. As soon as I do, you'll be the first to know."

Darling. Why did that sound so natural, and where had I heard it before? Certainly not from Stephen. "Why can't you tell me what this is all about?" I pleaded.

He ran his hand through his hair. "Because it's too absurd to even contemplate. You'll have to trust me."

"I want to," I began.

He dropped his arms and stepped back. "Christina, this isn't a game and this isn't America. I don't make a habit of seducing women on the riverbank."

I laughed. I couldn't help it. A tremendous weight had been lifted from my shoulders. "Not all Americans jump into bed on the second date, Ian."

"Do you?"

This was suddenly too important to take offense. "No," I said simply.

The brightness of his smile was like a living flame warming me inside. "Thank God for that," he said. "Now, let's go. It looks like rain."

Instinctively, I knew we'd weathered a crisis. When he kissed me good-bye at the door of Traquair House, I didn't mind leaving him. Our relationship had changed, and this time, I knew I would see him again. Dropping the basket in the kitchen, I greeted Kate and hurried upstairs to find Janet Douglas's diary. My shower could wait.

❊7❊

Scone Castle
June 1745

"Katrine," begged her mother, "be reasonable. You hardly know the man. If you marry him, he'll take you away to his home in England. You were born and raised in the Highlands. How can you even think of leaving everything you know for a man you met less than a month ago?"

"I've never known anyone like him," Katrine said simply.

"There's a brightness in him, a fire that pulls me." She looked directly at Janet Douglas. "Surely you know how it is, Mother? You married Father despite the disapproval of your families. I'm your daughter. Isn't it possible that I know my own mind as well as you knew yours?"

Janet wrung her hands. "It isn't the same at all. George and I are Scots. We share the same loves and loyalties, the same history and customs. The match would have been welcomed by both clans if it were not for—" She stopped and bit her lip.

"Go on," Katrine said curiously.

Janet sighed and sat down in the comfortable, unfashionably wide chair that she refused to leave home without. They were in the refurbished sitting room attached to her bedchamber. Despite her preference for everything Scottish, she preferred this room to any other at Scone, and it was decidedly English in flavor. Over the fireplace, the doors and bookcases, and in the marble-topped console with its carved eagle support, the impact of the Palladian revival was evident. Heavy pedimentation and richly framed mirrors accented the room. Niches filled with painted ivory, porcelain, and jade from China were set into the peach-painted walls. An Oriental lacquered screen shut out the light from one of the long windows and a large portrait of Sir David Murray, the first Lord Scone, hung above the fireplace. The only fault Janet could find with these Inigo Jones reproductions were the chairs. They were spindly and narrow with embroidered cushions that looked like the heavy tapestries that had covered the walls of Blair-Atholl for centuries.

Janet was a fashionable woman in all things except her comfort. The wide, high-backed chair with its sturdy arms had been with her most of her life. Here, at her mother's knee, she learned to set the neat, perfect stitches that had brought her fame in Edinburgh. It was to this chair that she brought the first glimmer of her love for George Murray, burying her flushed face against the worn upholstery, wondering if he felt the same heat that surged through her veins. Here she had nursed her children, coming to know for the first time the exquisite ache of a tiny mouth searching for sustenance. Curled up in the warm softness, she taught them their prayers, encouraged their dreams, listened to their confidences, and bandaged their hurts. In this comforting sanctuary from her childhood, awash in the happiness of her second pregnancy, she had experienced the onset of the terrifying nightmares.

She looked at her daughter. Katrine's light-filled eyes studied her as if she were an exotic bird perched on the mantel. "Are you all right, Mother?" she asked.

Janet's hand trembled as she smoothed the brocade of her skirts. "What will you do if your father forbids the match?" she asked.

Katrine's lips tightened. "He wouldn't. There is no impediment to the marriage. Father knows that. Richard is suitable in every way."

"You didn't answer my question."

"If I have to, I shall wait until I'm of age," said Katrine stubbornly. "Two years isn't such a great deal of time."

"We may soon be at war with England, my love. Would Richard agree to wait?"

Katrine's smile was both tender and proud, and her answer was very sure. "He will wait for as long as it takes. There is no one else for either of us, Mama."

Janet stared into the lovely, heartbreakingly earnest young face and relented. Perhaps it would be all right. Richard Wolfe could have no connection with an ancient Scottish prophecy. And even if he did, the course of fate could not be changed. "I'll speak to your father," she said at last. "However, it would help if your young man pleaded his own case."

"Richard rode to Edinburgh to see Papa this morning."

The light that burned inside Katrine flamed into a joy so intense, so vitally alive, that Janet couldn't bear to look at her. Turning away, she blinked back the tears that welled up in her eyes.

Less than one month later Katrine Murray married Richard Wolfe on the twenty-fifth day of July in the small, intimate chapel at Scone. It was a private ceremony with only family members present. Richard's family was not in attendance. They had not been expected. The political climate was too unsettled for a journey north. Janet held up well, smiling mistily through a veil of tears. Katrine's brother, Alasdair, stood in white-lipped silence, his thin Celtic face betraying none of the anger twisting his mind. But his thoughts were full. His sister married to a *Sassenach*. It was beyond endurance.

George Murray walked down the long, portrait-lined gallery with his daughter on his arm. His footsteps on the oaken floor, where so many kings had walked, were sadly resigned. Of all that were present that day, only he knew what had transpired and what was to come. Only he knew that the marriage of his only daughter, the laughing, flame-lit, wood-sprite Katrine, was doomed because of a tall, brown-eyed young man who called himself a prince and had all the romantic appeal of a hero.

Only days before, Prince Charles Edward Stuart, in the company of a few loyal men with a pitifully small store of arms and ammunition, set foot on the isle of Eriskay. Sir Alexander MacDonald of Boisdale, a gruff and practical Scot, advised him to go home. The prince eyed the gathered clansmen, bowed deeply from the waist, and said, "I am come home, sir." The men broke into a resounding cheer, and Scotland's fate was sealed.

By now his frigate had most likely reached the mainland at Loch nan Uamh near Arisaig. Charles would seek support from the Highland chiefs, and George knew that despite his new son-in-law, the Murray standard would rise with the prince. He would be very gentle with his daughter today. Holy God, she should know something of the happiness he and her mother shared. Before the flowers on her bridal bouquet wilted, her world would be torn apart, her loyalties divided. Her husband's troops would kill members of her clan. Perhaps the family she loved would make her a widow. It was enough to make a man drown himself in good Scotch whiskey.

No hint of the troubles to come intruded upon the young couple as they ascended the steps of the travel carriage for their journey to Blair Castle. George had insisted they go there after the wedding. He wanted Richard to see Katrine's childhood home. The couple would have complete privacy except for the servants. He and Alasdair were on their way to Perth to meet with the prince, and Janet would remain at Scone.

Richard's eyes widened at his first sight of Blair-Atholl. The startlingly white medieval towers against the green hills of Tayside were blinding in their brilliance. In full view of the surrounding countryside, the castle was unusual in that the courtyard and outer buildings were not protected by the usual wall and postern gate.

"Isn't it rather vulnerable to attack?" asked Richard, his military-trained gaze perusing the disadvantages of holding off an enemy.

"This is the eighteenth century, Richard." Katrine's gray eyes danced at his naïveté. "Clans no longer make war upon each other by besieging castles. Any skirmishes we've had recently have taken place in open fields."

Richard thought of the latest dispatch sent to him only yesterday. There would definitely be a war in Scotland. He was profoundly grateful that his marriage to Katrine had taken place before it was officially declared.

Later, after the last of the dinner dishes were removed, he looked down the long banquet table at his wife. Her face and the lovely line of her neck were framed by the light of twin candles. Her eyes glowed like diamonds, and a single black curl rested against her breast. She smiled, and his mouth went dry.

"Shall we go upstairs?" he asked in a voice he didn't recognize.

She nodded. "I'd like to go up first if you don't mind."

"Of course." He stood and walked to the other end of the table. Bending to kiss the nape of her neck, he caressed her bare shoulder. She reached up to thread her fingers through his hair. At the touch of her fingers, he pulled away, breathing raggedly. "You'd better leave now, darling," he said, "or I won't be held accountable for my actions."

Touching his cheek lightly, Katrine left the room and climbed the stairs to the bedchamber that had been prepared for them. A servant helped her out of the voluminous petticoats and panniers and pulled a simple cotton night-dress over her head. There had been no time for a trousseau. Katrine was sitting on the bed, brushing out her own silken curtain of hair, when Richard stepped into the room and closed the door behind him.

He walked over to Katrine and lifted a shining lock of hair. "I've never seen it loose," he said in wonder. "You must never powder it. Never."

"I won't if you prefer it."

Without a word, he shrugged out of his jacket and unbuttoned his shirt. Katrine swallowed. His shoulders were massive, and the deeply muscled chest was covered with a mat of the fairest hair she'd ever seen. He looked down at her, saying nothing, the blue eyes smoldering with passion. She recognized it immediately. Desire, instant and primal, rose within her, and she held out her arms.

He went into them. Bending his head, he kissed her, pushing her back on the pillows. A wave of white-hot sensation seared through her at the touch of his mouth on her throat. When his hands slid up under her gown, over her legs to her waist and then her breasts, she cried out and opened her legs, reveling in the heaviness, the power and strength of the rock-hard muscles, between them.

There was pain when he entered her, pain and splintering light and rocking waves of pleasure. Afterward, he lay spent on the pillow beside her, and she played with the loose silvery hair spilling across her shoulder. Without his clothes and his neatly tied-back queue, he no longer looked like an English gentleman. He looked primitive and uncivilized, like a Viking plunderer from a different age. She smiled widely.

Richard felt the movement of her mouth against his shoulder and raised his head. "Christ, sweetheart," he began.

"I know," she replied.

His lips found the sensitive spot on her throat. "Shall we try again with a little less intensity?" he murmured.

Her eyes, in the pale oval of her face, were wide with surprise. "Good lord, why? Have you heard me complain?"

Startled, he sat up on his elbow to look down at her.

Moonlight streamed in through the long window, illuminating the flushed skin, the high bones of her cheeks, and the clear gray eyes. There was nothing of guile or flirtation shining through the transparent depths, only trust and love and a pure, elemental gleam of anticipation. He did not deserve this woman. He, Richard Wolfe, known for his savoir faire in lovemaking, came to his wife in blinding need. He had taken her like a rutting bull or an unskilled boy with his first barmaid, and still, she held out her arms to him. He flushed, his fair skin darkening with shame.

Katrine sat up, bracing herself on her arms. The bedclothes slipped down and he saw something else: the full, parted lips and long eyelashes, the smooth column of her pulsing throat, the warm olive tones of her skin, and the full rise of her taut, young breasts.

She smiled seductively and lowered her lashes. His eyes widened as he watched her slide her hands down her own body, lingering on the curve of her hip and the flat plane of her stomach. When she returned to her breasts and cupped them, his mouth was completely dry. She was driving him insane. Where would an innocent girl learn to do that?

With a groan, he pulled her beneath him, and his mouth locked on hers. Her response was immediate, and it gentled him. Exercising the self-control for which he was renowned, he set out, for the first time, to arouse the woman he loved.

Brushing the hair back from her forehead, he trailed light kisses from her ear to the base of her throat, sucking gently at the point where the blood leaped to life. Running his hand down the slope of her breast, he followed with his mouth, flicking the sensitive tip with his tongue until he felt her nipple harden. She gasped and arched up to meet him, holding his head down. He filled his mouth with her, moving from one mound to the other until she cried out, begging him to end it.

He was fully erect. Sliding his hand between her thighs, he parted them and moved over her.

Katrine had never imagined her body capable of such magic. She was beyond thought, beyond logic, reeling in a sea of pure sensation. Heat pooled in her womb, and the delicious tension rose and rose until she wanted nothing more than to pull the hardened flesh now probing at the entrance to her womanhood as deeply into the heart of her being as it would go. Who would have thought a man's body, all hard lines and jutting angles, could hold such delights for a woman? She wanted him now. Boldly, she reached for him, her hand encircling the turgid flesh. He stiffened and froze, the veins in his neck standing out like cords. Instinctively, she move her hips. Richard's control snapped. With a shout of surrender, he drove into her over and over until the shattering pleasure of his release drained him completely. Raising his head, he looked down at her face. What he saw satisfied him and he joined her in sleep, their bodies tangled, for twelve dreamless hours.

Traquair House

1993

Janet's diary lay unopened beside me. It was no longer necessary for me to read. The images came from inside me, from my own mind. I managed the walk to my room in relative calm. Gathering my clothes, I made it to the bathroom and locked the door. But in the shower, as the soft spray of hot water hit my face, I lost control. If anyone had asked me to explain the wrenching sobs that wracked my body, I couldn't have done it. Maybe it was the beauty of Katrine Murray Wolfe's wedding night. Maybe it was the all-consuming desire of two doomed lovers or the piercing clarity of the selfless love they so obviously shared. Or maybe it was pain. Pain for the failure of my dreams and the realization that my own marriage, compared to the burning, heart-shattering passion of Katrine's, had been nothing more than an empty shell.

Later, instead of turning on the lamp on my nightstand, I lit the candles on either side of the bed and lay back against the pillows, pretending to be Katrine Murray waiting for her bridegroom. The flickering candlelight contributed to the feeling of mystery and age permeating the room. I could almost feel the centuries roll back and the faint crows-feet disappear around my eyes. I was suddenly, glowingly happy. I was a bride waiting for the husband I loved. Sipping Kate's still warm tea, I waited for the images to come.

Ashton Manor, England
September 1745

Katrine looked out the long, diamond-paned windows at the manicured lawns and graceful fountains of Ashton Manor. The Wolfes' country seat, with all its amenities, was as luxurious and dignified as a palace. The wide staircases, modern kitchen, well-lit bedrooms, and formal gardens bore no resemblance to her childhood home. Katrine bit her lip. She was dreadfully homesick. When Charles raised the standard at Glenfinnan and her father had agreed to become his field commander, she knew it was time to return to Scotland. Only the child prevented her. The child and the desperate, quicksilver brightness of the love she bore for Richard Wolfe. She had not yet told him that she carried his bairn. If he knew that, he would never allow her to leave. Only her mother knew and perhaps not yet. Mail was dreadfully slow, and the letter she had franked only two weeks before may have been delayed.

Richard walked into the room in his shirtsleeves. It was September and unseasonably hot. Without speaking, he rang the bell and waited for the butler to appear. "Send up a bottle of claret, Hastings," he ordered.

"Very well, sir." The servant bowed and left the room.

Katrine wet her lips. "It didn't go well, did it?"

Some of the grimness left Richard's mouth. She always knew, even without words. "No," he answered, looking at her steadily. "Charles captured Edinburgh without a fight after routing Sir John Cope and his troops at Prestonpans. Your prince is now residing at Holyrood."

"Holy God! What will the government do?"

Hastings returned with the claret and set it on the tea cart. "Will there be anything else, my lord?"

"No, thank you," said Richard, tossing down a quick glass and pouring another.

"We'll ring if we need anything else, Hastings," said Katrine. "You may leave us now."

The butler bowed and left the room. She turned to her husband. "Tell me, Richard. Anything is better than not knowing."

"Is it?" His mouth was twisted in a mocking grimace. "Parliament has issued orders for his arrest."

"On what grounds?" demanded Katrine.

"Treason." The ugly word echoed loudly in the still room.

"The punishment for treason is death," she whispered.

Richard poured himself another drink. It would be a relief to forget this madness and get thoroughly, blindingly drunk.

Katrine asked the question through stiff lips. "What of my father?"

"You're not stupid, Katrine," he lashed out angrily. "What do you think?"

Her pale lips tightened with resolve. "I want to go home, Richard. I must go home."

The face he turned to her was one of a stranger. "You are home, Katrine. Ashton is your home. Don't ever forget it."

"Are you forbidding me to see my parents?"

"Yes."

She stood, straightening to her full height. "When you can speak to me reasonably, m'lord, I shall be in my room."

"Dammit, Katrine." His fist crashed against the papered wall. "Scotland is in the midst of civil war. It will be a blood bath. The French have not come out for Charles, and half of Scotland opposes him. Only the clans remain faithful."

"It doesn't sound as if my country wants war," she said coldly. "We merely want our rightful king. It is the English that persist in this folly."

Richard did not miss the fact that she had allied herself against him. "The result is the same," he insisted stubbornly. "It is too dangerous to consider a journey into Scotland."

"That is only your opinion."

"I am your husband, therefore, it is the only opinion that matters."

She whitened, and her eyes blazed like twin diamonds in her angry face. Not trusting herself to speak, she left the room without a word.

Leaving the glass on the table, Richard picked up the bottle of claret, threw himself into the nearest chair, and proceeded to drink himself into oblivion.

Katrine sat on a low stool before her dressing table and stared into the glass. She closed her eyes, enjoying the gentle tug of the hairbrush as the maid ministered to the black curtain of silken hair that fell across her shoulders. The woman was very skilled and agreeably silent. For the first time, Katrine was grateful for her reticence. It would have been beyond endurance for anyone to expect conversation from her this night. Her marriage was over, and she felt nothing more than a curious numbness. She knew the strange lethargy wouldn't last. Soon, there would be pain and then anger and finally grief. She would let the depth of her despair wash over her, bleeding her of all emotion. Then she would plan her escape.

Katrine had known from the beginning that this day was inevitable. Richard had known it as well, but he was a man, and with a man's arrogant disregard for forces beyond his control, he had assumed that upon their marriage, Katrine's loyalty would belong only to him. Her smile was tender as she thought of her husband. She loved him so much, and their time together hadn't been nearly long enough. She would live on the magic and the memories for the rest of her life.

Later, when he came to her, she was reminded of their wedding night, when his hunger had been so great there was nothing left of control. He took her suddenly, quickly, without the skill to which she had grown accustomed. Katrine welcomed his passion. Desperate times demanded forceful measures. It was a primitive thing, this raging tidal wave of desire that had run through all men since the dawn of time. It was an act committed out of fear and for only one reason—to claim possession.

"I love you, Katrine," he said much later when her head was pillowed against his shoulder. "I couldn't bear it if you left me."

Her lips were cool against his skin. "It is you who will leave me," she whispered. "England will call you to lead her troops in battle, and I will be left alone."

"It isn't the same thing at all."

She smiled sadly. "Of course not. Go to sleep, my love."

Katrine's first London ball was unlike anything she had ever experienced. Carriages were lined up for blocks, the wait over an hour, as elegantly groomed guests stepped out on to the marble steps. Although it was after ten, the candles at the entrance to the duchess of Langley's gracious town-house gave off enough light to make the time seem closer to noon than midnight. Katrine smoothed her skirts and allowed her husband to help her out of their carriage. She looked around, surveying the enormous crowd with plea-sure. Katrine loved parties.

"What a miserable crush," he groaned, shaking his head at the noise. "Come, Katrine." He tucked her hand beneath his arm. "We are obligated to stay until midnight at least."

She stared at him in surprise. "Is it this ball you dislike in particular?" she asked. "Or do you despise entertainment altogether?"

"I hate crowds," he confessed. "All this milling about and pretending to feel pleasure toward those one would rather ignore. Everyone I care to see I visit on a regular basis."

He grinned suddenly, and the muscles in Katrine's stom-ach tightened. Richard's smile lit his entire face. It was one of the things she must learn to live without.

"I sound like a pompous ass, don't I?" he admitted sheepishly.

She laughed. "Rather. But the wonderful thing about you is that you recognize it."

He lifted her chin and looked down into her face. "That isn't all I recognize," he said softly. "You look beautiful, Katrine. There isn't a chance in heaven that I'll manage a single dance with you tonight."

It was true. Katrine did look beautiful. Her blue satin gown was cut low so that the fichu tucked demurely into the décolletage only served to emphasize the creamy swell of her breasts. Her skirt was fashioned with yards of material pulled aside by twin panniers so wide she just managed to walk into the ballroom without turning sideways. No evidence of the secret she carried showed in her small waist and still-flat stomach. Her hair was left unpowdered, the glossy curls pulled high on her head and allowed to cascade down her back. Her black eyelashes and the bloom on her cheeks were her own, but the patch placed just below her left cheekbone called attention to her clear, light eyes, high cheekbones, and expressive mouth.

Resting her cheek against his velvet-clad shoulder, she succumbed to the sudden, fleeting spasm of pain that twisted through her. They had so little time left together. "You shall have as many dances as you wish," she said fervently.

It was very clear to everyone who attended the duchess of Langley's ball that evening that Lady Katrine Wolfe would have an extremely successful London season. The circle of her admirers completely hid her straight figure from the man who had recently entered the room.

"Who is the latest toast?" he asked his hostess, beckoning a servant who carried champagne.

"Lord Wolfe's new bride," replied the duchess. She looked up through her lashes at the tall, aristocratic man by her side. "Shall I introduce you, Duncan? She is quite lovely, although I confess if you flirt with her, I shall be furious."

His lips twitched, and he brushed away an imaginary speck of lint from his shoulder. "Don't be absurd, Lavinia. Besides, I already know the chit. She is Atholl's daughter."

"Then you need no introduction," drawled the duchess. "I'm so relieved."

Duncan Forbes set down his champagne glass on a low table and bowed politely. "I believe I'll take the chance that she remembers me."

Lavinia Devereaux, duchess of Langley, watched him walk away with a puzzled frown between her brows. Duncan Forbes was an enigma. A passionate Whig, he had used his position in the House of Lords to plead for lenience toward the clans. His huge fortune and impeccable lineage made him a matrimonial prize. He was nearing forty, but so far he had shown no preference for any of London's reigning beauties. There were rumors of an unrequited love affair in Scotland, but those who were in a position to know refuted it. The duchess preferred to discount such a tale. Therē wasn't a woman in Britain who would refuse his title and lands, not to mention the extremely attractive person of Lord Duncan Forbes.

Without the slightest effort on his part, bodies seemed to fall away, allowing him a clear path directly to Katrine's side. Her eyes widened, and she blushed as he bent over her hand.

"What are you doing here, m'lord?" she asked in Gaelic.

"I might ask the same of you," he replied in the same language, noting with satisfaction her heightened color. At least the minx had the grace to be embarrassed for jilting him so abominably.

"My husband is in the card room."

"Do you require protection, Katrine?" His hands were at her waist.

"This dance is taken, m'lord," she said coldly.

He ignored her. "You haven't answered my question."

Aware that curious stares were upon them, she placed her hand upon his arm. "We cannot be private here." She nodded toward the French doors. "Take me to the balcony."

His thin, perfectly molded lips curved upward in a triumphant smile. There was nothing he would rather do than be private with Lady Katrine Murray. "I am yours to command, m'lady."

Once they were safely out of doors, she dropped her arm and whirled on him furiously. "How dare you embarrass me so. Why are you here, Duncan?"

"You have a short memory, Katrine. I live in London most of the year." His hand clenched over the snuff box in his pocket. "Did you also forget that you were promised to me?"

Her cheeks were flame red. "You are not being fair, m'lord. I told you I was not indifferent to you. That is all."

"It was enough to give me hope."

She spoke gently. "I'm sorry for disappointing you, Duncan, but I am married now. What was between us must be over."

He reached out, his fingers clamping down hard on her shoulders. "Why, Katrine? Richard Wolfe is a Whig and an Englishman. If you meant to change your loyalties, why him and not me?"

She lifted her chin in a haughty, defiant gesture. "I love him. But I have not changed my loyalties. If you care as deeply as you say, then be happy for me. The path I've chosen is not an easy one."

He dropped his arms and turned away, but not before she saw the pain in his eyes. His hands clenched until the knuckles showed white through his skin. "If you ever need anything—"

"I have everything I need," she broke in, "except—"

Quickly he turned to face her. "Except?"

"How is the situation in Scotland?"

Disappointed, he nevertheless answered truthfully. "If Charles would only stay in Edinburgh, he might have a chance. His march on London was a fiasco. He has no hope of support from England, and word has it that your father has quarreled with him over the Irishman, O'Sullivan." He laughed humorously. "Charles always was a fool. If he listened to George Murray, he might prevail. As it stands, he is doomed."

"That would suit your purposes, wouldn't it, Lord Forbes?" she said bitterly.

"I've made no secret of the fact that I'm a government man," he replied. "This isn't the Middle Ages, Katrine. The divine right of kings is an outdated tradition. The Stuarts would do their country a better service to remain in France."

"The Stuarts are kings of Scotland," she asserted.

"You are such a child, my dear. Haven't we executed enough of them to dissuade those remaining from making such a claim?"

"I'm leaving," she announced. " 'Tis enough to turn one's stomach to hear such treason from a Scot."

He stopped her with his hand on her elbow. "Remember, I'm here if you need me."

Pulling away, she returned to the ballroom. Katrine found Richard and, pleading a headache, asked to go home.

Alone in her own room for the first time since her marriage, she felt the child inside her quicken. And that night, in the frosty chill of an English winter, she experienced the first of the nightmares.

Traquair House
1993

The sun slanted through the window and rested on my face at exactly the same moment I heard the pounding at my bedroom door. I managed to open my eyes and look at the clock. It was well after nine. I had slept more than twelve hours. My body cried out for insulin. Dragging myself out of bed, I walked to the door and unlocked it. Holding a tray of tea and scones, Kate stared at me anxiously.

"I thought something happened to you," she said. "You've been asleep for hours. Why have you locked your door, Miss Murray?"

I covered my mouth and yawned. Apparently living with other people carried its own set of responsibilities. The woman really did look concerned. "I'm sorry for worrying you," I apologized. "I've lived alone for quite a while. Everyone locks doors in Boston. It's a hard habit to break."

"I suppose." She nodded and watched me while I pulled my prescription from the top drawer of my bureau, assembled the syringe, and injected myself. "Your father called," she said. "He sounded concerned when I told you were still sleeping. I offered to wake you, but he wouldn't allow it."

Knowing my father, the words *wouldn't allow* seemed out

of character. More than likely, Kate had decided I shouldn't be disturbed. "Did he say when he would call again?" I asked.

"Tonight or tomorrow morning." She poured the tea and buttered the scones after arranging them on the plate. "He said not to change your plans."

"Kate," I asked curiously, "if you wouldn't wake me for my father, why did you wake me now?"

"Mr. Douglas called," she said. "He wanted to know if you were available to drive into Edinburgh at ten." She looked pointedly at the clock. "It's nearly that now."

I sat down on the bed, tucked one leg under the other, and bit into the hot bread. "What did you tell him?" I asked, reconciling myself to the fact that this woman I barely knew had taken it upon herself to manage my social calendar.

"I told him I would check with you first," she replied primly.

She had told him no such thing, and I knew it. Otherwise, I wouldn't have been roused from a sound sleep to have breakfast in bed and Kate wouldn't be opening the armoire to inspect my wardrobe.

"I'm finished," I said quickly, brushing the crumbs from my lap. "Give Mr. Douglas some tea when he arrives and tell him I'll be down soon." I handed her the tray. "You can take this with you."

She frowned. "You didn't eat much, Miss Murray. Are you sure you're feeling all right?"

"Quite sure," I said firmly. Taking her arm, I led her to the door and closed it behind her. I stared at the lock for several seconds before deciding against it. Replacing the olive green jacket and slacks she had pulled from the closet, I chose a pair of loose-fitting jeans, a navy turtleneck sweater, and a camel-colored blazer. After washing my face and brushing my teeth, I looked critically at my complexion in the mirror. I definitely wouldn't pass for twenty but still not bad.

For a long time now, I'd subscribed to the old adage that "less is better" as one gets older. Keeping that in mind, I decided on nothing more than lipstick and a brush or two of mascara. "Thank goodness for a good haircut," I said out loud to the mirror as I brushed my shoulder-length hair into a smooth curve. Grabbing my purse, I reached for the blazer and headed for the stairs.

Ian was already seated in the drawing room with a pot of tea when I walked into the room. He stood immediately and, to my surprise and delight, closed the door behind me and pulled me into his arms. His kiss was hungry and demanding, and then his lips softened, moving gently against mine, expertly coaxing a response. When he lifted his head, my knees gave out, and I stumbled against him.

He steadied me with a hand at my waist. "Easy, Christina." His voice shook. "We'd better leave or Mrs. Ferguson will lambast me for compromising your reputation."

"Mrs. Ferguson?" I concentrated on the movement of his mouth, barely hearing the words.

"Your housekeeper."

"Oh, you mean Kate." I was suddenly embarrassed. "It never occurred to me to call her by anything other than her first name. Do you think I've offended her?"

He brushed my cheek with his hand. "She would have told you if you had. In case you haven't noticed, Kate Ferguson isn't reticent about speaking her mind."

"I wonder," I said slowly. Kate certainly ran things her own way, but she was extremely careful about expressing an opinion that conflicted with mine. Perhaps that was normal. Unemployment was high in Scotland. She was probably safeguarding her position.

Ian was speaking, and this time I listened. "I contacted Professor MacCleod," he said. "He's delighted that you're in Scotland again. I mentioned that you were interested in the inhabitants of Traquair, and he promised to tell you all he knew over lunch."

"He's a wonderful old man," I said warmly. "I can't wait to see him."

Ian held out his hand and I took it. "Shall we go?" he asked.

I was relieved that we didn't encounter Kate on the way out, although why it should matter that Ian held my hand, I couldn't explain. For some reason, I didn't want her to speculate on something I was not yet sure of.

We took the picturesque, single-laned road that was once

a medieval pony path to the connecting A7 Highway leading into Edinburgh. It had been several years since I'd visited Scotland's capital city, but the evidence of its history in the silent, brooding castle that hovered over the city never failed to stop my breath. Occupied since the sixth century, the castle site with its forbidding walls, formed by the core of an ancient volcano and wrought by glaciers moving east and west, claimed by Pictish, Celtic, and Saxon monarchs, had seen the rise and fall of countless dynasties.

The modern citizens of Edinburgh hurrying down High Street and the Royal Mile, past Lawnmarket and Canongate to the shops and restaurants, the pubs, offices, and tea-houses of Princes Street, rarely gave a thought to the fact that they lived in the shadow of a proud and tragic history. It was left to the tourists of the world, the Americans, Canadians, and Australians, those whose nations began less than two centuries before, to marvel and gape, to pay exorbitant fees and brave stifling crowds, to stand at the gravesites and worship the effigies of men and women who had long since vanished into the shadows of time.

Long before we reached the outskirts of the capital, I could see the nearly vertical north face of the castle foundations. This, with the south side a close second, was my favorite view. It looked more natural, more terrifying somehow, than the gradual western slope and the descending eastern ridge.

This was how an enemy coming up from England or down from the isles must have seen it, craggy cliffs slippery with ocean spray, primitive jutting rocks, biting winds whistling through the battlements. How they must have shuddered at the thought of scaling those granite walls. Those who were foolish attacked. The wise prayed for mercy and retreated. Every man with eyes in his head and the smallest claim to battle experience knew that laying siege to Edinburgh Castle was folly. As wonderful and mystical as it would always be for me, it wasn't the castle I wanted to explore today.

"You're awfully quiet," remarked Ian as he shifted to stop at a light.

"Ian." I clutched his shoulder. "Do you have to be back tonight?"

He gave me a long, assessing look before the light changed. "What did you have in mind?"

"I want to see Blair-Atholl," I said quickly. "It's the Murrays' castle, and it was Katrine's childhood home. I've got to see it."

"I might have known," he muttered.

"I beg your pardon?"

I could see the red creep up under his tan. "Never mind," he said. "I'm surprised you haven't visited it before this."

"I have, but it's not the same." I reached into my shoulder bag and took out the leather-bound book. "Now I have Janet's diary. I want to be where she wrote it."

A worried frown appeared between his eyes. "Let's talk to the professor first, shall we?"

"Why?" I demanded. "What has he got to do with Blair-Atholl?"

Ian sighed. "I'd prefer to let Professor MacCleod explain, Christina. He knows as much about the Maxwells and Murrays as anyone. It really will seem less absurd that way."

I settled back into the seat, resigned to yet another wait, to more polite greetings, the catching up on a two-year absence, the ordering of meals, the serving of drinks, the pouring of tea, and finally, when there was nothing left to discuss, the answers for which we had come. It was much more than my own curiosity about Traquair House that needed satisfying. Somewhere, in the last twenty-four hours, the stakes had changed. There was a connection between the three of us, Katrine Murray, Mairi Maxwell, and myself. And, somehow, that connection included Ian Douglas.

Turning down Giles Street into the Leith section of Edinburgh, Ian parked the car across from a restaurant I had never seen before. In the past, because I was often alone and on a limited budget, my tastes ran toward inexpensive, family-style pubs in the center of town. I could see immediately that the Vintner's Room was of a different caliber entirely. I looked down at my jeans and scuffed loafers and swallowed nervously. When the proprieter ushered us into a warm, sunlit room with tasteful plasterwork and wooden tables and chairs, I relaxed. The setting was definitely informal.

Professor MacCleod was already seated. When he saw us, he stood immediately and held out his hand. "How are you, my dear?" he said, his fingers closing around mine in a bone-crunching clasp.

"I'm fine, sir," I replied, kissing him on the cheek. "It's wonderful to see you again." It really was. The professor was the epitome of an English scholar with his rosy cheeks, patched tweed jacket, and thick white hair. I was relieved to see that the last few years hadn't changed him at all.

He pulled out my chair, and I sat down. "Ian tells me you've inherited a substantial piece of property. I had an idea you might be related to the Maxwells, but one can never be sure."

"That hasn't really been established yet," I said, pleased that he'd come right to the point. "I'd like to ask you some questions about the Maxwells and the Murrays."

"I thought so." The professor beamed and patted the briefcase beside his chair. "I'll be happy to tell you all that I know, but I printed a copy of my notes for you in case I leave anything out. The two families have a fascinating history."

"So I understand," I murmured, glancing sideways at Ian. His face was smooth, revealing nothing. "Shall we order first?" he suggested.

"A capital idea," said the professor. "The grilled oysters with bacon and hollandaise are wonderful," he said. "Have you eaten here before, Christina?"

"No, I haven't. I'm not really familiar with Edinburgh's finer restaurants. I usually eat in the pubs with friends, or if I'm staying longer, I cook something in my flat."

"I don't think anything with sauces is a good idea for Christina, Professor," Ian said. "She has diabetes."

Frowning, I glanced at Ian. Why had he pointed that out? I didn't ordinarily include my medical condition over luncheon conversation. I opened my mouth, ready to explain that diabetes wasn't the dibilitating illness most people thought it was, when I saw the professor's face. His ruddy complexion had paled and his water glass hung precariously in his hand halfway between the table and his mouth.

"Professor." I touched his arm. "It's all right. Really it is. I've had it all my life. You would never even have noticed if Ian hadn't told you."

"All of your life?" he whispered.

"Yes."

He raised the water glass to his lips with a shaking hand. When he placed it on the table, he appeared much calmer. "I'm terribly sorry, my dear. Ian's announcement shocked me, you see."

"But why?" I was determined to leave the restaurant with answers.

The waiter arrived, and once again I chose the salmon. Boston has its own wonderful seafood, oysters, scallops, and quahogs, a type of large clam that they serve fried in batter and sell in paper bags from concession stands all over the Cape. But there is nothing in the entire United States to compare with salmon caught fresh from the glassy waters of the River Tay.

Ian was content to drink his stout and let the professor dominate the conversation.

"Seven hundred years ago, Mairi Maxwell became the mistress of Edward I of England." He smiled. "I don't have to explain the difficulties of such a union to an expert in Gaelic history. Historians tell us that when the king tired of her, she became the wife of David, earl of Murray. David was a proponent of independence for Scotland and followed Robert the Bruce. Meanwhile, Edward became a strong king. For years he held off the Bruce. It wasn't until his death that Robert was allowed to take his throne." Professor MacCleod shook his head. "One can't help but wonder how the history of Scotland would have changed if Robert had died before Edward."

"What does this have to do with the Maxwells and Traquair House?" I asked, watching the waiter set the mouthwatering plates in front of us.

Ian was already sampling his scallops. For all his teasing about my eating habits, he didn't have what anyone would call a small appetite either.

The professor continued. "Don't forget that Robert the Bruce was once Edward's loyal vassal. When Robert was crowned king of Scotland at Moot Hill, Edward was furious. He rode into Scone, the Murray stronghold, with the intention of removing Scotland's Coronation Stone. It was his right, as overlord of Scotland, to remove the Coronation Stone of Scottish kings. When he learned that Mairi had taken it to Traquair, he followed her there. Most likely he was furiously angry to be thwarted by a woman, especially a woman who had once been his. David Murray was away with Robert, but Mairi was there. To save her life and the life of her child, she gave up the stone to Edward. There was nothing else she could do."

"No," I whispered. "She wouldn't have done that."

"I'm afraid she did, Christina," the professor said grimly, "and in the end, she paid a terrible price for her defection. David's mother, Lady Douglas, claimed she witnessed Mairi's removing the stone from Moot Hill. She told Robert, and he had her pressed to death before an angry mob of peasants."

The food tasted like chalk in my mouth. I knew for a fact that I had never before come across the story of Mairi of Shiels in my research. I was equally sure that this was the first time anyone had spoken of it to me. How, then, could the events of my nightmare at Traquair House so closely parallel the professor's story? Obviously, it was a tale he was very familiar with. But it wasn't exactly the way I remembered it. Had Professor MacCleod left anything out or was he relaying the facts as modern historians knew of them? I was willing to wager that they didn't have the same version of the story that I did.

"Is there anything else?" I prompted him.

He sipped his tea and peered intently at me over his old-fashioned spectacles. "There is. Lady Douglas placed a curse on the Murrays descended from Mairi Maxwell. We have no record of the nature of her curse, but in my research, I found some interesting similarities in the Murray women who died early." He laughed self-consciously and took out a handkerchief. Blowing long and hard into the worn linen, he wiped his nose and replaced it in his coat pocket. "This will seem absurd to you, Christina. It certainly did to me, but Ian insisted I tell you. In the entire line descended from Mairi Maxwell, only two women have died tragically and before their time. They were Katrine Murray of Blair-Atholl and Jeanne Maxwell of Traquair. Both, in addition to their descendency from Mairi and their Murray blood, had another Maxwell ancestor on their mothers' side of the family. Both were susceptible to terrifying nightmares that didn't begin until after they became pregnant."

Katrine Murray. The lovely girl who looked like me had died tragically. There was more. I knew it. There had to be. Why else would I feel a strange chill creep up my spine? Why would the hair stand up on the back of my neck and an eerie sense of inevitability temper my reactions, giving me this outward appearance of calm?

The professor reached out and covered my hand with his own. "Bear in mind that you're an American and that this is the twentieth century."

I laughed with a false bravado that fooled neither of the two men at the table. "Don't worry about me. If there is anything else, I'd like to know."

He drew a deep breath. "Katrine Murray and Jeanne Maxwell were afflicted with a disease that has all the symptoms of what we now call juvenile diabetes."

"Dear God!" I didn't realize I had whispered the words out loud until Ian leaned forward and gripped my wrist with his hand.

"It doesn't mean anything, Christina," he asserted fiercely. "It's absurd to even consider it. Your circumstances and those of the Murray women are nothing alike."

Just hearing the words and seeing his face settled my nerves. I turned toward the professor. "My mother is Irish," I explained. "I haven't any Maxwell ancestors, and it appears that I can't have children."

"But you do have nightmares?" he persisted.

I considered his question carefully before speaking. "They aren't exactly nightmares, Professor MacCleod. You see, I'm not in any of them."

"Who is?"

I inhaled deeply. Not for the world could I have turned away from his piercing, hypnotic gaze. "Katrine Murray and Mairi of Shiels," I said at last.

"Ah." He nodded as if satisfied. "I thought so."

"You did not!" Ian was visibly upset. "You knew nothing about Christina's association with the curse until I told you about her."

"That isn't true, Ian." The old man's voice was very soft. "I knew from the first moment I met Christina Murray ten years ago at the university that there was a strong possibility she would be part of this legacy."

"How?" Ian demanded.

"Traquair is a marvelous old house," MacCleod explained. "You really must explore it some time. Take the visitor's tour. It's really the best way to view the house. In the priests' room at the top of stairwell called the hidden stairs is a portrait of Jeanne Maxwell. It was painted at the beginning of the sixteenth century just before her death." His eyes were moving across my face, as if committing my features to memory. "You really must look at it, Ian. It's a haunting experience." Somehow I expected what was coming next. The professor's words only confirmed what I already knew. "Jeanne Maxwell looks exactly like Christina."

"There is something else," I said.

The glow of discovery illuminated his face. "Tell me."

"I know the nature of Grizelle Douglas's curse."

"You also know her first name," he observed. "I didn't and neither does anyone else alive today. Please go on."

"It has to do with the stone." I closed my eyes, trying to remember the words from my dream. "For your treachery the Maxwell women through David's line will never rest," I recited. "Their sleep will be haunted by ghosts of the dead who walk the earth until they die by foul and tragic means. Only when Scotland's Stone of Destiny is found and returned to Scotland, will the curse be lifted."

"Good God." The professor sighed. "We have about as much chance of lifting the curse as we have of going back in time to change the course of history."

"But Christina isn't a Maxwell," interrupted Ian. "Christ, MacCleod, she isn't even a Scot on her mother's side. Even if this preposterous theory is true, the Maxwell strain should be stronger. And what of the dreams? They came to Jeanne and Katrine while they were pregnant. Christina isn't able to have children."

Professor MacCleod looked at me and stroked his chin. "He's right, of course. Only your diabetes and your face links you to these women, unless—"

"Unless what?" I was having difficulty breathing.

He looked at the white ridge around Ian's lips and the hand that held my wrist in a desperate grip. "I don't wish to make this any more painful for you, Christina, but was your infertility diagnosed?"

I shook my head. "Not really. I had all the tests, but the doctors couldn't come up with any reason for Stephen and I not to have a child. It just didn't happen."

He smiled wisely. "I see. What about your family? Are you sure your mother has no Scottish blood?"

"Very sure." Susan Donnally Murray was as proud of her German–Irish ancestry as if she'd arranged the genotype herself.

"Well then, perhaps the reason for your dreams is that you have *an da shelladh,* 'the sight.' It's not uncommon in Scotland." He smiled at us both. "Shall I pick up the check?"

When Ian and I were back in the car and on our way to Blair Castle, I realized that I still didn't know the answer to the question that had been bothering me since we sat down to lunch with Professor MacCleod. "Ian," I said tentatively. He didn't really look like he was in the mood for conversation.

"What is it?"

"Grizelle Douglas was your ancestor too, wasn't she?"

"Yes."

"Does any of this have to do with you?"

He looked at me, and I could see the beginnings of fine lines etched into the skin around his eyes.

"Apparently so," he replied with a lightness that belied his expression. "I haven't sorted it out yet, love. But when I do, I'll tell you."

Love. He'd called me love. I closed my eyes, lingering over the word, repeating it silently to myself.

* * *

Two hours later, following the A9 into Perthshire, eight miles northwest of Pitlochry, we came to the Vale of Atholl and Blair Castle. I had seen it before and been impressed with the pristine whiteness of the castle walls, the magnificent parklands, and what surely must be one of the largest private historical collections on display in all of Great Britain.

Because I was a Murray, I knew that my ancestors had come from this area of Scotland. I had always assumed that my people were peasants forced to leave Scotland because of the clearances, hoping for a better life in a land of greater opportunity. Now, I wasn't so sure. If Katrine Murray and Mairi Maxwell were direct ancestors, some of my past was here in the castle of the duke of Atholl. I could feel my heart pound with excitement. It was already after four and the last tour left at five. I didn't want to rush this visit.

"Shouldn't we find a hotel first?" I asked. "It's too late to get a good look around."

Ian shook his head. "We aren't staying at a hotel."

"Why not?"

He drove past the coach park into a private road with a carport. Setting the emergency brake, he turned to face me, sliding his hand across the back of my seat to rest lightly on my shoulder. "George Murray and I shared a room at Harrow when we were children. We attended Oxford together before I left for America. I have a standing invitation to stay at Blair whenever I visit the Highlands."

"The tenth duke of Atholl is your friend?" He couldn't miss the incredulous wonder in my voice.

"His son is my friend. The duke is seventy-two years old."

For the first time I realized the differences in our backgrounds. He was a British gentleman, untitled, but still brought up with money and privilege to a lifestyle that was completely foreign to my middle-class American values. He was no longer wealthy, of course, and between the two of us, I had more formal education, but there was a chasm a mile wide between us. Was I in for more heartache? Chewing my lip, I stared at Ian's handsome, slightly worried face.

"Christina." His voice had a breathless, husky quality.

"Hmm?"

"This is your family home, not mine. George Murray, the man you are descended from, was the younger brother of the duke of Atholl. You have more right to be here than I do."

I looked around at the acres of green parklands, at the mile-long driveway, at the hundreds of windows and the towering turrets where the standard of the House of Murray waved proudly in the wind. Blair Castle had welcomed visitors for more than seven hundred years.

Closing my eyes, I pictured a girl in a beautiful evening gown, a girl with black hair and gray eyes. That girl had ridden across these parklands. She had danced in the ballroom, played in the nursery, learned her lessons in the wonderful old library, and drawn the cocooning curtains around her at night in a bedchamber somewhere up above the curving staircase. I was Katrine's legacy. I was also a Murray. Opening the door, I smiled across the chasm at Ian. "Shall we go inside?"

The family wasn't in residence, but it didn't seem to matter. Ian and I were treated like honored guests. We were ushered into the tea room for afternoon tea. In direct view of family portraits and armor, exquisite furniture, moldings, and a china collection my mother would have swum the Atlantic to possess, we were served cucumber sandwiches, scones, and tea.

My bedroom was something out of a Georgette Heyer novel. Elegant stucco scrollwork in the curving rococo style was evident in the mantel. Painted wallpaper decorated with flowers and brightly colored birds covered the walls. The furniture was Georgian with delicate Chippendale carvings in the bedposters and canopy. A commode in one corner of the room had ivory fittings and covered urns. The fender, grate, and fire irons were copied from Chinese designs, reminiscent of the Oriental craze dominating the middle of the seventeenth century. When I opened a door at the end of the room, I was relieved to see a modern bathroom, complete with a state-of-the-art showerhead, thick towels, and creamy rugs. There was another door at the opposite end of the bathroom. I opened it and found Ian in the next room, sprawled out on the bed, asleep. Closing the door carefully, I retreated to my own room.

It might be hours before he awoke, and I desperately wanted to get back to Janet's diary. Pulling up a comfortable chair to one of the floor-length windows, I looked out over the hills of Perthshire. There was something gracious and comforting and familiar inside these medieval stone walls of Blair Castle. They welcomed me just as Traquair had welcomed me. I opened the diary and began to read, but I couldn't focus on the words. My head ached and I felt dizzy. Suddenly the pain increased. I dropped the journal and let my head fall back against the chair. A terrifying wave of blackness engulfed me, and then, as before, the visions came.

Ashton Manor
February 1746

Katrine was very thin and unnaturally pale. For the first time in his life Lord Richard Wolfe was desperately afraid. Afraid he would lose her and the child she finally confessed to be carrying. Against his better judgment, he was almost convinced to allow her to return home to the loving ministrations of Janet Murray. The Highlands would bring the roses back to her cheeks. Now that she carried his child, he had no fear that she would leave him permanently. Katrine's sense of duty was too ingrained. He frowned at the glass of ruby-colored liquid at his elbow. The port was strong, and for weeks he had been drinking heavily. Leaving the wine untouched, he walked out of his study to the stairs. There was a loud commotion at the door.

"What is it, Hastings?" Richard asked, his hand on the railing.

"This gentlemen seeks speech with Lady Wolfe." The butler pointed to a bearded, disreputable-looking figure wrapped in plaid. "I told him she was unavailable, but he will not accept my answer."

Richard walked toward the door. "Perhaps he will accept mine. My wife is resting, sir," he said politely. "May I take her your message?"

"I canna' do that," the man said in a brogue so thick it was difficult to understand. "Wha' I ha' is for the lass, only. Do you ken?"

"Nevertheless, we will not wake her," insisted Richard firmly. "You may wait in the hall if you like."

"It's all right, darling. I'm up now." All heads turned to the voice at the top of the landing. Katrine, dressed in a loose-fitting gown of soft blue wool, appeared to float effortlessly down the stairs.

"Angus." She held out her hand to the clansman. "'Tis lovely to see you. Have you eaten?"

Richard's mouth twisted. Only Katrine, with the beautiful manners instilled into her from birth, would think to ask if this scowling, mud-stained peasant was hungry.

The man called Angus shook his head. "I'm to bring you to Scone, lass. Alasdair is dead and your ma beside hersel'."

Katrine whitened and swayed. Richard sprang to her side, holding her up with his arm. "Damn you!" he swore. "Can't you see that she is breeding."

"Aye." Angus nodded. "We'll need a carriage. I brough' only horses."

Katrine straightened. "I'll come immediately."

"Katrine," Richard protested. "You can't be serious. Of course you must go, but 'tis nearly night. A few more hours won't make a difference."

She shook her head, her rain-colored eyes filled with tears. "I must leave now, Richard. Please understand."

In the end, he let her go. It was after dark when the travel coach, emblazoned with the Wolfe crest, pulled out of the courtyard into the long driveway. Richard watched from the steps as the square-shaped cab pulled by six horses turned past the gates and disappeared into the mist. With a bleakness born of resignation, he knew that, given Katrine's poor health, his child had only a prayer's chance of surviving the journey.

Katrine's heart lifted as she crossed the borders into Scotland. It was early February and bitterly cold, but she was home. Her brother was dead and nothing would ever be the same again, but she was finally home. That, in itself, was nothing short of a miracle. Here she would heal. She would speak to her mother and learn the source of the frightening nightmares that sucked the sleep from her exhausted body.

Janet Murray took one horrified look at her daughter's emaciated figure with its large belly and another at her face, where the skin was stretched so tightly across the bones that the girl's every heartbeat was evident in the blue veins pulsing at her temples, and refused to answer any questions. Instead she ordered her to bed. It wasn't until later, weeks later, after fortifying broths and soothing plasters and honey-sweetened teas had added pounds to Katrine's slender frame and filled out her cheeks, that she relented and told her about Alasdair.

He had fallen at Falkirk on the seventeenth of January. The battle was a victory for the prince's army, but the advantage was not taken. In the confusion of a winter dusk, Alasdair was taken prisoner, marched to Edinburgh, and hanged on the gallows. There was nothing anyone could do. Stirling surrendered to the prince, but the castle remained in government hands. Charles was at Inverness waiting out the winter weather. The duke of Cumberland, second son of the English king, had reached Aberdeen on the twenty-seventh of February. His army had received five thousand German troops under Prince Frederick of Hesse.

Katrine knew the duke from her London season. He was a heavy, pompous young man in his early twenties with a tendency to overrate his own importance. Still, he was an experienced commander, and the fact that he was in Scotland to command the English troops did not bode well for the Jacobites.

"You should not have returned to Scotland at this time, Katrine," her mother admonished her. "What were you thinking?"

"I had to come," Katrine replied softly. "Even if it

weren't for Alasdair, I still would have come. Ever since the standard was raised at Glenfinnan, I planned to return."

"What does Richard say?"

Katrine bit her lip. "He was against it at first, but I think he was at the point of changing his mind. My illness frightened him. Of course, when Angus brought the news of Alasdair, he couldn't refuse."

"Angus went on his own," said Janet. "I would never have sent him. You were safe in England." She rose from the side of the bed and walked to the window. "I fear it is all at an end for the clans, Katrine. Your father is convinced that the retreat from London disheartened the troops. He has lost his hope of victory."

"I did not come home for Scotland or for the Jacobite cause, Mother."

At the odd note in her voice, Janet turned toward the bed and frowned. "What is it, Katrine? Why did you arrive here thin and pale, on the brink of death?"

Her eyes were huge and filled with terrible purpose. "'Tis the nightmares. They wake me night after night, always the same. Tell me, Mother. Tell me truly. Am I accursed? Am I destined to live the rest of my life with this fear of the night and my own sleep?"

Janet closed her eyes. *Oh God, no. Please, no. What have we done, George and I?* She looked again upon her daughter. "What is it that you see, Katrine?"

"I see two women from the past."

"Women?" asked Janet sharply. "There are more than one?"

Katrine nodded.

Her mother sat down beside her on the bed. "Tell me of your dreams."

Katrine closed her eyes and leaned her head back on the pillow. It was such a relief to confide in someone. Someone who carried the same dark legacy in her blood. "Do you know of Mairi of Shiels, Mother?"

"Aye." Janet's lips trembled. She knew more than she wanted of Mairi Maxwell of Shiels.

"She married David Murray before Bannockburn," Katrine continued. "But she loved King Edward of England.

She was killed for giving him the Coronation Stone and cursed by David's mother, Lady Douglas." Her eyes were huge in her too-thin face. "The woman was a witch, Mother. Her curse haunts us still. It comes through the women of the Murray line." In a hushed whisper she told of Mairi's deception, of how she switched the stones, of the long, narrow passageway, the flickering candles, the netherworld-lit stone in the burial crypt, and the desperate, persuasive power of Mairi's haunted eyes.

"You said there were two women," Janet reminded her. "Who else did you see?"

Katrine took several deep breaths, willing her thundering heart to calm itself. "Every night I see it over and over again. There is a wide moor filled with horses and armor and stained with blood. The wounded cry out. 'Tis a horrible sight. It smells of death and rotting flesh. Mountains overlook the moor on three sides." Katrine wrinkled her nose against the odor and swatted at imaginary flies.

Janet's hand rose to her throat. Flodden Moor! She could almost see the terrifying images Katrine described.

"A woman, richly dressed, walks among the bodies," said Katrine. "She searches the wounded on the field, turning them over, one after another, asking those who live, 'Where is John Maxwell?' Finally she finds the one she seeks. With a cry, she pulls his head into her lap. 'You're very pale, my love,' he says. 'You must eat. It isn't wise for you to go without food. Don't cry, Jeannie,' he begs her. 'Maxwells never cry.'"

Tears rolling down her cheeks, Katrine sat up and grasped her mother's shoulders. "'Tis my own face I see," she whispered. "Tell me why Mairi of Shiels and Jeanne Maxwell have my face."

Janet's eyes were wide with shock and startled recognition. "Of course," she said, tracing the bones of her daughter's face with wondering fingers. "How could I not have seen it? Yet, it was so very long ago when they last came to me."

"What are you saying?"

Katrine's horrified whisper pulled Janet back into the present. She sighed and explained. "I, too, was afflicted with the nightmares. They first came when I carried you. After you were born, they disappeared forever. I believe 'tis the curse."

"But you are a Douglas, not a Murray," Katrine protested.

Janet shook her head. "I cannot explain everything, my love. Lady Douglas was a Murray and also a Douglas by marriage. She gave her husband three children. Our families have intermarried so often that it would be an amazing thing were we not all related." Her hands clenched in her lap. "There was opposition when your father and I wanted to wed," she confessed. "I carry Maxwell and Douglas blood. Your father is a Murray from the line of David and Mairi. Although no one admits to actually believing the power of the curse, they all step carefully around it." She reached out and brushed the hair back from her daughter's brow. "I believe there are many who have had the dreams. Otherwise the curse would have long since been forgotten. It is only dangerous when all the conditions are present."

"What are the other conditions?"

"I'm not sure."

Katrine's forehead wrinkled in concentration. "There must be a reason we dream of only these two. Something about them was the same." She gasped and clutched her mother's sleeve as a thought occurred to her. Looking into Janet's dark eyes, she realized her mother had come to the same conclusion. "They have my face," she whispered. "They died horribly and they have my face."

"It means nothing, nothing at all." Janet was on the brink of hysteria. "When you have the bairn, this nonsense will stop just as it did for me."

Katrine kicked away the confining bedcovers. Taking Janet's hands in her own, she knelt beside her and spoke slowly and deliberately. "Don't you see, Mother? I am the one. I must prove Mairi of Shiels did not betray Scotland. I must end the curse or I will not live to bear my child."

Janet's eyes burned with an eerie light. For a moment, Katrine thought she recognized the fanatical glow of Grizelle Douglas's witchery in her mother's gentle face.

"No, Katrine," she said softly. "You have it all wrong.

The child will be born first. Mairi and Jeanne bore their sons. Otherwise you would not be here."

"Of course." Katrine barely whispered the words, but Janet, tuned to every nuance of her daughter's expression, heard them. "Alasdair will never sire children. There is no one left but me." She turned determined eyes on her mother. "Somehow we must find the stone. If my child is a girl, she will inherit the curse, and if it is not, then 'tis I who will die."

Janet did not tell her daughter that she had never seen Jeanne Maxwell in her dreams nor had Mairi ever drawn her down a cold, narrow passageway. Before Katrine had revealed the nature of the curse, she had known nothing of the stone. All that she knew of Mairi of Shiels was of the moments before her death.

There was compassion and pain and tremendous love in the kiss Janet placed on the young cheek beside her. She saw no point in telling Katrine that she was most definitely "the one" and that the child she carried was not a girl.

Blair Castle
1993

I don't know when I realized that the words in Janet Douglas's diary fell far short of the story that unfolded before me. The words were there, of course, and beautifully written but not the way I saw them. There was nothing in the black, carefully bound book that described the clarity of Katrine Murray's bones beneath her pale skin or the look of anguish in her eyes. Nor did the words describe the sudden meeting of minds between mother and daughter as they stared at one another. I knew what Katrine would do next as surely as I drew breath. I knew because it was exactly what I would do. *She would search for the stone.*

Brushing away tears, I stood and walked to the window. Rubbing my arms against the cold, I stared outside at green lawns and pine forests. Blair Castle was well heated. The sudden chill in the room had nothing to do with temperature. It had to do with my ability to see into an unalterable past. With an overwhelming sense of despair, I knew that Katrine Murray would fail in her quest. She would fail because I was alive with all the conditions she knew nothing about. All except one. I was not pregnant. Or at least I hadn't been when Mairi of Shiels first led me down the dark passageway to the stone.

Leaning against the window, I closed my eyes and let the visions clamoring for release inside my head envelop me.

April 1746

Katrine pressed the scented handkerchief against her nose and rubbed her enormous stomach. She was exhausted and longed to rest her aching back against the dungeon wall, but she dared not. The hewn stone ran wet with dampness, and the cold was so intense it seeped through her woolen cloak, past her gown and petticoats to the sensitive skin beneath. She knew she shouldn't be here. The slick stone stairway with its numbing cold and lonely isolation, with its scurrying rats and shadowed darkness, was no place for a woman in her last month of pregnancy.

The stone was not to be found here at Scone Castle, and it wasn't at Blair-Atholl. She had searched every room, every hidden stairway, every cell, every rank-smelling and musty dungeon, to no avail. Nothing even remotely resembled the hallways of her dream. The narrow passageway and large burial chamber filled with death masks and glowing light was nowhere to be found. Only Traquair was left to explore. Traquair with its secret stairs and hidden cellars, its ancient library, and tranquil, gracious public rooms. Traquair, a refuge for Catholic priests, a pleasure ground for Scottish kings, Jacobite seat of the Maxwells, and home to Jeanne Maxwell, direct descendent of Mairi of Shiels.

The thought of Traquair terrified Katrine. She and Alasdair had visited the house many times from early childhood. The Maxwells were cousins to both the Murray and Douglas sides of their family. But this was different. Traquair was where Mairi and Jeanne had been killed. It was also the last logical resting place for the stone. There was no other place she could think of to look.

There was another complication that Katrine refused to admit even to herself. Duncan Forbes was at Traquair. The persistence of his suit had not abaited even when her pregnancy became obvious. Her English husband was very far away, and his last letter was over four weeks old. It was rumored that Prince Charles was expected at Traquair. Duncan, a Whig and Hanover supporter, had been sent to persuade Charles that his cause was hopeless, to lay down his arms and return to France.

Richard Wolfe cursed fluently and kicked the rock under his boot. It had been weeks since he'd heard from Katrine. Now, when he was at Nairn and less than a day's journey from Blair, his position as aide to the duke of Cumberland made it impossible to go to her. The duke's army of nine thousand foot and horse soldiers was camped on Drumossie Moor, a wide bare plain that might have been made specifically for the maneuvers of the disciplined infantry.

To the south, across the River Nairn, was the broken, hilly ground George Murray had chosen for the battle site. He had been rebuffed by the Irishman, O'Sullivan. Prince Charles, blinded by the man's flattery, chose to accept his counsel rather than the hard-headed appraisal of Murray, who had proven himself to be a brilliant military tactician. Richard knew there was little doubt as to the outcome of the battle to come. The five thousand Jacobite troops, weak from lack of provisions, hadn't a chance.

He drew his cloak around him and looked disapprovingly at the primitive beauty of Drumossie Moor. If he never saw this godforsaken country again, it would be too soon. He missed the manicured loveliness of the England countryside. He missed his valet and his library and the gracious decorum of life at Ashton Manor. He missed breakfast in the sunlit room near the conservatory and the excellent claret waiting for him in his wine cellar. He missed discussing horseflesh with his groom and finances with his secretary. He missed clean sheets and feather mattresses and warm bathwater. Most of all, he missed Katrine. He ached for the mere sight of her. Christ! How had he, Richard Wolfe, become embroiled in this absurdity? He closed his eyes and prayed for the first time since he was a boy. If God was merciful, when next he stood before his wife, it would be without her father's blood on his hands.

"Richard?" The quiet voice interrupted his thoughts.

He turned, and his eyes widened. George Murray, immaculately dressed in wig and hat, stood before him.

"How did you manage to pass through our lines?" Richard asked.

Murray's smile was grim. "There are enough Scots in the duke's regiment to make one more nearly invisible."

"I'm sorry for this, sir." Richard's pain was genuine. Never, in his darkest moments, had he believed it would come to this.

George smiled again. "I didn't come to blame you, lad. I came to ask a favor."

"You know I won't let anything happen to Katrine or your family," Richard assured him.

"It isn't Katrine I worry about. 'Tis the clans. Cumberland knows that if the prince's cause is to find support anywhere in Britain, it will be the Highlands. Use your influence, Richard. Plead for mercy."

"You speak as if the outcome is a foregone conclusion."

Murray gestured toward the wide expanse of plain that was Drumossie Moor. "Have you ever seen a more inappropriate ground for Highlanders?" he asked the younger man.

Richard, who knew something of the Highland clans sole battle tactic, that terrifying uncontrolled charge followed by merciless work with a broadsword and dirk, had to agree. "I didn't realize O'Sullivan's influence carried such weight," he said.

"O'Sullivan has a way with words," replied George dryly, turning away.

"Wait." Richard's voice stopped him. "How did you leave Katrine?"

"She is well," replied George without turning around.

"Take care, lad. Every bairn needs a father to keep him in line."

Richard watched his father-in-law's tall, raw-boned figure disappear into the mists.

Charles Edward Stuart looked every inch a prince as he lifted Katrine's hand to his lips. "Your father never told me that you had married, Lady Katrine," he said. "Who is the fortunate man?"

She lifted her chin and met the dark eyes of her prince defiantly. "He is English, Your Grace. Perhaps you've heard of Richard Wolfe?"

"Indeed I have," replied Charles pleasantly. "A good man." He looked pointedly at Katrine's protruding stomach and grinned. "Apparently marriage agrees with you. In France you were not so encumbered."

She blushed. "I apologize for receiving you in this condition. My visit to Traquair House was unexpected."

His eyes twinkled down at her. "Apologies are unnecessary, lass. You are lovely as usual, and motherhood is a noble undertaking. May I escort you to dinner?"

At that moment Katrine realized what it was about this tall, slender young man that won hearts to his cause. She smiled. "I would be honored, Your Grace."

Dinner was excellent. His lordship's cook, upon learning that Prince Charlie himself would be dining at Traquair, outdid himself. The roasted lamb was pronounced delicious, the pasties light and rich, the black pudding and haggis the best the assembled guests had tasted.

Herbert Maxwell, laird of Traquair and an ardent Jacobite, was delighted. With the exception of Duncan Forbes at his table, the evening could not have been more perfect. If Duncan's mother had not been a Maxwell, the man would have been shown the door and hospitality be damned. Maxwell shook his finger at his unwelcome guest. "How dare you suggest that our prince will not be victorious?"

Duncan's mouth thinned. "Easily," he replied. "His forces are outnumbered by a highly trained, well-fed, well-paid army." He focused his attention on the prince. "I beg you, sir. Fall back. Disband your men and return to France.

Nothing will come of this but destruction of the Highland clans."

"Are you omniscient, Forbes?" The prince's brown eyes glinted with anger. "Can you assure the government forces their victory and my own defeat?"

"It does not take a genius to do so," Duncan replied bluntly, "only a man with his eyes and ears open."

The prince inspected his wineglass. "How interesting an interpretation."

Katrine saw the pulse leap in Duncan's throat and marveled at his ability to keep his temper. "Are you aware that Cumberland intends complete annihilation of the clans?" he demanded. "There will be no quarter given, not even to the wounded. Glens will be laid to waste and looting sanctioned. Leaders will be executed, and those that are spared will be stripped of their hereditary powers. Is that what you wish for those whose loyalty is yours?"

"Not even Cumberland would stoop to such butchery," protested Maxwell.

"Would he not?" Duncan spoke softly, but no one could mistake his meaning. "Why don't you ask Katrine what matter of man he is? She knew him in London. Perhaps another Jacobite can convince you."

"Katrine?" Charles smiled across the table at her. "Do you agree with Duncan? Shall I call an end to our cause?"

"Would you?" Her large, black-lashed eyes challenged him.

"No," he replied honestly and grinned.

She smiled wearily and rose to her feet. "Then I'll bid you good night." All three men rose, but she waved them to their seats. "Don't get up. I can find my own way."

Katrine climbed the stairs that led to the guest bedchambers. But instead of turning down the corridor that led to her room, she moved in the opposite direction toward the secret stairs that led to the hidden priests' rooms. Last night, in her dreams, Mairi had come to her once again. This time Katrine willed herself to stay calm, refusing to succumb to the terror of the dark passageway and steep, slippery steps. Instead she concentrated on landmarks, committing to memory every turn, every miss, every ancient smoking sconce, on her way to the crypt.

She had awakened early that morning alert and rested for the first time in months, her senses sharp with awareness. Her eyes sparkled, and the dark shadows beneath her lashes had disappeared altogether. Hope surged through her veins. She felt piercingly, vibrantly alive, like a felon destined for the gallows who is unexpectedly reprieved at the final hour. The answer had come to her when she tripped over a jagged irregular step. In a sudden rush of memory, Katrine realized that she had traveled this way before, first as a little girl with Alasdair and later with Gavin Maxwell, Herbert's oldest son. She knew where to find Mairi's passageway.

Now, all she needed was a chance to search the rooms above the secret stairway in privacy. The men were still arguing among themselves, and her pregnancy had given her the excuse to retire early. Her maid wouldn't look for her for another two hours.

Rubbing her arms against the chill, Katrine carefully climbed the twisting stairs. The well was so narrow that she found herself walking sideways in order to squeeze through the narrow turns. Her breath came in shallow gasps, and she stopped several times, bracing herself against the walls. Finally, she was at the top. She didn't bother to search the rooms but went directly to a rosewood panel near the mantel. Mairi had led her down, not up. Wherever the stone was hidden would not be at the top of Traquair House.

Using all her strength, Katrine pushed on the carved wood and held her breath. A door, cleverly carved to match the wall, opened onto a narrow stone tunnel. Sighing with relief, she leaned against the wall and pushed a tendril of hair from her forehead with a shaking hand. This was it. The passageway that led to the Stone of Destiny.

Breathing deeply, she straightened and looked around. Spying a footstool in the corner, she pulled it out, anchored the door open, and stepped inside the tunnel. She walked slowly, shifting her weight to accomodate the stitch in her side that grew more irritating by the minute. Ignoring the tightening bands of pain around her back and stomach, she continued down the passageway. Her excitement grew as she recognized the jagged irregular step from her dream. In the distance a pale glow beckoned her. The space narrowed and darkened. Katrine could no longer see the light. She hurried forward, gasped, and doubled over as a knifelike pain gripped her. Holy God! Could it be the child?

Katrine turned back, frantic with fear. The stone would have to wait. She stumbled as her foot searched the darkness for a hold on the step. How far had she come? Would there be time enough to return? Running her hands along the walls, she climbed, half walking, half crawling her way up, stopping only when the waves of pain rocked her with an intensity that sucked out her breath and drew the waning strength from her limbs. Her stomach felt very hard. Suddenly she gasped. A flooding warmth rushed down her legs, soaking her undergarments and ruining her satin slippers. Was it blood? Horrified at this unknown phenomenon, the fine edge of her control slipped away. Shaking with fear for her unborn child, Katrine cried out, "Help me. Oh, God! Someone please help me."

❧ 10 ❧

Duncan Forbes knocked softly on the door to Katrine's bedchamber. If she was already asleep, he would leave the message with her maid. Moments before, a Forbes clansman had arrived at Traquair, reporting that the Jacobite army under the command of George Murray had assembled at Drumossie Moor. The duke of Cumberland and his troops, which included Major Richard Wolfe, were still at Nairn celebrating the duke's birthday. Forbes grimaced. He did not relish the idea of telling Katrine that her child might share a birth month with the second son of England's king. He knocked again. Whatever his personal feelings, Katrine had a right to know that her father and husband would be on opposing sides of this battle.

A maid answered the door. When she saw who it was, her heavy-lidded eyes widened, and she curtseyed deeply. "I beg your pardon, sir," she stammered. "My lady hasn't returned yet, and I was busy with the clothespress."

His eyes, skimming over her dilated pupils and sleep-slack features, dismissed her excuse. "Has your mistress not returned from dinner?" he asked.

"No, m'lord."

Duncan knew she was not lying this time. He frowned and turned away. Where could Katrine have gone?

He walked past his own room to the end of the hall. The twisted stairway leading to the priests' room was illuminated by the flickering flames of the candle sconces mounted on the opposite wall. He hesitated, chiding himself. What possible reason could Katrine have for climbing the secret stairs in her condition? And yet she hadn't returned to her room and she wasn't in the library. He'd checked there first.

Lifting the candle branch from the wall, Duncan sighed and moved into the shadowed alcove, its confining space almost too narrow for the breadth of his shoulders. His instincts regarding Katrine had never been accurate. From the time she was fifteen years old, he had loved her to distraction. She had been half his age and he'd convinced himself it would be better to wait, at least until after her first season, to approach her with his regard.

For three years he'd bided his time, calling upon a lifetime of discipline, waiting and watching while younger, more ardent men claimed her dances, squired her to parties, and rode with her on the moors. It was only right, he argued with himself, that Katrine should have her youth. She was a beautiful, vibrant young woman. She was also fiercely patriotic and exceptionally intelligent. Duncan had counted on that. No callow, unschooled youth would satisfy her for long. In time, her eyes would turn to a man of experience, a man with influence, a man who had sewn his oats and would appreciate a woman with a mind of her own. Never, in his wildest dreams, had he imagined that he would lose her to an Englishman. He still refused to concede defeat. A battle lay ahead. A battle from which a great many would not return. It was entirely possible that Katrine would find herself a widow. Duncan was too honorable a man to wish death on anyone, but if fate were to decide Richard Wolfe's time was at hand, he would be there to help Katrine move on with her life.

The stairway was dangerously slick. She couldn't possibly have managed it. He would have turned around, but a single nagging doubt kept him moving upward. Finally he reached the top. Lifting the candles above his head, he looked around and froze. A wooden panel stood ajar, revealing a narrow passageway.

The muscles stood out on his neck. Drawing a deep breath, he strode forward holding the candles before him and pushed the panel wide open. "Katrine," he called loudly. "Katrine, are you down there?"

A sobbing moan reached his ears.

Uttering a vile expletive, Duncan forced himself to think clearly. She was obviously injured. He would need both arms. Anchoring the candle branch through a niche in the wall, he removed a single candle and forced himself to descend the narrow stairs carefully. When he finally reached her, he saw that his worst nightmare had come true. Katrine was in the throes of childbirth.

He looked at the narrow stairwell and cursed again. Carrying a woman swollen with child through that narrow corridor was impossible. There was no help for it. Katrine would have her child on this damp, vermin-infested floor, and he, Duncan Forbes, lord president of the Court of Session and a bachelor unaccustomed to children, would be her midwife.

She was barely conscious. "Duncan," she whispered, "is that you?"

"Yes, dear," he replied in a voice that was far calmer than he felt. "Don't be frightened. I'm here now."

She spoke through cracked lips. "The bairn will come soon."

"I know," he said hoarsely, reaching for her hands. "Do you know what to do, Katrine?"

She shook her head. "Do you?" she asked hopefully.

"Of course," he lied, placing the candle on an empty step and standing to remove his coat. "The first thing we must do is make you more comfortable." He bunched the coat into a pillow and placed it beneath her head. Reaching for the hem of her gown, he eased it up over her thighs, grateful for the shadowed darkness of the corridor. The desire of his life had been to lift Katrine Murray's skirts, to peel back her stockings and run his hands over the length of her long, slim legs. His mouth twisted wryly. He was doing exactly that, but it was in far different circumstances than he had imagined.

Her legs were wet with what could only be blood. Bile rose in his throat. He forced himself to look at the juncture between her thighs, but the single candle was inadequate to see properly. He needed the branch. "Katrine," he said, his voice low. "I need more light. There are candles at the top of the stairs. Can you manage if I leave you for a moment?"

He thought she nodded, but he couldn't be sure. He didn't wait to find out. Never in his life had he moved so quickly. Within seconds he was back and none too soon. Her stomach had tightened like the skin of a drum. She reached for him, and unreservedly, he gave her his hands. Lifting her head, she dug her nails into his skin and cried out, a frightening, primitive, unrecognizable sound that turned the blood in his veins to ice. Again she cried out, her head thrashing on his coat. Her eyes were wild, and there was blood on her lips. When it was over, she sank back against the steps, drained and white. Duncan reached for the candles when another spasm hit, racking her body and arching her back. Again she tore at his hands, crying out her pain, begging for release. He clenched his teeth, and the muscles tightened along his jaw. How could a human being bear such pain?

She clutched his arm. "He comes, Duncan. I can feel it." Her voice cracked. "Help us."

Unable to resist that piteous plea, Duncan squeezed her hand and nodded. Positioning himself between her knees, he waited for endless seconds until Katrine's tortured body expelled a wet, black-haired head. Gently he cradled it in his palm and with his other hand worked the infant's shoulders free. Finally, in a rush of blood, the rest of the body slid into his arms.

" 'Tis a boy," he announced and wiped the mucus from the tiny puckered mouth.

A healthy wail broke the anxious silence. Katrine laughed, a rich, silvery peal that sounded remarkably healthy.

Duncan stared down at her in surprise. That sound couldn't possibly have come from the torn body lying on the stairs. "Are you all right, Katrine?" he asked.

"Oh, Duncan. I'm so grateful. How did you know I was here?"

"Never mind. You need a woman to see to you." He looked at the cord still attached to the baby. "I've got to get you out of here. Can you wait until I go for help?"

"I can bear anything now." She held out her arms for her son. Balancing the baby in one hand, Duncan shrugged out of his shirt and wrapped the infant in the expensive linen. He handed him to Katrine and kissed her lightly on the lips. "I'll be back soon."

"I don't think this surprise march is a good idea, Murray," O'Sullivan remarked. "The men are tired and hungry. Why not let them have the night to rest?"

George Murray did not bother to explain that because of their inferior numbers and the Irishman's choice of battleground, a surprise attack was their only hope. "Cumberland will be celebrating his birthday," he said instead. "The soldiers will be drunk as beggars."

"I pray you may be right," said O'Sullivan. "The prince arrives tonight from Traquair. He won't be pleased if you muddle this one."

The entire rebellion had been a hopeless muddle from the beginning, reflected George as he walked, still in his kilt, through the columns of exhausted clansman. They had marched for two days without sleep, and their food and provisions had inadvertently been left behind at Inverness. The grumbling he heard among the ranks was not his imagination. The men were losing heart. If only they could fight from the hills where the ground was thick and marshy.

Because there was nothing else to do, George gave the order to march. It was eight o'clock and very dark, and he had only five thousand soldiers.

Cursing, the men complied.

They were to march around Nairn and strike the English under cover of darkness. After only an hour of marching, Murray found that nearly one-third of the men had left to forage for food. Precious time was wasted while officers rounded them up.

The ground was a giant bog, and more and more men, disgusted and nearly dead with fatigue, crawled under the bushes and fell asleep. The march was halted while O'Sullivan and Murray argued in the fog. Finally George cursed. "If we are to reach the English before dawn, there can be no more delay."

Again the troops moved forward, but this time pale streaks of dawn lit the sky. They could hear the English troops stirring in their camp. There would be no surprise attack on Nairn. Dispirited, George Murray gave the order to retreat, and the starving, weary soldiers marched back to Drumossie Moor. There was still no food. No longer able to stand upright, they fell where they stood and slept. Less than an hour later, the drums rolled signaling the call to order. The battle had begun.

"Why didn't you tell me before?" Katrine demanded.

Duncan Forbes grinned and gestured toward the child in her arms. "We were otherwise occupied," he reminded her.

Katrine's eyes softened as she looked down at the bundle nestled close to her heart. She touched her lips to the tiny head and inhaled deeply, loving the sweet baby scent of him. She thought of her aborted journey to find the stone and pushed it to the back of her mind. Scotland's Stone could wait. She smiled at Forbes. "'Tis true, we were. But now, I must see my husband."

"That isn't possible," replied Duncan flatly. "You've not yet recovered, and a battlefield is no place for a woman and child."

"Your house is there, Duncan," she coaxed him. "Surely, as guests of the lord president of the Court of Session, no harm will come to us."

He tried to reason with her. "I cannot guarantee your safety on such a journey, but I will take a message to your husband personally."

She shook her head. "No, Duncan. If you won't help us, I'll find someone else."

"Katrine," he begged her, "be reasonable."

She refused to listen, and when their conversation was over, Forbes retreated to his own room, where he threw himself, fully clothed, on top of his bed and cursed the hold Katrine Murray had over his heart.

Years later, when he stopped to recall the relentless pace of the next two days, he would shudder and wonder, not for the first time, if he'd been afflicted with temporary madness. Or perhaps the tales of witchcraft in the Murray family were true. From the first moment he had seen her, Katrine had bewitched him. There could be no other explanation for such a deviation in his normally excellent judgment.

At first light, they traveled north, skirting Edinburgh, and crossed the Firth of Forth at Grangemount. They spent the night at an inn near Dollar. The following day they passed through Perth and changed horses at Blairgowrie. Duncan argued for stopping at Blair Castle, hoping that Janet Murray would convince her daughter to end her journey there, but Katrine would have none of it. She ordered the coachman to continue on to Drumossie.

And so it was, that in the early hours of April 16, the Forbes travel coach bearing its long-suffering master, a squalling infant, and his bone-weary mother, rolled into the courtyard of Culloden House. It was close to dawn.

Bidding her host good night, Katrine closed the door of her room and, for one blissful moment, closed her eyes and leaned her cheek against the engraved wood. Thank God the bairn was taken care of. After feeding him, Katrine had handed him to Duncan's housekeeper with a sigh of relief.

There was no time to lose. Pushing away from the bracing support of the door, she looked for her trunk. It was tucked away in an alcove beneath the window. She knelt before it and lifted the lid. Every muscle in her aching body protested as she pulled on a warm cloak, woolen stockings, and sturdy boots. She stared down at her belly, the puckered flesh extended from childbirth, and grimaced. The breeks would never fit. She must brave the cold in the loose dress she had worn on the journey from Traquair.

Less than a quarter of an hour later, in the light of a brilliant dawn, she rode her horse past the rallying Jacobite troops toward Nairn. Foot soldiers were drawn up in two lines, the cavalry in the rear. The prince's meager artillery, only thirteen assorted guns, were on the left, center, and right of the front line. Even an inexperienced observer like Katrine could tell that the men had lost heart. Many were still asleep. She bit her lip and urged her mount forward, praying that Cumberland's army had not yet begun their march.

On the knoll near Leanach Holding, Katrine heard the unmistakable sounds of horses' bridles and boots marching in cadence. She reined in her horse and listened carefully. It could only be the government troops. She was too late. Richard would never leave his command, even if it meant facing her father across a broadsword. Patting her mare's heaving flanks, she turned back toward Culloden. There was a vantage point near Leanach Cottage, where she could watch the battle undisturbed.

The two armies did not face one another until almost eleven o'clock. Katrine caught her breath when she recognized the man on the gray gelding. Charles Stuart in his tartan coat and cockaded bonnet looked as jaunty as ever. His front line consisted almost entirely of clansmen, standing from three to six deep. On the right of the front line, Katrine recognized her father commanding the Atholl Brigade, which included Camerons, Stewarts of Appin, and Frasers, all wearing their clan tartans. In the center, she saw the Chattans, MacLachlans and MacLeans. She frowned. What were the MacDonalds doing on the left? Since Bannockburn, their position had always been on the right. Katrine knew what such a mistake would mean to the proud Highland MacDonalds. More importantly, the position put them at a serious disadvantage. The two front lines were not equal in length. The right of the prince's army was perhaps one hundred yards nearer Cumberland's front line than the left. In a charge, the MacDonalds would be slaughtered.

Katrine bit her lip and narrowed her eyes, squinting at the lines of Cumberland's men. Where was Richard? She searched the six regiments from right to left. On the flanks were the cavalry and then came the second line of infantry. It was then that she saw him, and her heart turned over. His hat was off and his fair hair glinted silver in the sunlight. The Campbell militia was positioned behind the prince's right flank.

The first shots came from a Jacobite gun. The duke's gunner opened fire with devastating results to the Highland ranks. The tartan-clad line, with wind and gunpowder blowing in their faces, stoically suffered the assault. Cumberland was too good a general to allow his men to engage in hand-to-hand combat before his artillery had done their job. With the Jacobite ranks standing six men deep, cannonballs wiped out entire regiments in seconds. Still the Highlanders stood, waiting for the signal to charge.

"Please," Katrine prayed, "give the order, give it now."

The fury of a Highland charge was legendary. There were few English troops that could withstand a hoard of screaming men bearing down upon them with broadswords drawn and claymores swinging. But the order never came. The prince was too far behind to see what was happening to his front line.

Something was definitely happening. Katrine clenched her fists. Richard's troops were moving forward to a position in front of the wall. When the Highland charge came, her husband's men would sweep the clansmen with bullets from end to end.

There was confusion in the Jacobite ranks. The MacIntoshes of Clan Chattan rushed forward, and the men of Atholl followed. Richard's men poured forth their fire. The carnage was appalling. Katrine closed her eyes and willed the nausea rising in her throat to depart. When she opened them, it was to see her father, his wig and hat blown off, fighting his way from the rear of the duke's army to the head of the second line. But it was already too late. Defeated, the clansmen were moving back. The moor was covered with the blood of the dead and wounded. Cumberland's cavalry rode forward, pursuing the retreating Jacobites. Katrine could no longer see her father. The entire battle had lasted less than one hour. On the moor and on the road to Inverness packed with fugitives, Cumberland's dragoons began their indiscriminate slaughter.

Katrine's breasts ached and the bodice of her gown was wet with leaking milk when she maneuvered her mare down the gradual slope to the bloodstained moor. She could not return to Culloden House until she knew the worst. On the battlefield, surgeons cared for the government injured while Cumberland's dragoons bayoneted and clubbed to death the wounded of the prince's army.

She must find Richard. He would stop this senseless massacre. Praying that he was still alive, Katrine slipped from her horse and walked amidst the bodies strewn haphazardly across the field. Her eyes burned with the effort of holding back tears.

It was April, and all around her the heather bloomed in glorious profusion. Wrapped in a clan tartan, the Cameron standard-bearer, MacLachlan of Coruanan, lay stiff in the dirt. Robert Mor MacGillivray, his arms and legs severed from his lifeless body, lay nearby. With a sob, Katrine rested her aching body against the flank of her mare. These were her people, the men she had grown up with, danced with, teased and laughed and joked with since before her earliest memory. Hot tears flowed down her cheeks. Shoulders shaking, she slid to the ground and buried her face in her hands.

A sharp pain pricked her shoulder. She turned quickly, surprising a youth dressed in the despised garb of a government soldier. Fury drowned out her reason. Rising to her feet, she pushed aside the point of his sword. "How dare you," she hissed. "Do you know who I am?"

"You are a Scot, madame," the soldier replied. "The duke's orders are to give no quarter to the enemy."

"Does the English army stoop to making war on women?"

The man nodded. "We do now. Ever since George Murray's orders to give the enemy no quarter."

Katrine's eyes flashed. "That's a lie. Lord Murray is an honorable man. He would never issue such an order."

"He did indeed," the man argued.

Katrine straightened. "I am Katrine Wolfe. Perhaps you know my husband, Lord Ashton?"

The man whitened under his tan, and she saw that he was little more than a boy. "I know Lord Richard Wolfe, m'lady," he said. "If you'll allow me, I shall take you to him."

Under different circumstances, the expression on her husband's face when he looked up and saw her would have been worth everything she'd been through. He was in his tent, signing some last-minute dispatches before returning to the battlefield.

"My God," he said hoarsely, rising to his feet. "Katrine, is it really you?"

She burst into tears and threw herself into his arms. The soldier, showing exceptional tact, retreated hastily.

"Oh, Richard," she sobbed, "I can't believe you're alive." The feel of his mouth on hers after so many long and lonely months was like a small taste of heaven.

Shocked at the raw emotion that threatened to wreak havoc with his military discipline, Richard tightened his arms around her and buried his face in the dark cloud of her hair. "Did you see it?" he asked gruffly.

She nodded against his shoulder. "Everything."

"I'm so sorry, Katrine," he murmured, inhaling the fragrant scent that belonged to her alone. "If I could have done it differently, I would have. Please believe that."

She looked up at him, her cheeks streaked with tears. "Have you seen my father? Is he still alive?"

His face was ravaged. "I don't know."

She swallowed and pulled out of his arms. He looked at her, seeing for the first time the purple shadows under her eyes and the full, almost shapeless gown concealed beneath her cloak. His eyes widened in shock. Katrine was no longer pregnant.

"Do you have something to tell me, my love?" he asked gently.

She smiled. "I'd almost forgotten. We've a son, Richard, a healthy son. I'd like to name him after my brother."

"Whatever you like," he replied. "When was he born?"

"The day before yesterday."

Richard stared at her. "Good God, Katrine! You should be in bed. Whatever possessed you?"

"I couldn't bear not to know what was happening."

"Where are you staying?"

"At Culloden House."

"I'll take you back immediately. I want to see my son. When this is over, we'll go home."

She said nothing.

He frowned and stepped forward, drawing her back into his arms. "You do want to come home with me, don't you, Katrine? We'll go back to England and forget all of this."

Her smile held no gladness. She lifted her hand to touch his cheek. "Oh, Richard," she whispered as he led her to her mare. "Don't you see? We'll never forget any of it for as long as we live."

They were mounted and on their way when Katrine remembered the soldier's words. She urged her mount forward until she rode directly beside her husband. "Richard," she began, wetting her lips. Anxious as she was to learn the truth, she knew the answer might prove distasteful. "The soldier who brought me to you said my father had issued an order of no quarter to the enemy."

Richard's lips tightened, and he cursed softly. "No, Katrine," he said at at last. "It was a forgery. Cumberland inserted the no quarter phrase himself to encourage his troops in their slaughter. George Murray never gave such an order."

"Thank God," she said fervently.

"Don't thank Him yet," warned her husband as a very large, very heavy man in the frocked coat of an officer approached them. Richard looked around quickly. "Take your horse and wait behind that rock. I don't want Cumberland interrogating you."

Katrine did not question his orders. Pulling on the reins of her mare, she dropped back into the shelter of an enormous boulder and waited.

"The enemy has been routed, Major Wolfe," said the duke. "It is said that the prince has fled the field." He could not keep the scorn from his voice. "We leave for Inverness tonight. I've a mind to take up residence in the house my dear cousin has recently vacated. Are you agreeable?"

"Of course," replied Richard. "I must decline for myself, however. My wife has just given birth and is recovering at Culloden House. I wish to spend tonight with her and our son. I'll join you tomorrow."

"Very well and please accept my congratulations, Major. It isn't every day that an heir is born."

A moan interrupted them. Cumberland's eyes dropped to the badly wounded man lying only a few feet from his horse's hooves. His lip curled. He raised his sword and then appeared to change his mind.

From her place behind the rock, Katrine released her breath, offering a silent prayer of relief. She had recognized the man immediately. It was Charles Fraser of Inverallochy, commander of the Fraser contingent.

Again Cumberland spoke. "He's yours, Wolfe. Kill the insolent rebel."

Katrine's eyes widened in horror. Would Richard refuse such an order? Could he and still live? The distance between her hiding place and the open field where the two men faced each other was not great. She saw Richard straighten and face his commander. In the deep tan of his face, his eyes glittered an angry ice blue.

Pride and relief surged through her veins. This was her husband and despite the fact that they had known very little of each other on their wedding day, her instincts had prevailed. She had seen something far greater and worth much more than his ancient title, his handsome face, and courteous manners. Richard Wolfe had courage and character. Katrine had chosen well. She knew what his answer would be even before he spoke.

"The man is wounded," he replied scornfully. "Murder does not sit well with my conscience. I would rather resign my commission than carry out such an order."

For a long time the two men stared at each other. Cumberland's handsome, fleshy face was stained a dark red. "Never mind then," he said stiffly. "I'll find someone else to do it." With that he rode away.

Katrine came out from behind the rock. Silently, she positioned her mare beside her husband's mount and placed her hand over his. She nodded toward the wounded man. "We can't leave him, Richard. He'll be killed."

"He's dead already," her husband answered bitterly. "Damn Cumberland's soul."

He saw the tears slide down her cheeks, and the anger left him. He smiled reassuringly. In silent communion, they rode side by side until they reached Culloden House. Together they walked through the door and up the graceful, winding staircase into the sunlit room that served as a nursery. Dismissing the servant, they leaned over the cradle where their son lay sleeping.

Richard couldn't explain the thundering of his heart or the clammy coldness of his hands as he looked down into the face of the child Katrine had borne him. Alasdair Wolfe did not look like an English baby. Long black lashes rested against olive-tinted cheeks. His mouth was like Katrine's, and the delicate bones of his cheeks and chin promised the slender sharpness of his Celtic ancestors. Just then, the baby's eyes opened, revealing where the Murray lineage had given way to his own. Long lashes surrounded eyes as true and deeply blue as any Wolfe who had ever lived.

A lump rose in Richard's throat. This was his child, his son. He was unprepared for the rush of love that swept through him, wiping away the cultivated inhibitions of a lifetime. His mouth opened, but he couldn't force the words past his lips. For one horrifying moment he felt like weeping, and then Katrine's hand slipped into his. He looked up to find the strength he needed in her gaze. It would be all right. They were in this together. When the score was settled, he would resign his commission and they would return home to raise their child.

For Richard, the night was too short. Lying next to Katrine for the first time in months, holding her close, breathing in the clean scent of her hair was like a restoring tonic. He didn't want to waste one precious moment in sleep. But in the end, he succumbed to his exhausted body's need. His eyes closed, and his breathing deepened into the rhythmic cadence of the unconscious.

Katrine awoke first. It was just before dawn. She propped herself up on her elbow and looked down at her husband. His bare chest was tanned, his stomach lean and tight with muscle. He was thinner than she remembered. The golden hair spread across the pillow was bleached almost white from the sun. Something dark and elemental stirred inside of her, something she hadn't thought about in the long months of her pregnancy and confinement. Regret washed over her. It was too soon after Alasdair's birth. With a sigh, she pulled the covers over the two of them and nestled against the comforting warmth of his body.

She thought of the baby. Instantly, wet circles dampened her gown. Richard smiled in his sleep and pulled her into a possessive embrace. Burrowing her head against his shoulder, she closed her eyes. Just this once, Alasdair could wait.

The next time she woke, Richard was completely dressed, except for his boots. Katrine watched him as he pulled on the right one first and then the left.

"Were you going to wake me before you left?" she asked.

"I was hoping to return before you noticed I was gone," he confessed.

Katrine frowned. "I don't want you to feel as if you must leave anything unfinished because of me, Richard."

He leaned across the bed and cupped her chin in his hand. "I want us to go home, Katrine. My heart isn't in this anymore. I'm a husband and a father, not a soldier."

Her eyes glistened. Of his own free will, Richard was making the commitment she had waited so long to hear. More than anything in the world, she wanted to throw herself into his arms and tell him nothing mattered but the life they would have together. But it wouldn't be true. There was much more at stake than just the two of them. Richard did not yet understand the significance of what had happened at Drumossie Moor that day, and Katrine did not have the courage to tell him. Instead she said, "I could never leave without first seeing my father."

Richard nodded. His eyes were very blue as they searched her face. It was as if he were trying to imprint into his memory every curve and line of the fine narrow bones, the clean planes of her cheek and chin, the tilt of her nose, the sweep of black lashes against olive skin, and the clear, fathomless gray of her eyes. His kiss was swift and hard. "I love you, Katrine," he said hoarsely. "Whatever happens, remember that. God willing, I'll spend the rest of my life proving it to you."

"See that you do, Richard Wolfe," she said gravely. "Come back to me in one piece."

Tucking his hat under his arm, he smiled at her one last time before leaving the room.

That morning, Katrine breakfasted alone. Duncan had already left when she came down the stairs. His message, telling her he had been summoned by Cumberland, was a cryptic one. He must have realized that Richard had survived the battle and spent the night in her room. She sighed. Duncan had proven himself to be a dear friend, but Richard was her husband. Sooner or later, Duncan would have to come to terms with that fact.

Katrine was halfway through her second cup of tea when a loud pounding at the door interrupted her. She stood and walked into the entry. Duncan's butler and a blood-smeared clansman she recognized as Gillies MacBean of Clan Chattan argued loudly.

Quickly, she intervened. "May I help you?" she asked politely.

"Don't listen to him, m'lady," entreated the butler. "Lord Forbes specifically instructed me to see that you remain inside today. Cumberland's troops are killing everyone in sight, no questions asked."

"I appreciate your concern, Holmes," replied Katrine, "but I must hear what Gillie has to say."

Gillie MacBean straightened his shoulders and stepped forward. "'Tis Ewan Douglas who sent me to fetch you, lass. His wound is poisoned, and he wishes to leave your mother a message."

Katrine's hand flew to her throat. Ewan was her uncle, her mother's only surviving brother. "Can you wait until I get my cloak?" she asked.

The man's worried countenance relaxed, and he nodded. "A moment more will make no difference."

"'Tis not safe, m'lady," the butler repeated. "I wish you will reconsider." His words followed her as she ran up the stairs, found her cloak, and hurried down again.

"Tell Lord Forbes where I've gone," she said, pulling on her gloves. "If my uncle is well enough, I shall bring him back with me."

The servant bowed his head in defeat as the burly clansman lifted Katrine to his own saddle and climbed up behind her.

"Where are we going?" she asked.

"To a barn near Balvraid," the man replied. "Ewan made his way there last evening."

Her eyebrows lifted in astonishment. "Are there no surgeons to see to the wounded?"

"Aye," said Gillie bitterly, "to the government wounded. Those fighting for the prince can expect nothing more than the sharp end of a bayonet."

"Even those who surrendered?" Katrine refused to believe the men her husband commanded were capable of such cruelty.

"This isn't a tea party, lass. The charge against us is treason, and the penalty is death."

Katrine could think of nothing to say that would soften the horror of such a fate. She remained silent until they pulled up beside what appeared to be a deserted barn.

Her uncle was still conscious, but his eyes were closed. He was alone, and the blood staining his shirt came from a wound in the center of his chest.

Katrine knelt beside him. "Uncle Ewan," she whispered, "'tis Katrine. I've come to take you away from here."

Slowly the dying man's eyes opened. His breath was loud and rasping, and the bubbles forming at his mouth were filled with blood. With enormous effort he formed the words. "Tell Janet—"

Katrine bent her ear to his lips. "Tell her what?"

His words were the barest whisper. "Tell her to go to France. Take my son, his wife, and the child." His breathing altered for a moment and then continued. "They mean to kill all of us. No one in the Highlands is safe."

She drew back in horror. "We've had uprisings before," she argued. "Why is this different?"

For a man at the end of his strength, his grip on her wrist was amazingly strong. "Do as I say, Katrine. Promise me."

She stared down into the face that was as familiar to her as her own father's. Slowly she nodded. "I promise."

"Good girl," he rasped and turned toward the wall.

Gillie MacBean leaned forward and placed his fingers against the wounded man's throat. He shook his head.

Tears rolled down Katrine's cheeks. She dropped her head into her hands and sobbed.

"He waited for you, lass. I'm sure it was a great comfort to him to have you here."

She opened her mouth to speak when a noise outside the barn stopped her. Gillie held his finger against his lips, picked up his broadsword, and flattened himself against the barn wall. The door burst open, and a dozen horses filled the entrance. There were a dozen more behind them.

"What have we here?" A large heavy-set man with a long nose and double chin stared first at Katrine and then at the lifeless body of Ewan Douglas. He frowned. Katrine's face, in the dark shadows of the barn, was unrecognizable. Gesturing toward one of his men, he ordered, "Bring her outside."

She lifted her chin. "That won't be necessary," she said and walked between the sweating horses into the dim light of an April day.

"Who are you?" asked the duke of Cumberland.

Smiling disdainfully, she spread her bloodstained skirts in a mocking curtsey. "Don't you recognize me, Your Grace? I am Katrine Wolfe."

His eyes narrowed. "May I ask why you are here giving aid to a rebel?"

"Ewan Douglas is my uncle," she said shortly. "I could not refuse him."

He toyed with the black rosette on his hat. "George Murray is your father, is he not?"

"He is."

"Have you Jacobite sympathies, Lady Wolfe?"

Across the distance that separated them, he could see the flashing silver of her eyes. "I do, Your Grace."

"Are you aware that the penalty for treason is death?"

Something clicked in the back of her mind. This scene had been played out before. She closed her eyes, and the memory of another woman and another time flooded her consciousness. Words, clear and proud, resounded in her head. Katrine's eyes opened, and her faintness cleared.

Her voice was strong with purpose. "I am no traitor," she said, "for I did not betray my king."

Cumberland could not mistake her meaning. His face turned a dark purple. "In that case, m'lady," he said, "you shall join your fellow Jacobites. 'Tis a pity we have no gallows, but I've heard death by sword is far more merciful." He turned to the men mounted beside him. "Seize her," he ordered.

In unison they moved forward. Gillie MacBean, brandishing his broadsword at the duke, stepped out from inside the barn. "Touch her and I'll spear you through the heart."

Cumberland's face twisted in fury. "Kill him," he shouted.

Two dragoons positioned themselves beside Katrine. The rest moved forward. She closed her eyes, praying for a miracle. The odds against Gillie were twenty to one. The minutes seemed like hours, but finally it was silent again. Katrine opened her eyes and gasped. Thirteen government soldiers lay dead and with them the trampled and dismembered body of Gillie MacBean. Tears pricked her eyes. If there had only been more men like Gillie, yesterday would have turned out quite differently for the duke of Cumberland. His attention had returned to Katrine.

"Save your tears for yourself, Lady Wolfe," he said. "You shall join him shortly." Dismounting, the duke pulled out his sword and advanced toward her.

"What in bloody hell are you doing?" A voice, ice cold and deadly with rage, froze Cumberland in his tracks.

Slowly he turned around and looked across the clearing into Major Richard Wolfe's forbidding blue eyes. He was alone and on horseback. Somehow, during the fray, he had come unnoticed upon the duke and his men.

"Your wife is guilty of giving aid to the enemy," Cumberland announced. "She is also an admitted Jacobite. The penalty is death."

"She is my wife," said Richard through gritted teeth. "As the countess of Ashton, she is an English peer. That entitles her to a trial."

"Not in time of war."

"This isn't a war," replied Richard scathingly. "'Tis a

bloodbath. You'll be remembered throughout history as a butcher."

Both of Cumberland's large chins quivered with anger. "Major Richard Wolfe, you will be placed under arrest for insubordination."

Richard's eyes challenged him. "I'll not allow you to harm my wife." He drew his sword. "You'll have to kill me first."

Cumberland stepped back. "Restrain him," he ordered his men.

The dragoons looked doubtfully at each other. More than one face held a troubled expression. Major Wolfe was a superior officer and a favorite among the men.

Richard grinned. "Come, lads. I'll take you together or one at a time."

Two horsemen moved forward.

"No," Katrine moaned, pulling out of the grasp of her captors. She could not bear to see Richard's lean, beautiful body torn into pieces before her. Rushing forward, she grabbed Cumberland's sleeve. "Stop please," she begged.

Surprised at the unexpected contact, he turned quickly, his sword extended. The blade, cold as ice, sliced deeply into the soft flesh of Katrine's breast.

A look of astonishment crossed her face. She stepped back and touched her hand to her side. Blood stained her gown and seeped through her fingers. With a gasp, she crumpled to the ground.

Shocked, Cumberland dropped his sword just as Richard's hands found his throat. The choking pain had given way to a sweet lassitude before his men pried him loose. When at last he sat up, he saw Major Wolfe riding away, cradling his wife in his arms. No one attempted to stop them. Looking into the accusing eyes of his men, Cumberland knew that any order to apprehend the couple would be disobeyed.

Richard Wolfe had seen enough of war to know that Katrine's wound was fatal. It was amazing that even now she lived. Blood poured from the gash like a fountain. His jacket and shirt were already drenched, and he could feel the familiar wetness beneath his clothing, warm against his skin. He refused to succumb to his pain. There would be a lifetime for anguish. Now, he must be strong for Katrine.

"Richard." Her voice was faint. "Save my family. See that they leave for France."

"You know I will." Not for one moment did he consider lying. Katrine, straightforward in the throes of death as she was in life, would be spared the effort of pretense. They both knew she was dying. Any comfort must be taken in these last few moments together. He stopped the horse. They were far from Cumberland and his men.

"Take care of Alasdair," she whispered. "Later, when the troubles are settled, bring him to Scotland. My mother has no one left."

Richard tried to contain his grief, but the pain was too great. Burying his head in her hair, he wept. Her hand slipped away and her head fell back, and still he wept. He knew from the frightening limp weight of her that she was gone. He knew night would soon descend and that a lone man on horseback was a target. He knew that his life would be worthless if either Cumberland's troops or Jacobite marauders came upon him. But none of it mattered. He had lost Katrine Murray. Nothing would ever matter again.

❧ 11 ❧

Blair Castle
1993

An insistent knocking brought me back to the present. Crossing the room, I unlocked the door to find an anxious Ian Douglas staring back at me.

"In another minute, I would have forced my way in," he said. "Are you all right?"

Shaking my head, I stepped back and leaned against the door. I opened my mouth to speak, but the words wouldn't come. Tears choked my throat and paralyzed my tongue.

The worry on his face deepened. He stepped forward and reached for me. Closing my eyes, I leaned against him, giving way to the searing grief I could no longer hold back. Deep inside me, from a source I didn't know existed and hadn't yet begun to tap, the heaving sobs began. Gathering me against his chest, Ian let me cry for a long time, rubbing my back and the crown of my head, murmuring Gaelic words of comfort into my ear.

Much later, when my storm of emotion had passed and his sweater was damp with tears, I pulled out of his arms, wiping my nose with the back of my hand. He handed me his handkerchief, and I accepted it with a self-conscious "Thank you."

Ian waited until I'd restored some semblance of calm to my tear-streaked face. Then he led me to the armchair, pressed me down into the cushions, and asked, "Are you ready to tell me what that was all about?"

I looked away from the concern reflected in his face and closed my eyes. For some reason I was exhausted. What I wanted more than anything in the world was to go home. Edinburgh and the luncheon with Professor MacCleod seemed like weeks ago. I chewed the inside of my lip. What would Ian say if I asked him to take me back after coming all this way? There was nothing else to do but tell him how I felt.

Opening my eyes, I spoke directly. "I want to go back to Traquair, Ian. There is nothing here at Blair-Atholl."

He frowned. "How do you know?"

I hesitated. How much would he accept?

"Christina." He knelt beside me, his blue eyes very intent. "I'm not as skeptical as you believe. Trust me."

My eyes moved over his face. It was a strong face, confident and sincere. A muscle throbbed at the corner of his mouth.

"Mairi hid the stone at Traquair," I blurted out. "Katrine found the passageway, but she went into labor before she could explore it."

His voice was very controlled. "You've been dreaming again."

"They aren't dreams. They're visions. Katrine Murray died at Cumberland's hands. She had a child. A boy." I could hear the hysterical quality to my voice. "She had diabetes, and she saw everything exactly as I've seen it." Sitting up, I clutched his sleeve. "I've got to find the stone, Ian. Don't you see? If Mairi's name is cleared, the curse will end."

Perspiration beaded his forehead. "Haven't you forgotten something?"

"What?"

"If, as you say, the pattern holds true and you believe everything you're telling me, you are in considerable danger, Christina."

A cold prickling sensation made its way up my spine. He had voiced what I'd refused to admit for some time now. "I know," I whispered.

Errant raindrops dripped down the chimney and fell into the flames of the fire. A log hissed and sputtered and then broke in two. Ian spoke softly, but his eyes never left my face. "Mairi and Katrine died at the hands of their enemies." He reached over to the desk and picked up Professor MacCleod's envelope. "I think you'd better read this. It's the biography of Jeanne Maxwell, compiled from letters found after her death."

"She's the one I know nothing about. Why is that, I wonder?" I looked inquiringly at Ian.

He shrugged. "Maybe something we know nothing about triggers a particular association or maybe the mind can only take in so much information at a time."

"Or maybe Mairi is controlling us all, allowing only so much to happen at a time." I shivered and ran my fingers over the envelope. "Have you read this?"

He nodded and brushed his hand against my cheek. "I have. And if you come to the same conclusion I did, we're in this together."

My mouth felt dry. "Why?" I whispered.

He smiled, and once again I felt a tiny flutter of pleasure in my stomach. "Let's just say that I've a small stake in your future. You'll know more when you've finished reading."

He stood up, pulling me with him. "Shall we take a break and go down to dinner?"

Apparently dinner at Blair was never informal, even when the host was absent. I counted seven courses in all, from the salmon in wine sauce and clear dill soup to the dessert, which was a custard-filled bread pudding.

"Excuse me, Miss Murray." The butler bowed slightly. "I called Traquair as you requested and explained that you and Mr. Douglas would not be returning this evening. Mrs. Ferguson wanted me to tell you that your father called from America. She said his message was urgent."

I could feel myself pale. "Did she mention why?"

"No, miss." He shook his head. "Would you like to use the phone in the library?"

"Yes, please." I pushed back my chair and stood. "If you'll excuse me, Ian, I'll be right back."

He stood. "Of course. I hope there's nothing wrong."

"So do I," I muttered.

My hands shook as I dialed the operator for instructions on how to complete a trans-Atlantic call. Within seconds, the sound of my parents' telephone rang in my ear. Two rings, three, four. Where were they? It was eleven o'clock in the morning in California. They always ate an early lunch on the patio after walking the dogs. The answering machine picked up the call, and my father's familiar recorded voice explained that no one could come to the phone and to please leave a message. After hearing the beep, I explained where I was and that I would be returning to Traquair in the morning. Hanging up the phone, I walked back into the dining room.

Ian held out my chair, and I sat down. The fragrant smell of hot coffee coming from the shining silver coffee service was too tempting to ignore. I waited in silence as the housekeeper poured the dark brown liquid into a delicate china cup, placed it on a matching saucer, and handed it to me. She repeated the process for Ian. After asking if there would be anything else, she discreetly left the room.

"Is everything all right at home?" he asked.

I sipped my coffee. "I don't know. No one was there."

He frowned. "Do your parents normally call you when you visit Scotland?"

I shook my head. "Never. I'm not always sure when I'll be in. I usually call them every Sunday night."

"Why don't we call Kate and ask if your father mentioned where they might be?"

"I don't think that would help," I replied. "My father is a lawyer, Ian. He doesn't leave anything to chance. If it was important that I know where they were, he would have left a specific message." I looked up to meet his worried expression. His concern had a reassuring affect on me. I smiled. "Thank you for caring, but I'm sure nothing is seriously wrong. He would have told Kate if it was a real emergency."

He looked relieved. "If you're sure—"

"Very sure," I said firmly. "I'm curious, nothing more."

We left the dining room, and Ian reached for my hand. "There's a comfortable sitting room at the other end of the house," he said. "It even has a television."

I looked up into the sculpted perfection of his face. What I saw there stopped my breath. It was surprising that I recognized it at all. I had seen it only once before in the last several years and that was yesterday on the riverbank. It was the look of a man in need and hungry—for me.

When my heart resumed its beating, I answered him. "It sounds wonderful, but do we really need a television?"

He grinned and slid his arm around my waist. "Follow me."

The sitting room was as modern as my mother's California living room. The twin sofas were large with plush, comfortable pillows and stylish upholstery. Recessed lighting gave the room a cozy glow. A sleek wooden coffee table in front of the fireplace carried copies of popular magazines.

Ian dimmed the lights and lit the fire while I sat on the couch and thumbed through a copy of a women's magazine not sold in America. Soon he joined me and, as naturally as if he'd done it every day of his life, pulled my head against his shoulder, and kissed me.

Who can explain why one particular man instinctively knows the secret of setting a woman's body aflame when another can try time after laborious time and never quite get it right?

Ian's hands moved across my skin like a concert pianist, while his lips and tongue played havoc with the dips and scooped-out hollows of my cheeks, my throat, the curves of my breasts, and the sensitive spot where my neck and shoulder met. I couldn't stop the moan of sheer animal pleasure when he pressed me back against the pillows and covered my body with his. He was lean and hard and warm and beautiful, and I wanted him with a desperation completely unfamiliar to me. Shamelessly I encouraged him, urging him on with words and gestures I would never have imagined myself capable of before this night. My body took on a life of its own, moving and opening with wanton abandon under the sensual, drugging magic of his skilled hands and seeking lips.

"My God, Christina," he said and surged inside me. He stiffened, and I could feel the cords stand out on his neck. "I'm sorry, darling," he gasped, "but I can't wait any longer." At his first swollen thrust, my pleasure peaked. Sensation consumed me and for the first time in thirty-seven years, I came to know the meaning of the words *white hot* and *rocking waves of passion.*

Later, when the fire was nearly out and Ian's chest moved in the steady rhythm of the nearly unconscious, I lifted my head from his shoulder and asked the question I had wanted to ask since yesterday on the riverbank. "Why do you know so much about my family history?"

His eyes flew open, and for the barest instant I could feel resistance in the sudden tightening of his arms. Then he relaxed and settled my head back into the hollow of his shoulder. I held my breath, hoping that this time he wouldn't put me off. My patience was rewarded.

"You'll think I'm mad," he muttered.

I lifted my head to stare at him in astonishment. "After everything I've told you? Don't be ridiculous."

He still looked unconvinced.

"Ian," I said softly, using his words, "please trust me."

He sighed, and I could feel the tension flow out of his body. In the lyrical, hypnotic voice of a Highland bard, he began to speak. "My family is descended from the Black Douglases through the illegitimate line of Sir James Douglas."

I knew something of the history of that ill-fated family as

well as that of the Red Douglases who came later, but I didn't interrupt. I had a feeling that Ian's story might be a great deal different from the textbooks.

"From our earliest history to the time when Sir William Douglas was imprisoned inside the Tower of London after fighting with Wallace at Falkirk, we had the usual triumphs and tragedies that most clans experienced. But after that, when the Bruce came to power, things changed. The family fortunes deteriorated, the line died out, and Douglas men fell out of favor."

When the Bruce came to power. I felt a chill run down my spine. The Bruce had come to power during the lifetime of Mairi of Shiels.

"Sir James Douglas had two sons," Ian continued, "one illegitimate. His brother Archibald had one as well. As you know, James died in Spain while attempting to bury the Bruce's heart in the Holy Land. His son fell fighting the English at Halidan Hill. Archibald also died at Halidan. William, Archibald's son, became the earl of Douglas. He died at Otterburn without an heir."

I remained silent, asking no questions, hardly daring to breathe. Scotland's history had always been a rocky one, her people's disagreements settled at the point of a sword. It wasn't completely clear as to where Ian was going with his litany of tragic deaths, but as I listened, my suspicions grew.

"Archibald the Grim, a bastard, came to power as the third earl of Douglas. His oldest son died in battle, and his grandsons were lured to Edinburgh and executed in the castle. The title went to Archibald's second son, James, and then to his son, William. William renewed his allegiance to the earls of Crawford and Ross. King James II sent him a safe conduct and invited him to Stirling, where he had William stabbed and his body flung over the battlements, where it was found by his brother, the new earl.

"Three years later, King James charged the family with treason and brought an army against them. The entire Douglas estates were forfeited and the earldom extinguished. The earl fled to England with one of his brothers, leaving his wife behind. She was called the Fair Maid of Galloway. The king arranged for her divorce, married her to his own half brother, and gave them the Douglas lordship of Balveny. They became the earl and countess of Atholl. So you see, Christina, the Murrays prevailed after all."

Ian had related his story as if everything had happened in his own lifetime, to people he knew and loved. But I knew that the final curtain had come down on the Black Douglases in the middle of the fifteenth century, over five hundred years ago. I still had no clue as to why this had anything to do with the twentieth-century Ian Douglas. I was about to interrupt his reverie and ask when he started to speak again.

"I know this background history must seem tedious to you, but I had to establish a reference. For years descendents of the Douglases fostered themselves to other clans, hiring themselves out to sympathetic families. In the middle of the sixteenth century, an enterprising Douglas married into the Murray clan and was gifted the home that now belongs to my family. By staying neutral during most of Scotland's wars, a Douglas heir has always managed to survive there."

I couldn't miss the hostility in his voice or the bitter twist to his mouth.

"When other estates had difficulties, we had disasters. Somehow the Douglas lands have always been in the path of marauding armies and crop-destroying storms. Our fortunes have always been explained away as chance or unusually bad luck until the First World War when my grandfather was decorated for heroic service. He was a career officer and rose steadily in the ranks until it was time for his appointed promotion. They passed him over for a desk officer who had never so much as left the country. He retired immediately and drank himself into an early grave."

"I don't understand," I began.

"You will when I'm finished," he promised. "My father ran for a seat in the House of Commons. He was a popular man, respected by everyone in Innerleithen and Peebles. His opponent, an Englishman from York who had recently moved into the area, accused my father of molesting his fourteen-year-old daughter. I was in America at the time and didn't know the exact details until after it was all over.

My father had too much pride to speak in his own defense. They found him the morning after the trial with a bullet hole in his head."

"Oh, dear God." My eyes swam with the tears I couldn't hold back. "I'm so sorry, Ian."

"I didn't realize any of it was connected," he continued, "until I met Professor MacCleod. We met on the road. His car battery broke down, and I stopped to help him. When he realized who I was, he introduced himself and explained that he was interested in Scottish antiquities. We had tea, and I drove him to Traquair. By the end of the day, he must have decided that I wouldn't accuse him of insanity because he confided in me. It was then that I learned about the entire history of the Maxwells and the Murrays and my own ancestor, the woman who placed her curse upon the two clans."

He held me away from him, his eyes searching my face, willing me to understand and accept. "She was my ancestor, Christina, and impossible as it appears, from the very moment she accused Mairi of Shiels, her descendents have lived under a black cloud."

How could such a thing be possible? Every ounce of sanity in my brain protested. And yet, why not? I had seen it all, much more clearly than Ian. I was present when Grizelle Murray Douglas condemned Mairi to death. I had seen the pain in David Murray's eyes and watched his pleasant features twist in hatred when he met his mother's triumphant gaze.

"What can we do?" I whispered.

With a hoarse cry, Ian pulled me against him and buried his face in my hair. "Bless you, Christina," he murmured in relief, "and thank you for believing me. It sounds so outrageous that half the time I don't believe it myself."

I smiled into his shoulder, but the pleasure of being in his arms was diminished by the urgency of our problem. "There must be something we can do," I repeated.

"Perhaps there is, now that you're here."

"What do you mean?"

"You have an unusual gift, my love. I'm not sure what it all means, but wherever it takes us, we're in this together."

Something bothered me, and I had to voice it. "Why me, Ian? Why do I have the sight?"

He folded my hands between his own, and when he spoke, his voice was gentle and patient. "I believe that whatever forces of goodness exist on earth gave us this chance, just as it gave Katrine Murray, two hundred years ago, and Jeanne Maxwell, two hundred years before that. The incredible part is that we have a chance neither of them had. They were alone. We found each other."

The fire was completely out, and the air had grown cold. I shivered, and Ian pulled a woolen afghan over me. "It still doesn't make sense," I persisted. "Not everything fits. My mother is Irish, and the dreams didn't come to Katrine until after she was pregnant. Was it that way for Jeanne Maxwell?"

He shook his head, his forehead wrinkled in thought. "Jeanne's circumstances were different. She didn't have the first of the nightmares until after her son was born. I don't have all the answers, Christina. We'll just have to go along with the facts we have."

"I can't have children," I reminded him.

With the tip of his finger he traced my cheekbones, the bridge of my nose, and the line of my mouth. My lips parted, and I tasted the salty flavor of his skin. He bent his head, and I felt his breath against my ear. "Wrong, Christina," he whispered, pressing his mouth against the sensitive lobe. "You just haven't had them yet."

Later, we made our way up to my bedroom and together opened Professor MacLeod's envelope. Ian positioned the feather pillows behind his head and settled me against him so that my back rested against his chest. Surrounded by the security of his arms, I read aloud the documents so painstakingly collected for me. The dry expository prose wasn't nearly as enjoyable to read as Janet's diary had been, but it didn't matter. Before long, Ian fell asleep and I must have also because, like a dream, the shockingly visual story of Jeanne Maxwell of Traquair unfolded before me.

❧ 12 ❧

Edinburgh
June 30, 1509

"There he is, Jeannie. I told you he would come." Moira Sutherland squeezed her companion's arm in rapturous excitement. "Don't look now." She gasped, staring at the lean, black-haired figure maneuvering his way expertly through the crowded great hall. "Sweet Mary. He's walking toward us."

Jeanne Maxwell lifted her chin and removed her arm from her friend's painful grip. "Don't play the fool, Moira. 'Tis only John Maxwell. He's my cousin and I've known him since I was born."

"But he's so very handsome, and you haven't seen him for years," Moira protested.

Jeanne sniffed. "He was always a braggart. I doubt if the English court has improved him."

From behind them an amused voice interrupted. "Turn around, Cousin, and see for yourself."

Moira gasped and turned quickly, stammering an awkward greeting. Jeanne took a moment to gather her composure. Slowly, she turned to face her boyhood champion, and her eyes widened in disbelief. So the rumors were true. John Maxwell was a man that would make a woman's gaze linger. He was taller than she remembered with wider shoulders, and his features had lost their bluntness. Now they were sharply defined as if they'd been sculpted by a craftsman with a finely honed blade.

"Welcome home, John," she said cooly. "We've nothing so grand as Whitehall here in Edinburgh, but I'm sure you'll be comfortable."

Moira's face flamed. Jeannie Maxwell, the kindest and most loyal of friends, was behaving like a shrew to the most engaging young man who had ever graced the court of King James IV of Scotland.

John Maxwell grinned. To Moira's amazement, he didn't appear in the least offended. "'Tis good to be home, Jeannie," he said. "I've missed your tongue-lashings."

Jeanne's eyes moved over him, noting the changes of the past five years. "You've cut your hair," she remarked disapprovingly.

"'Tis the fashion in England."

"This is Scotland. You would do well to remember that."

Moira's misery was complete. She nearly swooned with embarrassment. John was so kind, so courteous, and so amazingly like Jeanne in appearance. Beneath lowered lashes, Moira stared curiously at the two of them. The Maxwell strain was clearly stamped on their faces. The thin, Celtic features, olive skin, and pale gray eyes could not be denied. Neither could the hair framing their faces. It was shining and black as a raven's wing, unusual for a Scot. Jeanne's was long, hanging free to her waist in the manner of unmarried women. John's was shorn close to his head, an unusual style not yet fashionable at the Scottish court.

Moira's hands clenched with resolve. It wasn't right. This handsome young man with the pleasant smile and laughing gray eyes didn't deserve the stinging thrusts Jeannie leveled at him. Taking a deep breath, Moira threw herself into the middle of the fray. "Tell us about King Henry's court, m'lord. Is it as frivolous as they say?"

Surprised, John looked down at her, noticing her presence for the first time.

Jeanne stared at her friend. What could have possessed the painfully shy Moira Sutherland to call such attention upon herself?

John recovered first. His smile gentled, and he reached for Moira's hand. Lifting it to his mouth, he brushed his lips across the back. "I'm terribly sorry for my rudeness, lass. Perhaps Jeanne will introduce us when she remembers her manners."

"My manners are not the ones in need of attention," Jeanne snapped, glaring at Moira.

The girl's lip trembled, and suddenly Jeanne was ashamed of herself. "Never mind, love. John always did bring out the worst in me." Quickly, she introduced them. "Moira Sutherland, this is my cousin, Lord John Maxwell of Traquair."

Moira glanced shyly up at his face. "How do you do, sir?"

"Very well, thank you," John replied. "But I find myself in something of a quandry, Mistress Sutherland."

"How so, sir?"

"How is it that a termagant like my cousin can be found in the company of such a sweet and gentle lass as yourself?"

Moira's pansy brown eyes widened, and she blushed adorably. "Jeannie is no such thing, m'lord. I've never before seen her behave rudely."

The light-filled eyes looking down at her flickered thoughtfully. "Is that so?"

"Oh yes," replied Moira loyally. "She's the best and kindest of friends. Why—"

"That will do, Moira," interrupted Jeanne. "Why don't you continue your conversation with Lord Maxwell while I seek the punch bowl."

"I've a better idea," cut in John. "Why don't I call on you tomorrow, Mistress Sutherland? I'll tell you tales of the English court that will make your head turn. But now I must be private with Jeanne. 'Tis a family matter." He smiled charmingly, and Moira blushed again, tripping over her skirts as she backed away.

"How could you?" Jeanne spoke through clenched teeth.

John pulled her into a small retiring room off the main hallway and looked around. It was furnished with a table and chair. He waited to release her arm until he'd closed the door tightly behind them. "How could I what?" he asked.

"Moira Sutherland is little more than a child. You deliberately set out to win her regard with no thought for her feelings at all." Jeanne was furious. "She's half in love with you already. You, the greatest profligate in Scotland."

He looked bewildered. "You wrong me, Jeanne. I was merely being polite."

"Polite!" She pronounced the word scathingly.

He watched in fascinated silence as her breasts rose and fell beneath the square décolletage of her gown.

"Have you no shame, John? You kissed her hand. You wooed her with your smile and promised to see her again.

Women far more experienced than Moira have succumbed to your charms."

His eyes widened in mock horror as he clasped his hands across his heart. "Will her father be posting the banns then?"

It was then that Jeanne Maxwell, a woman known the length and breadth of Scotland for her beauty, her wit, and her cool self-control, lost what was left of the last tenuous threads of her temper. Taking the steps necessary to bring her within inches of his face, she lifted her hand and slapped him, hard.

His eyes narrowed to mere slits in the dark tan of his face. Jeanne was suddenly, desperately afraid. John Maxwell had spent five years at the English court, but he was still a Scots border lord. Such an insult demanded swift retaliation. Her hand flew to her throat, and she swallowed. What could have come over her? Only once, in her entire memory, had she behaved so outrageously. That was the day, five years before, when John had left for England. Her face was pale and her eyes wide as she waited to see what would happen next.

He lifted his hand to the mark already reddening his cheek. Slowly, the fury faded from his eyes. "I was told you had outgrown that temper of yours."

Relieved, she asked, "Why would anything about me be of interest to you, John Maxwell?"

"You know the answer to that as well as I."

She could no more stop the blush from rising to her cheeks than she could deny the dawning awareness in his eyes.

He laughed triumphantly. "You can't hide from it, Jeannie. I knew in London when stories of the 'ice maiden' began to surface. I could scarce believe they were speaking of the Jeanne Maxwell I knew."

She lifted her chin and stared defiantly into eyes the exact color and shape of her own. John Maxwell was only a second cousin, but he looked enough like her to be her twin. "What are you suggesting?" she asked calmly.

The wary look on her face stopped him. Jeanne still didn't trust him. She wasn't ready for a declaration. Perhaps she never would be. Pushing aside the cold fear that always accompanied such misgivings, he smiled gently. "I meant no harm, lass. Can't a man miss his favorite cousin and ask of her now and then?"

"It isn't at all like you," she said doubtfully.

He lifted her chin, forcing her to meet the silver purpose of his gaze. "Perhaps you don't know me as well as you think."

"I know you well enough," she muttered. "What did you wish to tell me?"

Frowning, he dropped his hand and stepped away from her. "I merely wished to pay my respects," he replied. "How is your mother?"

Jeanne stiffened, and her face assumed a cold, implacable expression. "Very well, thank you."

John nodded. "I'm glad. She's had a difficult time of it."

Two red spots of color stained Jeanne's cheeks. "I might have known your first consideration would be for my mother."

There was no mistaking the rage in her voice. Faith, what ailed the woman? He had merely asked about her family. "Flora was always good to me," he began. "Is it wrong that I ask after her well-being?"

Jeanne's eyes were the color of ice above a frozen gray tarn. "Not at all," she said. "Perhaps you'll be pleased to hear that she is now a widow."

John's forehead wrinkled in confusion. "Why in the name of heaven would I be pleased to hear such a thing? I admired your father. He was a great friend to me."

Her face was a still, pale oval. "Were you worthy of that friendship?"

He stared at her, a thoughtful expression in his eyes. "What is it, Jeanne?" he asked softly. "What is it about me that you find so distasteful?"

She lowered her eyes but not before he saw the tears she struggled to hide.

His mouth tightened, and a thin white line appeared around his lips. "I have no wish to upset you, but what lies between us must be said. I've come home to collect what I left behind, Jeannie. If it takes time to accustom yourself, so be it." Nodding briefly, he walked to the door.

"John." Her voice stopped him, but he did not turn

around. "I'm promised to George Gordon. We await Jamie's approval before posting the banns."

When he spoke again, his voice had an odd, husky quality. "There is more to the king's approval than a promise between a man and a maid."

Her hands clenched. "Leave us alone, John Maxwell. Take your comfort with my mother. I'm sure she'll be pleased enough to see you."

At that he turned to face her, a puzzled expression on his face. "What's gotten into you, lass? I told you of my way of thinking in my letters. Once a week, I wrote you. 'Tis a long time for a man to remain constant without a reply."

Her eyes challenged him. *"Were* you constant, John? Do you even know the meaning of the word?"

He grinned, a mocking flash of white in his sun-browned face. "Aye, lass. I do." With that he opened the door and left her standing alone in the retiring room.

Jeanne sank into the only available chair, surprised that her legs hadn't given way beneath her. John Maxwell was most definitely a man to be reckoned with. Her fingers drummed nervously on the table. Why had he come back now, after all this time? And what was that foolishness about collecting something he'd left behind? A picture, ugly and persistent, formed in her mind. She tried to resist, but the image remained. It had occurred long ago, but the memory was as clear as if it had all happened yesterday.

Her father, Donald Maxwell, had been away when his infant son died of the pox at Traquair House. It was only natural for fifteen-year-old Jeanne to think of her childhood friend in times of trouble. She sent for John. He arrived shortly after the burial. Her mother was incoherent with grief. She couldn't be blamed for throwing herself into the young man's arms. John, however, should have known better. Jeanne turned the corner from the landing in time to see him pull her distraught mother into his arms and take her lips in a kiss that only a nun, cloistered from childhood and exceptionally naive, would have called comforting. Frozen into immobility, Jeanne watched as John led her mother, her arms still locked around his neck, into her bedchamber and closed the door.

Given the scene she had witnessed, John's unexpected

marriage proposal on the banks of Saint Mary's Loch came as a horrifying surprise. What shocked and dismayed her was her own unexpected response to his kiss. The firm warmth of his lips as they moved against hers and the hard muscles under his linen shirt left her breathless and confused. Could a man who kissed a woman that way be in love with another? Would he tell her of the years he'd waited until she'd finally grown up, only to creep into her mother's chamber at night?

Jeanne had almost convinced herself that he was sincere when word came that he'd left for London. At first, she'd welcomed his weekly letters, greedily taking them to her chambers to read alone, searching between the lines for proof of his regard. It wasn't until he'd been gone almost two years that Jeanne learned the truth.

She was seventeen and newly arrived at the royal court at Stirling. It wasn't long before the rumors reached her ears. John Maxwell was a favorite at the English court. Reports had it that his string of mistresses rivaled that of the English king Henry VIII.

And now he was back. It hadn't taken long for Jeanne to realize that his proposal five years before had been a sham, made for the purpose of hiding his true reason for coming so often to Traquair. That reason had everything to do with her mother. Not only had John Maxwell inherited Traquair and the title upon her father's death, he had also inherited his wife. It was all so despicably convenient. Jeanne tightened her lips. She would never again fall for the easy charm that came so readily at his command.

Smoothing her thick, knee-length hair, she stood and walked back into the main hall of Edinburgh Castle, biting her lips to restore their color. She must find George immediately. Perhaps he could persuade Jamie Stewart to agree to a wedding date. The sooner she was married and away from the temptation of John Maxwell's soul-destroying smile, the better. Faith, the man could coax the kelpies from their watery resting places.

" 'Tis said the people go hungry and Parliament grumbles while Henry spends the royal treasury on outrageous schemes. What say you, John? Is that a fair assessment of the English mind?" James Stewart, king of Scotland, fixed his heavy-lidded eyes on the tall young man beside him. He wanted an answer and he wanted it now.

John hesitated. His face assumed the pleasant, implacable mask of the courtier while his mind sifted through and discarded a dozen different replies. There were spies at Jamie's court. Any answer he gave would be whispered into Henry's ear in less than a fortnight. He decided on the truth, although a diplomatic version of it. "Never think that the English will not support their king, Your Grace. Henry is a favorite with the nobles and yeomen alike. He rides, reads, and rules with equal aplomb in all areas."

The king's night-dark eyes appraised him carefully. John met his searching gaze without challenge or fear. Finally, Jamie nodded. "Well spoken, lad. Well spoken, indeed. You shall make a full report to me tomorrow." He looked down at his queen. "You are very quiet tonight, Margaret. Do you agree that your brother is deserving of such flattering words?"

Margaret Tudor lowered her eyes and flushed painfully. There was nothing of the charming and confident Henry in the shrinking figure of his older sister. John's heart softened with pity, and when he spoke, it was far more gently than he had replied to his king.

"There is no shame in finding virtue in a beloved brother, m'lady," he assured her. "I'm sure were Henry here, he would speak as highly of you."

Margaret straightened and flashed him a look of gratitude. "You are most kind, sir," she said graciously. "But my lord forgets that I have been queen of Scotland for many years. My brother was little more than a child when I left England. I have no opinion as to what kind of man he has become."

John's expression remained as courteous as ever, but in truth, the queen's answer surprised him. It was every bit as diplomatic and carefully worded as his own. Sweet Jesu! The woman knew something of deception. What kind of life was it to be always mindful of one's tongue? Five years of watching his back at the English court was enough. John asked nothing more than to settle his affairs, marry Jeanne, and spend the rest of his years living quietly at Traquair, watching his children grow.

A young man whispered into the king's ear. John recognized him at once and studied him curiously. The passing years had changed George Gordon immensely. The earl of Strathbogie was a tall, lean young man with the feline grace of a cat. His thick, tawny hair and golden eyes reminded John of Mary Gordon. He had seen much of George's younger sister at Whitehall.

Jamie frowned and spoke aloud. "You are too impatient, George. Give me time. A Stewart marriage cannot be taken lightly."

"I am a Gordon of Strathbogie, Your Grace," the young man reminded him.

"Your mother was a Stewart, rest her soul," pronounced the king. "She would wish this matter to be given the consideration it deserves."

"Jeanne Maxwell is suitable in every way," insisted Gordon.

Jamie's obsidian-bright eyes glittered dangerously. "I'm well aware of that, Cousin. Mistress Maxwell's suitability is not the cause for my delay. Have your manners gone begging, m'lord?" He nodded at John. "Here is the Lady Jeanne's kinsman after five years in London."

Gordon acknowledged John Maxwell with a brief bow and immediately turned his attention back to the king. "If it is not a question of her name, what is it, Your Grace?"

Jamie grinned. "There is another suitor for her hand. I've not yet decided which alliance would serve me best."

George Gordon's eyes narrowed, and his hand moved to the hilt of his sword. "I insist that you name him."

"I beg your pardon?" Jamie's teeth were set, and his face was white with rage.

"Lord Gordon," interrupted the queen. "I don't believe you've asked me to dance this entire night. You must tell me what you think of the improvements my husband has made to the great hall." Chatting brightly, she maneuvered Gordon across the enormous room into the circle of dancers taking their places.

"Insolent puppy," growled James. Draining his goblet, he motioned for a servant to take it away. "Have you nothing to say, Maxwell?" he demanded. "The man seeks to wed the wench who holds your heart. If it were I, he would be cut in two on this very floor."

John grinned. "I am not king of Scotland, Your Grace, and Jeanne is not so obedient as your Margaret. Were I to make such a public declaration, she would spite me by taking the Holy Orders."

"I can forbid the marriage," suggested James.

John shook his head. "Not yet. I would rather her hand be freely given. An unwilling wife makes a poor bed partner."

Jamie laughed. "From what I've heard, lad, you should know."

"I wish you had not heard such a great deal, Your Grace," John said wryly. "Not everything is always as it seems."

"No matter, lad." Jamie clapped him on the back. "Come to me tomorrow and we'll speak of London. I'll keep young Gordon at bay until the Lady Jeanne is of a kinder frame of mind."

John's eyes warmed with laughter. "My thanks, Jamie," he drawled softly. "Perhaps someday I can return the favor."

"You will, lad. Never fear. You will."

Lord Home stepped forward to claim the queen's hand for the next set, and George Gordon relinquished it gratefully. He could not be comfortable with Jamie's shrewish wife. Searching the room, his eyes settled on the woman he could be comfortable with.

Just looking at Jeanne Maxwell revived him. He could forget he was here, in the filthy city of Edinburgh with its twisted wynds and overflowing gutters reeking of offal. The clear, calm beauty of Jeanne's face was like a rain-scented wind blowing across the ramparts of Strathbogie.

She leaned against a piling beneath the ferocious boar's head, the remains of a trophy that Jamie had killed and carried single-handedly back to Edinburgh. The blood-encrusted head and curved teeth contrasted hideously with the pale loveliness of Jeanne's ermine-trimmed figure. Her gown was white. The pristine color suited her. The deep square neck and long full sleeves set off the slenderness of her arms and throat. A kirtle of twisted pearls gathered the flowing skirt around her slim, boyish hips. The only color about her was the rich darkness of her hair and the pale pink of her cheeks and lips.

His hands clenched. He wanted this woman more than he'd ever wanted anything in his life. He wanted her serenity, her quick understanding, her unusual Celtic beauty. The touch of her long, cool fingers, the sweep of her lashes, the untapped mystery behind her diamond gray eyes, set a fever in his veins that neither time nor distance could assuage. Jeanne Maxwell belonged to him. God help the man who stood in his way.

He crossed the room to her side.

Jeanne smiled. George was very handsome. In the light of the flickering torches his hair gleamed like burnished gold. "You look serious, m'lord."

George grimaced and shook his head. " 'Tis the queen. In her eyes, Jamie can do no wrong."

Jeanne's eyes widened. " 'Tis most unwise to tell the queen you find fault with her husband. Despite their differences, she adores him."

He rubbed the back of his neck and sighed. "I tire of this delay, Jeannie. Why won't he consent to our marriage?"

Jeanne bit her lip. "Has he refused?"

"Almost." His laugh was bitter. "There is another suitor for your hand."

"Jamie cannot force me."

"If the marriage furthers his cause with the pope, you will have little choice."

"I shall seek sanctuary with the Sisters of Llewellyn Mar."

George took her hands in his own and smiled down at her. "I am truly touched," he said gently. "But that is a sacrifice I cannot accept."

"Why not?"

"You have no calling, Jeannie."

"How do you know?"

His eyes moved from her face to linger deliberately on the

swell of her breasts above the white gown. "Your body was made for a man's enjoyment," he said bluntly.

She flushed and pulled away. "You insult me."

"Nay, lass. But to become a bride of Christ without a true calling is a mortal sin. I will not have that on my conscience."

Her smile confused him. It was small and sad and held nothing of warmth or amusement. When she spoke, her words chilled his heart. "It is my conscience we are speaking of, m'lord, not yours."

Something flickered in the depths of her eyes, something dark and forbidden that he didn't understand. Unwillingly, his sister's warning flashed through his mind. Jane Hepburn had not approved of Jeanne. Witchcraft ran in the Maxwell line. George had refused to countenance such absurdity. Jeanne was the purest, most devout woman he knew. He saw her at Mass every morning. Still, her eyes were the illusive, netherworld gray of the hill people, and her friendship with the *calliach*, Grania Douglas, was spoken of at court in hushed whispers.

Pushing his misgivings aside, he took her arm. "There is no need to speak of this now. Come, let us find a place in front before the singing begins."

Jeanne allowed him to guide her into the crowd clustered at the end of the hall. A hush blanketed the room as the melodic notes of the troubadour echoed against the wood-beamed ceiling and filtered down, filling the appreciative ears of the guests. Closing her eyes, Jeanne allowed the powerful notes of the border lament to seep into her consciousness, filling her mind with the tragic story of unrequited love.

The performer was particularly skilled. When Jeanne opened her eyes, she was not surprised to see more than one woman surreptitiously wiping her eyes with a lace-trimmed handkerchief. She looked around for George and saw that he was listening to the woman beside him. It was Jane Hepburn. Jeanne frowned. She did not care for George's sister.

She backed away, bumping into a figure behind her. She turned with an apology on her lips and blushed. John

Maxwell looked down at her. From the expression on his face, she knew his eyes hadn't missed a single detail of her appearance, including the telltale track of tears winding their way down her cheeks. Before she could move away, he reached out and wiped them away with a gentle finger. "'Tis only a ballad, lass," he murmured. "The bards will sing a happier tale of Lady Jeanne Maxwell of Traquair."

"Traquair is your home now," she reminded him. "You are the new laird since Father died."

The gray eyes gleamed like liquid silver in the torchlight. "Traquair needs a mistress," he said softly.

"Then you must seek a wife."

He smiled, and the lean planes of his face gentled into the boyishness she remembered. "I already have, Jeannie. All I need is her approval."

Shock drained the color from her cheeks. Was the man daft? Did he really think to convince Jamie that he was a more suitable mate for Donald Maxwell's daughter than George Gordon? Another thought occurred to her. Perhaps he meant something else entirely. Perhaps he'd found someone else. The room was suddenly cold. Her stomach burned. John and another woman. Only once before, in her twenty years, had she felt so miserable and alone.

❦13❦

John ignored the guards flanking the ornately carved door and knocked loudly.

"Enter," a booming voice called out.

He turned the handle and stepped inside. The king was

seated in a wide-backed chair by the fire, a jeweled goblet in his hand. "Welcome, John," he said and gestured toward a stool directly opposite his chair. "I've been waiting nearly an hour, lad." He waved his arm to encompass the small paneled room. "As you can see, we are alone. Now tell me of my dear brother-in-law's plans."

"I apologize for the delay, Your Grace," replied John. He seated himself on the stool and stretched out his long legs. "I'm afraid my news isn't good."

Jamie nodded. "I thought not. Tell me everything you know."

"His Holiness seeks to twist Louis of France in a powerful noose," said John. "Henry encourages this hatred of his enemy by sending Rome huge sums of gold. There will be a time when you must choose, Your Grace."

"Bah!" The king threw the remains of his wine, goblet and all, into the blazing fire. "I'll not take arms against Louis. He is my ally. We've a treaty between us."

"Even if it means war with England?"

"Julius is a sorry excuse for a clergyman," Jamie muttered. "The last thing Christendom needs is a warrior pope. He should concern himself with the Vatican. If he wants to lead an army, why not send a crusade to the Holy Land? God's blood! There isn't a man in Scotland who wouldn't vie for the privilege of taking up such a cause."

John could think of nothing less appealing, but he knew better than to disagree with Jamie when he started on the subject of a holy crusade. "Julius II is a selfish man, Your Grace," he said instead. "There will be a Holy League, but it will not be against the infidels. It will be directed against our ancient ally, the most Christian king of France."

Jamie drummed his fingers on a small side table. "Louis will not stand for such nonsense," he said. "He will appeal for a general council against the pope."

A taut white line appeared around John's lips. "It would be most unwise for Louis to set himself against the pope."

The king gave him a sharp look from beneath his heavy eyebrows. "I do not believe you are at all concerned for Louis, my friend."

John grinned. "You are always astute, Your Grace."

Jamie leaned forward. "You have been five years at the English court. Where will you stand, John Maxwell, if Scotland allies herself with France?"

An angry wind moaned against the parapets and stirred the tapestries lining the paneled walls. In the fireplace, a log cracked and split, sending a shower of sparks onto the hearth. No one looking at the handsome, chiseled features of the laird of Traquair would have guessed at the enormity of the decision weighting his mind. There was the power and might of the English king allied with Ferdinand of Aragon, the emperor Maximilian, and all of Christendom against a weakened Louis VII and the tragically loyal, recklessly brave Jamie IV of Scotland.

A flash of lightning illuminated the room, throwing the king's features into bold relief. John was shocked. For the first time, the fleshy, handsome features of the man who had wrested a kingdom from his father at the age of fifteen reflected uncertainty. In that instant, John made his decision. With everything to lose and nothing to gain, he knelt at the feet of Scotland's king and bowed his head in deference.

"I am a Scot, my liege," he said. "Command me as you will."

With a deep, rumbling sigh, Jamie offered his hand. John kissed the royal ring with its raised pelican crest, symbolizing the Stewart dynasty.

"Stand, m'lord." The king's voice was gruff with emotion. "I'm not foolish enough to believe your words come easily. For that I thank you."

Tall and lean in the leaping light of the fire, John looked down at his king and nodded. Jamie was charming and fickle, not unlike the others of his line who had ruled this kingdom to the north of England. He was also inspirational, rash, daring, and willful, the kind of leader men took into their hearts, worshipped, fought with, and willingly died for. John was no different. Against his better judgment, his sword was forever pledged to the House of Stewart.

"Where are you going at this hour? 'Tis after four." Flora Maxwell's smooth brow wrinkled in dismay as she stared at the back of her daughter's head.

Jeanne was almost out the door. Her hands clenched on the folds of her skirt, but she did not turn to face her mother. "I go with Sim to carry peat to Grania's cottage," she said. "The nights are cold for an old woman."

"Send Sim alone," begged Flora. "The moors are no place for a woman and a lad not yet grown."

Jeanne turned impatiently, her lovely face set as if carved in marble. "We've been through this before. I will not be ruled by you, Mother. Not in this. Not in anything."

Flora's face paled, but she stood, determined to have it out between them. "Why do you hate me so? You are my only daughter, my only living child. What have I done to earn your contempt?"

"Don't be ridiculous." Jeanne's smile did not reach her eyes. "You are imagining what isn't there."

"Am I?" Flora's eyes narrowed. She took a deep breath and said out loud the words she'd carried in her heart for such an endless length of days and nights. "Is it I alone who imagines what isn't there, Jeannie?"

Jeanne lifted her chin and studied her mother's face, carefully noting the trembling Cupid's bow mouth and the pink blush on her unlined cheeks. Flora Maxwell looked much younger than her thirty-five years. John was twenty-seven. It would be a match made in heaven. Bile rose in Jeanne's throat. "Don't play games, Mother," she lashed out. "Say what you mean."

Flora traced the embroidered edge of a high-backed chair with slender fingers. "John Maxwell has returned from England," she began.

Jeanne remained silent.

"Before he left, he asked for your hand in marriage. I told him the match had my approval if you agreed. You were very young and five years is a long time." Flora lowered her lashes over brimming tears and bit her lip. "There was a time when I believed you were not indifferent to his attentions."

Jeanne could contain herself no longer. "That was before you made your preference quite clear."

Bewildered, Flora stared at her daughter. "I beg your pardon?"

"I saw you." Jeanne's eyes were the dark, stormy gray of

the North Sea. "My brother's body was still warm when John carried you into the bedchamber you shared with Father. Did you believe I was too young to know what went on inside that room, *Mother?*" She spit out the last word in a scathing blast of contempt.

White with shock, Flora listened to the blasphemous words. "No," she whispered. "No, you don't understand. It wasn't that way at all." She held out her hand imploringly. "John was your father's friend, nothing more. John wanted *you,* Jeannie. He loved you from the beginning when you were children together. I've always known that. How could you think either of us would betray your father in such a way?"

"I don't believe you."

"Why?" The single word was a cry of agony.

"He didn't come home when Father died," said Jeanne. "He waited until you were free."

"Donald died two years ago," Flora reminded her. "Why would he wait so long to claim me?"

"Any sooner would seem improper to the church and the king."

Flora's lip curled. "Since when has Jamie Stewart been concerned with propriety?"

Jeanne frowned. If what her mother said was true, she had much to think about. The wounds she'd nursed for five years wouldn't heal with a single explanation. Besides, even if John and her mother had not been lovers, his reputation at the English court was enough to make him an unsuitable choice for a husband. "It grows late and Sim waits below with the horses," she said shortly, turning the door handle. "I shall stay the night with Grania."

"There are those who believe she is a witch, Jeannie," Flora warned. "Be ruled by me in this. Do not go to her this night."

"Do you believe such an absurdity?" Jeanne asked, her expression contemptuous.

Flora shook her head. "Of course not. But it matters not what I believe. There are those with far greater influence than I who swear she deals in magic."

"I need to think," Jeanne explained. "Grania's cottage is good for thinking."

"And Traquair isn't?" her mother challenged.

Jeanne stopped, and when she spoke, her voice was very low. "You forget, Mother. This is no longer our home. It belongs to John. We are allowed to remain only because of the affection he bears our family. It would be unwise to become too fond of Traquair House." With a whisper of velvet skirts against the stone floor, she was gone.

Three hours later, a servant ushered John Maxwell into a small, dimly lit sitting room at the back of the house. There, he found the mistress of Traquair lying on a leather settle, one arm thrown across her face in a gesture of despair. Leaning against the door jamb, he crossed his arms. "Is this any way to greet the head of your family, m'lady?" he teased.

Flora dropped her arm and sat up immediately. "John," she cried and started to rise. He stopped her by striding across the room to sweep her up into a choking embrace. They stood close together for a timeless moment, the dark head bent protectively over the light one. Finally, laughing breathlessly, Flora pulled away. "Stand back and let me look at you," she ordered.

He moved away allowing her sight-starved eyes to look their fill. "Oh, John." Her eyes filled. "You've grown up into a shockingly handsome man."

His eyes, so like Jeanne's, twinkled down at her. "I'm glad you approve. I hope your daughter's taste is the same. Where is the lass?"

Flora wrung her hands and sat down on the settle. "She left three hours ago to pay Grania Douglas a visit."

John's eyes widened. "Sweet Jesu," he marveled. "Is Grania still alive? She was ancient when we were children."

"I'm afraid so," replied Flora. "Jeanne visits her often. I'm afraid the woman may be dangerous."

John sat down beside her and took her hand. "Grania is a harmless old *calliach*, Flora. How could she possibly harm Jeanne?"

"You've been away a long time, John," explained Flora. "I hardly know Jeannie anymore. 'Tis difficult for us to speak without tension between us. Perhaps she finds Grania's advice to be more satisfactory than mine."

He grinned. "Jeanne never appreciated advice, no matter who it came from."

Flora shook her head. "You don't understand. There are rumors that Grania deals in witchcraft. She was ordered by the prelate to appear before him once already. The next time she will be brought to trial. Jeanne refuses to stay away from her."

John lifted her chin, forcing her to meet his thoughtful, light-filled gaze. "Jeanne was devoted to you before I left Scotland," he said gently. "How is it that the two of you have come to such a pass?"

Flora opened her mouth to protest her own innocence when she happened to glance down at the hand that held hers. It was a thin hand, long fingered and finely made, the skin dark against her own. She blushed. How could she tell him of Jeanne's doubts when they came so near to the truth? Flora knew John Maxwell had never considered her to be anything more than a beloved aunt or older sister. It was Jeanne he loved. It was Jeanne he would wed. During the long, cold nights of winter when he stood his watch or walked the battlements of Dunaverty Castle, where he had been fostered, it was Jeanne's face he called to mind. Through the five years in England, it was Jeanne who received his letters. Her gray-eyed, black-haired, unconventional daughter had captured his heart when she was scarcely more than a child.

Still, a woman could dream, especially a woman married to a man twice her age. Flora's dreams were filled with a dark-haired boy with thick straight brows and beautifully chiseled features. A boy with the lean rippling muscles of a warrior. A boy who moved with the grace of a cat and used his voice like a sword, clear and coldly disciplined. A boy who loved her daughter. A boy who would be the father of her grandchildren. A boy who was now a disturbingly handsome man.

Flora bit her lip. She loved John Maxwell, but she loved Jeanne more. If there was to be any happiness in this life for her daughter, it would be with this splendid young man now seated beside her. Whatever it cost, whatever look of horror it brought to his face, he deserved the truth. "Jeanne believes we betrayed her," she began. "When my son died, she saw you carry me into my bedchamber and believed the worst."

John's expression was incredulous. "That can't be," he denied flatly.

"'Tis true, John. At fifteen, a woman is no longer a girl. Indeed, I was already a mother. She must have loved you, even then, to believe such a thing and to feed her jealousy for so long." Flora lowered her eyes. "Our embrace could not be called platonic, even to one so inexperienced as Jeanne."

"You were hysterical," he reminded her. "Donald was expected. When I touched you, naturally you assumed I was your husband."

Flora had assumed nothing of the sort. Wisely, she remained silent.

John stood and paced the room. Suddenly he stopped and ran his hands through his hair. "It makes no sense. I spoke to Jeanne of my intentions before I left for England. She led me to believe my feelings were returned."

A fierce, stabbing jealousy burned in the pit of Flora's stomach. It was a long moment before she trusted herself to speak. "There have been rumors about your activities at Henry's court. Jeanne is very proud, m'lord. You will have to convince her the others meant nothing."

"Others?" A deep frown settled between John's brows.

Flora laughed. "Come now, John. Even a saint would not claim to have practiced celibacy for five years."

His cheeks darkened. "I make no false claims," he muttered, "but neither am I accustomed to debauchery."

"Explain that to Jeanne."

"God's wounds, madam. No other woman would blame me for satisfying an occasional need."

"Jeanne is not like other women. If you don't know that by now, I suggest that you turn tail and run back to Edinburgh. Telling her she should hold you blameless for taking women to your bed will gain you nothing. She would most likely ask how you would feel if she had done the same."

"The situation is different."

"How so?"

"Jeanne is a lady."

"And you are a gentleman."

John grinned. "I wouldn't stake my honor on it, madam. Tell me whether I should seek out this strong-minded daughter of yours or wait until she returns."

Again, Flora hesitated.

"What is it?" he asked.

"It would be unwise for Jeanne to learn you stayed the night at Traquair House, m'lord. Seek out Grania Douglas and bring my daughter home."

John slipped the reins of his horse over the stunted branch of a black oak and walked to the door of Grania's hut. Nestled in the bosom of twin hills, it was pitifully small, even smaller than he remembered. He paused at the door, remembering the enthusiasm of Grania's welcome when he and Jeanne were children. The pathetic croft had been a haven of blessed warmth to the two of them, an orphaned boy and a wild, leggy girl, grass-stained and smeared with peat from the bogs.

The old woman had offered nothing more than companionship, oatcakes, and new milk thick with cream and frothy warm to satisfy their ravenous appetites. Somehow it had been enough just to sit across the scarred table and watch her button-black eyes as she regaled them with ancient tales of Scotland's glories. John was seven years Jeanne's senior, much too old to be anything more than pleasantly entertained by Grania Douglas's stories. But Jeanne had listened and believed, her eyes gleaming like liquid silver, absorbing the woman's words with rapt attention. John closed his eyes, recalling the glow of that childlike elfin face, pointed and high boned with the promise of beauty not yet realized.

He thought of Jeanne Maxwell as he had last seen her in Edinburgh and frowned. He had waited an ungodly length of time for her to grow up. Now that she had, he didn't know if he preferred the ice princess of Jamie's court or his childhood shadow with her bare feet and a mouth stained with Grania's blackberry jam.

The windows of the croft were mere slits, thick with smoke and the smell of peat. Taking a deep breath, he pounded at the door. Immediately it swung open, revealing a dark, shrunken figure silhouetted against the fire-lit room.

"Granny," he said gently, "'tis I. John Maxwell."

The old woman reached out to touch his face. Slowly, her fingers traced his nose, his lips, the bones of his cheeks, his chin. "There be no denying yer a Maxwell," she said, stepping back to wave him into the room. "Jeannie, lass. We've a visitor."

Across the room, wrapped in a woolen plaid, Jeanne rested on a mattress of freshly cut rushes. Her black hair was loose, flowing thick and long without a whisper of curl across her bare shoulder, pooling in a fall of ebony silk on the floor. She lay on her side, propped up on one elbow, and stared at him for a long time. Finally, she swept the hair from her forehead and sat up. "What are you doing here?" she asked.

The lie came easily to his lips. "To see Granny, of course."

"You didn't care to see her before this. Why now?"

"I was in England."

"You never wrote."

"Can she read?"

Grania laughed. "He's got ye there, lass. Even before I lost my sight, I couldna' read."

With a shock, John realized the old woman was blind.

Jeanne flushed and turned to stare into the flames of the small hearth. What was the matter with her? Only John provoked her to such rudeness.

"Will you ha' some *usquebaugh,* lad?" Grania asked. "'Tis a cold night."

John nodded, reaching for the cup. "I thank you," he said, draining the fiery liquid in one gulp. He gasped, and his eyes burned. Five years had passed since he'd sampled Scotch whiskey, and Grania's batch was strong.

Jeanne watched in amusement from beneath lowered eyelashes. John's courteous reply to Grania's offer of refreshment had softened her outrage. Now she was merely annoyed that he'd followed her. The time she spent with the hill woman was hers along. Here, no one frowned disapprovingly when her hands fell idle. No one inspected her food, carefully removing every crumb of the sugary sweets she craved. No one bothered about her hair or her clothes or the fact that she was twenty and not yet wed. Here, she was only Jeanne Maxwell, the inquisitive lass from Traquair House. Her presence was enough. She turned back to look at the fire, not realizing that John had crossed the room and stretched out beside her.

"Grania sleeps," he whispered, nodding toward the table where the old woman sat, her head pillowed in her arms.

"I'll put her to bed," Jeanne said and started to rise.

John's hand on her arm stopped her. "Don't get up. I'll see to her." He stood and walked to the table. Carefully slipping one arm behind Grania's knees, he cradled her against his chest and lifted her to the crib pushed against the opposite wall. Gently, he tucked a blanket around her frail body. Jeanne watched as he stared down at the old woman's wrinkled face.

"Has she changed so much?" she asked softly.

John shook his head and turned to look at Jeanne. "Probably not. She was always old, although I don't remember her being so small."

From her place by the fire, Jeanne smiled, and his breathing altered. Like a moth to a flame, he was drawn to her. Crossing the room, he stretched out once again by her side.

"Thank you for being so good to her," Jeanne said. "She was pleased to see you."

"I didn't come for her," John replied.

"I know." Her voice was so low, he could barely make out the words.

Her face was very close to his own. He turned to look at her. She was beautiful. The clean, chiseled planes of her features, the sweep of black lashes, the sensual mouth. "You are so lovely," he murmured and, without thinking, bent his head to her mouth. Incredibly, her lips parted, and her arms slid around his neck. A fierce joy blazed up within him. She was soft and welcoming, and it seemed as if he had waited his entire life for this.

Much later, with her head pillowed against his chest, he said, "I'd not expected that."

"Liar." Jeanne's voice was soft and amused. "I knew what you wanted from the moment you entered the room."

"I didn't say I didn't want it," he corrected her. "My intentions were to woo you slowly. We've been apart for a long time."

Her fingers made small, circular motions against the wool of his tunic. "What are your intentions now, John?"

"The same as they've always been. I came home to wed you, lass."

There was no mistaking the satisfaction in her voice. "Was there no one at the English court suitable enough to be the countess of Traquair?"

He smiled into her hair. She'd finally come out with it. He considered telling her the truth immediately and decided against it. She deserved a moment of worry for believing the worst of him.

"Aye," he replied promptly. "There were many who were suitable."

She pulled out of his arms and turned to face him, her gray eyes bright with anger. "Why didn't you wed one of them?"

"No one would have me," he lied.

Her mouth dropped open in surprise. Quickly, she recovered. "I don't believe you."

"I'm flattered."

"Don't be," she countered. "It isn't your handsome face or your charm that I find so irresistible."

"What is it then?"

She stood, pulling the plaid with her, and ground her fists into the curve of her waist. "Nothing," she said. "There is nothing about you that appeals to me."

Slowly, he sat up and squinted into the flames. "I love you, Jeanne Maxwell," he said quietly. "I've always loved you. Not a day went by that I didn't think of you. I wondered why you didn't write or if the spells you had as a child came more often now that you were grown. Most of all, I feared you had wed and that no one had bothered to tell me."

With her heart in her throat, Jeanne watched the austere beauty of his profile highlighted by the flickering firelight.

"There has never been anyone else for me," he continued, "not at the English court and not here, in Scotland. I know nothing of what you've heard, but this I can swear before everything that is holy. My heart is yours, lass. No other woman will ever claim it." He rose to his feet and stood looking down at her. "Now, Jeanne Maxwell, I ask you once again. Will you marry me?"

She closed her eyes and waited. Moments passed. Why in the name of heaven didn't he touch her? She opened her eyes to find a bleakness she hadn't expected in his eyes.

"Is it so difficult an answer?" he asked gently. "Yes or no. Tell me, Jeanne."

"Yes," she whispered at last. "I'll marry you."

He frowned. The words were everything he'd hoped to hear, but something was wrong. Stepping closer, he took her hand. "What is it, my heart? Tell me why you are still not sure."

She had to say it or for the rest of her life remain silent and wonder. Taking a deep breath, she uttered the words she had carried in her heart for five long years. "Were you ever in love with my mother?"

He smiled, and her knees weakened. Reaching out, he pulled her against him, his thin, muscular hand firm on her back. "I shall always love your mother, Jeannie," he murmured close to her ear, "but not nearly as much as I loved your father. He raised me as if I were his own son. I could never have betrayed him, not even if I hadn't fallen desperately in love with his daughter."

The tears welled up under her eyelids and slid down her cheeks. "I love you so much and I missed you terribly," she confessed.

"Does that mean you find me appealing after all?" he teased.

She laughed shakily. "You know exactly how appealing you are, John Maxwell. Has no one ever told you that modesty is a virtue?"

"I had an unusual childhood," he replied. "I trust my wife will teach me the art of becoming a country laird."

Her eyes held a wicked glint. "Shall I begin now?"

He looked at the pile of rushes on the floor and then at the sleeping woman on the bed. Shaking his head regretfully, he said, "Not now, lass. But after we're married, I promise to be a most dutiful pupil."

Pulling him down on the rushes beside her, Jeanne wrapped the plaid around the two of them and buried her face against his chest. Who would have thought the night would end like this? She smiled. Grania always brought her luck.

❈14❈

Blair Castle
1993

I awoke completely rested with a smile on my lips. The morning air was unusually warm, and I was very aware of Ian's lean, bare body next to mine. Propping myself up on one elbow, I studied his face, relaxed in sleep. With his hair falling over his forehead, his sun-dark chest against the bleached-white sheets, the stubble of a beard covering his cheeks and chin, he looked different, less civilized, more vital than the sophisticated gentleman I knew by day.

His eyes opened to my admiring gaze. Smiling, he held out his arms. I blushed and looked away, embarrassed by the circumstances. Never before, in my entire life, had I spent an entire night with a man who was not my husband. In the deceptive shadows of darkness, a middle-aged woman might flatter herself into believing that the crow's-feet around her eyes and the sagging flesh on her neck and kneecaps wouldn't be noticed. But in the merciless glare of daylight such deception is impossible. Every widening pore, every smudge of leftover mascara, every line and dark circle, every blemish, is sharply and painfully evident.

I drew a deep breath, deciding then and there that this time, with this man, I would make no excuses for my imperfections. Forcing myself to meet his eyes, I allowed Ian Douglas to look his fill. For a long time he didn't speak. His fingers sifted through my hair, catching in the thick tangle at the back of my head. Then he traced my nose, my lips and chin, lingering on the hollows of my cheeks. Carefully, like an artist, his palm molded my face and throat, resting at last on the flesh covering my pounding heart.

"Do you have any idea how lovely you are?" he asked, his voice hoarse and breathless.

I laughed, shaky with relief. Burying my head against his chest, I erased from my mind the fact that we had known each other only a few days, that the differences in our backgrounds were as great as two people's could possibly be, and, at this very moment, the forces of a seven-hundred-year-old curse were aligning themselves against us.

His lips were warm against my throat. "Are you ready to go home?"

"Uh-hum," I answered, intent on the feel of his lips as they explored the sensitive skin behind my ear, the column of my throat, and the slope of my shoulder. I shivered as they moved lower. Suddenly, there was a knock on the door. Ian tensed.

"Who is it?" I asked, looking at the clock. It was after nine.

"I'm sorry to disturb you, Miss Murray, but it's the cook's day off. Would you like breakfast before she leaves?"

I looked at Ian. He shrugged his shoulders and bent his head to my mouth. "Tea and toast will be fine," I managed to call out before Ian's lips closed over mine. For a moment, I was lost, caught in the incredible sensations of pleasure and passion that his presence managed to evoke.

"Ian," I gasped, pulling away. "It doesn't take any time at all to make tea and toast. The maid will be back in a few minutes."

He relaxed against the pillow. "I hope she'll bring more than that. I'm starving."

I sat up, pulling the covers around me. "We should get dressed."

Ian frowned. "Why?"

"I don't want her to find us like this."

"Good Lord." He looked genuinely surprised. "Why not?"

I didn't answer, but my incredulity must have been obvious. His eyes danced with amusement. "Don't tell me you're embarrassed in front of the servants."

"Aren't you?"

He laughed. "Not at all. There isn't a person in this entire castle who doesn't know where I spent the night. Why do you think no one knocked on my door to ask if I wanted breakfast?"

I could feel the deep blush staining my chest and shoulders. Opening my mouth to speak, I was silenced by another knock.

"Your breakfast is here," announced a feminine voice.

"Do you want me to leave?" Ian mouthed the words. I nodded. He threw back the covers, gathered his clothing, kissed me briefly on the forehead, and exited through the adjoining door.

"Come in," I called out as the knock resounded once again.

The maid, carrying a tray of silver-covered dishes; two plates, cups, and saucers; and two sets of silverware, entered the room. She placed the tray on a nearby table and looked around. "Will you be breakfasting alone this morning, Miss Murray?"

"Yes."

"Where will Mr. Douglas be eating?"

"I beg your pardon?" I couldn't help myself. I was unprepared for such a matter-of-fact attitude toward sex.

"Where shall I take Mr. Douglas's breakfast?" she asked, not at all disconcerted by the tumbled bedclothes, my bare shoulders, or chapped, kiss-swollen lips.

"He's in the bathroom," I muttered, acknowledging defeat. Ian was right. The habits of the duke of Atholl and his guests didn't concern the servants in the least.

"Will he be returning or shall I take a tray to his room?" she asked politely.

Enough was enough. Wrapping the sheet around me, I stood, grateful for my inches. I was in control once again. "I'll see that Mr. Douglas gets his breakfast," I said firmly. "Now, if you'll excuse me, I'd like to dress."

"Of course, Miss Murray." With a pleasant smile, she left the room. I didn't relax until I heard the click of the bolt.

Pulling on a robe from the armoire, I walked to the bathroom and opened the door. Ian was shaving at the sink. He looked rested and healthy from the tracks in his shower-damp hair to the towel wrapped around his waist. "There's breakfast for two in my room," I announced.

He grinned, and I relaxed. "How did you know it wouldn't matter?" I asked, leaning against the marbled sink.

He wiped the shaving cream from his face. "British society is still very status conscious, Christina. Those in service to the upper classes regard everything their employers do with a certain detached amusement that wouldn't be tolerated within their own order."

"Are you telling me that the duke of Atholl's servants wouldn't be comfortable associating with us?"

"Exactly."

"Isn't that a rather outdated assessment? After all, I'm a history teacher and you're a farmer."

Ian laughed. "True. But in this case, it makes no difference how we earn our living. On this island and in much of Europe, family is everything."

"Do you approve of that philosophy?" I asked curiously.

"It doesn't matter whether I do or not. I live here and change doesn't occur overnight."

He was wrong. It did matter, but I wasn't sure how much. He turned away from the mirror and folded his arms across his chest. His face was smooth and completely expressionless. "Will you pour me some tea?" he asked.

I nodded and walked back into my room, conscious of his presence close behind me. He slipped beneath the bed-covers, while I poured the dark, fragrant liquid into a cup, added milk, and handed it to him. Ian ate and drank the same way he did everything, quickly and efficiently with a minimum of wasted motion. I watched him swallow his tea and wield a knife, carefully spreading the delicious Golden Shred marmalade across his toast with blunt, capable fingers. A sweet, piercing ache rose up inside me. There was something deeply personal about the sharing of breakfast after lovemaking. It was a promise, a sense of completeness, of well-being and security, that I hadn't felt in a very long time.

Later, after we'd dressed and were on our way back to the borders, I asked Ian about Jeanne Maxwell. "Did Jeanne die at Traquair House?"

He reached over and squeezed my hand. "Yes, but I wouldn't call it dying exactly."

"What do you mean?"

"She was murdered, accused of witchcraft and hanged."

I could feel the color leave my face. "Before or after she married John Maxwell?" I asked.

"After. I believe she had her share of happiness even though she came to such a tragic end. The marriage was a good one. After John died at Flodden, she was arrested and executed." He glanced at me curiously. "Were you able to read through most of MacCleod's information last night?"

Leaning back in my seat, I fingered Professor MacCleod's envelope and looked out the window at the golden greens and bright russets of the countryside. "I don't need to read anymore, Ian," I said slowly. "She comes to me whenever I'm alone."

His hands clenched, and the knuckles on the steering wheel whitened beneath his skin. "Are you frightened?" he asked quietly.

I shook my head. "I know what's going to happen. So far the documents seem to be historically accurate. What terrifies me is the pain. I can feel her hurt and her joy. It's only logical to assume that I should also be able to feel her pain."

"Did you feel it when Katrine died at Culloden?"

"No," I said. "I felt sorrow and compassion for another's suffering. But this isn't the same. The images of Jeanne Maxwell are much clearer. This time, I can feel textures and smell cooking from the kitchen. I feel her relief when she takes down her hair and the warmth of a fire after coming in from the cold. I can *feel* everything." I leaned my head against the window, grateful for the coolness against my forehead. "Ian?" I whispered. "Am I losing my mind?"

He smiled reassuringly. "No one who asks such a question is ever in danger of that, darling. You've been through quite an ordeal, and it isn't over yet." His hand reached out to cover mine. "Don't worry. We'll make it through this."

And then what? I wondered. Would I be the next in line to fall victim to Grizelle Douglas's curse, or would we solve it, Ian and I, and then go our separate ways? Suddenly, I wanted very much to be alone in the privacy of my own room at Traquair.

The first thing I did, after being kissed good-bye at the steps of Traquair House, was to search for Jeanne Maxwell's portrait. Later, after Ian had returned, when I could think logically, I would find the stone.

Ignoring Kate's curious stare, I brushed aside her questions and headed for the secret stairs. The halls were narrow here in the east wing, and every floorboard creaked under my feet. I wondered how the structure managed to survive the hoards of tourists that descended upon it every year.

The priests' hidden chamber was long, with whitewashed walls and an uncarpeted floor of English oak, dark and stained with age. It was late afternoon and the room lay steeped in shadows. The air was still with a dank, musty smell reminiscent of mold and age and closed-up rooms that had outlasted their purpose. The furniture was sparse, and the only paintings on the walls were those of churches and village scenes. Where was Jeanne, and where was the entrance to the hidden stairs?

Baffled, I returned to the main hallway and walked down to the kitchen. Kate was basting a huge chicken with a clear liquid that could only be drawn butter. Thank goodness I wasn't overly concerned with cholesterol. Diet drinks and aspertame had not yet made their way into Scotland. She looked up when I walked into the room. Was that a flicker of apprehension I saw in her eyes?

Her voice gave nothing away. "May I help you, Miss Murray?"

Why did I feel as if I were intruding in my own kitchen? "I was wondering if my father called again," I said.

"Not yet." She closed the oven door and wiped the perspiration from her forehead with the back of her hand. "I would have told you if he had."

For some reason, I didn't want to broach the subject of Jeanne Maxwell's portrait, but I was impossible at deception and I'd run out of conversation. "I'd like to see the hidden stairs," I blurted out.

She opened her mouth as if to speak, then apparently thought better of it. Instead, she gave me a long, searching look and removed a key from the large ring hanging on the wall. Removing her apron, she hung it on a hook. "Follow me," she said. "You'll never find it unless I take you there."

Silently I followed her through the beautifully appointed rooms, up three flights of stairs, down the narrow hallway I'd seen in my dream to the priests' room. There, she pushed at a panel hidden inside a tiny alcove. The wall swung open, revealing a hidden door.

"We keep this open when tourists visit," she informed me. "The stairs have never been reinforced. It's too dangerous for a large group to go up, but they can look past the rope up the stone stairs. I don't think a slightly built person like yourself would come to any harm." She looked at me with a smile that didn't reach her eyes. "I imagine it's quite a sight for some, especially those whose history didn't begin until George Washington."

For a moment, the venom in her words didn't register. When it did, I was coldly, furiously angry. But it was too late. She had already handed me the key and walked away. Her voice floated back into the room. "If you have any trouble locking up, call me."

I didn't move until the sound of her footsteps had faded away. If I hadn't been sure before, I was now. Kate Ferguson was no friend of mine. The awareness hurt me more than I thought possible. It was important enough that I considered going after her to be sure my impression was accurate, but on second thought, I decided against it. Confrontation had never been my style.

Instead, I peered up the narrow passageway at the curving steps. It didn't look at all familiar. Cautiously, I climbed the first step and then the next and the one after that until I reached the top. Turning the corner into a tiny room crowded with antique furniture, I glanced at the walls looking for the portrait. There was nothing except a faded spot where a large floor-length frame must once have hung. It was an unusual place for such a large painting. Curious, I stared at the naked wall for a long time before I turned to walk back down the stairs. It was then that I saw it. A cloth-covered object the size of a door balanced against the opposite wall. Quickly, I crossed the room and pulled away the covering. I could feel a loud roaring in my ears and the sledgehammer slamming of my heart against my rib cage. Here, at last, was Jeanne Maxwell exactly as I'd seen her in my dreams. The artist commissioned to paint her had broken with tradition and eschewed the dark colors typical of the sixteenth century. Instead, he'd painted her as she was, a tall slender figure in a gown of deep rose set against a colorful backdrop of heather and gorse.

I knew now why Ellen Maxwell's heart had failed after taking one look at my face. Of the three women who were my ancestors, Jeanne Maxwell was most like me. From the night-dark hair and wistful mouth to the hurt expression in her pale gray eyes, looking at this woman was like facing a mirror image. Here was no confident girl like Katrine Murray or lady of legend like Mairi of Shiels. This was a woman unsure of herself, a woman who had suffered agonies of uncertainty.

I studied the portrait for the familiar signs of anguish. They were all there; the bitten-down fingernails, the bluish shadows around the eyes, the aloof smile and too-pale skin, the prominent collarbones rising from the rose material of her gown. My heart ached for her. What could have caused a woman of birth and beauty, a woman who had married the man she loved, to experience such heartbreak?

I thought I knew, but I couldn't be certain. The light was poor. I pulled the painting, frame and all, across the room and leaned it against the wall beneath the tiny window. It was in remarkable condition for its age. Carefully, I studied the delicate lines of Jeanne's gown, from the square bodice to the sweeping train of the skirt where it lay in folds around her feet. There could be no mistake. The skirt was full, gathered beneath the bodice with a ribbon instead of hugging the hips in the fashion of the day. I glanced at her left hand. A ring encircled the third finger. Jeanne was married, and if I knew anything about sixteenth-century clothing, she was also most definitely pregnant. Despite what Ian had told me, I knew that by the time this portrait was commissioned she'd either had the first of the nightmares or something else was very wrong.

After pulling the painting back to where I'd found it, I wrapped it up in the concealing cloth and started down the stairs, deep in thought. Why was a valuable sixteenth-century painting hidden away in a tiny attic room where no one would ever see it? And how had Professor MacLeod found it? More importantly, where was the passageway Katrine Murray and I had seen in our dreams? Running my hands over the walls, I could detect no indentation, no hidden panel or alcove, nothing that would lead me to believe this room held the secret of the tunnel.

Kate was nowhere in sight when I replaced the key. I thought about keeping it in my room and decided against it. There was no reason to assume that my housekeeper couldn't be trusted to open the door in the morning for tourists and lock it up at night. She probably had no idea that the portrait even existed.

Back in my room, I pulled on a robe and began brushing out my hair when a thought stopped me. Professor MacCleod said he had first seen the portrait over ten years ago hanging at the top of the secret stairs. Kate had lived at Traquair all of her life. She must have seen it. Why, then, hadn't she reacted when she saw my face for the first time? She must have noticed. The resemblance was unmistakable.

In the hall, the phone rang. I tensed, waiting for the second ring. Then and there, I decided that the first thing I would do with Ellen Maxwell's money would be to install a telephone in my bedroom. It rang a third time. Tossing the brush aside, I walked into the hall and picked up the phone before the fourth ring.

"Hello."

"Christina," a familiar voice said.

"Dad." Relief flowed through me, weakening my knees. I had to sit down. "I've been so worried. Is everything all right?"

"I'm not sure."

I frowned. "What's wrong?"

"Is there something wrong with your phone, Chris? It sounds as if someone else is on the line."

Immediately there was a telltale click. "I think we're all right now," I said dryly.

"Never mind. I'd planned on telling you the news personally."

The muscles in my back tensed. "Is anything wrong? It isn't Mom, is it?"

"There's nothing wrong, honey. Your mother's had quite a shock, and strangely enough, it has to do with the house you've inherited."

"Do you want me to come home?" I asked.

"No, of course not. We're coming there the week after next. I'll call you when we reach Edinburgh. Don't change your plans. If we can't track you down, we'll rent a car."

What could possibly be shocking enough to convince my thrifty father to buy two plane tickets to Edinburgh during the peak of the tourist season?

I hung up the phone, tightened the sash of my robe, and walked downstairs. There was a phone in the kitchen and another in the library. I unplugged the cords and stuffed them into my pocket. It was a futile gesture, really. Kate probably had a phone in her suite. But she would know why I'd done it, and she would know that I wouldn't stand for her interference. There were other housekeepers in Scotland, and even if the position proved hard to fill, middle-class American women weren't as helpless as British ladies. If the situation called for it, I wasn't above scrubbing out a toilet or two myself.

The next morning I arranged for my own private phone line to be installed in my room. Two men came out that afternoon. I answered the door myself. Ushering them past a white-faced Kate, I led the way up the stairs to my bedroom. Thirty minutes later they were gone, and I walked back downstairs for the confrontation I knew would come.

Kate sat on a chair, her hands folded in her lap. I sat on the sofa across from her and picked up a magazine. I didn't have long to wait.

"Are you unhappy with my services, Miss Murray?" she asked, her lips tight and angry.

"Not at all." I closed the magazine and placed it on the table. "Why do you ask?"

Two bright red spots appeared on her cheeks. "In the past, it has been my responsibility to arrange for all services necessary here at Traquair."

"What services are you speaking of?" I asked, meeting her gaze across the coffee table.

"Repairs, utilities, ordering supplies, paying the invoices for utilities." She waved her hand in a nebulous arc. "Everything."

"I'm sorry, Kate. I didn't mean to offend you," I said steadily, "but I'm neither elderly nor an invalid. You will be paid your customary salary, but I'll approve and pay all other expenses at Traquair myself. If that arrangement isn't satisfactory to you, I'll understand if you choose to give your notice."

"You mean leave Traquair?" Her voice cracked. "Why, I've lived here all my life."

"The choice is yours," I said gently. "You're a wonderful housekeeper; however, I am not Ellen Maxwell. You must learn to take direction from me or else find another position."

The eyes that stared at me were black with rage. A flash of memory awoke inside me. Once again, she reminded me of someone. Who was it? For a moment I wondered if my decision allowing her to stay was wise. Kate Ferguson looked dangerous. Immediately I dismissed the thought. Naturally, she was resentful. It wasn't easy to lose an employer of twenty years. Kate would need time to acclimate. With a firm smile, I rose and looked down at her. "Take the rest of the evening off to think about it," I told her. "Let me know what you intend to do as soon as possible."

The kitchen was warm and dark. The only light came from the smoldering peat logs in the fireplace. After turning on the flame under the teakettle, I pulled up a chair near its delicious warmth. A fireplace in the kitchen was a lovely idea.

Hundreds of years ago, when Traquair was first built, the kitchen had been a structure separate from the rest of the house. A large hearth was necessary for both cooking and heat. With the advent of gas and electricity and the fear of burning down the main house nearly obsolete, a kitchen fire was no longer practical. Whoever had ordered the renovation of Traquair had chosen to leave the original chimney structure alone and I was grateful. Slipping off my loafers, I held my feet toward the flames. The heat, through my woolen socks, was sheer bliss.

I stayed there a long time, warming my feet and sipping tea. In hindsight, the conversation with Kate seemed almost unbelievable. I was not a woman who welcomed confrontation. In my experience, a conciliatory approach reaped far more reward. I couldn't explain the stand I had taken. It was almost as if I'd assumed another identity, stepped into a stronger, more confident woman's shoes. Maybe it was Traquair that changed me. Traquair and the essence of Mairi of Shiels that lingered everywhere around me.

Seven hundred years ago she had walked these floors, climbed these same stairs, overseen the making of perfume and candles in this very kitchen. She had prayed in the chapel and ridden on the moors, picked gorse and heather in the fields, and laughed and played and loved in the room I now occupied upstairs. Her blood flowed through my veins. She had passed down to me her eyes, her hair, her skin, and the long, loose-limbed elegance of fine bones and straight teeth. With such a heritage, how could I not, in some small way, try to measure up.

I knew that having words with my housekeeper could not be compared to what Mairi had done, but it was no small thing for a woman who had given up everything she owned in an uncontested divorce settlement for the sake of keeping the peace. If it turned out that I was unsuccessful, if the location of the stone remained a mystery, I did not want another Murray woman two hundred years from now to look at my picture and feel only disappointment.

In the darkened room, the fire glowed, blue tipped and orange. I felt as if I'd been awake for a long time, and when my head began to ache and the strange, unsettling dizziness washed over me, I wasn't at all surprised. My last conscious memory before I drifted off was the figure of Jeanne Maxwell beckoning me from the flames.

❧ 15 ❧

Traquair House
1509

Flora Maxwell stared at the two of them standing hand in hand before her. She was not surprised to hear their news. Few could resist John Maxwell's appeal once he made up his mind. Just now, he appeared lit from within with such happiness that it was difficult to look at his face. She turned to Jeanne. Her obstinate, defiant daughter actually looked pleased. Holding out both hands, Flora smiled. "You've made me very happy. I congratulate you both."

With the generosity typical of his nature, John reached out immediately, clasping Flora's hand to bring her into the circle of his warmth, but Jeanne hesitated. When her mother would have gathered her into an embrace, she pulled away, searching Flora's face for signs that the match did not meet with her approval. She found none.

John frowned. He had not missed his betrothed's withdrawal. She carried more resentment toward her mother than he thought. He only hoped it would not extend to him.

"I suppose Jamie's approval is a mere formality," Flora continued, brushing aside her daughter's rejection.

"Jamie owes me a favor," John replied with a grin. "I made sure of his approval before I left Edinburgh."

Jeanne's eyes widened. "How is that possible? George Gordon said Jamie had not even made a decision on a match between us."

"George is presumptuous." John cooly dismissed his rival. "He should know that the king dislikes committing himself unless 'tis to his own advantage."

Jeanne smiled mischievously. Forgetting her audience, she slipped her arms around John's neck. "What hold do you have over our liege, m'lord, that he so willing granted your heart's desire?" She spoke very near his ear, punctuating each word with a tiny breath of air.

His eyes narrowed, and the skin across his cheekbones, already dark from the sun, reddened. Sliding his arms around her waist, he spoke gruffly. "Perhaps 'tis because Jamie understands what it is for a man to lose his heart's desire."

Flora looked away, overcome with need and ashamed of her jealousy. The mood was no longer teasing. Jeanne was too young to remember the love affair between Maggie Drummond and the boy-king Jamie Stewart, but Flora knew that Masses were still purchased for Maggie's soul and, on winter nights, just before dusk, the king could be seen kneeling at her grave.

"I'll leave you alone," she interrupted, moving toward the door. For Jeanne's sake, she would pretend only pleasure, but it was too much to watch the man she burned for make love to her daughter before her very eyes. At the door, curiosity overcame her. She turned back one last time. Intent only on each other, neither one noticed her departure. With a sad smile, Flora left the room.

A bright summer sky and warm winds heavy with the scent of heather heralded Jeanne's wedding day. She woke early, with the first streaks of dawn, but made no motion to rise. The ceremony would begin at ten. It was good to lie back on her pillows and do nothing. For the first time in six weeks, she had a moment to herself. John had insisted on marrying as soon as possible, and the preparations had taken every waking hour.

Jeanne grudgingly admitted that her mother had been

wonderful. Perhaps she had misjudged her after all. Could a woman in love with a man marrying another enter into his wedding preparations with such enthusiasm? Could she debate the benefits of serving ale or spiced wine for the banquet? Would she sigh over the ermine-bordered wedding dress or giggle like a girl when she saw the nearly transparent gown designed specifically for the wedding night. Jeanne flushed. She owed her mother an apology. But not today. Nothing would spoil today.

A knock sounded on the door. She sat up, propping herself on her elbow. Her hair, black and shining, spilled over the mattress and onto the floor. "Enter," she called out.

Four servants carrying a wooden tub entered the room and placed it near the fire. Four more carrying steaming buckets of water followed. Jeanne watched as they poured the steaming liquid into the tub and scattered rose petals across the surface.

Kicking aside the bedclothes, she stood, pulled off her nightshift, and stepped into the heated bath. She would have liked to lie back and let the warmth seep into her bones, but her hair needed washing. Brushing it dry would take most of the morning.

Leaning forward, Jeanne felt a rush of warm liquid through her hair. Water dripped over her forehead and into her eyes and ears. When she had only caught her breath, another pitcher was poured and then another until her entire head and fall of hair was soaked completely through. She breathed in the familiar scent of roses and felt the slick, perfumed soap on her forehead, around her ears, and at the back of her neck. A soft moan escaped her lips as the competent, familiar fingers of the maid rubbed her scalp.

More water was poured and still more until every strand of hair, pulled between two fingers, vibrated like the strings of a lyre. A maid dragged the ornamental screen from across the room, shielding her mistress from the eyes of the servants. When it was securely in place, Jeanne stood and rubbed the soap over her entire body, concentrating on her ankles and the backs of her knees. After rinsing herself with more bathwater, she picked up a towel from the floor and wrapped it around her. As if on cue, the maid appeared from behind the screen to wrap another towel around her hair.

Jeanne stepped out of the tub and slipped her arms into the sable-lined robe held out before her. Tying the sash, she sat on a low stool facing the glass while the same maid worked at her hair with a comb. It was pleasant sitting here, feeling the gentle tug of the comb, lapping up the warmth of the fire like a cat who has had more than her share of stable mice and cream. When every tangle had been combed free, her hair was brushed dry until it hung straight and thick to her knees. The entire process had taken over two hours.

She noted the time and shivered with delicious anticipation. After today she would no longer be a maid. Her hair would never again hang unbound to her knees. Thoughts of the night to come consumed her. Despite the stories she had heard, sharing the marriage bed with John Maxwell did not frighten her. In fact, she welcomed it.

Jeanne was not completely ignorant of sexual matters. She had grown up in the country, and the habits of animals were familiar to her. She had also come of age during the reign of Jamie Stewart. It was impossible to visit the royal court without acquiring a rudimentary knowledge of sex. However, the act itself had never been explained to her satisfaction, and when she stopped to consider it, it seemed physically impossible. She was anxious to see for herself how it was done. Instinct and of course the rumors told her that John would be an excellent teacher.

A soft murmur interrupted her thoughts. The maid was holding out her shift. Jeanne stood and untied the robe. It fell to her feet, and the cloth was pulled gently over her head. The material was of the finest linen, thin and so tightly woven it felt like air when she moved. Then her dress was eased over her shoulders, the tight busk was adjusted across her breasts, and the soft folds were gathered around her waist with a diamond-studded girdle. A train, with a footwide border of snowy white ermine, flowed out behind her.

Pulling the sleeves off her shoulders, Jeanne turned to the glass, and her eyes widened. Staring back at her was a woman, tall and willowy slim, with hair that glowed like black fire where the sun touched it. Her chin was up, and her cheekbones were very pronounced beneath eyes that flashed as clear as the diamonds at her throat. For the first time Jeanne realized that she was beautiful. She smiled triumphantly. John Maxwell would not be disappointed in his bride.

A hint of color was applied to her lips and perfume touched to her throat and wrists. Slipping her feet into soft-soled shoes, she turned toward the door. It opened unexpectedly, and her mother stepped into the room. Jeanne stiffened.

"Please wait outside," Flora ordered the servants.

They were quick to obey.

Her eyes were misty as she looked at her daughter. "You are the loveliest bride Traquair has ever seen."

Jeanne relaxed.

"I came to tell you—" Flora stopped. The tears rose in her throat. "Never mind," she said, "'tis time."

"Mother." Jeanne placed her hand on Flora's arm. "Thank you," she whispered, "for everything."

Tears welled up in Flora Maxwell's eyes, streaking through the rouge and rice powder so artfully applied to her face. Breathing a prayer of thanks, she gathered her daughter into her arms. The soft kiss pressing against her cheek more than made up for her pain. Finally, she pulled away. "Come," she said, "the archbishop waits."

Moving aside, she watched Jeanne walk down the stairs. Four servants carrying the heavy train accompanied her to the landing. From there, she went on alone, down the stairs and across the wide courtyard to the chapel.

John stood at the altar, his face very serious and terribly handsome in its gravity. Jeanne's heart nearly failed her. The distance she must walk to reach his side seemed insurmountable. Her step faltered. She couldn't do it. Then, as if he knew her troubled thoughts, John's eyes met hers. Across the long, carpeted aisle, she felt him reach out. Smiling tentatively, she moved forward again, her eyes riveted to the lifeline he held out to her. Just as she reached his side, he winked and grinned broadly. A bubble of mirth welled up in her chest. *Dear God,* she prayed silently, *keep me from disgracing myself in the presence of an archbishop.*

Her prayer was answered. The Mass seemed incredibly short. In almost no time at all, they exchanged their vows in low, solemn voices. The air inside the chapel was very still. The sun rising into the sky hovered for a moment outside the small, etched windows. At the very moment John slipped his ring on Jeanne's finger, a shaft of light penetrated the glass and found the diamonds in the pendant at her throat and waist. A collective gasp swept through the congregation as it split into a thousand colors, surrounding the couple in a gleaming arc of netherworld light.

Murmurs circulated through the crowd. "Surely, 'tis a sign," they whispered. "The union is blessed by God, the Holy Virgin, and all the saints."

Flora Maxwell closed her eyes as John bent his head and briefly kissed her daughter's mouth. With a firm shake of her head, she opened them again and looked back at the altar. Jeanne was married and, from the looks of it, happily so. There would be children at Traquair again. Flora imagined herself bending over the cradle of a black-haired baby, a baby the image of John. The bairn would be doubly dear because it would be Jeanne's child as well. She smiled and disregarded the idea of going away. Jeanne would need her, and the feel of a sweetly scented bairn against her breast after so many years was a temptation too great to withstand. Fate had decreed that she would never marry John Maxwell, but she could still love his child.

The wedding couple sat in the banquet hall on a raised dais. It was almost evening. Serving the food had taken a long time. For hours to come, wine would flow and the merrymaking continue until none the length of Scotland would forget this day. There were dancing girls from France and trained bears restrained by leather leashes. Musicians played and troubadours sang ballads honoring the beauty of the bride, the courage of the groom, and the loyalty of the entire House of Maxwell. There was braised fowl and roasted mutton and enough fiery *usquebaugh* to keep every man drunk for days to come. Men and women alike, their faces flushed, mouths smeared with grease, and lips stained with wine, dropped to the floor in exhausted stupors. Beside their alcohol-dazed bodies, dogs growled and fought for bones dropped on the rush-strewn floor.

The food was superb. The cooks of Traquair had outdone themselves. By decree, the first of every course was served to the king. Jamie waved his knife and lifted his trencher in approval. As each new dish passed inspection, the crowd roared and the music played on.

Jeanne stared at the uneaten food on her plate. The torches had been lit hours ago, and on the cloth-covered tables, candlewicks drowned in wells of melted wax. A curious numbness invaded her body. Despite her intentions and her curiosity, she was suddenly afraid. Soon the door of the laird's bedchamber would close and she would be alone with her husband. For the first time in her life, she would share a man's bed. That the man was dearly loved and had been her friend and childhood companion for every conscious moment of her life mattered not at all. Her hands were icy cold, and the food tasted like ashes in her mouth. Even the music and the dancers seemed very far away. Jeanne closed her eyes, alone in her own private terror.

John lifted the heavy goblet emblazoned with the Maxwell creed, *Reviresco,* "I deliver," to his lips. He was truly enjoying himself. The entertainment was marvelous and the food better than anything he had tasted in England. He turned to compliment Jeanne, and his eyes narrowed. Her skin was paler than the ermine-bordered sleeves of her gown, and her eyes were closed. He could see the fluttering of her pulse in the delicate skin at her temple. His lips turned up in a tender smile. Poor lass. She was terrified.

John Maxwell was not an arrogant man, and he had never before bedded a virgin, but he was confident of his ability to arouse his young wife's deeply passionate nature. After all, she loved him. He was sure of that. And although his experience would never rival either Jamie Stewart's or Henry Tudor's, the women who had shared his bed seemed anxious to return, sometimes embarrassingly so.

Jeanne's hand rested on the table. He placed his own over it. Startled by the contact, she opened her eyes and looked at him. What she saw in his expression caused her to tremble. Wetting her lips, she whispered, "How long?"

"An hour."

She nodded, and together they stood. A hush fell over the

banquet hall. He slid his arm around her waist, and a great cheer rose from the crowd.

"Our bridegroom grows impatient," Jamie called out from the dance floor.

John acknowleged his words with a grin. "Go now," he whispered to Jeanne. "Perhaps I can hold them off for a while."

She knew exactly what he meant. Gathering her train, she stepped down from the dais and tried to slip unobtrusively out the door. But the crowd would have none of it.

"Run," cried Flora into her ear. "They will not be denied their sport."

Jeanne ran down the hall to the stairs with her mother and Moira Sutherland close behind. The crowd followed. Jeanne reached the first landing without mishap. Down the hall she fled, flushed and breathless, pushing open the door to the room she would share with John. Moira threw herself down on the bed while Flora slammed and bolted the latch behind them. Howls of laughter and ribald jokes penetrated the thick wood. For several moments the women waited while their drunken pursuers serenaded them. Finally, they heard the sound they waited for: boots descending the stairs. Then all was silent.

"They're gone," Flora announced, moving away from the door. "Hurry. We've no time to lose." She looked at the nightgown lying on the bed and then at Jeanne's face. Quickly, she moved forward, reaching for her hands. "There, there, darling," she said. "Everything will be all right." She turned to the younger woman. "Fetch my daughter a draught of wine, Moira. Her hands are cold."

Moira moved to do her bidding. "Whiskey would be better," she said, handing Flora the goblet. "You aren't frightened, are you, Jeannie? Sweet Mary, I'd give much to be in your shoes tonight."

"Hush." Flora silenced her. "You know nothing of it." She pulled her daughter into her arms. "John loves you," she whispered. "He will be gentle. By this time tomorrow, you will have found a pleasure greater than any you've imagined. 'Tis what we are made for, Jeannie, to love a man and bear his children. What else is there for a woman?"

The wine brought the color back to Jeanne's cheeks. She stood and smiled tremulously at her mother. "Help me out of this, please" she said, lifting her arms.

Flora drew Jeanne's gown and undershift over her dark head and hung it in the clothespress. Then she held out her arms. "Hand me the nightdress, Moira."

With an envious glance and a final stroke of the luxurious fabric, the girl complied. The garment had been fashioned in France and made of black silk with three tiny ties, one at the breast, another at the waist, and, the last, several inches above the knee. Flora slipped it over her daughter's head. Moira took one look at Jeanne's slender, elegant body so daringly revealed in the exquisite garment and gasped.

Jeanne glanced at herself in the mirror and blushed. "It is rather indecent, isn't it?"

"Never mind," said her mother wryly. "There will be little left of it in the morning." She poured water into the basin and motioned for Jeanne to bathe her face and hands. Moira was busy slipping the warming pan between the sheets. Everything was ready, the scented candles, the bed made ready with turned-back covers and plump pillows, the wine on a small side table. Suddenly, her eyes swam with tears. It was exactly right. With one helpless, apologetic glance at her daughter, Flora left the room.

Moira smiled in sympathetic understanding. "Your mother is very fond of you. 'Tis difficult for a mother to lose her only child."

"I go nowhere," replied Jeanne shortly. "John and I will continue to live at Traquair. My mother will live with us."

"Then why—?"

Jeanne shrugged. "Perhaps she is tired. The last weeks have been difficult for her."

Moira nodded. "She's worked hard on the wedding."

Jeanne did not contradict her.

A heavy knock and muffled laughter sounded at the door. "Open the door, lass," the king's voice called out. "Your bridegroom awaits."

"He comes," Moira whispered.

Jeanne's hand closed tightly over the back of a chair. "Let him in."

Moira opened the door and several pairs of arms pushed John inside. His shirt was torn, and he breathed as if he had run a great distance. He stared at the scantily clad figure of his wife, and his eyes widened.

With reflexes born of years on the border, he reached out instantly to slam and bolt the door against the brawny arms pushing against it. Ignoring Moira, he crossed the room to tower over Jeanne. She was tall for a woman, but he was half a head taller still. Lifting a lock of black hair, he twisted it around his finger.

"I'm flattered, lass," he said silkily, "but were you really going to show yourself in such a garment to all the king's men?"

"I'll wager that I'm more decently clad than half the women in Henry's court."

"You would lose," replied John promptly.

"Are you criticizing my gown, m'lord?" she asked icily.

He bent his head to her lips. They were so close they shared the same air. "Not at all," he murmured. "I like it so long as I am the only man to see it. What I object to is your displaying your charms in such a public manner."

Jeanne could not believe her ears. "You dare to criticize me?"

"I am your husband."

She lifted her chin. "I see. Apparently your idea of marriage is different from my own."

"Don't be absurd." This was not the way John had envisioned his wedding night. Why couldn't she have waited for him in the customary manner: in bed? He was sorry he'd mentioned the cursed gown.

Moira cleared her throat and edged toward the door. "I'll be leaving now," she announced. There was no answer from either man or woman in the tension-thick room. Sliding the bolt, she escaped into the hall. It was empty. She breathed a sigh of relief and made her way back to the banquet hall.

Back in the laird's bedchamber, the two faced one another like antagonists readying for battle. John relented first. Sighing, he turned away and walked to the small table near the bed and poured himself a goblet of wine. Swallowing a long draught, he replaced the goblet and turned back to his bride. Her face was wet with tears. In two strides he crossed the room and took her in his arms. "I'm sorry, love," he murmured, kissing her nose, cheeks, and chin. "Don't cry. I can't bear to see you cry."

She wept against his shirt. "I wore it for you. I wanted the wait to be worthwhile."

Silently, he cursed himself. "I know, darling. I know."

"You shouted at me." Jeanne, worn out by weeks of strain and anticipation, was sobbing in earnest.

John lifted his head in bewilderment. "I did?"

She nodded. "Yes."

Wisely, he remained silent.

"Do you think I wanted to wear this ridiculous gown?" she railed at him. "I was terrified to face you." Lifting her head, she stared at him with reddened eyes. "Have you any idea what the first time is like for a woman? Can you even imagine it?"

Fascinated at the thought of Jeanne imagining anything of the sort, he shook his head.

"Of course not," she said scornfully. "I realize that this isn't an unfamiliar experience for you, but please remember that it is for me."

The injustice of her words stung him. "What in the name of heaven do you mean by that?"

"Do you deny that you've bedded other women?"

"That is hardly a subject for our wedding night," he replied angrily.

"Why not?"

Mustering the last remnants of his self-control, John counted to ten. Lifting Jeanne's chin in his hand, he forced her eyes to meet his. "I cannot change my past, Jeannie," he said softly, "nor will I defend it. There is nothing of shame in what I've done. I am a man, not an unschooled boy. 'Tis an unimportant matter but one that I believe you will be grateful for in time. I will not lie and say there have been no women before you, but I can promise that from the day you agreed to be my wife there has been no one else, nor will there be."

Her eyes, swimming in their sea of tears, fixed themselves hopefully on his face. Catching her bottom lip between her teeth, she clutched his shirt in a desperate grip. "Truly, John?" she asked.

He was helpless against the tiny catch in her voice. With a groan, he set his mouth against hers. It was a long, drugging kiss, and when he lifted his head, his breathing was heavy. Swinging her into his arms, he carried her to the bed and laid her gently on the sheets. Turning away, he shrugged out of his clothes and doused the candles. In the dark, he made his way to the bed and slid in beside his wife. Heart hammering, he reached out for her.

Innocently, she nestled against him, molding her body to his. Willing himself to proceed slowly, he waited for several moments, and then brushed back her hair and touched his lips to the curve of her throat. There was no response. He lifted his head and stared down at her face. In the darkness he could barely make out her features. She was sound asleep.

With a sigh of resignation, John gritted his teeth. His body throbbed with need. Gently, he extricated himself from the tangle of Jeanne's arms and moved to the other side of the bed. He was quite sure the night would be the longest he'd ever known.

❋ 16 ❋

The following morning Jeanne hovered on the brink of consciousness, aware of an unusual weight warming one side of her body. She opened her eyes to find John propped up on his elbow. He had obviously been watching her sleep. She flushed, uncomfortable with such intimacy. Yesterday's events came back to her in a rush of memory, the wedding, the banquet, the dim rose-scented room, and her fear of the night to come. She frowned. That was all. Nothing else came to mind. Cautiously she moved her legs, shifting to one side. Again nothing. Her body felt completely normal, better than normal. The fatigue that had plagued her for weeks before the wedding was gone.

She smiled lazily at her husband. "Did you sleep well?" she asked.

John's eyes widened. Was she serious? No flesh-and-blood man could have slept a wink. He searched her face for signs of amusement. There were none. "Not entirely," he answered.

"I'm sorry. We can change the mattress if you like."

"Jeanne," he said, exasperated. "My discomfort has nothing to do with the mattress."

Her smile faltered. "I don't understand."

He stared at her in amazement. Was she really as naive as she seemed, or had the wine affected her more than he realized? Another thought occurred to him. If she truly didn't remember the events of their wedding night, perhaps he could use it to his advantage.

"I'll help you understand, *mo chridhe,*" he murmured huskily. Reaching under the bedclothes, he parted the ridiculous nightgown until he felt the smooth skin of her thigh. Slowly, sensuously, his hand slid up her leg to the curve of her waist. She shivered, and the breath caught in his throat. Bending his head, he found her mouth at the same moment he untied the ribbon at her waist.

Jeanne's pulse leaped at the touch of his lips, the feel of his hand on her hip, then her stomach, and, finally, her waist. When it closed over her breast she refused to breathe, afraid of the overwhelming sensations consuming her. Could this really be John, her childhood champion, whose seeking lips and skilled hands were bringing her to a state of frenzied need? How could she have grown up in his presence without realizing the magic his touch would bring? Wrapping her arms around his waist, she arched her back to bring him closer.

His kiss deepened, and his hands moved over her, familiarizing himself with every hollow and curve of her body.

His jaw clenched and the cords of his neck were slick with sweat as he struggled to maintain control. She was soft and warm and sweetly damp beneath him. Her breathing came in short, shallow gasps and her hands played along his spine and hips, too shy to explore further. He nuzzled her neck. It tasted of salt and roses. He adjusted his body, causing her hands to slide lower. Immediately, they froze, and he held his breath. Tentatively, they moved again in small circular motions, testing the skin and hair beneath her palms. John pulled away to look at her, elbows locked, resting on his hands. Her eyes were closed, and a flush covered her face and chest. She was ready for him.

Gathering her close, he kissed her deeply and slid one thigh between her legs. She accepted him willingly. He tightened his arms and waited no longer.

Jeanne gasped and opened her eyes. The sensations were no longer pleasant. The burning pain between her thighs was close to unbearable. She pushed at John's chest. Instead of pulling away, he lifted her hips, and with one swollen thrust, filled her completely. Jeanne cried out and dug her nails into his back. Tears coursed down her cheeks and still the arms of steel held her prisoner. Strange vibrations pulsed in the most private part of her body, and she realized that John was shuddering. Twisting her neck, she struggled to see his face. It was buried against her throat. The pain inside her had lessened, but the pressure was still very great. Cautiously, she shifted her hips.

John groaned against her throat. The tiny movement was his undoing. He came at once, thrusting inside her over and over until he collapsed against her breast.

Jeanne stared in fascinated horror at the limp body on top of her. The pain between her thighs had diminished to an aching soreness, and the pressure had disappeared completely. The pushing, thrusting body of her husband was once again nothing more than a comforting weight warming the front of her. He looked completely spent and satisfied as if he had fought a great battle and won. Could he possibly have enjoyed himself?

John opened one eye and grinned at her. She was suddenly, illogically angry. "You hurt me," she accused him.

"I know." His eyes danced with flickering lights. "I'm sorry, love. It won't happen again."

"How do you know?" she asked suspiciously.

He lifted himself off of her. "It only hurts the first time when the maidenhood barrier is torn."

She blushed, embarrassed at discussing such matters openly. Then she thought of something else. "Why wasn't it torn last night?"

He looked amused. "Because you fell asleep on me. I spent my wedding night in a state of torment."

Humiliation flooded through her. She tried to turn away, but he would have none of it. Turning her chin with his hand, he said, "It doesn't matter, lass. What happens between the two of us in the privacy of our bedchamber is no one's business but our own. Do you really believe I would tell the world my lovemaking skills are so inadequate that my bride fell asleep on our wedding night?"

Jeanne hadn't thought of the matter in that light before. He made it seem as if the failure was his own. Immediately, she felt better. Reaching down to straighten the sheet, her hand came in contact with something wet.

Frowning, she threw back the covers and sat up. "I'm bleeding," she said with a gasp.

John could no longer control his amusement. Was there ever before a woman who had been raised in such ignorance? Throwing back his head, he laughed, a full-bodied, deep-chested sound that swayed the tapestries lining the walls.

Jeanne looked at him indignantly. "Will you please explain what is so amusing?"

When he had finally contained himself enough to speak, several moments had passed. "'Tis proof of your virginity."

She was too surprised to feel embarrassed. "Do all women bleed?"

"I believe so," he answered.

"Don't you know?" she asked curiously.

This time it was he who reddened in embarrassment. "Not really."

"Why not?"

"By all that is holy, you are the most frustrating woman I've ever known," he cried.

"'Tis said you've known many." Her voice was sweetly sarcastic.

"I've never, until this morning, bedded a virgin."

"Oh."

John eyed her uneasily. She looked almost disappointed. He sighed. "What is bothering you, Jeanne? Tell me now, and we'll be done with it."

"Why have you never bedded a virgin?"

He thought carefully before answering, afraid of offending her. There was no way around it but the truth. "A man thinks of pleasure when lying with a woman," he answered. "There is no pleasure for a woman the first time."

Her forehead wrinkled as she considered the matter. "Does it matter to a man that a woman feels no pleasure?" she asked at last.

He nodded. "Aye. The enjoyment is lessened if a woman leaves unsatisfied."

Jeanne moistened her lips and closed her eyes, unable to look at his face when she told him. "I'm sorry, John. But I don't believe I'll ever enjoy what we did."

The silence was heavy between them. Gathering her nerve, she opened her eyes. He did not look at all devastated. In fact, he looked positively cheerful.

He lowered his head so that his lips played along the curve of her throat. "Was it all bad?" he murmured between kisses.

"Not entirely." Jeanne was feeling strange. When his hand stroked the side of her breast, she felt tiny flutterings in the pit of her stomach. "I like this very much," she confessed.

He smiled into her neck before moving to the slope of her breast. She sighed and closed her eyes, welcoming the weight of him against her body. Stretching seductively she clasped her arms around his neck.

Once again, John was filled with need. But it wasn't the raging tide of the previous night. This time he could wait. His eyes lingered on her parted lips. Bending his head, he kissed her, his tongue tracing the polished teeth, the line of her mouth, and the sweet flesh within. When her hands twisted themselves in his hair and her tongue followed his, he pulled away well satisfied. Better to wait and leave her with the memory of pleasure. Perhaps in a day or two, she would reconsider her opinion of lovemaking. He smiled wryly to himself. This business of marriage was more than he'd bargained for.

Traquair House
1993

My father called at nine in the morning. He and my mother had flown all night and sounded exhausted on the telephone.

Kate had spent the last few days preparing for their arrival. A huge bedroom, which I learned was traditionally the laird's suite, had been cleaned from top to bottom, the mattresses turned, rugs pounded, and sheets hung outside to absorb the scent of pine and clean wind. Bouquets of heather were set on the mantel and both end tables, and thick, freshly laundered towels hung in the modern master bath.

I was grateful that the road was deserted. The car I'd rented the day before was a Sierra, a model I'd never seen in the States but close enough to an American car to feel and look familiar. The steering wheel, however, was on the right and the roundabouts with their spokelike directionals came too quickly to make driving completely comfortable. Thankful that I didn't have to worry about those until I reached the city, I looked around at the scenery and thought about Jeanne Maxwell.

According to Professor MacLeod's research, she had confided in her husband, telling him of the nightmares that came to her with such terrifying clarity. But, unlike Katrine, she had not experienced them during her pregnancy. Jeanne's visions of Mairi's death had not come until three years after her marriage, well after her son was born. Everything else fit perfectly. Her diabetes, the combination of Murray and Maxwell blood in her gene pool, the incredible similarity of features. Something was missing. What was it? What could have occurred in her life to give her that look of wariness I'd seen in her portrait? Had her marriage turned out to be unhappy?

I thought back to her wedding night. It hadn't lived up to her expectations, but it wasn't an unusual experience for a woman who knew next to nothing about sex. From the beginning of time, women had suffered through much worse and gone on to have satisfying relationships. John Maxwell didn't strike me as a man who couldn't arouse his wife, or any other woman for that matter. No, I decided. The problem couldn't have anything to do with their marriage.

The turnoff to the airport came sooner than I'd expected. Signs for arriving flights were posted on the side of the road. I took the next exit and maneuvered my car into the parking lot near the British Airways terminal.

I saw them before they recognized me. Relaxing on a bench in the airport lobby, my mother looked smaller and older than I remembered. It had been almost six months since I'd last seen her. A wave of guilt surged through me. Boston was only three thousand miles from California, five hours by plane, hardly an insurmountable distance. I should have visited more than I had.

Thank goodness for my father. I couldn't help smiling when I saw him. He never changed. The cowlick that wouldn't lie flat stuck straight up on top of his head, and he'd buttoned his sweater unevenly. Retirement certainly suited his personality. Dad never cared much for appearances. My smile died. Mother, always the perfectionist, didn't seem to care either. She looked dazed, as if the airport activity was too much for her.

Slowly, I approached them and rested one hand on each of their shoulders. "Hi, you two," I said, folding my mother into my arms. "How was the flight?"

"Just fine," said Dad heartily, relief in his voice. "We didn't expect you so soon. Traquair must be closer than it looks on the map."

"There isn't any traffic here," I reminded him. Slipping my mother's bag over my shoulder, I linked my arm through hers. "Let's go. I can't wait to show you the house." My usually opinionated, sharp-tongued mother allowed me to lead her through the airport like a lost child.

I opened the door to the front passenger seat, but she refused to sit in front. "If you don't mind, Christina, I'd rather take the backseat. I'll just throw my jacket over my bag and get some sleep. I don't think I can sit up another minute."

"You shouldn't have taken such a late flight," I scolded my father on the drive south. "It's not as if you couldn't afford to fly first class."

"We had some business we had to take care of in Boston first," he replied. "It was the only flight we could get."

"What's going on, Dad? Why the urgency?"

"Your mother's had quite a shock, Chris. I promised to let her tell you. She wants to see Traquair first."

I glanced in the rearview mirror. Her head was on the makeshift pillow, and her eyes were closed. She obviously needed rest and more than just the hour it would take to reach Traquair. Patience was a virtue, I reminded myself. One more day would hardly make a difference.

Mother seemed to know where we were the moment we reached the gates of Traquair. Rubbing her eyes, she sat up and stared at the lush grounds and high stone walls. "I can hardly believe it," she whispered. "I never knew."

I opened my mouth to ask what she was talking about when I glanced over at my father. He shook his head, and I remained silent.

Kate opened the door as we climbed the front stairs. "Welcome to Traquair, Mr. and Mrs. Murray. Would you like some refreshment before I show you to your room?"

"That would be lovely." Mother's smile changed her features completely. Her austere demeanor softened into an expression of such breathtaking warmth that no living being, human or otherwise, could resist her.

Kate looked at her and then looked again, more closely this time. Her eyes widened as if she couldn't quite believe what she saw, and then she smiled. It was the most genuine expression I'd ever seen on her face.

"I'll bring a pot of tea into the sitting room and some freshly baked scones to go with it," she said.

"Thank you. That sounds wonderful." Mother laid her hand on my shoulder. "We'll let you get started while Christina shows us where to go."

For some reason Kate's unusual servility bothered me. The woman was in my employ, and yet in the three weeks I'd known her, she had never treated me with anything close to the ingratiating submissiveness she had shown my mother.

"I thought you were tired," I said as I led my parents through the hall into a room with comfortable furnishings and a well-laid fire.

"I am," Mother replied, sinking into a chair with plump cushions. "But first, I have something to tell you. Otherwise, I won't be able to sleep at all."

"And neither will I," Dad groaned, stretching out on the couch.

"Christina," Mother began and hesitated, biting her lip.

I was more than a little worried by this time. "Is it that bad?"

"Not really," she answered. "It's just very unexpected." She sighed. "All right, Chris, here goes. After your phone call telling us you had inherited an eight-hundred-year-old house, Dad did some checking around. We both thought it extremely odd that someone we didn't know would leave you something so valuable." Her voice had risen to a high-pitched excitement. "Your father logically assumed, since Traquair was in Scotland, that your inheritance came from someone on his side of the family. But nothing turned up. That was when he spoke with my parents." She sat up, her back very straight, her hands clasped tightly together. "I'm adopted, Christina. Ellen Maxwell's husband, the late laird of Traquair, was my father."

My heart stopped. The conditions of the prophecy pounded in my brain. A daughter bearing both Maxwell and Murray bloodlines. The room turned, and I heard a roaring in my ears. I know I must have spoken, but I couldn't hear the words.

Apparently my mother did, because she answered me. "I don't know who she was. My parents believe she was some unfortunate girl who became pregnant by a married nobleman, made her way to America, and gave me up for adoption."

My father spoke for the first time. "The real question, as far as I'm concerned, is why Lord Maxwell left Traquair to you, Christina."

I could have told him, then and there, and maybe I should have. But something held me back. Something more than my fear that they wouldn't believe me, although that was a foregone conclusion.

Kate came in with the tea tray. We made polite conversation while she served and poured. Again, the tea was unusually spiced and delicious. After setting the tray on the table, she picked up two more embroidered pillows and placed them behind my mother's back.

"If there is anything else you need, Mrs. Murray, just ring the bell."

"Thank you. I'll do that," Mother answered. After Kate left the room, she lowered her voice and asked, "Is it my imagination or is she being overly solicitous to me?"

"It isn't your imagination," I said dryly. "She seems like a completely different person."

"Maybe you resemble someone, Susan," my father said. "After all, servants tend to stay with families for generations."

I could feel my mouth drop open. Of course. Why hadn't I thought of that? Kate had told me herself that her mother had been the housekeeper at Traquair before her death. If Lord Maxwell's indescretion had been with a servant, Kate's mother would probably know. Maybe she'd even kept in contact with the woman. My thoughts came quickly, tumbling over each other in their hurry to materialize. Maybe that was the reason Kate was so resentful. Class differences were stringently maintained here in Scotland. Kate obviously resented working for a woman from the same social order as herself. I breathed a sigh of relief. That I could handle. It was ancient curses and death threats that bowled me over.

Mother loved the bedroom. Dad opted for a shower before his nap, while she stretched out on top of the high four-poster bed. "There's more to tell you, Chris," she said, "but the most important part is over with. I'm just too tired to go into it any further today. If I sleep through dinner, don't wake me."

It was early still, only a little past noon, but I was exhausted. Ian had called earlier to say he would give everyone a day to adjust to the time change before inflicting himself upon us. I was grateful that he wasn't coming over. I didn't think I had the strength or the enthusiasm to tell him about my mother's startling revelation. He must have suspected the truth long ago. I thought back to our first conversation at the tearoom in Peebles, where he'd hinted at the rumor that I was the earl's illegitimate daughter. I didn't think he would be terribly surprised to learn I was his granddaughter.

There could no longer be any doubt. Like puzzle pieces, everything fell into place. Everything was there, exactly as it had been with the Murray women who came before me. My features, my Maxwell strain, my diabetes, everything except the most important factor.

I picked up my bedroom phone and dialed the Peebles operator. "I'd like the number of the medical clinic please."

"I'll connect you," she said.

In less than a minute, a pleasant voice answered the phone. I started to explain what I needed when she interrupted me. "There's no need for an appointment. Just come in and take your turn unless you have an emergency. This isn't an emergency is it, dear?"

"No," I replied, "no emergency at all. It's just that—"

Her voice changed. "Is this Traquair House calling?"

"Yes," I said, surprised.

"I recognized your voice, Miss Murray. It isn't everyday one hears an American accent. Of course, I'll make you an appointment. When would you like to come in?"

The sooner the better. "This afternoon if possible."

"Will four o'clock be suitable?"

"Yes. Thank you."

Apparently privilege still had its advantages, even in modern-day Scotland. Fluffing my pillow, I buried my nose in the fragrant linen. I wasn't used to sleeping in the middle of the day, but I couldn't shake this unusual lethargy. I yawned. Four o'clock was hours away. If I closed my eyes for just a minute, there would be plenty of time to make the drive into Peebles.

❖17❖

Traquair House
May 1510

John Maxwell stared at the twin bundles in his wife's arms. "Two of them?"

Jeanne, her face framed by two neat plaits of black hair, glowed like a Byzantine madonna. "They are wonderful, are they not?"

"By God, 'tis you who are wonderful, Jeannie. However did you manage it?"

She smiled demurely, but her eyes danced with mischief. "I had a bit of help, m'lord. You were not exactly lax in your duty." To Jeanne's delight, her husband's face reddened. At night, with the candles dimmed, John was creatively uninhibited when it came to sexual matters, but speaking of them by day embarrassed him. Jeanne had quickly discovered this unusual personality trait and teased him unmercifully.

As for herself, circumstances had turned out better than she could possibly have imagined. Whoever would have guessed after her disastrous wedding night that she would acclimate so quickly to the pleasures of the marriage bed? For in truth, she could think of no greater joy than having the lean muscular length of her husband's body stretched out beside her own. The touch of his lips, the feel of his strong narrow hands on her skin, the whispered urgency of his words, ignited a fire in her that could only be quenched by the age-old ritual of possession. She sighed and looked down at the babies in her arms. It had been too long already.

John interrupted her thoughts. "Are they boys or girls?"

"Both." Jeanne indicated the bairn on her left. "This one is the boy.

John reached for the infant on her right. "A man has a lifetime with a son, but only a few short years with his daughter." Gingerly he held the precious bundle. "Hello, sweetheart," he crooned. "Have you a smile for your sire?"

A tiny fist butted his chin. John laughed and unbelievably, the baby opened her eyes. Small, as an infant born three weeks early inevitably is, the features of her face were already clearly defined. The lines of what would one day be brows were sweeping arcs against the fairness of her skin. Her nose was firm, her chin determined, and her cheekbones high and ridged, proclaiming her Maxwell ancestry. The hair on her head grew counterclockwise in a black whorl on the delicate skull. Her eyes were already the clear winter gray of her mother's.

"Good Lord," exclaimed John. "She looks exactly like you, Jeannie."

"I know." Jeanne frowned. "There are those who say all the Maxwells resemble one another, but that isn't true, is it? I can see it here, in their faces. Our son has the same hair and eyes, but he looks nothing like me."

John bent over his son. It was true. The bairn's hair was black, and although his eyes were closed, John knew they would be the same clear gray as his sister's. But there, all resemblance to the women in his family ended.

John felt his chest swell with pride. This was his son, a child created in the image of himself. He could see it in the squareness of the miniscule jaw, in the set of the mouth and the flare of thin, aquiline nostrils. There was the promise of strength in the tiny hand clenched around his mother's finger. In this determined mite, born after two grueling days of childbirth, John Maxwell had a worthy heir.

"I thank you from the bottom of my heart, Jeannie." His voice was hoarse with emotion. "Two healthy children and you look as if you've done nothing more than gather heather on the hill."

Jeanne knew she looked nothing of the sort. She was more tired than she'd ever been in her life, and her glass told her the dark circles under her eyes made her look ten years older. Thank God for John, she thought gratefully. He had never once, not even in the screaming throes of childbirth, found her anything less than perfect. "What have I done to deserve you?" she asked quietly.

Their eyes met over the heads of their children. "'Tis I who should be asking that question, lass. Whatever it is, I'm very glad of it."

There was a soft scratching at the door. "Enter," Jeanne called out.

Flora Maxwell peeked into the room. "There is someone at the door to see you, John," she said in a hushed voice. "She wishes to pay her respects to Jeanne and the bairns."

"I'm very tired," Jeanne protested. "Please tell her tomorrow would be better."

John leaned over the bed to kiss his wife. Handing her the blanketed infant, he walked to the door. "I'll speak to her, love. Give the bairns to your mother and try to rest."

With a grateful sigh, Jeanne did as she was told.

John walked down the stairs with a light heart. Two babes and Jeanne was well. Surely it was a fortuitous beginning. The birth had been hard, but the midwife assured him that with rest, Jeannie could have a dozen more children. He thought of the clear, austere beauty of his wife's face, and a huge weight lifted from his heart. Children were important to a man, but nothing was as important as Jeanne. To stay away from her willing young body just when he'd learned the art of pleasing her would be a fate worse than death.

In the entry at the bottom of the stairs, a woman waited. Her shawl covered her head, but John knew instantly who she was. "Welcome, Grania," he said gently. "'Tis a long way for a woman of your years and affliction."

"I ha' to come," she said, nervously fingering the brooch on her bodice. "Last night I ha' the vision. Yer lass must be told."

John frowned. "What did you see?"

"No, no," Grania shook her head. "I canno' tell ye. 'Tis Jeanne, I must see."

"Jeanne sleeps," explained John. "The birth was hard."

"Aye," the old woman nodded. "I saw it. Two bairns for Traquair."

John took a step forward and took Grania's arm in a warning grip. "My lady bears you great affection, Grania Douglas, and for that you are welcome here. But know this, if you disturb her with tales of woe, your life will be worthless."

"I would ne'er harm the lass," Grania whispered. "'Tis only wha' I see."

"Tell her nothing of what you see," ordered John.

Grania's eyes bore through him, and he swore he saw pity in their sightless depths. "Do ye no' know yer own wife, lad? She will see whe'er I tell her or no'."

"I want you to leave my house," he said through clenched teeth.

Grania nodded. "Aye, I shall for now. But ye canno' keep her from me fore'er. She will come t' me."

He watched as the old woman felt her way toward the door, the gnarled old hand guiding her past the paneled wall, down the stone steps, and into the courtyard. Instantly John was ashamed of himself. She couldn't see, and he had made no move to help her. Jeanne wouldn't thank him for treating her guest so shabbily.

"Grania," he shouted, following her out the door. "Granny, wait." A thick concealing fog swirled around his head, muffling his voice and hiding from view everything farther than an arm's length away. The old woman shouldn't be out on a night like this. The borders were dangerous at this hour. Then he remembered that Grania was blind. All nights, fog laden or clear, were the same for her.

Traquair House
1993

I jackknifed to a sitting position in bed, consumed with an urgency so great it woke me immediately. My heart pounded as I attempted to calm myself and concentrate.

According to the professor, Jeanne Maxwell gave birth to a son. There was no reference to twins. Was it possible that such a thing could have been overlooked? I discounted it immediately. In medieval Scotland, women of high birth were prized for their dowries. The daughter of an earl was too important to be ignored. Somewhere, there must be a reference to Jeanne's daughter.

I looked at my watch. It was early afternoon, plenty of time to tear apart the library. Pulling a sweatshirt over my leggings and turtleneck, I slipped into comfortable loafers and made my way downstairs. As I'd expected, the vents in the library were closed, a concession to Kate's notions of conservation. I lit the fire and warmed my hands before beginning what I knew would be a lengthy search. The number of books was enormous.

Luck was with me. Two hours later, I found what I was looking for. A Bible, handwritten in ancient Latin script, the spine cracked and dusty with age, had the entry I needed.

On the third page, halfway down, written in a firm, masculine hand, was a birth entry that could only refer to Jeanne Maxwell's twins. *"On the twenty-fifth day of May, in the year of our Lord 1510 a son and daughter were born to John Maxwell, Earl of Traquair, and his wife."*

My fingers shook as I traced the thin, delicate parchment and ancient binding. The people I saw in my dreams had actually existed. They weren't myths or figments of my imagination. Here, in this very house, they had lived and walked and eaten and slept. In the hushed quiet of the library, it seemed as if their spirits surrounded me, urging me on, encouraging me to complete their story.

Curious to know more of my Maxwell ancestors, I read farther down the page. The next line stopped me cold, like the shock of ice water on bare skin. It was an obituary. *"Isobel Maxwell, beloved daughter of the Earl of Traquair and his wife, died in her fourth year, on the thirtieth day of July, 1513."*

I remembered the look of wonder on John Maxwell's face as he held his infant daughter for the first time. The words on the page blurred, and tears gathered in my throat.

Pressing my fingers against my eyelids, I managed to control myself. Isobel Maxwell had died nearly five hundred years ago, and there were other, much more important issues at hand. I still had no idea how the curse had affected Jeanne or if she even realized that she had a connection to Mairi of Shiels. Another thought occurred to me. Was it possible that Jeanne's small daughter, by her death, had lifted the curse from her mother?

Quickly my finger slid down the page, searching for Jeanne Maxwell's name. Nothing. There were no other entries at all until fifty years later. What could have happened to Jeanne's family?

There was only one way to find out. I swallowed, and in spite of the cold, perspiration gathered in the hollow of my throat. Slowly I closed the book and climbed the ladder to replace it carefully on the shelf. Hugging myself against the chill, I walked back to my room and sat down on the bed. The ticking of the clock disturbed me. Without thinking, I reached over to pick it up and noticed the time. Disappointment washed over me. It was nearly four. If I left immediately, I would just make my doctor's appointment. The mystery of Jeanne and her family would have to wait.

Conscious of the time, I hurriedly changed into a sweater and skirt, pulled a blazer from the armoire, and started down the stairs.

The doctor's office was just off the main street, near the post office. I pulled over to the side of the road and parked the car. As I turned the key in the lock, I felt a hand on my shoulder. A familiar voice spoke. "It appears that wishes sometimes come true," Ian murmured into my ear. "I was just thinking of you."

I laughed nervously, wondering how I could escape and slip into the office unobserved.

"What are you doing here?" Ian asked. "I thought you would be up to your ears in a family reunion, or are your parents tired of you already?"

"They are tired but not of me. I decided to let them rest while I came into town." The post office loomed before me. "For stamps," I announced, pleased with my sudden inspiration. "I need stamps."

Ian looked at me thoughtfully. "That shouldn't take long. Will you join me for tea after I've made my purchases?"

"Of course." I hoped my relief didn't show. "When will you be finished?"

"A half hour should do it. Shall we meet here, at your car?"

I nodded and watched to make sure he crossed the street and disappeared into the hardware store.

Hurrying to my appointment, I opened the door into a cozy sitting room, complete with fireplace, large bay windows, and a rolltop desk. Seated behind the desk was a cheerful-looking woman with gray hair and round cheeks. She peered at me over the rims of her glasses.

"Miss Murray?" she asked.

"Yes."

"Come right in. The doctor is expecting you."

Apparently, I was the only patient. The apple-cheeked woman ushered me into an immaculate examining room and handed me a cotton gown. "Remove your clothing, dear. The doctor will be in shortly."

I shed my skirt and sweater as quickly as possible and perched on top of the table, holding the back of the gown closed. Sooner than I'd expected, the door opened and a man walked in.

My mouth dropped open, and I felt the hot, humiliating flood of color start at my chest and move up. I recognized him immediately. He was the doctor from Traquair House, the same one who gave me insulin the day of Ellen Maxwell's funeral. Inching forward until my feet touched the floor, I slid off the table and stood before him.

"I must have dialed the wrong number," I stammered. "I wanted a gynecologist." He looked very young in spite of his gray hair.

"I am a gynecologist. I'm also every other type of physician you can think of. That's what general practitioners are, Miss Murray, jacks-of-all-trades. This is a clinic, and it happens to be the only one in Peebles."

I backed up to the chair where I'd draped my clothes. My face flamed with embarrassment. "I think I should make an appointment in Edinburgh."

He smiled. "Don't you trust me?"

"It isn't that," I assured him.

"Why don't you tell me why you came."

I thought of the friendly banter exchanged between Ian and the doctor at the foot of my bed in Traquair House. Shaking my head, I said, "It isn't important."

"Are you ill, Miss Murray?"

There was genuine concern in his eyes. Miserably, I shook my head.

He crossed his arms and leaned against the sink. "In Scotland as well as in the United States, doctors are required to honor patient confidences. I take my profession very seriously. Nothing that happens here will ever leave this room."

Had he guessed? I looked directly at him. There was nothing but compassion in the thin face that looked back at me. What difference did it make? If it were true, everyone would know soon enough.

"I came for a pregnancy test," I confessed.

"Shall I take a look and tell you for sure?" That was all. No look of surprise, no judgmental flaring of the nostrils or pursing of the lips. No look of censure. Just a simple question and a friendly smile.

I smiled back and walked over to the examining table.

Twenty minutes later I was dressed and on my way back to Traquair. Somehow, my mind registered road signs and traffic lights. Otherwise I would never have made it home safely. The impossible had happened. I, Christina Murray, a thirty-seven-year-old divorcée, was going to be a mother for the first time. All those miserable years of thermometers and mechanical sex, the bitter arguments and cold silences, the harsh accusations and bruised egos, had resulted in nothing more than the dissolution of a fifteen-year marriage. And now, in less than a month, the few magical, frantic couplings of unprotected intercourse between Ian and myself had accomplished this miracle.

Ian! I'd forgotten all about him. There were no other cars in sight. I swerved to the left, made a U-turn, and accelerated considerably over the speed limit back to Peebles. He was gone, of course. I thought that he would be, but I had to be sure. He would understand my absentmindedness once he heard the news.

There was no question that Ian would insist on marriage. He was born into a culture and tradition that assumed gentlemanly behavior long after the age of chivalry had been reduced to a brief salute consigned to the pages of ancient history books. But I had already been through one bad marriage, and although I was sure there would never be anyone else like Ian Douglas for me, I also knew that my judgment where men were concerned wasn't always the best. This time I had choices. I didn't *have* to be married although I desperately wanted to be. But more than that, I wanted Ian to ask me to be his wife without pressure or ulterior motive. But if he didn't, I'd waited half my life to have a baby. Nothing was going to spoil it for me.

On a more practical note, I needed Ian. It was more important than ever to solve the mystery of the stone. Any last, lingering doubts about coincidence and the possibility that my fertile imagination had taken control of my mind disappeared at the confirmation of my condition. Everything was finally in place for the fulfillment of the legacy. But now I wasn't alone. I knew without a doubt that besides Ian and myself three women who had transcended the portals of time, shared their lives, their hopes, their innermost secrets, were also with me.

Before today, I had been anxious to see justice done, to reveal that Mairi of Shiels was not a traitor to her country. The threat of danger to me, Christina Murray, a twentieth-century woman, seemed too incredible to believe. Now it was different, more personal. Now everything was possible. This Murray of Traquair was determined to watch her child grow up.

"Miss Murray," Kate called after me as I started up the stairs to my room, "Mr. Douglas called. When I told him you had just arrived, he said to tell you he was on his way over. Shall I serve tea in the sitting room?"

I looked at my watch. It was after five. "I suppose so," I replied. The sooner I told him, the better it would be for all of us. "Kate," I said, stopping her as she started to walk away, "are my parents still resting?"

"I believe so," she answered. "I've seen no sign of either one since shortly after their arrival."

I muttered a grateful "Thank goodness" under my breath. The last thing I needed was an audience. "Did Ian say when he would be arriving?"

"He called from Peebles, but I believe he meant to stop off at home to drop off his purchases. I'll have tea ready at five-thirty. That should give him plenty of time."

Twenty minutes. I had twenty minutes to collect my thoughts and plan how I was going to tell him about the baby without sounding desperate for a wedding ring. I knew not to underestimate Ian. He could be very persuasive when he wanted something and I was the last person to withstand his personal appeal especially when it was something I very much wanted myself.

In the bathroom, I pulled back my hair, secured it with a barrette, and splashed water on my face. The hollows under my eyes looked like giant bruises against my skin. I frowned and studied my reflection in the mirror. Fatigue had done its worst. Where was the glow pregnant women were supposed to radiate? I looked every bit of my thirty-seven years. Releasing the clip, I finger-combed my hair into its usual neat bob. How was I going to make it through the next hour?

Glancing at my watch, I saw that I had ten minutes. Ian was never late. I debated between changing my clothes or putting my feet up. As always, comfort prevailed over ego. With a sigh of relief, I climbed up on the high bed and pulled the pillows into a comfortable position behind my head.

Almost immediately I felt it, the aching temples, the dizziness, the pull of the past. Across the centuries, Jeanne Maxwell called to me. Her thoughts, her words, her laugh, were so like mine, she no longer appeared as an apparition. The dreamlike quality of my earlier visions had completely disappeared. I saw and heard and smelled and touched with the brilliant, diamond-edged clarity of a never-to-be-forgotten moment in time.

❈18❈

Traquair House
July 30, 1513

"How does it flatten out so easily for you?" Jeanne asked as she pulled impatiently at the clumps of wool balling up on the spindle. "I've two good eyes, and all I get is a sticky mess."

Grania Douglas smiled indulgently. "Ye ha' no patience, lass, and with a hundred servants, ye ha' no need."

Jeanne frowned and rescued the ball of yarn from her daughter's berry-stained hands. "I hate it when you say that. It makes me feel as if I were a stranger." Her eyes held a curious, hunted look, like that of an animal caught in an awkwardly sprung trap. "I'm the same person I always was."

Grania chuckled. "Aye, tha' ye are, lass. But I canno' remember that ye e'er enjoyed spinnin'."

Jeanne looked down at her oily hands and laughed. "I never did," she admitted. Throwing aside the pin, she lifted her daughter to her lap. " 'Tis time you joined your brother, my love." She glanced over at the crib, hidden behind a hanging blanket that divided the living quarters from the sleeping area.

"He sleeps like the dead," she whispered to Grania. "There were times, just after he was born, when I would rest my head on his chest to be sure he still breathed."

Grania nodded. "The bairn is a restless lad. He sleeps t' renew the blood in his veins." She nodded toward the black-haired child in Jeanne's arms. "Do no' make the mistake o' believing wha' is righ' fer the lad is the same fer Isobel. Mark my words, yon lass is different."

A chill ran down Jeanne's spine, and she hugged the tiny

girl to her breast. "You've said that before, Granny, but I cannot believe it. She is no different than I was. Mother told me so."

Grania's sightless eyes narrowed. "Ye were no' in the common way yersel'. Yer mother ne'er wanted to see it."

Jeanne changed the subject. "John doesn't like it when I come here."

"Does he forbid ye?" Grania's skillful fingers continued their task as she spoke.

"He would never do that," Jeanne was quick to assure her. "But the talk about your healing grows uglier by the day."

Grania sighed. "Do no' concern yersel', lass. T'was always the way."

"The king is very superstitious," Jeanne continued. "Now that he plans to invade England, you must be more careful than ever. Stay home," she pleaded. "There are healers to care for the villagers. In every corner, spies wait like vultures to pick over the carrion. Do not give them a reason to question you."

"Yer a dear lass t' be so concerned, but here in the hills, nothing changes. Do no' worry so."

Jeanne sighed. This argument between the two of them was an old one. As usual, Grania would do as she pleased. Isobel's weight in her lap felt heavy. Peeking around the black hair framing the child's face, Jeanne saw that her eyes were closed. Carefully, so as not wake her, she carried her to the crib and laid her beside her brother. She looked down on her children and smiled. They were so alike in appearance and yet so different in temperament, much like John and herself, she admitted.

Andrew was a child of light and laughter. His moods were predictible, his temper even. He ate and slept as he did everything, with great gusto and total appreciation. Isobel was completely different. Wraithlike and delicate, she moved with an instinctive grace that was unlike any child Jeanne had ever seen. Her quicksilver moods and frequent bouts of temper kept the entire household in a state of nervous anticipation. Difficult as it was to admit, there were times when Jeanne did not enjoy caring for her only daughter. Those nights when Isobel screamed relentlessly in her arms, she would pace the nursery floor, teeth clenched, nerves stretched taut like the strings of a lyre, believing she would never know the comfort of a full night's sleep again.

Only John could calm the child. He would take her in his arms and kiss the tears on her small, contorted face and whisper soothing words into her ear. Jeanne would creep away for a few hours of much-needed rest, grateful for his tolerance, yet resentful at the same time. When she questioned him, begging to know the secret of his skill, his eyes would dance with amused laughter. He would stroke her cheek and say, "I am adept at handling Maxwell women, Jeannie. As I recall, you were very like Isobel when you were small."

Her eyes softened as she looked at her sleeping daughter. Isobel Maxwell was a lovely child. She tucked the blanket around her daughter's body and bent down to kiss her cheek.

A gurgle of laughter interrupted her. Jeanne looked at her son. Andrew was awake. She held her finger warningly against her lips. Andrew rolled over to look at his sister. Satisfied that she slept, he held out his arms to his mother. Sighing, Jeanne lifted him over her daughter. Andrew was much heavier than the slender, small-boned Isobel. Why had no one ever told her that rest was a forgotten luxury for mothers?

"'Tis a lovely day, sweetheart," she whispered. "Would you like to pick some flowers?"

The child nodded and squirmed to escape from her arms. Hastily, Jeanne set him on the floor and took hold of his hand. "'Tis a warm afternoon, Granny," she said, careful to pitch her voice low so as not to disturb her daughter. "I'll take the horse and walk Andrew down to the burn. Isobel should sleep for now."

Grania smiled and nodded as they walked out the door. The sun was warm on Jeanne's head as she lifted her son to the saddle of her mare. Andrew clutched the leather of the pommel and looked around delightedly. It wasn't often that he was allowed to ride without the restraining arms of an adult around him.

Andrew Maxwell was three years old, but already he knew the measure of his own importance. As heir to the earldom of Traquair, his very existence was the beacon upon which his household revolved. He had only to thrust out his lower lip or stamp an insistent, sturdy foot and whatever he wished for was instantly realized. Oddly enough, the knowledge of his power made him reluctant to use it. The servants, his nurse, his mother, even his father, were like dry leaves before the storm of his strong-willed, yet personable charm. The only one to ever thwart him was Isobel. As is often the case with those who have everything, knowing that he could not control his tiny, imperious sister made her all the more appealing to him.

Intuitively, Andrew knew that she was not as important to Traquair House as he was, and his sensitive heart ached for her. By the time the twins were two years old, it was not unusual to see the small boy offer his smaller sister the use of a toy or a choice bit of sweetmeat. He preferred her company over everyone else's. The two of them could often be found digging in the garden or mounding hay in the barn. Andrew's face lit with joy at the sight of a smile on his sister's small, serious face.

Although he did not realize it, caring for Isobel was a tremendous strain for such a small boy. A ride in the country with his mother meant freedom, and he reveled in it.

Jeanne smiled at her son. He looked unusually content, his small body swallowed up by the too-large saddle. The sun touched his hair, picking out strands of fire in the night-dark cap hugging his forehead and cheeks. He grinned down at her, caught up in the warm wind brushing his face, the smell of pine and marshland, the cry of the lone curlew circling overhead, and the trickle of a burn over the next hillock.

Following the pony path, they reached the shaded banks in less than an hour. Jeanne lifted her son to the ground and wound the reins of her horse around the sturdy limb of a black oak tree. Testing the ground for dampness, she curled up in a sunny spot at the base of a weathered rock.

Andrew picked up a stone and threw it into the water,

close to his feet. The splash drenched his trousers. He laughed, a cheerful infectious sound that warmed Jeanne's heart. She laughed with him. "Be careful, love. We've no other clothing for you until we go back to the croft."

Andrew ignored her. He lifted another stone and again threw it into the sparkling burn. Wiser this time, he stepped back, escaping the leaping stream of water. Again and again he threw the stones, fascinated with the response of the crystalline drops, until his supply was exhausted. Chewing his lip, he looked at the opposite bank and then at his mother. Jeanne shook her head.

Disappointed, Andrew busied himself with throwing sticks into the current and watching them float. Finally, he grew bored. Climbing up the bank, he curled up against his mother's legs and fell asleep. Within moments, Jeanne's eyelids drooped and she too drifted into a contented slumber.

The smell of charred wood woke her. Cocking her head to one side, she inhaled tentatively. The scent was too acrid for a peat fire. No, it was definitely the smell of burning wood, and it came from the direction of Grania's croft. Shaking Andrew awake, she scooped him into her arms and walked swiftly to her horse. Settling the child in the saddle, she climbed up behind him and set out at a full gallop.

By the time she reached the rise, the cottage roof looked like an angry ball of flames against the darkening sky. Her blood froze at the sight below her. Men on horses, wearing the king's livery and carrying torches, circled the dwelling. Where was Grania? Dear God, where was Isobel?

Knowing she was already too late, Jeanne raced her mare down the hill, her arms locked like a vise around her son's middle. Less than fifty paces from the inferno, she drew up her horse. A guard carried a struggling Grania from the flames. Before Jeanne's horrified gaze, he held the old woman's arms behind her while another leaned from his horse and with the tip of his sword, sliced her open from throat to belly. Bile rose in Jeanne's throat and her stomach churned.

"Mama." Andrew's anxious voice pulled her from her state of frozen immobility.

"Hush, darling." Jeanne looked around frantically. The rain-damp soil had muffled the sound of their approach. The guards hadn't yet spotted them. Jeanne knew she couldn't hope to outrun the men. Turning the mare around, she rode for the cluster of trees at the bottom of the rise. Her heart pounded, and a cold sweat drenched her skin. Taking deep breaths, she forced herself to remain calm. Logic told her that Isobel was dead and she must not risk her son's life. But she pushed the thought away. No power under heaven could make her ride away without knowing the fate of her daughter.

When they reached the safety of the trees, she lifted his chin. "Andrew," she said, her voice very calm. He looked back at her with round, solemn eyes. "You must allow Gwenhara to take you home. She knows the way." Desperately, Jeanne fought back tears. "Do you understand, my love? Mama will not be with you, but you must go home. Tell Da-Da we need him at Grania's croft. Can you do that, Andrew?"

He nodded.

"Very well then." She slipped to the ground and coiled the reins loosely around a bridle strap. "Gwenhara is a gentle horse," she reminded the child. "Speak to her quietly and she'll not harm you."

The mare's ears twitched. She turned her head to look back at her mistress as if to assure herself that the curious lightness in the saddle was intentional. Jeanne gave her a gentle tap on the flank and watched as she carried her precious burden out of the clearing and up the hill.

Biting her lip, Jeanne gathered her skirts, forcing herself to walk out of the shelter of trees toward the croft. Every instinct urged her to run, to fly on the wings of falcons, to dive into the the very heart of the flames and search the ruined croft for her child. Instead, she walked, head held high, chin lifted in haughty arrogance. The men before her were guards, unruly men who responded to only one thing: authority. She did not want them to think even for a moment that she was a peasant out for a walk on the moors.

Like a cold stone weighting down her chest, Jeanne knew that if Isobel were inside the cottage, there was no longer any hope for her. There was nothing left of the thatched roof. Jeanne prayed that somehow Grania had seen what was coming and hidden the child in the hills. Intent on their grisly business, the men did not notice Jeanne's approach until she was almost upon them.

"What have we here?" A guard with blackened teeth leered at her.

"I am the countess of Traquair," she announced. "This is my land. What are you doing here?"

Another man, obviously the leader, turned his horse and scowled down at her, noting her simple gown and lack of jewels. "'Tis a strange countess who travels alone on the moors without even so much as a horse to her name."

"Nevertheless," insisted Jeanne, "my husband is John Maxwell, earl of Traquair. The woman you killed is his tenant."

"We but follow the king's orders," the man growled.

"Since when does Jamie Stewart make war on old women and children?"

"There are no children here," he insisted, "only a witch whose time had come."

Jeanne nodded toward the burning croft. She spoke clearly, emotionlessly. "The woman you killed was minding my bairn. If her body is found inside, you will hang."

The guard looked down upon the slender, arrogant figure standing before him. It didn't occur to him to doubt her. There was something about her carriage and the regal tilt of her head that spoke of noble blood and centuries of command. He frowned and considered his situation. She was obviously alone. If the remains of her child were discovered in the croft, his life wouldn't be worth a single copper. Still, he wasn't a butcher. The thought of bairns and murder in the same breath left a sour taste on his tongue.

He issued a terse command. "Search what is left of the dwelling. Do not spare yourself."

Without a word, two men dismounted and ran to the back of the croft. Agonizing seconds passed. Jeanne's hands were bloody from deep wedges carved with her own fingernails. Finally, she heard a shout. Her heart pounded against her ribs. The two men, one half dragging, half carrying the other, came around the building. The one who gave the order dismounted and walked over to them. Jeanne couldn't hear their conversation. At last, he turned and walked toward her.

"There is no sign of a child in the croft," he said.

Jeanne searched his face, noting the averted eyes and the dull red staining his cheeks. He lied. She was sure of it.

She could bear it no longer. Isobel would not be buried in a crypt of flames. Without warning, she lifted her skirts and ran straight toward the burning door.

"Seize her," someone shouted.

Just as she reached the threshhold, strong arms pulled her back. Desperation gave her strength. She struggled, pulled away, and was seized again. Tears of pain and frustration coursed down her cheeks. "Please," she sobbed, twisting in the steellike grip. "Let me go."

"Do as she says," a voice cried out. "If she is who she claims to be, we are dead men."

"Nay," another protested. "We are the king's messengers. The child's death was an accident."

The leader stroked his chin thoughtfully. Perhaps there was a way out of this after all. Would Jamie Stewart not question why the countess of Traquair allowed her child to keep company with a known witch?

It was nearly dark. The borders at night was no place for a small company of men. "Bind her," he ordered. "We shall take her to Edinburgh."

"No." Jeanne's voice cracked. "I won't go."

The man's massive hands clenched. He drew his dirk and approached the spot where she stood between her captors. Deliberately he ran his thumb down the deadly blade. A small red line appeared on the fleshy pad. "Lady," he said, his voice low and ugly, "you shall come with us or prepare to end your life as you stand."

She spat in his face. "I would rather die than travel one league in the company of murderers." There was no trace of fear in Jeanne Maxwell's eyes. She glared at him openly, not bothering to hide the hatred in her heart.

Sweet Jesu, the man thought, she was lovely! For a moment, he allowed himself the normal appreciation of a man for a beautiful woman. With her disheveled hair and plain gown, she looked very much like a lass of his own order. He wondered briefly what it would be like to have such a woman for his own. He discarded the idea immediately. The Maxwells were kin to the Stewarts. It was blasphemous to think such thoughts.

He turned away. "You will ride with me."

Suddenly, a voice rang out in the darkness. "Unhand my wife."

Jeanne closed her eyes and nearly sobbed with relief. Andrew had found John. Her son was safe.

A hand closed around her throat. "Safe passage for my men, or the lady dies."

"I think not, lad." Amusement colored John Maxwell's words. "Every man with me is skilled in archery. At this very moment an arrow is aimed at your heart. I'll take the chance that it finds its mark before you carry out your foul deed."

Reluctantly, the hand loosened from around Jeanne's neck. She took a deep, cleansing breath and walked past the frozen guards to her husband's side. Her mouth opened to tell him about Isobel, but the words wouldn't come. Tears crowded her throat and spilled down her cheeks.

John's smile turned to concern. Leaning down, he lifted her into his arms. "What is it, love?" he asked. "Are you hurt?"

She shook her head. If it were only that. If only she didn't have to tell him. He would surely blame her for leaving the child with Grania. The ache in her heart was unbearable. Burying her head in her husband's shoulder, she sobbed uncontrollably.

Frowning, John looked at the burned-out croft. His jaw hardened. "Where is Grania?" It was too dark to see the old woman's dismembered body lying on the ground.

"Dead," Jeanne whispered. Her fingernails dug into his hands. She couldn't bear for him to ask the question that would surely come. Gathering her courage, she looked directly at him. "Isobel was asleep in the croft."

At first, her message didn't register, and then, all at once it did. Jeanne watched as his eyes reflected the stages of his loss. First, bleak understanding, then pain, and finally rage.

Without looking at his wife's face, he deliberately lifted

one arm and signaled to the men who followed him. Immediately, Jeanne felt a rush of wind against her face. She heard a cry and watched Grania's murderer crumple to the ground with an arrow in his heart. John signaled again. Another man fell, this time without a sound. Again and again, John lifted his arm until every man who wore Stewart colors lay lifeless in the dirt.

Only then did John walk his horse to the croft and dismount, reaching up to untie the rolled-up plaid behind his saddle. The shooting flames were out, leaving only the charred remains of a mud wall and a smoking wooden frame.

Jeanne watched as her husband disappeared behind the wall. Moments later he reappeared, carrying a plaid-wrapped bundle. She slid to the ground and held out her arms. John walked into them, refusing to relinquish what was left of his daughter.

Pressing her face against the plaid, Jeanne breathed in deeply. Beneath the acrid smell of smoke and death, she detected the faintest scent of blackberries. Her eyes burned as the tears welled up again. Clinging to the familiar plaid, she gave herself up to a heartbreak too vast for words.

❋ 19 ❋

Traquair House
1993

"Miss Murray," Kate called through the door. "Mr. Douglas is here to see you."

I sat up, groggy and disoriented. My eyes burned, and I was conscious of a weariness more profound than anything I'd experienced before. I rubbed my cheek, and my fingers came away wet. The ache in my heart wasn't imaginary. I felt a deep, soul-consuming loss for Isobel Maxwell. For me, the events leading to her death happened just moments ago, not five hundred years in the past.

Kate's knock was more persistent.

"Tell Ian I'll be down in a minute," I said. There was silence and then the sound of her footsteps as she walked down the hall.

Fortified by a hairbrush and a splash of cold water, I followed her down the stairs. Ian stood when I entered the sitting room. He studied my face, and his eyes narrowed.

I saw no point in postponing the inevitable. "I'm sorry I missed our appointment, but I had some shocking news."

"At the post office?" he asked dryly.

I blushed. "No. At the doctor's office." Taking a deep breath, I walked over to the couch and sat down, motioning for him to sit beside me. "We're going to have a baby," I announced bluntly.

Other than a sudden tightening of his jaw, his face didn't change. "I see," he replied.

It wasn't the reaction I'd expected, and suddenly I was as desperately insecure as the day Stephen told me our marriage was over. Looking away from Ian's handsome tight-jawed face, I realized, miserably, that I'd once again taken too much for granted. It would be better to get this entire conversation over with. I swallowed and mumbled. "Aren't you going to say anything?"

"That depends."

"On what?"

"On your plans," he said, keeping his voice even. "I believe I've already declared myself more than once, but I haven't heard you respond. I noticed that you said *we* are going to have a baby. Does that mean I'm included?"

I stared at him in surprise. Was it possible that he was as unsure of me as I was of him?

"Well?" he persisted.

"I don't know," I whispered. "Do you want to be included?"

"Are you serious?"

I nodded.

Ian sighed and stood up. Balling his fists, he thrust his hands into his pockets and walked over to the mantel. For a long time he stared into the fire. Finally he spoke. "What are you afraid of, Christina?"

"Nothing," I began.

"Stop it!" He had never used that tone of voice before, and it startled me. "Tell me the truth, for God's sake. You've told me everything else."

"All right," I said, carefully. "I will tell you."

He turned around, his eyes fixed on my face.

"For fifteen years I was married to a man who was cold and selfish and dishonest. The greatest gift he gave me was when he walked out of my life. But for that, I'd still be with him, suffering in silence, believing I was the one with the flawed personality. Is it any wonder that I need it spelled out for me?"

"Do you really believe that has anything to do with me?" Ian spoke slowly, controlling his temper.

"No. But I'm not really a very good judge of character. Before I married Stephen, I thought I knew him as well as I knew myself." I was crying now, and my nose began to drip. Ian reached into his pocket and without saying anything crossed the room to hand me his handkerchief.

"Thank you," I mumbled, wiping my nose. "The worst of it is, I would still have been there if he hadn't left me."

"Christina." He knelt at my feet and took my hands in his. "It isn't that way with us. You must know that."

"How do I know it? You've never really told me."

He started to smile, then thought better of it. I sniffed and returned his handkerchief. He stuffed it into his pocket. "I won't press you for an answer now, but I want you to marry me." He hesitated briefly. "I'd planned to ask you anyway, even before I knew about the child. Do you believe that?"

I nodded, unable to meet his eyes, feeling more miserable than ever and not sure why.

"I know things are different in America, but this is Scotland and Peebles is a small town," he continued. "If you intend to live here, I ask you to consider our child's future. Will you do that?"

I stared at him. "Would that be enough for you, a

marriage based on the fact that you accidentally fathered a child?"

He dropped my hands and stared at me, dawning realization on his face. "I'm not doing this very well, am I? Surely you know that I love you. And whether you admit it or not, you love me. I can't think of a better reason to go through life together. Can you?"

"May I come in?"

Ian and I turned at the same time. My mother stood framed in the doorway, a wooden smile on her face. My cheeks burned. How long had she been there?

"Am I interrupting anything?"

Ian took the initiative. Walking toward the door, he held out his hand. "You must be Christina's mother. Welcome to Scotland, Mrs. Murray. I'm Ian Douglas, a neighbor."

"Thank you." She took his hand for the briefest of exchanges.

I had known her long enough to understand what she was up to. In the most subtle and ladylike way, she was expressing her disapproval. Only an idiot would misunderstand her message, and Ian was no idiot. The tiny seed of antagonism that was inevitably present when my mother decided to turn unreasonable sprouted into a desire to defend Ian. I found my voice. "Ian was proposing to me, Mother."

"Really?" The blond eyebrows lifted. "Proposing what?"

"Marriage."

"Oh." She was definitely not happy.

"Why are you looking at me like that and why are you so surprised that someone wants to marry me?"

"I'm not at all surprised," she said coolly, seating herself on the couch beside me. "You are a lovely, intelligent woman, Christina. What surprises me is that anyone would be foolish enough to consider such a commitment after only a brief period of acquaintance." She poured herself a cup of tea. "Unless I'm mistaken, the two of you just met, didn't you?"

"We did," Ian interjected smoothly. "Was yours a long engagement, Mrs. Murray?"

I stared at Ian. How had he known?

Mother's voice was strained when she answered. "I knew

my husband only two months, Mr. Douglas. But I had not been recently divorced, and I was not at all vulnerable to the first man who showed an interest in me."

"I don't believe Christina is all that miserable over her divorce," replied Ian. "I'm not exactly a fortune hunter, you know, and even if I were, her father acting as her lawyer could assure that I would have no access to her inheritance. I believe it's called a prenuptial agreement."

"I wasn't suggesting that at all," Mother said so hastily that I knew he'd pinpointed exactly what she'd been thinking. "The mistake would be just as devastating for you if Christina decided she'd made a mistake."

"I'm willing to take that risk."

I could see the white caps of her knuckles as her hands clenched the handle of the teacup. She was losing the argument, and there was nothing that made Susan Murray angrier than someone who disagreed with her and won.

"Why not wait?" she asked. "Surely, six months or a year isn't too long to decide if marriage is in your best interests."

I looked up and found Ian's eyes on my face. We stared at each other for a long time. I knew exactly what he was asking. Finally, I sighed and nodded. He smiled, a brilliant, blinding smile of relief that altered my breathing and made everything else in the room dim in comparison. When he spoke, his words were exactly the ones I needed to hear. No one, not even my skeptical, suspicious parent, could doubt that he was sincere.

"I've loved your daughter from the very first moment I saw her, Mrs. Murray. If we waited six months or ten years to marry, it would make no difference to me. My feelings won't change. But the fact is, Christina and I are going to have a child and I very much want my name on his birth certificate."

Until now, I believed that I'd experienced every reaction possible from my mother's considerable repertoire of disapproving emotions. I'd expected anger and disgust, even outrage. At best, I'd hoped for coldness and long telephone silences across the Atlantic when I broke the news. Nothing, in all the years of our relationship, prepared me for what happened next.

Her hands shook as she set her cup and saucer on the tea tray. She placed both palms against my cheeks and looked at me. Then she swallowed, looked away, and then looked back again, searching my face with a look of yearning hunger that I couldn't begin to explain. I watched her color come and go and her eyes fill with tears. She tried to speak and couldn't and then tried again. "Are you sure, Chris?" she asked haltingly, brokenly, as if afraid to hope.

"Yes."

"How did it happen?"

For the first time in that entire tension-filled afternoon, I laughed. No one, with the exception of a woman who'd reconciled herself to never becoming a grandmother, would have posed such a leading question. From across the room, Ian grinned at me. I decided to lighten the mood.

"The usual way," I said. "Ian and I—"

"Never mind," she interrupted in a voice much closer to her normal tone. "I didn't mean that."

"I know." I covered her hands with mine. "Miracles do happen. Maybe it just wasn't right before this."

"And now it is?"

"Yes," I replied. "Now it is."

She stood, her emotions once again completely under control. "I don't think your father should be the last to know. I'll wake him, and we'll celebrate. You do have champagne, don't you, Christina?" she asked, stopping briefly on her way out the door.

I shrugged my shoulders. "Probably. Ask Kate."

She disappeared into the hall. "Oh, Kate, there you are." I heard the surprise in Mother's voice and assumed that Kate had been eavesdropping again. "My daughter and Mr. Douglas have announced their engagement," she continued. "We need a bottle of champagne immediately."

"Of course, Mrs. Murray," I heard Kate reply. "I'll bring one up right away. May I offer my congratulations?" The woman actually sounded delighted.

"I think Kate approves," I said to Ian.

He sat down beside me and pulled me into his arms. "Everyone approves, especially me. What made you change your mind?"

"Mother," I confessed. "Every time she states her opinion, I disagree. Things haven't changed much since I was a little girl."

He chuckled, and his lips brushed against my hair. "I have a feeling that she's bested you this time."

I pulled away to stare at him. "What do you mean?"

"Your mother is an intelligent woman, Christina. I can't say for sure, but I believe she heard a great deal before she made her presence known. What I am sure of is that she understands the relationship between the two of you much better than you think. She doesn't strike me as a woman who would encourage you to raise a child alone when there is a man anxious to marry you."

He was right. I'd been the victim of reverse psychology, hoaxed by my own mother in the most transparent of ploys. I wasn't as indignant as I pretended to be. After all, the outcome was something that I really wanted. Mother's nudge had clarified my feelings. I was actually grateful to her, but I didn't plan on telling her that. She'd tasted enough victory for one day.

I leaned into Ian's embrace, content to let the events of the day rest, when I suddenly remembered that he didn't know about Jeanne Maxwell's twins. Tilting my head back, I looked up at his face. His forehead was smooth, and the white line that appeared so frequently around his mouth had disappeared altogether. Poor Ian. For the first time I realized that I wasn't the only one experiencing the strain of our predicament. Should I tell him now, or wait? I hesitated. One more day wouldn't make a difference. I relaxed against his shoulder and felt his arm tighten around me.

"Is it me or is it unusually cold in here?" he asked.

I laughed. "It's never warm enough for me unless it's eighty degrees outside. Shall I turn up the thermostat?"

"Don't bother," he said. "I'll add more peat to the fire."

He was right. It was cold. Uncomfortably so. I felt it as soon as he stood up. Scooting over to his place on the couch, I curled up in the leftover warmth of his body and watched as he rebuilt the fire.

I frowned. Ian's movements were very strange, like a frame frozen in slow motion. The block of peat he'd tossed into the flames seemed to float on the air and bounce several times before settling on the grate. Slowly, very slowly, he turned around. His eyes, distinctly blue across the length of the room, found mine and widened. Like an old movie reel on a projector operating at the wrong speed, his arm reached out, fingers extended in a desperate appeal.

I tried to stand, to reach out to him, but an enormous pressure held me back. His face contorted, and he cried out. The words he shouted were lost forever in a rush of darkness and roaring wind. Spinning, spinning, over and over, I lost all sense of up and down, dark and light. The walls turned around me, and I felt as dizzy as if I'd already imbibed more than my share of the promised celebratory champagne.

Finally, after a bout of nausea stronger than any I'd ever experienced, the room and my stomach settled themselves. I sighed with relief and turned to look for Ian. He wasn't there. In his place by the fire, a much larger and brighter one than I remembered, stood a lean, black-haired young man with eyes the color of clouds.

I stared at his clothes, at the jewels winking in his scabbard, at the cut of his hair and the shape and cast of his features. A long, silent moment passed before the drumming began in my head. This couldn't happen. It wasn't possible. What was I, Christina Murray, a twentieth-century woman, doing in a room with a man who'd been dead nearly five hundred years?

He looked concerned, as if something about me troubled him, and when he spoke, his words froze the blood in my veins.

"Not all the tears in Christendom will bring her back, Jeannie. Andrew needs you, and there is the new bairn to consider."

A surge of emotion swept through me at the sound of his voice. That lilting accented speech, the way he rolled his *r*'s, and the barest lift of his voice at the end of a syllable had disappeared from Scottish dialect centuries ago. That, more than anything else, convinced me that the impossible had happened. *One of us had transcended the barrier of time.*

I looked around at a Traquair I'd only seen in my mind.

There were tapestried walls, high-backed chairs, and embroidered pillows, the torches smoking in their sconces on blackened walls, the rush-strewn floors and above the mantel, the door-length portrait of Jeanne Maxwell that I'd seen, only this time it wasn't five centuries old. It looked newly painted, the colors brilliant and vivid, the woman breathtakingly alive against the radiant splendor of a Scottish spring.

"Jeanne." The timbre of his voice was low and terrifyingly intimate. I shivered. Reality splintered around me like a blast of icy air. It was as if I'd come out of a warm movie theater into the cold rain of a New England November. This man was John Maxwell, earl of Traquair, and he believed, without a doubt, that I was his wife.

I watched in fascinated horror as he pushed away from the mantel and walked toward me. Each controlled, deliberate step brought him closer to the settle where I sat. My mouth tasted like steel wool, and my hands shook with fear. I looked up, sick with the knowledge that any moment I would be exposed as an impostor. He would know the moment he touched me. Jeanne and I might look alike, but that was all.

A man who had lived with a woman, shared her bed, and given her children would know much more than the shape of her features or the color of her hair and eyes. He would know the feel of her lips under his. He would know her laughter and the familiar weight of her body in sleep. He would know every mark and line, every mole and curve, that made her who she was and infinitely unique from every other woman who walked the face of the earth.

Without speaking, he looked down at me for a long time. Then, with no hint or warning, he scooped me up in his arms and strode out the door and down the hall. I held my breath, afraid to speak, fearing the telltale evidence of my accent would damn me immediately, wondering how I could possibly explain the truth. *I'm terribly sorry, Lord Maxwell, but I'm not your wife. I just look like her. Actually I'm Christina Murray, one of her descendents, which makes me yours, too. I was born in the year 1956.* Of course, that didn't explain where Jeanne Maxwell was and why I was here, taking her place in the sixteenth century. Somehow I didn't think this determined young man who managed my weight as easily as if I were a five-pound bag of coffee would believe me.

I recognized the hallway immediately. There were no runners on the wooden floors and it was much darker without modern lighting, but the lovely carved doors inlaid with brass and the wooden floors were unmistakable. John Maxwell was taking me to bed.

He kicked the door open with his boot and closed it behind us the same way. Carrying me to the enormous curtained bed, he dropped me into its middle. Before I had time to react, he lowered his body on top of mine and pressed his mouth against my throat. I tensed, every muscle stiffening against the onslaught of his searching lips.

"Don't fight me, Jeannie," he begged, his breathing harsh against my ear. "Holy God! I'm not a monk. Let it go, love. Let it go and come back to me."

It was too much. Whether he believed me or not, I had to tell him. "I'm not—"

His lips stopped my words, and his hands moved skillfully, possessively over my breasts, evoking sensations that were both new and familiar. I felt free and unusually light and very unlike myself, half of me reveling in the sensuality of the moment, the other half detached and observant, seeking answers to this impossible new development.

Possibilities danced through my consciousness. Was I really here or was this an incredibly realistic dream that I would come out of with some new insight into the mystery of the stone? Why were John Maxwell's carresses so achingly familiar, and how did he know exactly what to do and where to touch with those lean, brown hands that brought such exquisite and long-forgotten pleasure? Memories danced through my consciousness. Memories of events the woman Christina Murray could never have experienced and yet were undeniably part of that other woman, the wanton one with her head thrown back, her lips parted and breasts arched, the one responding so completely and instinctively to John Maxwell's lovemaking.

At any moment, I could have gone over the edge. I know it

now, just as surely as I didn't know it then. Christina Murray would cease to exist. It was so close to happening, the assuming of another woman's identity, the entering into her mind and body, the swallowing of myself into that dark and misty portal of time from which there was no escape. I would have done it, knowing I was doomed to a miserable death, knowing I had no hope of returning to my life as I knew it. For that moment, it was enough to be held and soothed and possessed by a man I'd never dreamed could exist for me. Lured by the spellbinding magic of his touch, call it immoral or depraved, I would have given all I knew of heaven and earth to stay wrapped in his arms for whatever time I had left.

Some time later, I wasn't sure if it was moments or hours, he rolled off of me and pulled my head against his shoulder. "I love you, Jeannie," he murmured. "Don't ever leave me again."

My heart plummeted and then righted itself. This man knew nothing of Christina Murray. It was Jeanne Maxwell he loved. I had no place here in this vision I'd created for myself. Jeanne's life was over no matter what direction mine would take. As much as I longed to change the path of destiny, it was impossible. There was no going back for Jeanne or myself. The realization came suddenly on the wings of that strange rushing darkness and the spinning tunnel of wind.

Somewhere, in the wind and darkness, we passed each other, Jeanne and I. Somehow our thoughts connected, merged. We became of one mind, one consciousness. I, with a greater knowledge of the past and future, wondered what confusion she must have felt as we exchanged lives and she viewed my world as I viewed hers.

❈20❈

Traquair House
September 1513

Jeanne stirred in the large bed and flung her hand to the side where John usually slept, searching for the reassuring warmth of his bare skin. Finding nothing but smooth sheets, she sat up and looked around. He was seated in the only chair in the room, pulling on his boots. His sword and targe lay nearby. Wearily, she pulled a quilt around her and slid off the bed to stand beside her husband.

"Don't get up," he said. "'Tis still dark and much too cold."

"You've decided to go," she said accusingly. "Without even telling me, you were going to ride out like a thief in the night."

His jaw tightened, but he answered patiently. "I would hardly call bringing five hundred men into Jamie's army the work of a thief. I had no intention of deceiving you, Jeanne. Everyone at Traquair will hear us leave."

"I don't want you to go," she insisted stubbornly. "You said yourself that it was a fool's errand and there isn't the slightest hope of victory. Must I lose my husband as well as my daughter?"

His eyes softened, and he stood up, fully dressed for travel, and clasped her shoulders. "We won't speak of the worst," he said. "God knows I've been in enough battles and come away with no more than a scratch. This one will be the same." His words sounded hollow even to his own ears.

"This battle is different. You said it yourself. Ten thousand men against an English army of twice as many. 'Tis a death wish. Don't go, John," she pleaded. "This time Jamie Stewart asks too much of us."

"You know I cannot do that." He brushed her lips with his. "Come. Walk with me downstairs. The men wait."

She summoned her last argument. "John, I'm afraid. The dream I told you about came again and another one with it. This one was even stranger than before. 'Tis almost as if someone is trying to warn me."

He sighed and sat down on the chair, pulling her to his knee. "Tell me what you saw."

She settled against him, breathing in the reassuring warmth of his scent. "First, the same as before," she began. "I saw my own face, and yet I knew the lady was not myself. She beckoned me down a tunnel here at Traquair. It looked like the cellar where the wine is stored. She refused to speak, but I knew her thoughts. At the end of the tunnel was a large antechamber and a flat gray stone set in a place of honor. The stone glowed with a light that came from nowhere. We knelt together, the lady and I. I knew her mind as well as I know my own." She turned to him, flushed with excitement. "It was the Stone of Destiny, John. The stone that sits under the Coronation Chair in Westminster Abbey is not Scotland's true stone. The lady in my dream was Mairi of Shiels, and she did not give the true stone to Edward the Hammer."

John took her hands and rubbed them between his own. They were very cold. "Why is this so important to you? The deed is done. Mairi's guilt or innocence makes no difference to us now."

Her eyes, wide and gray as the North Sea, entreated him. "We must find the stone. If we do not, something terrible will happen. I know it." She saw the doubt in his face, and frustration surged through her. "Trust me in this. Please, John."

"What of your other vision? Was that one a warning as well?"

Jeanne frowned. "I know not. I was here at Traquair but in a room I've never seen before. There were people wearing strange clothing and speaking a language that was familiar and yet different from ours. I saw myself in the glass." Her voice grew whispery soft. "It was a wonderful glass, like looking into the clearest stream. Again, my face was the same, and I carried a bairn. I could feel him close to my heart." She rested her hand on her stomach. "My clothes were odd. I wore hose like a man that made my legs look long and thin, and my hair was clipped close to my head."

John frowned. The hour grew late, and he hated to leave her like this. Ever since Isobel's death, Jeanne had suffered from nightmares. Jamie's invasion of England could not have come at a worse time for Scotland and for his family. At first, the news that Jeanne was carrying a child had seemed like a godsend, but now he wasn't sure. She seemed so distant, so removed from life at Traquair. Even Andrew could no longer coax a smile from her. She woke at night, slipping out of the great laird's bedroom to walk aimlessly through the freezing corridors, a silent, wraithlike figure in a white nightshift, ethereally pale, her figure slight as a child's except for the small mound at her belly. In moments of despair, John feared that her trauma had been too great and that the woman he had loved for most of his life was lost forever. He looked at her now, her cheekbones striking and carven in her still face.

"Jeannie," he murmured. "I must go. Do not make it more difficult than it already is."

She looked at him, her eyes darkening briefly with the old rebelliousness he remembered so well. His breath caught in his chest, hoping against hope that his wife had returned to him. The look faded, replaced by the vacant stare he had seen so often in the past weeks.

"I'll watch from the window," she said. "You know how I feel. 'Tis too much to ask anything more."

He nodded and held her chin so that she looked directly at him. "Take care of yourself," he ordered gruffly, "and don't forget to eat. You're dreadfully thin. A man wants more in his bed than skin stretched over a bag of bones."

She looked mutinous again, and again his heart rejoiced at her words. "You told me you preferred a slim lass," she retorted, "and I'll eat when I feel like it."

"Tell me that you'll sit down to a meal three times a day."

She hesitated and then realized how foolish it was to resist. He had her interests at heart. Slowly, she nodded. "I promise."

Having won the match, he decided to press his advantage. "No sweets, Jeannie. Give me your word that you won't touch the sweetmeats."

"I'm not a child, John," she reminded him haughtily.

He smiled tenderly. "No, you are not. Kiss me good-bye, love. With luck, I'll see you within a fortnight."

It was the hardest thing she had ever done to watch him ride away. He was a wonderful horseman. From her room, she could see him stop at the Bear Gates and rein in his mount. Tears burned her eyes as he lifted his arm in farewell. He couldn't possibly see her, but he would know that her eyes were upon him until the last possible moment when he and his company of men disappeared into the distance. His horse reared and danced back on two legs. She saw his brilliant smile flash before he turned south toward the Cheviot Hills and Jamie's army. Jeanne's throat tightened. She knew deep in her bones that it was the last time she would watch him ride out from the gates of Traquair House.

With cold-numbed fingers, she dressed quickly, struggling to pull the tunic over her bulging stomach. Cursing under her breath, she threw the garment aside and pulled on the high-waisted gown and woolen stockings. Summer had lingered on through early September, warming the rolling border hills and farmlands to a comfortable temperature. But where Jeanne planned to go, beneath the ground into the dank cellars of Traquair House, down treacherous steps and thick, dripping walls, it was cold as the depths of winter. She plaited her hair, tying it off with a velvet ribbon, and pulled on her boots. Her ermine-lined cloak, a present from John, hung in the press. Slipping it over her gown, she picked up a candle and tinder box and hurried down the hall to the landing.

No one was about. She descended the stairs and pushed open the door to the wine cellar. Ice-cold air stung her face and burned her lungs. Clutching her cloak tightly around her, she made her way down the stone steps. The hall twisted and grew narrow. Jeanne stopped to light her candle and look around. She frowned. This hallway was lighter in color and wider than the one in her dream. Perhaps she had mistaken the direction and there was another way to the room she had seen. Another few steps and she would turn around. The candle flickered as she continued down the stairs. The air was cloying and stale, but that was all. There was no evidence of the strange light or the ghostly presence Jeanne had seen in her dream.

Where was the passageway? Frustrated, she stopped and thought. If anyone knew every corner of every room, every secret panel and tunnel, every escape hatch in this house, she did. Twenty-five years ago Flora had given birth to her upstairs in the laird's bedroom Jeanne now occupied with John. Traquair House had always been her home. There must be something she had overlooked. She clasped her hands together until her knuckles showed white beneath her skin. Time was running out. There was no explanation for how she could know such a thing, but she did. From the time she was a child, Jeanne knew she had been given the gift of *the sight*. Only Grania had understood, and she was dead, killed along with Isobel, by order of the king.

Wearily, Jeanne turned back and climbed the stairs. There were moments, they came more frequently now, when nothing mattered at all, when she considered allowing destiny to take its own course with no help from her. It would be so easy, she thought, to lay down the burden of the stone, of Scotland's destiny, and the future of the Maxwells, to close her eyes and sleep forever. Her daughter, her beloved Isobel, was dead, and if her instincts proved true, her husband would not survive Jamie's battle.

She paused at the door of the nursery. Andrew would be awake by now. He never slept past the first light of morning. She paused before opening the door. Did she have the strength to see her son? She was exhausted. The bairn affected her strangely. While carrying Andrew and Isobel, she had never felt so tired.

Before she came to a decision, the door opened, and a beaming Andrew, clutching the hand of his nurse, appeared on the threshhold. He had not expected his mother. His smile wavered.

Since the fire at the croft and the loss of his sister, his mother's moods were no longer predictable. There were long periods when she sat in silence, seeing and hearing nothing around her. Andrew was four years old. The events of the past weeks seemed liked a lifetime ago. At first, he had missed Isobel terribly, but as time passed, he grew accustomed to her absence. There were tenant children to play with, and although they could not replace the constant companionship of his sister, they did not burden him either. He no longer worried whether Isobel was content or warm or fed or whether some thoughtless act would bring on one of her tantrums. Isobel's death dissolved his restraint. Andrew was liberated. He became more childlike, more impulsive, more inclined to laugh. For that, his mother condemned him.

Riddled with guilt, Jeanne could not bear the sight of her son. Andrew had been her favorite, her even-tempered child, the apple of her eye. She would never forget the circumstances of Isobel's death. Lured by a few precious hours alone with her son, she had left her daughter to die. Whenever she looked at Andrew's sturdy body, heard his laugh, watched his cheeks glow with health, the lump of misery that never left her rose in her throat. The thought of another child, a son like Andrew or, God forbid, another Isobel, made her sick with despair.

"Hello, Mama." Andrew's voice lifted bravely. "I'm having breakfast."

Over his head, Jeanne's eyes met those of his nurse. "That's fine, love," she said. "I haven't eaten yet. Why don't I join you?"

The servant's face softened. Without a word, she transferred Andrew's hand from her own to his mother's and stepped back into the room.

Tears misted Jeanne's eyes as the small fingers grasped hers and she looked down into the trusting eyes of her son. "Shall we eat in the hall or the sitting room?" she asked.

Andrew cocked his head to one side. "In the garden," he said at last. "I want a picnic in the garden."

The heaviness inside Jeanne's chest lightened. For the first time in weeks, she laughed, a clear pure sound that delighted her son and rattled the diamond-paned windows above their heads. "Very well, Andrew. We shall picnic in the garden."

Sometime later, in the middle of salting her healthy portion of oats, it came to her like a streak of light illuminating the night sky. The passageway was not in the wine cellar; it began at the very top of the house in the priests' sanctuary. She could hardly contain her excitement. She looked across the table at Andrew. He smiled engagingly, and her heart melted. Despite everything that had happened, perhaps happiness was possible after all.

"Hurry and finish, love," she said. "Mama has something to do this morning, but later we'll take out your pony." She reached over to caress his cheek. "Would you like that?"

Andrew's brow wrinkled as he considered the matter. The ride across the moors on Jeanne's full-sized mare had ruined him forever for the small Highland pony he called his own. He wanted to ride a horse. Should he tell his mother and remind her of the nightmare that had taken Isobel from her? He chewed his oatcake and looked across the table into the wide, light-filled eyes fixed on his face. "Yes," he said at last. "I would like that."

After breakfast Jeanne left Andrew with the maid and proceeded up the stairs to the top of the house. Carefully she climbed the twisting stairs, turning sideways to squeeze through the narrow turns. The climb was steep. By the time she reached the top, she was out of breath. Bracing herself against the wall, she stopped to rest and look around.

The sanctuary looked very much as it had when she was a child, dark and old and very quiet. Jeanne could not remember the last time services had been held here. An altar with a statue of the Blessed Virgin stood against the far wall. Stunted candles, their wicks dark, stood in congealed pools of wax near a brass urn, empty now but at one time most likely filled with holy water. Stained glass covered the small windows and pillows for kneeling were scattered across the wooden floor.

Jeanne drew a deep breath, pushed herself away from the wall, and walked directly to a rosewood panel near the mantel. She knew exactly what she was looking for. With all her strength, she pushed at the carved wood and then stood back. A door, carved to match the wall, opened onto a narrow, stone tunnel. Her hand shook as she smoothed a loose strand of hair away from her face. She was sure this was it.

With her foot, she slid a pillow between the door and the wall to anchor it open and then stepped into the tunnel. It was very dark. Using the tinder box, she lit her candle and waited for her eyes to adjust to the meager light.

The passageway was narrow. A fully grown man with the shoulders to lift a broadsword would not squeeze through. Holding the candle above her head, Jeanne slowly made her way down the steep stairs. The air grew steadily colder as she traveled deeper into the ground. A dank smell of mold and airless caverns surrounded her. The hem of her skirt dragged heavily in the dampness. She wrinkled her nose, allowing herself only enough air to continue downward.

Moments later, or was it hours, she faltered, her foot stumbling on a jagged, irregular step. Dropping to her knees, she moved the candle over the stone. The pounding of her heart sounded thunderous in the silent darkness. It was the step from her dream. Out of the corner of her eye, Jeanne saw something flicker. She looked up, startled to see a pale glow in the distance. Clutching her cloak, she stood and moved forward toward the light. The space narrowed and darkened. The light disappeared. Frantic to find it again, she continued quickly down the twisting stairway. Suddenly the tunnel widened, and there were no more stairs, only a wall of granite with a narrow opening on one side. Turning sideways, Jeanne managed to squeeze through.

The room was massive and bright as day, lit by torches mounted on the walls. Tombs, embedded in the granite, were lined up side by side. The air smelled of herbs and candle wax. A small altar with a figure of the Holy Virgin and hundreds of flickering candles was set above a large irregular stone.

Jeanne's eyes widened as realization washed over her. This was the ancient burial vault of the Maxwells, sealed off more than two hundred years ago after the Black Death had swept throughout Scotland. The hair rose on the back of her neck. There was no logical way to explain the torches and candlelight after so many years had passed. Instinctively, she knew she was not alone in this granite kingdom of the dead.

She turned toward the Stone of Destiny. What she saw did not surprise her. She had seen it all before in her nightmares. A woman shrouded in a dark cloak, her face hidden, knelt and pressed her lips to the stone. Suddenly rays of light, warm and brilliant, illuminated the rock. She turned toward Jeanne and beckoned her forward. Together they knelt. Together they placed their hands on the stone.

The pulsing began in Jeanne's fingers, spreading to her temples and throat and chest. She could no longer separate it from the pounding of her heart. An explosion of light rocked the room and then a sensation of heat and she was alone, standing in the midst of a bloodstained battlefield.

Severed bodies, both human and animal, their extremities blackened with old blood and swarming flies, lay piled on top of one another. Groans of delirious men calling for water and pleading for a merciful death assaulted her ears. All around her she recognized the thick, heavy accents of the Highlands and the Isles, the more refined tones of Edinburgh, the border brogues. The flower of Scotland lay dying at her feet. Dear God, where was John?

Stepping over the dead and wounded, her eyes wet with tears and horror, she searched the field, stopping only to look carefully into a darkly tanned face, turning over the bodies of lean, black-haired figures, closing eyes that were brown or hazel, blue, green, and gray, but never John's. She saw Lennox and Argyll and Jamie's favorite, Lord Bothwell, lying in the dust, their lives forfeit to the king they loved.

Biting her lip, Jeanne continued on toward Pipers' Hill when her eye was caught by a winking jewel, brilliant in the afternoon sun. It was a rich, clear purple, the color of kings, and it adorned the hilt of a sword. Heart hammering, she knelt by the thick body of the man who clutched it even in death. She turned his head and brushed aside the graying hair. A low moan, more animal than human, welled up from her chest. Jamie Stewart, that gallant, brave, and impetuous monarch, had led his last charge. There was no hope for Scotland, no hope for those who fought the English at Flodden Moor.

❋21❋

As suddenly as it came, the vision disappeared. Once again Jeanne was in the brightly lit burial chamber. The woman with the Maxwell features was still there, gazing at her with compassion. Jeanne marveled at the lady's likeness. Looking at Mairi of Shiels was like staring at her own reflection in Saint Mary's Loch on a day without wind.

"Was that destiny I saw?" she whispered to the ghostly figure.

The woman remained silent.

"Speak," Jeanne cried in desperation. "Tell me what you want of me."

Mairi stared at her with haunted eyes. Jeanne's forehead wrinkled in concentration. What was the woman trying to tell her? "Help me, my lady," she begged. "Give me a sign."

A gust of cold wind blew back the folds of Jeanne's cloak and set the candle flames flickering. Suddenly, inspiration seized her. She reached out to clutch the woman's shoulders, but her hands touched only air. Mairi was gone as were the torches and glowing candles. Only the stone remained, bathed in the strange netherworld light that came from within.

Jeanne's single candle seemed to burn more brightly as she climbed the twisting stairway back to the sanctuary. She was filled with hope and brave new resolve. If what she believed was true, the battle had not yet been fought. It could still be stopped. Only then would it be safe to return the stone to Moot Hill and the throne of Scotland. She knew that her country's fate was sealed if Jamie Stewart fell in battle. His heir was a mere bairn and the queen was English. Fortunately, the king was a superstitious man, known for his fear of spirits and witchcraft. Jeanne, Grania's pupil, knew exactly how to prey on those fears.

Traveling alone, dressed in a man's breeks and jack, Jeanne guided her mount to the pony path leading to the gentle green gold hills of West Lothian and Linlithgow Castle. The road north was empty. All men of fighting age were camped in the Cheviot Hills, awaiting Jamie's arrival. He remained at the palace until the final hour. Indeed, it was what she hoped for. Tonight, at Saint Michael's Kirk, he would be at vespers in the royal stall. There, she would go to him.

Leaving her horse in the capable hands of the castle linkboy, Jeanne crossed the wide lawn leading to the twin turrets guarding the entrance. Wind from the loch pulled at her jack and twisted loose tendrils of her hair into knots. Clutching the bundle that carried her change of clothing under one arm, Jeanne walked past the guards into the receiving hall. It was completely deserted. She was relieved but not surprised. Most of the nobles had already left for England, and the queen's attendants were preparing for the evening meal.

Jeanne climbed the wide stairs to the second landing, where the Maxwell apartments were kept in readiness for an unexpected arrival. She opened the door and bolted it behind her. The room was cold as ice. After lighting the fire, she walked to the window and looked out, rubbing her arms against the chill. The view faced south toward the loch. Leaning against the frigid panes of glass, she gave herself up to the still, heart-wrenching beauty of her homeland and the memories it evoked.

To the west, as far as the human eye could see, wheat and millet swirled like golden waves in a churning tide. To the east, where the land was left uncleared, black oak and maple forests shadowed marshland rich with quail, wild duck, and curlew. To the south, the silver blue waters of Loch Lothian shone clear as glass beneath a summer sun. Years ago, armed with fishing poles and bait, a black-haired boy and his small companion had comandeered a boat nestled in the brush. Jeanne's mouth watered. She could still taste the crisp skin and the soft buttery flesh of their catch. Nothing before or since had tasted more like heaven than the speckled brown trout she had helped John pull from the watery depths.

Jeanne looked around the well-appointed bedchamber and her heart sank. The optimism of the day before had long since disappeared. If only her husband were here safe beside her. The room was warm. It was nearly dark. Vespers would begin in less than an hour.

Jeanne shook out her cloak and gown and laid them on the bed. She had chosen black to blend with the darkness in the kirk. Quickly, she unplaited and brushed her hair, allowing it to hang loose for the first time since her marriage. With nimble fingers she unbuttoned the jack, folded it away, and stepped out of the breeks. The dress was overlarge and flowed loosely around her body, concealing the child she carried. Looking into the glass, Jeanne smiled grimly. She had chosen well. With her long black hair, cloak, and gown, she truly looked like a harbinger of death.

She did not take the main hall to the kirk. Linlithgow was over two hundred years old and, like most ancient castles, had its share of hidden tunnels and passageways. Jeanne knew the one leading past the wall to Saint Michael's Kirk could be reached from the rooms near her own.

Taking a deep breath, she slipped out of the room and looked around. Again, she saw no one. Without a sound, she tiptoed to the door leading to the next room and leaned her ear against the wood. It was unlikely that the room was occupied, but Jeanne took no chances. She heard nothing. Pushing open the door, she stepped inside. Like her own, the room was dark and very cold. It was also unoccupied. Congratulating herself on the smooth flow of events, she walked to a painted frieze on the east wall. It was a depiction of the death of Wallace at Smithfield after the Battle of Falkirk. Normally Jeanne would take a moment to reflect on the silent agony of his face at the moment of death, but today she did not. Today she had no time to waste on past heroes. She pressed the center of Wallace's targe, and the hidden door cracked open.

Jeanne pushed it gently. It swung open, wide enough for her to step inside. She closed it behind her and waited until her eyes adjusted to the darkness. No one had traveled through this passageway for some time. In her youth, the occupants of this room made use of it often, and flaming torches lit the way. Now there was only darkness. She had not thought to bring a candle, and time grew short.

Bracing her hands against each wall, examining each new step with an exploring foot, Jeanne made her way through the sloping tunnel. Gradually, her feet moved more quickly. There were no steps and no unusual turns, just straight empty darkness. At last it was finished. The dark was not so absolute now. She had come out into the night, its blackness tempered by starlight and a full, silvery moon. The outline of Saint Michael's steeple loomed ahead.

Jeanne pulled up her hood to hide her face and hurried across the road into the rear door of the kirk. The royal stall was far to the front, near the altar. She must pass the posturing clergy and those few nobles who remained in Linlithgow to accompany their king. Not one of the worshippers kneeling on the granite floor of the kirk that night noticed the slim, dark figure slip behind the velvet curtains into the sanctuary where the king worshipped alone.

His eyes were closed. In the flickering candlelight, Jamie Stewart appeared much younger and very troubled. Jeanne was moved to pity. This man, this king so suited to rule, had made an irreversible error. He was intelligent enough to realize the enormity of his blunder. If he were a lesser man, if he had held another position, amends could be made, feelings pacified, the hurt assuaged. For James IV of Scotland, the rules were different. Jeanne knew it. She had always known it, but try she must.

Dropping to her knees, she crawled to the high altar and shook her hair over her face, hoping he wouldn't recognize her. It was a sin to disturb the king at Mass. Resting on the damask altar cloth was a silver bell. She grasped the handle and rocked it gently. The clear, high sound echoed like music throughout the chamber. Slowly, Jeanne stood, staying clear of the wedge of light thrown by the fire. The hood of her cloak hid her face, and her shadow loomed menacingly, larger than life on the stone wall.

Startled, Jamie looked up. Ever the warrior, his hand dropped to the hilt of his sword. "This is a private service, mistress," he announced. "Declare yourself and then depart."

She pitched her voice low. Fear gave it an unusual huskiness. "I am but a loyal subject, Your Grace. I come to warn you of your fate on the morrow."

He was on his feet now, his brow furrowed. "Tomorrow I meet the English at Flodden Moor."

"You will not be victorious," warned Jeanne. "You will die in battle and the flower of Scotland with you. Your son is but a child and your wife English. Think again, Jamie Stewart. Would you condemn your country to such a fate?"

"'Tis too late. I cannot withdraw now," insisted the king stubbornly.

"Holy God!" she whispered fiercely. "Would you have us English satellites subject to the will of an English king?"

Jamie's eyes narrowed suspiciously. "Who are you who speaks blasphemy to the king?" he demanded. "By what right do you come here during prayers and speak to me of treason?" He drew his sword and advanced toward her.

Jeanne shrank back, pulling the hood farther in front of her face. "Halt," she cried, holding her hand out before her. "Would you profane the House of God?"

"You've done that already, lass," said the king, lifting the wool from her face with the point of his sword. "Come. Step into the light. I wish to see your face."

Jeanne had lost, and the only emotion she felt was overwhelming weariness. She knelt at his feet. Her hood fell back, revealing her raven-black hair. Defiantly, she looked up, waiting for the look of shocked recognition in his eyes.

"By the blood of Christ," he gasped. "'Tis Jeanne Maxwell."

"Aye, Your Grace."

"Why do you do this?"

Slowly, she stood. "This meeting with the English is illfated. Many will die and Scotland will be destroyed."

Until now, he'd ignored the rumors linking Jeanne's name with witchcraft. His voice shook. "How do you know this?"

She stared at him, saying nothing, her face so still and pale it could have been sculpted from marble.

With an imperious gesture, Jamie waved away his knights. They moved back, and he lowered his sword. "Where is your lord?" he asked her.

"At Flodden Moor."

He nodded, satisfied. "I might have known John would not desert me. Does he know you are here?"

"No, Your Grace."

Something in her direct, clear-eyed gaze disturbed him. Jamie Stewart was king of Scotland. Before the age of sixteen, he'd outwitted men years older than himself, plunged into the very heart of political intrigue, and wrested the throne from his weak, ineffectual father. He could smell fear and deception from across the length of a room. Jeanne Maxwell was not afraid nor was she lying.

He cleared his throat and spoke softly so that only she would hear. "I would ask you a question, Lady Maxwell. You may refuse me. But know this. Whether you answer or no, you will be detained in the castle until after the battle. I have not yet decided what to do with you."

She smiled, and for a moment Jamie forgot he was a king. Holy God, the lass was lovely. He stepped closer and reached out to touch her cheek.

She turned her head. "What is your question, Your Grace?"

He dropped his hand, ashamed of his weakness. "Will I survive Flodden Moor?"

Jeanne paused for a long moment, wondering whether to spare him. "No," she replied at last.

He looked at her, the heavy-lidded eyes hard and black as coal. Finally, he nodded. "So be it." He motioned to a guard.

"Wait." Jeanne clutched his sleeve. "What I see is only a vision of what might be. It is not yet written in destiny. Change your fate and that of all those who die at Flodden Moor. Recall your men before the English army arrives."

This time he did touch her, his hand resting on the shining crown of her hair. "You are very lovely, Jeannie," he murmured, "and very brave. I envy your husband." The thought of his wife or any other woman braving his wrath to demand a war be stopped was both absurd and amusing.

" 'Tis too late," he continued. "Surrey has already arrived with twenty thousand British troops. At this moment the English army prepares for battle. If we retreat, they will follow us into Scotland and cut us down. Our towns will burn, women and children will die. No." He shook his head. "The time for retreat has passed. We will stand and fight. My men would have it no other way."

"Then you are doomed," she whispered.

He grinned, and the years disappeared from his face. "Miracles happen, lass. God knows I deserve one."

Jeanne did not protest when the noble she recognized as Sir David Lyndsay led her away to a small room inside the castle. It wasn't as large or elegant as the Maxwell chambers, but at least it was comfortable. A huge mantel covered one entire wall and heavy curtains enclosed the bed. Colorful tapestries kept out the drafts, and a small window set high in the wall provided air and light. She held her hands close to the blazing fire, hungry for the sustaining warmth of the flames. It was a pointless gesture. The ice around her heart had extended to every part of her. For Jeanne Maxwell there was no warmth in all the world.

Jamie Stewart's mood on his way to Northumberland was not pleasant. Against the better judgment of his magnates, namely Bishop William Elphinstone of Aberdeen, he was attempting the impossible, something no Scottish monarch had ever done before. He had turned his back upon a classic tradition and moved his men out of their own natural fortress to take on an enemy, rich, impetuous, powerful, flushed with victory, and tired of peace. In defense, the Scots had a chance. As the aggressor, victory was impossible. All this and more Jamie knew, and his heart was heavy.

He rode quickly, holding his mount to a pace few men could best. Before dawn, he'd passed through the valley of Whiteadder in the Lammermuir Hills and left Norham Castle and the River Tweed in the distance. The first light of dawn streaked the sky when at last he crossed Till and joined his forces in the Flodden Hills. Reining in his exhausted stallion, the king surveyed his battleground with satisfaction. Protected by three significant mountains, it was unassailable from the southwest, equally impossible from the south, and to the east an advancing army would have to cross the River Till. The only viable approach was from the southeast along the flat ground between the foot of Flodden Hill and the river. This narrow precipice with its marshy ground was much too dangerous for an army to attempt their attack.

Jamie had already decided to stay put on the hill and draw out his enemy. With Huntly covering Branxton Hill and Maxwell on Flodden Edge, the Scots could last until summer without losing a single man. Surrey, the English commander, encamped at Woller Haugh seven miles to the south, would not willingly walk into such a trap. If he failed to show this morning, the ninth of September, the Scots could retreat with honor. This was Jamie's only hope.

John Maxwell looked over his troops from his vantage point on Flodden Edge. Hundreds of peat fires flickered in the predawn darkness. Across the Till he heard the English army readying for battle. The night before, he'd sent a company of men across the border to pillage an English village. This act of destruction, in full view of the English army on English soil, was an attempt to provoke the earl of Surrey into an early battle. It was a masterly move. Had the earl been a less experienced man, the ploy would have worked. As it was, it did nothing more than cement him in his purpose.

Before John's astonished eyes, the English army now moved out of the range of Scottish cannons, moved northward into Scotland. For more than an hour he watched until the entire army disappeared behind the hills. A messenger on a lathered horse rode up.

"The king orders you to move your men to Branxton Hill. Burn the camp behind you."

John frowned. Surrey would hardly be foolish enough to leave the rear of his army open to attack on foreign soil. If Jamie was shortsighted enough to believe such an absurdity, he must be reasoned with. John ignored the order. "Where is the king, lad?" he asked.

"At Branxton Hill."

John's heart sank. Only an idiot would move his troops away from the natural fortress of the mountains to engage an army four times the size of his own. Digging his heels into the sides of his mount, John headed for Branxton Hill. Halfway there, he met the king, surrounded by a company of men riding south at a furious pace. They reined in their horses when they saw him.

"The English have doubled back across the Till," Jamie panted. "'Tis a trap. Secure your positions on the slope. Home and Huntly on the left. Errol, Crawford, and Montrose to the right, and you, Maxwell, shall ride with me in the center. Lennox and Argyll with the Highland divison on the extreme right and Bothwell will command the reserve behind the line."

"Please, Your Grace," John interrupted. "May I make a suggestion?"

"Speak," ordered the king.

"Your person is too valuable to lead a charge. If you should be wounded or, God forbid, killed, there is no victory for Scotland. Stay back with Bothwell and the reserves."

Jamie straightened in his saddle. "I am the king of Scotland. What kind of king sends his men into battle while he cowers behind the lines?"

John hesitated. By the day's end, they would all be dead. He had nothing to lose by speaking his mind. "What kind of king risks the future of his kingdom? Should we die today, will there be a Scotland for our sons?"

For a long moment Jamie stared into the icy gray eyes of the man before him. There was nothing the king admired more than courage, and it appeared that John Maxwell had more than his share. "Save your temper for the battlefield, Maxwell, and I'll bestow an earldom on you."

John's lips twitched. "I already have one, Your Grace."

Jamie threw back his head and laughed. "You're a right one, John Maxwell. Collect your troops and meet me on the slope."

John acknowledged defeat. The king was beyond reason. "Aye, Your Grace," he said flatly. Turning his mount, he returned the way he came.

Much of Flodden Edge was obscured by smoke from the campfires, but high on the ledge, he saw the remnants of the British army. Surrey's move was masterly. By pretending to invade Scotland, he'd doubled back and cut James's lines of communication, severing any potential retreat to his own country. The men, however, were in poor condition, tired looking, their feet dragging. When they marched into battle, they would not have the advantage of high ground.

By the time John rallied his troops and marched them to Branxton Hill, the English were filing over by the Pallinsburn Causeway. The blood drummed in his temples. This opportunity was too good to miss. He looked around. Where was Jamie? He saw him farther up on the slope. Urging his stallion to higher ground, John reined in beside the king. He spoke without using the formal address. "We can pick them off with our guns one at a time. Give the order, Your Grace."

Jamie shook his head. "No. I want no piecemeal methods. They shall be lined up before me in the hollow of my hand before we shoot. Let them come on to their slaughter."

John watched in horror as the English army swung right and then westward beneath them, to disappear out of sight. Another surge of Englishmen, led by Sir Edmund Howard, advanced over the Pallinsburn to join their brethren. Still Jamie did nothing.

The armies, although invisible to each other, were very close together. A shot was fired, and the Scots' master gunner fell to the ground. The enemy came from below, a surging wave of disciplined manhood shooting with the executed precision only battle-trained troops in the best of conditions occasionally acquire. They stayed well out of range of Scottish gunfire.

On the brow of the hill, Jamie's men were shot to pieces. In his rage and panic, he did the only thing possible given his nature and the position in which he found himself. He ordered a descent from the hill to engage the enemy directly, with himself at the head of the attack.

The simmering anger inside John's head burst into white-hot fury as he watched the king commit his suicidal charge. With short, clipped syllables, he ordered ten of his finest soldiers to his side. Drawing his sword, he raised his targe, gripped his reins, and charged down the hill with grim determination. There was no going back now. No quarter would be given. They must follow their valiant, foolhardy ruler and die.

An unforseen dip in the ground put them at a disadvantage, forcing them to come up in front of the enemy. The Scots had spears and swords, but the English were armed with deadly billhooks. The king's standard went down. Reaching to within a spear's length of Surrey, John Maxwell was stabbed through the chest by a savage sweep of a billhook. He killed five Englishmen before his spear broke in his hands. By nightfall the massacre was complete, and the English general claimed his victory.

Jeanne sat up on the bed and listened. The voices outside her chamber door sounded loud and angry. She was sure one of them belonged to a woman. Kicking the blankets aside, she climbed out of bed and looked up at the window. The light was dim and the air misty. It was early morning, the day following the battle.

The door opened and a woman stepped inside. Jeanne's eyes widened. It was Jane Hepburn, countess of Bothwell. She had not seen George Gordon's fiery-tempered sister for years. They had never been friendly, and from the look on Jane's face, it was clear that her sentiments remained unchanged.

" 'Tis over," she said. "Jamie is dead. All is lost."

Jeanne nodded.

"I've come to ask you a favor." Jane bit her lip. "My husband and my brother are at Flodden. We've had no word, and I cannot leave the queen. She is distraught with grief."

"What can I do?"

"Ride to Flodden. The English won't harm a woman. Find out what has become of our men. Send back word with a courier. There is no need to return."

"I am a prisoner," Jeanne reminded her.

Jane's mouth twisted with pain. "You are no longer of any significance," she said wearily. "We are all prisoners. Go now and godspeed."

For Jeanne, lost in her own thoughts, the miles passed swiftly. She stopped only to water her horse and gnaw at the fruit and bread she'd remembered to stuff inside her pack. She approached Flodden slowly, up the right bank of the Till, and looked across the river. To the southwest was Monylaws Hill, to the north Branxton, and to the south and southeast, Flodden Hill and Flodden Edge. The green-gold beauty of the borderlands on the cusp of autumn made the sight that greeted her eyes even more heinous than it already was.

Day-old bodies, their limbs severed, their wounds covered with maggots and black with old blood, littered the field. Beggars swarmed over the battleground, claiming their spoils, rifling through pockets, prying jewels from targes and swordhilts, pulling boots and weapons from men who had breathed their last breath. Moans of the wounded echoed among the hills. The stench was nauseating. Jeanne pressed the folds of her cloak against her nose. Her stomach hovered on the brink of rebellion.

Slowly, she crossed the river and slid from her horse. Once again she saw the blood and the flies. She heard the cries of dying men pleading for water, saw the bodies of Lennox and Argyll and Jane Hepburn's husband, Lord Bothwell. Fighting helplessly against a force she could not control, Jeanne moved on toward Pipers' Hill, stepping over maimed clansmen, staring anxiously at tanned, dark-haired men until again she saw the jeweled swordhilt and the beloved gray-streaked head of Scotland's hope twisted at an unnatural angle. She had seen it all before, but this time the pain was too great. The lump in her chest made it difficult to breathe. Where was John?

At the bottom of Branxton Hill, she found him. He was alive. Kneeling down in the thick mud, Jeanne pulled his head into her lap.

His eyes opened, and he smiled. "You're very pale, my love," he said. "Have you eaten?"

Jeanne sobbed and bit down on her bottom lip. He was nearly dead and still he worried about her health. The tears rolled down her cheeks. "Yes, John. I've eaten."

" 'Tis not wise for you to go without food. You must think of the bairn."

Unable to speak, Jeanne leaned over to kiss his forehead. Her tears wet his skin.

He lifted his hand to touch her face, but the effort was too great. "You're crying, Jeannie. Don't cry, love. Maxwells never cry." A bubble of blood formed at his lips, and his eyes closed.

Jeanne didn't know how long she sat there holding his lifeless body in her arms. Night fell. She must have slept because all at once it was morning. Sunlight blinded her, and at first she didn't see the circle of men on horseback surrounding her.

"'Tis Jeanne Maxwell," a familiar voice spoke. "What are you doing here?"

Mutely, she looked up at the man who would have been her husband.

"Come, lass," George Gordon said. "Speak. The last I heard you were imprisoned at Linlithgow."

Jeanne eased the blood-encrusted head from her lap and stood up. "Jane sent me. She wished for news of you and her husband."

The brown stallion pawed the ground. "Bothwell is dead," replied George Gordon shortly.

"Aye." Jeanne's pain-filled eyes were on his face. "Others share his fate."

His eyes flickered over her and dismissed the man at her feet. "Scotland has suffered a greater loss than your husband or Jane's. Where is your mount?"

"I left her at Piper's Hill yesterday."

George Gordon, the earl of Huntly, reached down to lift her to his saddle. "We shall find her, and then I'll escort you home."

The men around him murmured angrily. "She is evil, Huntly, a weaver of spells, a witch," one of them said. "The king would be alive today if she had not cursed the battle."

George sighed. He had been educated in Italy and spent three years as ambassador to France. Sometimes it was difficult to remember that his fellow Scots were not all enlightened men. "The king would be alive today if he'd listened with his head," he explained patiently. "Surely you don't need a witch to tell you that an army of five thousand has little chance of victory against one four times as large?"

Another man spoke. "What of Bannockburn? The odds were greater against Robert the Bruce."

George's thin lips twisted contemptuously. "Jamie Stewart was not the Bruce."

Sir David Lyndsay opened his mouth to speak, but Huntly's raised hand silenced him. "The flower of Scotland died yesterday, m'lords. Our minds should be occupied with more pressing matters. After I escort Lady Maxwell to her home, I shall ride for Strathbogie and do what I can to save my lands. I suggest you do the same."

The men looked at one another, nodded, and turned their horses northward. Sir David was not convinced, but now he was alone. At last, he too turned his mount and rode away.

"You might at least have thanked me," said George wryly as he watched the last survivors of Jamie's army disappear over the hill.

"For what?" asked Jeanne dully.

"For saving your life. They wanted to hang you."

"It no longer matters what happens to me."

After a moment of startled silence, George swore long and fluently. "You little fool," he said at last. "What of your son, the heir to Traquair, and the child you carry within you?"

Tears welled up in her eyes, spilled down her cheeks, and dripped off the end of her nose. "You don't understand," she said.

"Of course I understand. Do you actually believe no one else has suffered? There isn't a family in Scotland who won't mourn a loved one this day." His fingers bit painfully into her shoulder. "Come, Jeanne. Our fight is just beginning. I expected more of you than this."

"Why?"

"Not so very long ago, we were betrothed," he reminded her. " 'Tis a grave disappointment for a man to learn he was so lacking in judgment as to love a woman who wished for death in times of trouble."

Jeanne turned to look at him, her eyes wide and troubled. "You're a good man, George. I'm sorry if I hurt you."

He shrugged. "I survived my pain and so will you."

"It isn't the same."

"Isn't it?"

"Of course not," she said angrily. "John was my husband, the father of my children. You have a wife. How can you compare what we had to the love you share with her?"

He looked at her thoughtfully. "Of course, you are right," he said at last.

She knew he didn't believe anything of the sort, but the argument was over and she was grateful. It made her uncomfortable to be reminded of the disgraceful way she'd treated George. There had been no help for it, but it embarrassed her nonetheless.

He left her at the gates of Traquair. The journey home took longer than usual because they stopped several times to eat. George remembered her condition and watched carefully for her skin to pale and the blue color to appear around her lips. The first time it happened, only minutes after they'd found her mare, he'd given her food from his pack. After that, whenever a croft or farm loomed in the distance, he insisted they refurbish their supplies.

Jeanne was grateful for his solicitude. The weight of the child and the effort of keeping her emotions under control had taken their toll. She was exhausted. Without George, she would never have managed the journey.

For days after her return, Jeanne searched once again for the stone. She found nothing. Each time, she'd ventured further into the darkness of the same tunnel, only to be disappointed again and again. She was sure she remembered the way. The passage was the same, as was the staircase with its irregular stone steps, but the light was gone and the room with it. It was as if it had never existed outside of her own mind. Finally she gave up, and with her decision, all emotion seemed to leave her. She walked and talked and slept and ate with a curious detachment that terrified everyone around her.

A fortnight later they came for her, a company of men mounted on horses and dressed in full mail. Bonnets hid their faces, and she didn't recognize their voices. With trembling lips, Flora announced their arrival, and Jeanne went out to meet them.

"Lady Jeanne Maxwell." A man in gray armor seated on a dancing brown stallion spoke. "You are under arrest."

"On what charge?"

"Witchcraft."

The word hung, suspended on the air between them.

"I am no witch," Jeanne said at last.

"Do you deny that Grania Douglas was your teacher?"

Jeanne lifted her chin. "Grania was my friend. She was no witch."

"Do you deny that she claimed to have *the sight.*"

"Every woman in the Highlands claims it," said Jeanne contemptuously.

"Do you have it, Lady Maxwell?"

Instant denial sprang to her lips, but the words were never spoken. Images of Flodden Moor filled her mind. Her hesitation sealed her fate.

"Seize her," the man ordered.

Two men dismounted and held her arms. Jeanne did not struggle. "Where will I be tried?" she asked their leader.

The man looked at her for a long time. The hard-bitten brown of his eyes glittered through the slit in his bonnet. The stallion fidgeted and pawed at the ground. With a harsh command and a swift jerk of the reins, the man brought him under control.

"You've already been tried," he said shortly.

"By what law?"

"Mine."

"Why do you do this?" she whispered.

He didn't answer. She saw his eyes move over the walls and gables of Traquair House. "Prepare the scaffold," he ordered.

Within moments a rope was twisted and thrown over the oak tree she and John had climbed as children. There was no platform, no keening of the pipes, no jeering crowds. The face of her accuser was unknown. Jeanne looked upon the proceedings as a curious observer with the same cloudy detachment that had governed her actions for the last several weeks. Even when she was lifted to the saddle of the brown stallion and the rope was placed around her neck and tightened, she did not protest.

The brown-eyed man shouted the command and flung her from his saddle. The rope was pulled taut. Searing pain closed around her throat, her neck snapped, and there was no more pain, only darkness. Jeanne Maxwell was dead.

Traquair House

1993

I walked Ian to his car, conscious of the possessive curve of his hand under my elbow.

"Are you going to tell me what happened in there?" he asked.

"Maybe you'd better tell me," I said, looking at my watch. An hour and a half had passed while I had watched Scotland fall to her knees.

He frowned and leaned against the car. "You were unusually quiet when your parents first came down," he told her. "Do you remember that?"

I shook my head. "The last thing I remember is your face after you finished stoking the fire. You looked as if you were in shock."

The look on his face told me he knew much more than he was saying. "You're tired," he said, kissing me on the forehead. "This business about your mother must have affected you more than you realize. I'll see you tomorrow."

His back was toward me as he opened the door of his car.

"Jeanne Maxwell is dead, Ian." My words stopped him cold. There was no need for further explanation.

The silence stretched out between us. "I know," he said at last, his voice low.

"What are we going to do?"

He must have sensed my desperation because he turned back to me and took me in his arms. "We'll work it out, Christina," he said. "Somehow we'll get to the bottom of this."

"Jeanne found the stone," I whispered into his shirt. "But it wasn't there when she looked for it again. Why wasn't it there?"

"I don't know," he confessed. "Maybe the timing was wrong for her. Maybe it was already too late."

"How will we know when it's too late for us?"

"It won't be," he said fiercely. "Trust me. It won't be. I'll come back tomorrow, and we'll look together. Do you remember enough to recognize familiar landmarks?"

"I think so."

"Good." He squeezed my hand and released me. "Get some rest. I'll be here early. Ask Kate to fix her famous scones but tell her—"

"What?"

He shook his head. "Never mind. I'll tell her myself."

I wasn't sure that I wanted to tell Kate anything, but since I really had nothing but intuition on which to base my suspicions, I kept silent. When Ian's car disappeared through the gates, I walked back into the house.

"He's certainly a personable young man," my father said, "but marriage? Are you sure, Christina?"

"Why do you ask?"

He frowned. "You didn't say a word the entire time he was here."

"I'm perfectly sure. We have a lot in common," I assured him.

"Such as?" My mother smiled expectantly.

"An interest in history, our ancestry, the fact that our families have been neighbors for centuries"—I ticked each attribute off on my fingers—"books, food, music, education. Just about everything."

She sighed. "Your living in Scotland will be hard on us. Boston was far enough, but Scotland." She looked at me and smiled tremulously. "I'm very happy for you, Chris. Now, before I get emotional, I'd like to look around the house."

I left my mother to her wandering, said good night to my father, and started up the stairs to my room. The day had been too long already. At the landing, I turned and nearly bumped into Kate. The moment stretched out, and neither of us spoke. Finally, it was too late to pretend politeness. Without a word, I moved around her and continued down the hall toward my room.

"May I offer my congratulations, Miss Murray," she called after me. "Your mother told me the news."

There was no reason to keep silent. After all, neither Mother nor I had done anything to be ashamed of. I turned around. "Do you know who my grandmother was, Kate?"

Something flickered in her eyes and then disappeared. "Why would I know anything of the sort?"

"We both know Lord Maxwell was my grandfather. You must have known it from the beginning. I want to know who my grandmother was."

"I couldn't tell you."

"Don't you know, or are you honoring a confidence?"

"My loyalties are to the people of Traquair."

She had cleverly twisted her answer, but I was too tired to pursue the issue. I rubbed my aching temples. "Ian will be here early tomorrow," I said. "I know you'll be busy fixing breakfast for everyone else, but he'd like a batch of your scones if it isn't too much trouble."

"Ian Douglas has never caused me trouble, Miss Murray."

Obviously my engagement had her approval. "Oh, by the way." I'd almost forgotten. "Tomorrow the house will be closed to tourists. Ian and I will be working upstairs."

"You're looking pale, Miss Murray. Is there anything I can get you?"

Was it my imagination, or had she deliberately ignored my comment? She didn't seem at all curious to know the reason Traquair would be closed or what Ian and I would be working on. It was very unlike her.

I looked at her closely, hoping the implacable calm of her face would crack and reveal something of her thoughts. She stared back without blinking. Her eyes glittered. Kate Ferguson reminded me of a witch in a fairy tale. Suddenly, I

was afraid. I turned away. "No, thank you," I murmured.
"All I need is sleep."

"Good night, Miss Murray."

I closed the door and, for the second time since I'd
arrived at Traquair House, slid the lock into place. The
woman was evil. I could sense it. The pieces were coming
together. I knew there wasn't much time left. I sensed that
Kate knew it too.

The headache came just as I was drifting off to sleep. This
time I was ready for what came with it.

Shiels Castle, Scotland
1278

> "Ring around the rosies,
> Pockets full o' posies,
> Ashes, ashes,
> All fall dead."

The circle of children dropped their hands and fell to the
ground, shrieking with laughter. The air smelled of smoke
and charred flesh. White flakes, soft and warmer than snow,
drifted down, settling on their heads, their clothes, the grass
where they played. Clouds of ashes rose where they fell,
burning their lungs, rendering them invisible from ten feet
away.

At first, caught up in their private world of illicit glee, no
one noticed the small boy standing by himself, his brow
furrowed, his bottom lip thrust out in a scowl. Finally, a girl
smaller than the others turned around and saw him.

"There you are, David," she called to him. "Come and
play."

Mutinously, he shook his head.

"Come," she begged. "We are uneven without you."

"I don't want to," he mumbled.

Another boy with thick legs and matted hair rose to his

feet. He swaggered toward David Murray until he stood within an inch of the smaller boy's chest. Thrusting out an accusing finger, he poked him roughly. "What's the matter with you?" he asked. "Annie wants you to play."

David's stomach clenched. He was only twelve, no match for the burly fourteen-year-old Donal MacPhee. The bully outweighed him by more than a stone, but today it didn't matter. Today, David wanted to use his fists, to feel bones snap and skin give way. Today, he wanted to assuage the ache in his heart with physical pain.

He took the first hit directly in the face, and his nose broke. There was no pain. Anger gave him courage. Clenching his fists, he charged the bigger boy and knocked him to the ground. Instantly, the children rallied around, urging them on, the blood lust strong in their hearts and voices.

Out of nowhere, into the concealing circle of ash and smoke, ran a child, a girl of no more than eight years. Her eyes blazed with fury. Fearlessly, she threw herself into the midst of the writhing bodies. "Stop," she shouted. "Leave him be. Leave him be, at once."

Instantly, the circle of children backed away, their eyes lowered. Donal MacPhee, his hand raised in a punishing fist, looked up through a swollen eye and grimaced. Slowly, he lowered his arm, pulled away, and stood up. David lay on the ground, his face a smear of blood.

Trembling with anger, the girl turned on the children. "Go away," she said through clenched teeth. "All of you. Go away."

Without question, they obeyed. All except David. She was Mairi of Shiels, daughter to the laird. It was unwise to cross a Maxwell of the borders. It was the height of stupidity to cross Mairi. She had a dreadful temper and a powerful father. There were those who swore she was possessed, not in the presence of the laird, of course, but in the whispered darkness and flickering fires of small crofts that dotted the countryside. Already, Mairi had enemies. There were only a few who called her friend and no one more than the boy with the bloodied face who lay at her feet.

From that first day at Shiels when David had found her in the woods, sobbing wildly as she attempted to free the mangled carcass of a rabbit from a poacher's trap, she had claimed his loyalty and his love. That was two years ago, when he'd come to the borders to be fostered to the laird.

For David Murray, the only child of a kindly, but distant father and a self-serving mother, Mairi's penchant for championing the abused and the lonely was a balm to his bruised spirit. The children were never far apart. When Mairi's mother died, only David could comfort her. When David's puppy was found in the woods, its small body dismembered by wolves, only Mairi had the nerve to brave the boy's white-faced stillness and offer him another hound. When Mairi learned to ride her pony, it was David who boosted her to the saddle. When David learned his letters, Mairi sat at his feet. When he practiced his swordplay, she watched from her perch on the wall. When the fledgings she saved from the cat died in her hands, it was David's arms that soothed her. Neither child minded not having anyone but each other. Together, they were enough. Until yesterday.

Yesterday, David's father rode across the drawbridge into the courtyard of Shiels. One look at his face had sent the servants scurrying to heat water for poultices. Their efforts were wasted. He lasted less than ten hours, and because of the nature of his illness, his remains were burned immediately. Nothing Mairi could do or say made a difference to David. He was an orphan, a child. Without a father, he was nameless and alone. What would become of him without his father? His mother would remarry. There would be other children. Her allegiance would be to them and to her new husband. He didn't blame her. What else was there for a woman? But how could he bear to leave Shiels? How could he bear to leave Mairi? He could smell the fragrance of her hair as she bent over him.

"David," she murmured, touching his swollen face with cool hands, "are you hurt?"

He turned his head to the side, avoiding her eyes, and kept silent.

"How dare they do this? Those, those—" she fumed, searching her eight-year-old vocabulary for language strong enough to suit the occasion. "Vermin." She spat out the word. "I shall ask my father to kill them."

Against his will, David started to smile, then grimaced. The side of his cheek throbbed unbearably. Mairi's passions frequently took a violent turn.

"Are you too hurt to walk?" she asked anxiously.

He shook his head and sat up. "What are you doing here, Mairi? Your father will skin you alive if he finds you outside the gates."

"I was worried about you," she replied.

"You needn't be." He tested his cheek and the skin around his eye gingerly. "I can take care of myself."

"I can see that," Mairi retorted. "Where would you be if I hadn't come?"

"I didn't ask you to follow me," he lashed out.

Tears sprang to her eyes.

Remorse flooded through him. "Don't cry," he said hoarsely. "I am not myself today." He stood and held out his hand. "Come. I'll take you back to Shiels."

She took his hand. They walked in silence through the powdery grayness. "Are you dreadfully sad?" she asked at last.

David shook his head. "I hardly knew him."

Mairi frowned. "Then why did you run away?"

He sighed. His nose throbbed, and he felt as if he'd aged a lifetime in the last day and in doing so left her far behind. "I didn't run away."

"What is the matter, David?"

Mairi knew nothing of subterfuge. She always came directly to the point and expected others to do the same. She would know if he lied.

Haltingly, he spoke. "Now that my father is dead, I am heir to Bothwell."

She did not understand. "That is good. As the earl, you can do as you please."

Gently, he tried to explain. "My mother will send for me, Mairi. I must leave Shiels at her command."

Mairi's face paled. Her fingers tightened over his palm. Words were beyond her. Only death would be worse than losing David.

One look at the despair in Mairi's eyes chastened him. He uttered a curse he'd overheard from the groom. Whatever turn his future took, he had no right to wound Mairi.

Clumsily, he attempted to reverse his mistake. "Pay me no mind, lass. I know nothing of what my mother intends. Worrying will do only harm."

Her smile was a wonderful thing to behold. David, on the verge of burgeoning manhood, caught his breath. Mairi was still a child, but someday soon she would be beautiful. The promise was already there in the thin bones of her face, in the elegant sweep of her brows, in the perfectly formed lips and wide, clear eyes. He swallowed and looked away. There, on the ash-covered pony path leading to the castle, with the odor of smoke and death filling his nostrils, David Murray made a promise to himself. He vowed to return to Shiels when Mairi was a woman.

Traquair House
1993

For the first time since I was a little girl, I longed for the comfort of my parents' king-sized bed. Snuggled between their bodies, wrapped in the warmth of unconditional love and a down-filled comforter, I knew that nothing would harm me. Now I had no such assurances. Mairi would find me no matter where I was. Her life would unravel before me in living color like a videotape whether I liked it or not. And with every heightened, larger-than-life experience, my time dwindled. What if I failed?

Cold sweat gathered in the hollow between my breasts. My heart pounded. I was afraid with a gut-wrenching, despairing kind of paranoia I'd never experienced before. I was afraid to sleep, afraid to confide in anyone, afraid to be alone. Good Lord! What was happening to me?

I looked at the clock. It was after eleven, and I couldn't sleep. Hot tea and the warmth of the kitchen hearth appealed to me. The hall was dark as I closed the bedroom door and felt my way along the wall, down the stairs, and into the kitchen. The glow of the banked fire cheered me. I filled the teakettle with water, turned on the burner, and pulled the rocker close to the hearth. It was easy to think here in the cozy darkness with the fire throwing an arc of light across the ceiling, leaving me and the rest of the room in shadow. Tomorrow Ian and I would begin our search. I shivered in anticipation. Somewhere inside these walls lay the secrets of my ancestors. With luck and perseverance, those secrets would be revealed for the first time in seven hundred years.

I lifted the kettle off the burner just before it whistled. Shaking out the loose tea, I spilled some on the counter, swept it into my hand, and dumped it into the teapot. The tea had steeped and I had poured the first hot, sustaining cup when I heard them.

Voices raised in argument, loud at first and then lowered in furious whispers. They came from the entry near the main stairs. My hand trembled as I placed the pot on the counter. There could be no mistake as to the identity of the two engaged in their private battle, but I had to see for myself to remove the last shred of doubt.

Slipping out of the kitchen, I flattened myself against the wall, inching my way slowly toward the entry. Pale fingers of moonlight lit the hall, illuminating Ian's blond head. Kate's hand was clenched on his arm, and the features of her face were twisted in desperation. The intimacy of their position shocked me. Obviously they knew each other much better than I had realized, and whatever their disagreement, it wasn't a small misunderstanding.

He shook his head. "Don't be absurd," he said in an angry whisper. "It isn't the same thing at all. I had no idea what you intended. You lied to me. What you've done is dangerous, not to mention illegal. You told me you only wanted to know her, to convince her of your claim. For Christ's sake, she's pregnant. If the child is damaged in any way, you'll be responsible."

"You knew from the beginning what the outcome would be," Kate reminded him. "Nothing's changed."

"Everything's changed." He ran his fingers through his hair. "Your request sounded reasonable and harmless. Now I find that you're playing with her mind. She actually believes in all this."

"Don't you?"

He was silent for a long time, and when he spoke, his voice was low and careful. "I don't see what she sees and neither do you. We both know that everything has a logical explanation."

She refused to answer and gave him a long, assessing look instead. Finally, she spoke. "What I believe is that you're a fool, Ian Douglas."

He swore softly. "Christina had nothing to do with Maxwell's will and neither did her mother. Everything is perfectly legal. I'm serious about this, Kate. It must stop immediately."

"I won't give up now." Kate's fingers curled around his arm. "Traquair is mine. No one else has worked for it as I have. I won't have it go to someone who didn't know it existed until a few weeks ago."

"Aren't you forgetting her mother? Surely, you can't dispute her rights."

"It's mine." Her voice was almost a wail. "It belongs to me and to my heirs."

"Kate." Ian's voice had gentled, as if speaking to a child. "You have no heirs. Christina would eventually inherit everything that belongs to you."

The woman tilted her head, measuring him with her sharp dark eyes. "On the contrary, Ian. You are my nearest blood relative."

My heart raced. What could their disjointed conversation possibly mean? How was Kate playing with my mind, and how were they related? I nearly strangled from the effort to control my breathing.

"It's all the same now," Ian continued patiently. "My child will inherit Traquair. My child and Christina's."

In the faint light, I could see her eyes narrow and a small gloating smile transform her face. "How do you think she would feel if she knew your involvement in this, Ian? Do you really believe she would marry you?"

His expression was grim. "Are you planning to tell her?"

"Should a marriage begin with deceit?" she countered.

"No." He stepped back, away from the touch of her hands. "But I don't want you telling her. I'll do it the first thing tomorrow. I hope you realize what this means. You'll be forced to leave Traquair. You could go to prison." He sighed. "You're ill, Kate. You may even be mad. I understand your disappointment that Maxwell didn't do enough for you, but life has its share of disappointments. You'll have to live with it. I suggest you go somewhere else. Somewhere far away. Start over again." He walked out the door, leaving it ajar behind him.

For a moment that lasted a lifetime, Kate stared out the door. Finally, muttering under her breath, she closed and locked it and climbed the stairs.

I waited a full fifteen minutes before even thinking of moving. Tiptoeing upstairs, I sat down and wrote a quick note to my father. Then, gathering my keys and purse, I made my way downstairs, unlocked the door, and crossed the courtyard to the carport.

An hour later I checked into an inconspicuous hotel outside of Edinburgh, turned up the heat, and stretched out between unfamiliar sheets. There was no point in thinking any further than I already had. It was nearly two in the morning. Exhaustion claimed me, and I fell asleep.

Traquair House
1286

"David." Mairi's eyes glowed with pleasure. Quickly, she hid the honey-coated *criachan* behind her back. "Why have you returned so soon from London?"

"I came to witness the wedding of Alexander and Jolande of Dreux," he explained. "Edinburgh is so close. I'd not miss an opportunity to see you, lass." Casually he reached behind her, his hand closing over the sweet clutched in her fist. He removed it from her hand and frowned. "You promised me you wouldn't do this. Is your word worthless, Mairi?"

"The batch was made fresh this morning, and I've only had one. 'Tis my first in a very long time. Truly, David."

He relented. "I suppose one will do you no harm. But 'tis dangerous to indulge yourself." The lines around his mouth deepened with worry. He would never forget the first time he'd witnessed one of Mairi's spells. They were children, and it was the first warm day of spring. Armed with a basket of food from the kitchen, they'd spend the afternoon in the marshes. Generously, David had offered Mairi the additional sweetbun the cook had packed and more than half of the *criachan.* She'd hesitated only a moment and then greedily consumed it all. Less than an hour later, her skin had paled and around her lips was a frightening blue shadow. He'd carried her halfway to the house before her father found them. Taking one look at his nearly unconscious daughter, the laird had lifted her to the back of his stallion and galloped back to Traquair, leaving David on the moor, a forlorn heap of misery, praying more desperately than he'd ever prayed before in his life. It had never happened again, but the experience had terrified him to such an extent that he'd never forgotten it.

She touched his cheek. "If it upsets you that much, I won't eat it."

"Please don't."

Looking up at him through her lashes, she tactfully changed the subject. "I've heard the women are lovely at the English court."

David caught his breath. This was a new, flirtatious Mairi. Perhaps she had grown up at last. Hope flooded through him. "There is no one for me but you, Mairi. You should know that by now."

She laughed with the crystalline purity of a choirboy. "What I know is that you've mastered the art of flattery, my friend. Tell me of Jolande of Dreux. Is she as beautiful as they say?"

David looked down at the face he was sure had been

sculpted by God Himself and swallowed. "Aye. I've heard that she's lovely enough, but it matters little. Alexander needs an heir of his own body. Jolande is young. There is a chance now."

"What does the English king think of Alexander taking another bride?"

"Edward is no fool. He knows that ten years is long enough for a man to mourn his wife, especially if that man is a king."

"Still," Mairi reflected, "Alexander has an heir."

"A child hidden away in Norway is hardly an heir," David protested. "Besides, Scotland has never been ruled by a woman."

She tilted her head to one side, a pose she adopted whenever her thoughts ran deep. David knew better than to interrupt her. "Until the matter is settled, Edward is overlord of Scotland," she said at last. "What manner of man is the English king?"

"He is a warrior," David replied promptly. "No one mistakes Edward for anyone other than he is. I would such a man could be found for Scotland."

Mairi shook her head. "I didn't ask if you admired him, David. What is he like?"

David frowned. "I don't understand."

"Is he tall and well favored? Are his teeth straight? Does he laugh often?"

"Only a woman would notice those things," David protested, laughing, "although I'm sure the lassies find him well favored enough. I've heard he keeps a mistress in every castle in England and finds time to satisfy his wife as well."

"'Tis possible his rank keeps him well supplied with women," Mairi suggested.

David shrugged. "Perhaps."

Mairi sighed and slipped her arm through David's. "How long can you stay?"

"Only the night." He hesitated and pressed her hand. "I'm sorry about your father, lass."

The winged brows drew together, and her chest constricted. Her father's death was still very new. "Thank you," she whispered.

"Will you stay here, at Traquair?"

She nodded. "My father's holdings belongs to the crown, but Shiels and Traquair belonged to my mother. They are mine."

David lifted a lock of silken hair and wound it around his finger. "I'll always think of you as Mairi of Shiels. Do you remember when we first met?"

Mairi smiled her generous, heart-wrenching smile, and David was reminded of the bard who sang of her beauty in the great hall in the Tower of London. King Edward had smiled indulgently, but even he was intrigued. There were beauties to spare in Londontown, but none could rival Mairi of Shiels.

"You've changed, David," she said, looking up at him with solemn eyes.

Her words startled him. He'd forgotten what he asked her. "How so?"

"You aren't listening to me."

"I'll warrant there's not a man who would."

She drew herself up to her full height and lifted her chin. "Why not?"

"Faith, Mairi. You are lovely enough to take a man's breath away. I no longer know what to say to you."

Her eyes widened. "Why not?"

He grinned. "When a man dallies with a beautiful woman, 'tis not conversation that comes to mind."

"What does?"

He reddened. "I'll tell you later."

"When?"

"Enough," he exploded. " 'Tis not the time."

Her outraged expression shamed him. One did not shout at Mairi of Shiels. Mutely, he appealed for peace. She ignored his outstretched hand.

He cleared his throat. "I apologize, lass. I did not come to argue with you."

"Why did you come?"

"To spend the day with my most loyal friend."

The corners of her mouth turned up. "You can be very disagreeable, you know."

"I know."

She forgave him completely. "Well then, what shall we do?"

"Do you still like to fish?"

Her eyes glowed with anticipation. "Above all things."

He slipped his arm around her waist. "Let us delay no longer."

Once again, in perfect accord, they made their way to the stables to fashion their poles and dig for bait.

Hours later, they lay on the bank, faces tilted to absorb the last rays of setting sunlight. Their hands were linked, their baskets filled with brown-speckled trout. Mairi broke the silence. "Isolde thinks I should marry."

David tensed. "Since when do your stepmother's wishes weigh with you?"

Mairi sat up. "Isolde is my dearest friend, next to you," she protested.

"Aye," agreed David, "but she hasn't the sense of a peahen. When have you ever been ruled by her?"

"Never before," Mairi admitted. "Still, this time she speaks the truth. Traquair and Shiels cannot be managed by a woman alone. They are too near the borders for safety." She bit her lip. "I am fifteen, David. At my age, most women are already mothers."

"Have you decided then?"

She hesitated. "I've had several offers."

"Your dowry is large."

Her eyes flashed like hammered silver. "How dare you?"

David saw his error immediately. "I spoke without thinking, lass," he apologized. "Your glass should tell you what every man sees when he looks upon you. What I meant was your lands alone would make you desirable even were you anyone other than you are."

"I do not wish to be married for my land."

"Why not?" he demanded reasonably. "If your heart is not involved, 'tis as good a reason as any. You say you wish to marry to protect your land. Why not marry a man who desires it as much as you do?"

She stared down at him, an arrested expression on her face. Coming from his lips, it sounded more reasonable than mercenary. "I had hoped for a man who desires me as much as my property," she admitted at last.

David crossed his arms behind his head and opened one eye to look at her. "There should be a few of those as well."

"Aye," Mairi nodded.

"Well?"

She bit her lip. "I cannot like any of them," she confessed. "Marriage is so . . . so—"

"Permanent?" he finished for her.

"Aye," she sighed with relief. David always understood. He sat up and took her hands. His heart slammed painfully against his ribs. "Do you care for me, Mairi?"

"Of course," she said impatiently. "You are my dearest friend. I would rather be with you than anyone."

"Then why not marry me?"

She sucked in her breath. "You cannot mean it."

"I do."

Her eyes widened. "Why? You have no need for land."

He laughed. "What I need, what I've always needed, is you."

Shyly, she met his eyes. "Truly, David?"

The expression on her face was too much for him. He flushed and spoke more earnestly than ever before in his life. "I've loved you since we were children. Do you . . . Can you care for me, Mairi?"

"Oh, I do," she hurried to reassure him. "'Tis just that I've never thought of you as a husband."

"Will you now?"

"I don't know," she answered truthfully. "You are my dearest friend, but is that enough to be wed?"

David frowned. With every breath in his being, he wanted Mairi for his bride but not without love. Tugging at her hands, he pulled her close to him and kissed her. At first she stiffened, but as his kiss deepened, her lips parted and moved against his. Relieved, he ended the kiss and pulled away. Mairi had responded.

"I love you," he said, his face flushed and humble. "I've always loved you. I can make you love me."

Mairi pulled her hands away and looked up at the sky. "It would be a relief to know 'tis settled," she said. "Still, I am in mourning for Father. Will you wait for my answer, David?"

His dark eyes glowed with pleasure. "If I must, I shall wait forever."

She laughed, and once again, her eyes met his. "I don't deserve you," she admitted. "I promise it won't be that long. Come. The fish will spoil."

Feeling as if he'd weathered a crisis, David took her hand and led her back to the house.

Edinburgh
1993

I awoke before dawn. It wasn't my normal type of awakening, where consciousness is welcomed and immediate, where the very idea of a new day, a new beginning, bursts upon the senses like fireworks on New Year's Eve. This time my awakening came slowly, miserably, my body reluctantly bracing itself for the memory of the previous night. It was happening all over again, the inevitable bone-weary dawns following my separation from Stephen. The feeling that if I could only hold on to that tenuous time between waking and sleeping when the mind knows that something is wrong but hasn't yet identified what that something is, if I could only prevent my sated body from waking completely, I could hold at bay the ache of betrayal.

Of course, it never worked. I was no more capable of stopping time than the next person. In the past two years I'd learned that pain can't be outdistanced. It must be faced head-on like all other seemingly impossible challenges. After the pain comes rage and after rage a kind of balancing as if the entire world shifts a bit and resettles to accomodate a new perspective. Only then, after pain and rage and acceptance, does the healing begin.

I was thirty-seven years old. If Ian Douglas wasn't the man I thought he was, weeping into a hotel pillow wouldn't help. Determined to get on with it, I showered, dressed, injected myself with insulin, and ordered breakfast. By eight o'clock I was on my way.

By American standards, the Hall of Records was old. In a city where time is measured in centuries, it is a large, modern building equipped with comfortable furniture, spacious rooms, and state-of-the-art computers. The clerk, a friendly woman seated behind a beautifully carved oak desk an American antique dealer would pay a fortune for, smiled at me.

"I've located the files you asked me about, Miss Murray. There are quite a few of them, I'm afraid."

"Thank you," I said, gathering the mountain of paperwork she'd collected. The desks were small, semiprivate cubicles with just enough space to stack books on one side. I selected a file from the top of the stack and pushed the others away.

Three hours later, I found what I was looking for. The baptismal records from a small church in Selkirk showed the baptism of a girl, Katherine Douglas, born in the year 1946 to Miss Morag Douglas and the laird of Traquair. The birth certificate from the hospital listed only the child's birth and the mother's name but not the father. Morag Douglas had kept the father's identity a secret from the hospital, but she could not lie to her God. There, in black and white, was the evidence that Kate Douglas Ferguson was the daughter of James Maxwell, laird of Traquair—my grandfather. Kate was my aunt, my mother's halfsister. She was also, it seemed, related to Ian, but how closely I didn't know.

Rifling through the newspaper clippings, I almost missed it. If the man hadn't looked so much like Ian, I would have skipped over it completely. The headline read, "Local Landowner Indicted." Skimming the page, I read the grim details of the evidence leading to the arrest of Ian's father, his subsequent suicide, and the return of his son. My eyes moved quickly over the page, discounting most of it, looking for something, anything, that would give me a clue as to why Kate and Ian had allied themselves against me. I almost gave up and moved on when a name in the last paragraph jumped out at me. I stopped, reread it, and moaned. It was worse, much worse, than I thought.

Closing my eyes, I rested my forehead against the wooden

divider and cursed. I was a fool, and my judgment was terrible. The last thing in the world I wanted to do was face Ian Douglas, but there was no helping it. I needed answers and only he had them.

Traffic was unusually heavy on the 703, and the drive to Peebles took over an hour. Located at the junction of Innerleithen and the 7062, Ian's home was a comfortable, stately manor house with straight, lichen-covered walls and a gabled roof. I parked the car in the graveled lot and walked to the door. Taking a deep breath, I lifted the knocker and let it fall. He opened the door immediately, and his face lit up with delight.

"What a pleasant surprise," he said, pulling me into his house and then into his arms. "I called this morning, but Kate said you were out. Did you forget we were to meet?"

For a moment I was tempted. The feel of his arms around me, the soapy smell of his skin, the rough comfort of his sweater against my cheek, almost broke my resolve. Would it hurt to forget everything I knew, to pretend that yesterday had never happened, that Ian and I were just another happy couple with ordinary differences and once they were solved we would go on just as before? He nuzzled my neck.

I stiffened in his arms.

Surprised, he lifted his head and looked at me. "Is anything wrong?" he asked softly.

I nodded, and he released me.

"Perhaps you'd better tell me what's happened."

Rubbing my arms, I followed him into a book-lined room. He closed the door and leaned against it. Folding his arms, he looked directly at me. "What's troubling you, Christina?"

There was no point in dissembling. "I want you to tell me exactly what your relationship to Kate Douglas is."

For a long time, he continued to look at me. At last he spoke, and his words condemned him. "How did you find out?"

"It doesn't matter. Just tell me."

He frowned and walked to the window. Pulling back the heavy drape, he stared out at the green-gold hills. "Kate is a distant relative. She's a Douglas, descended on her mother's side from the line that supposedly died out in the fourteenth century."

"Go on."

"Her father was James Maxwell, your grandfather."

"Why didn't you tell me?"

He turned around and came toward me. Backing away, I held out my hand to prevent him from coming closer. He stopped several feet from where I stood.

"Believe it or not, I was going to tell you."

I did believe it, but only because I'd eavesdropped the night before. "Why didn't you tell me in the beginning?"

His face was pale. "Kate wanted a chance to know you, to convince you that she had earned a part of Maxwell's legacy." His face reddened, and he hesitated. "I'm not proud of this, Christina. I was supposed to entertain you, keep you contented while you stayed at Traquair. That's all, I swear it. I didn't plan on falling in love with you, and I had no idea Kate was planning anything else until she told me last night."

"And then what?"

"I beg your pardon?"

"What was supposed to happen after I was entertained?"

He looked bewildered. "I don't understand."

"Don't you? Weren't you planning to end our relationship, hoping I'd go home brokenhearted and more than willing to leave Kate her house?"

"Don't be absurd. No one would give up an inheritance like Traquair, no matter how brokenhearted."

"I suppose you think Kate should have received a portion of the estate."

He nodded. "As a matter of fact, I do, and it isn't all that outrageous. Your mother and Kate were both Maxwell's illegitimate daughters. I can understand how Kate feels. Why should one daughter have inherited more than the other?"

"Neither of them inherited," I reminded him. "I did."

His hands clenched. "What do you want me to say, Christina? I had no part in Kate's scheme other than a very innocent one. What can I do to convince you?"

"Why don't you start with the truth?"

He looked startled. "What do you mean?"

"Isn't there something else you should be telling me?"

His eyes moved over my face. Finally, he nodded as if he'd come to a decision. "Very well," he said, his voice low. "I blame James Maxwell for my father's death. Maxwell spoke at the trial. He was the chief witness. His testimony assured my father's conviction. The following day, after the jury found him guilty, they found his body."

"Maybe your father was guilty."

Ian nodded. "He was, but not of the crime for which they accused him. He was guilty of loving Maxwell's wife."

"Ellen?" I barely whispered her name, but Ian heard.

"Yes." His eyes were haunted. "For years Ellen put up with Maxwell's womanizing. She'd decided to leave him right around the time that the scandal involving my father and the girl was made public. The details no longer matter, and I won't go into them. It's enough to say that Maxwell planned well. His wife stayed with him, and my father killed himself."

I refused to allow sympathy to interfere with my purpose. "What does any of that have to do with me?"

"I assumed that you wanted to know what I had against James Maxwell," he answered.

"You've explained," I said, turning to go.

"Christina, wait." His hand closed around my arm. "I never intended for you to be hurt. I love you. You must believe me."

"Don't say anything more. I suppose Kate was going to divide her share with you." Tears burned the insides of my eyelids.

"I don't want your money."

Unbidden, the words of our first conversation came back to me. *I hope you appreciate what you've been given.*

I turned on him, pain thickening my voice. "Don't you? If I hadn't overheard the two of you last night, you would've had the whole pie for yourself. Kate was no longer necessary."

"It isn't like that at all."

"You never believed any of it, did you?"

"What are you talking about?" He looked confused.

"You pretended to accept everything I told you, about

Katrine and Jeanne and Mairi of Shiels. Everything you said was a lie to convince me that you cared."

"That isn't true."

"Isn't it?" I felt the tears well up and spill down my cheeks. "Just which part of it isn't true?"

He ran his fingers distractedly through his hair. "I do believe you. At least, I believe that you believe it. Oh, hell." He gave up. "I don't know what I believe any more. Kate is drugging you, Christina. These hallucinations you're having may be a combination of what you've read about the Maxwell–Murrays and whatever it is that Kate is giving you. Who knows what effect this has had on you? I swear to you I knew nothing about it until yesterday when Kate told me what she'd done. I believed her when she told me she'd discussed your inheritance with Ellen Maxwell before she died and the two of them had agreed to ask you for her rightful share. I would never have allowed her to put you or the child in danger."

I could feel my face pale. *My baby. The drug may have affected the baby.*

"Until yesterday, time travel was nothing more than fiction to me," he continued. "But then I saw you fade before my eyes, and when you came back, you weren't yourself. I can't explain it. Maybe we're both crazy."

"I'm not crazy." I didn't normally raise my voice, but I was past logic. Ignorance was no excuse. He'd helped to harm my baby. "You're despicable. I don't know you at all. The only regret I have is that my child was fathered by someone who doesn't know the meaning of the word *character.*"

The tears were flowing freely now. I don't remember leaving the house or getting into the car. I'll never know how I found the road or negotiated the twisting turns back to Traquair House. It was late afternoon. No one was in sight. I walked up the stairs. In the comfort of my own room, behind the privacy of locked doors, I looked longingly at the bed. I needed rest, hours of it. Climbing, fully clothed, beneath the feather comforter, I closed my eyes. Pregnancy was exhausting. Later, much later, I would decide what to do with Kate.

❧24❧

The Borders of Scotland
1290

Edward gritted his teeth. The stallion's steady canter jarred his arm. A handful of moist peat pressed against his wound and held in place with strips of bloodstained linen cooled the fiery pain in his shoulder. Drops of sweat broke out on his forehead. The royal standard had fallen hours ago along with the bodies of ten knights who would be sorely missed in future battles.

Closing his eyes, he leaned forward to rest his head against the lathered neck of his mount, giving himself up to the endless swaying, the pounding in his head, and the sickening nausea that threatened to overtake him with every step. Soon, very soon, consciousness would leave him. There was no help for it. He would have to trust the boy.

Thomas led the way, urging his own mount and his master's forward, worried that their forced haste would unseat his lord, more worried that the border rogues who attacked them would follow. He had never traveled this far into Scotland. No Englishman would dare without a full retinue behind him. Thomas was afraid. Scotland was a wild, uncivilized country filled with men who fought in their bare feet and covered themselves with little more than ragged blankets. Rumors of torture and mutilation flickered through his brain.

He glanced behind at the still, hunched-over figure of his lord. His fear intensified. "Holy God and all the saints," he prayed reverently, "please don't let him die. Please help me find shelter."

Hours later, his prayer was answered. Rising from a blanket of fog so thick it muffled all light and sound was a massive iron gate. Thomas pulled up his mount and sighed with relief. The border code of hospitality was strong. No one would turn away a wounded man.

"Where are we, Thomas?" The voice was thick with pain.

"I know not, Your Grace," the boy replied honestly. " 'Tis the house of a great lord from the size of it."

Edward, king of England, grunted. The effort required to speak was too great. Once again, he closed his eyes. The lad had done well. If the house was truly the abode of a peer, he had nothing to fear.

Thomas shouted loudly and rattled the gate. It swung open. Guards bearing torches and spears materialized out of nowhere. Thomas waited, his heart in his mouth, as they positioned themselves in a menacing circle around him. He wet his lips. When he spoke, his voice cracked. He stopped and began again. "My lord is hurt." He nodded toward his king. Instinct told him not to reveal the identity of his master. "We ask for shelter and bandages for his wound."

Out of the mists came a rider on an enormous white stallion. The human circle parted, and the horseman stopped directly in front of Thomas. He was in full mail. Only his eyes, flat and expressionless, were visible through the slit in his bonnet.

"Who are you?" he demanded.

"I am Thomas Droune and this man," he nodded toward the king, "is Lord Durbridge of Surrey. We were set upon by thieves, and his lordship was wounded."

"For what reason does a gentleman from Surrey travel to the borders?"

Thomas sucked in his breath. He wasn't proficient at lying, and this man was no fool. "My lord inherited property in Northumberland," he improvised. "He came to oversee the sale."

The man's eyes narrowed as he considered the boy's answer. It was unlikely and yet possible. The jewels in the lord's sword hilt proclaimed his wealth. He was also mortally wounded. Most likely, he wouldn't last the night. "Follow me," he said at last.

Thomas sighed with relief. His ruse had worked. Still holding the king's reins, he followed the man across the grounds and into the courtyard. Something at the top of the stone steps caught his eye, something white. He turned to look, and his mouth dropped open. Did angels visit the borders?

"On your knees, knave," the man ordered. "'Tis the mistress of Traquair."

Clumsily, Thomas dismounted and fell to his knees.

"These men seek shelter, m'lady," the man explained to his mistress. "Lord Durbridge of Surrey was set upon by border rogues. He is wounded."

"Rise, lad," the lady said. "Bring your lord inside."

Edward lifted his head as Thomas attempted to pull him from his mount. "Easy, lad," he mumbled. "I'm not so weak that I cannot stand without a bit of help."

"I told them you were Lord Durbridge," Thomas whispered. "This is Traquair House. The mistress bids us enter."

The king nodded. Leaning heavily on his squire's arm, he walked around the horses and looked up at Mairi Maxwell. For the first time in his life, Edward I of England, overlord of Scotland, defender of the faith, conqueror of Wales, father of a dozen bastard children, looked at a woman's face and forgot to breathe.

The bards sang of this woman around a hundred great hall fires. They sang of great beauty and unusual virtue, of eyes filled with mystery and hair soft as silk and black as a crow's wing in the shadows, lit with a hint of fire in the sunlight. For once, they had not exaggerated. Indeed, they had not begun to do her justice.

Eyes, clear as glass and framed with thick, sweeping lashes, assessed him gravely. Her hair hung unbound to her knees. She was more than lovely, Edward admitted to himself, with a kind of ageless beauty found in chiseled bones and clear skin and perfectly proportioned features. This was no Englishwoman who stood before him in her pink and white glory. Mairi's Celtic ancestry was obvious in her long hands and pale olive skin, in the blue veins pulsing at her temples, in the thin, angular beauty of her face and the odd tilt at the corner of her enormous eyes. She was dressed in white, the shapeless gown pulled taut by the wind until every slender curve was revealed in the moonlight.

He drew a deep shuddering breath. "My lady," he began, "I beg—" He stopped and bit his lip. The searing pain, his loss of blood, the wild flight across the moors, the chill night air, and, now, this woman. Blackness swept through him. There was no more pain. The ground rushed up to meet his head, and he crumpled in a heap at her feet.

Mairi stood in the doorway and looked at him, lying motionless in the great bed. He opened his eyes, and she could see their startling color from across the room. The tension deep inside of her eased, and she released her breath. For three days, she had watched helplessly as the dreadful fever took its toll, racking his body with tremors and soaking the sheets with sweat. She could offer no more than sips of cool water and a cloth to wipe his forehead and chest. Late last night, the fever broke, and for the first time since he'd fallen at her feet, he slept without moving. Now he was awake, and she could think of nothing to say.

Until this moment, Mairi had no idea why keeping this man alive was so important to her. There were others who had clung to life just as tenaciously and by the slimmest of threads. Some were strangers, others she had known quite well, but it had never been like this.

Never before had she knelt near a bed for hours on end, inhaling the acrid scent of an herb strewn floor. Never had she fallen asleep with her head on a stranger's pillow. Never had she lit candles and offered Masses to the saints for their intervention in keeping safe a man she had never seen before. He was just a man, larger and fairer than most she knew, but still a man, until he opened his eyes. Then she knew, and the knowledge tied her tongue into knots.

"My thanks, lass," he said in a rasping whisper. "Thomas tells me you saved my life."

Mairi flushed. "You did that yourself, sir. I merely offered you shelter."

He lifted his head and groaned, dropping back on to the pillow.

She hurried to his side and rested a restraining hand on the bare skin of his chest. She felt the muscles clenched beneath her palm. "You mustn't," she warned him. "Give it another day at least."

His eyes moved over her features. "They were wrong, you know," he mused.

"Who?"

"The bards. They say you've the face of an angel, but it isn't so. 'Tis a temptress I see before me."

She laughed, her voice low and amused. "You're delirious. I'm just a woman like any other, neither angel nor temptress."

"Oh no, Mairi of Shiels." His voice dropped. She leaned closer to hear his words. "No man alive would name you a woman like any other." By the time the last word left his lips, he was asleep.

Mairi looked down at him for a long time. She had never seen hair of such color in her entire life. It was a shade between silver and flax, as pale and cool as the moon in winter. His face was brown from the sun, but the skin on his chest and arms was ruddy and fair. A Saxon, a *Sassenach* prince, untainted by Norman blood, a sworn enemy of her people. His chest was wide and furred and deeply muscled, his shoulders massive. Even in sleep, he was larger, more vital, than any man she'd ever seen.

So, she thought, *this is how it happens. A stranger at the gates, and a woman's life is changed forever.* Shaken to the core, she left the room and climbed the stairs to her solar.

The next day, when Mairi came to his room, he was stronger. He sat up in bed, his bare chest and shoulders propped up by pillows. He smiled at her, the brilliant turquoise of his eyes glinting with light.

"At last, you've come," he said. "I'd begun to think you were a vision."

Nothing of what she felt reflected itself in her still hands and implacable expression. "You are better today. I'm glad," she said gravely.

"Are you, lass?" He patted the side of the bed. "Then sit beside me. I've never been so bored in all my life."

Mairi approached the bed, but she did not sit. "You nearly lost your life," she reminded him. "Sleep will help you regain your strength."

"I've slept enough. What I need now is entertainment. Tell me about yourself. God's wounds, I've heard enough about you, but I never believed it. Why have you never been to court?"

Her lip curled. "An English court is no place for a Scot."

"You do not approve of England, m'lady?" he asked casually.

She lifted her chin. "Here in Scotland, we prefer independence, m'lord."

"I see." His eyes were on her face, noting the defiant tilt of her chin, the winged brows, and the pulse beating erratically in her slender throat. He did not want this woman to disapprove of him. Reaching out, he took her hand and pulled her down so that she sat beside him. "I am English, lass. Surely I've given you no cause to despise me."

"I do not despise the English," Mairi was quick to assure him, "however, I would prefer that they stay in England and leave the governing of Scotland to us."

"Margaret of Norway died," he reminded her.

"Aye, but there is still John Balliol and Robert the Bruce."

"Both excellent men," Edward agreed. "But neither has a strong following."

"Only because the king keeps them in England," Mairi countered.

Edward grinned. "A clever move on his part, do you not agree?"

She nodded. "Aye. A clever move for a man who seeks to rule both countries."

He shrugged. She tried to pull her hand away, but he tightened his hold. Laying his palm flat across her own, he threaded his fingers through hers and rubbed the sensitive skin with his thumb. "Perhaps he only seeks to keep the peace."

Mairi could barely think. "Edward is not a peaceful man," she managed in a strangled voice.

He looked at her, an arrested expression in his eyes. "What do you know of Edward of England?"

It was her turn to shrug. "Only what I've been told. He is forceful in battle, merciful to the conquered, wise in council, but happiest on horseback with his dogs behind and a hawk on his wrist. He is a brave and gallant knight, and his reputation with women is legendary. Besides his wife, he has a slew of mistresses throughout England." Her forehead wrinkled. "I suppose he is handsome, but I can't say for sure. David Murray would never notice such a thing."

Edward watched her carefully as she described his character traits. The light played over her face, illuminating the flawless skin and light, expressive eyes. Below his waist, the tension in his body was tight as the skin of a drum. Her informant had flattered him. For that Edward was grateful. If the truth were told, he was not always wise in council. His temper was inconsistent, and he hated muddle of any kind. He ruled with an impetuous decisiveness that inspired others to do as he commanded. His strengths were his battle strategy and his enviable charm. Without exception, those who disagreed with his decisons eventually came around to his way of thinking. It did not concern him that Mairi of Shiels believed him to be a womanizer. He had no intention of revealing his true identity. What puzzled him was her interest. It was obvious that her curiosity had passed the bounds of idle diversion.

"It sounds as if King Edward is highly regarded by your David Murray."

Mairi nodded. "David admires him greatly." A thought occurred to her. "What of yourself, m'lord? Do you admire the king?"

Edward's skin reddened, and he shifted uncomfortably under her innocent gaze. "He is a man much like any other," he muttered.

"Surely not like any other?" Mairi teased.

"Aye, he is," he assured her. "He stands taller than most by half a head, and he is very fair." He frowned. "There are those who consider him well favored."

Mairi's mouth turned up at the corners. "Why, Lord Durbridge. I do believe you are jealous of him."

Edward's eyes widened, and the flush in his cheeks moved to include his shoulders and chest. "Indeed I am not," he protested, shocked that she could conclude such a thing. "Edward is a strong king, but he is not a god, mistress. Do not for one moment mistake him for one. He would not thank you for it."

"Do you know him well?" she asked curiously.

Edward nodded, and when he spoke, his voice was low and gruff. "Aye. As well as I know myself." Never in his life had he pretended to be other than who he was, and he didn't like it. This pretense was becoming difficult to manage. Perhaps he should speak and end it now. "Lass," he began, his eyes meeting hers across their clasped hands.

"Yes?"

He opened his mouth to confess, but the words wouldn't come. Faith, she was lovely. What would she do when she found out? Would the trust shining forth from those incredible eyes fade and disappear forever? Nay, he couldn't risk it.

From the time Edward was fourteen years old, women came willingly to his bed, grateful for his attention for as long as it lasted. Occasionally he wondered if seduction came as easily to every well-favored man who wasn't king of England. Just once he would like to find out for himself what it felt like to be an ordinary man alone with a pretty maid.

He swallowed. "You are very lovely."

She did not blush or simper or even look away. "Thank you," she said instead.

"Are you betrothed?"

She thought of David Murray and the excuses she'd come up with over the years to put him off. Deep in the furthest recesses of her soul, Mairi knew that she would not marry him. Not now. "Not really."

"What does that mean?"

"Only that I've been asked and, until now, had considered the possibility."

"What changed your mind?"

She looked directly at him. "You."

He stared at her, aghast. "Lass," he croaked, searching desperately for a safe reply. "I can't—I didn't—"

Her eyes danced with laughter. "You needn't panic," she teased. "I won't post the banns until you are completely well."

Drawing a deep, restoring breath, he settled back against the pillows. "You are a minx, Mairi of Shiels," he said when he could trust himself to speak again. "Have you no scruples? You nearly stopped my heart."

"Would it be so dreadful?" she countered.

Once again heat rose in his loins. His eyes moved from her face to the sweet curve of her breasts. What would it be like to take her here and now, when the singing of her blood reached out to him, demanding fulfillment? It wasn't possible. He hadn't the strength for it. The scent of roses wafted from her hair. She was direct and unafraid. He would be direct in return. "Are you a maid?" he asked gently.

She did not look away. "Aye. Does it matter?"

"The issue is of some importance," he replied. "There are those to whom an untouched bride is a necessity."

"What of you, m'lord?"

He considered her question carefully. For purposes of succession, virginity was required in a queen. He thought of his wedding night with Eleanor. Three lords, the high chamberlain included, had waited and listened outside the cloistering bed curtains. The consummation of a royal marriage was an affair of state. He had acquitted himself admirably and taken her no less than three times that night. Poor lass. She hadn't enjoyed it nearly as much as he had. Not that the night had been particularly memorable for him either. Untouched virgins were not the most satisfactory of bed partners. Edward preferred lustier wenches who knew what a man expected between the sheets.

Mairi's expression was serious as she waited for his answer. Her eyes held a question in their depths and something else that could not be denied. Suddenly, it meant a great deal that she had never known another man. Edward felt the racing of pulse. Blood drummed in his temples. What had come over him? He was no debaucher of innocent virgins. He was the king of England, and Eleanor waited for him in London. Mairi of Shiels wasn't a woman to be tumbled for a single night's easy sport, and he knew, without a doubt, she would never agree to be any man's mistress. His eyes moved over her face. It was no wonder he had considered it. A saint would be tempted by this woman with the face of legends.

He cleared his throat and answered her question. "Virginity is less important to me than loyalty. It matters little whether a woman has known another man before she takes her vows as long as she knows only her husband after."

"Well spoken," said Mairi, her smiling lighting the still beauty of her face. "If all men had your tolerance, more women would be happy in their marriages."

He sighed with relief. The moment of tension had disappeared and with it the necessity of confessing his own marital state. He did not intend to bed this fascinating woman, but he saw no need to disclose his true identity or the fact that he already had a wife. Mairi would never travel to London, and he would never see the gates of Traquair House again. No one would be harmed if he carried on this flirtation for a bit longer. It suited him to be an ordinary man cossetted by a pretty maid.

Edward awoke for the second time that day. He could see from the light in the small window above his bed that it was no more than dusk, but it would be dark soon. Night fell quickly on the borders. He was no longer tired, and for the first time, hunger cramped his stomach. He couldn't remember the last time he'd been hungry. It was an unpleasant sensation. God's blood! Where was Thomas?

Cursing loudly, he threw aside the blankets and sat up. A wave of dizziness washed over him, and his shoulder ached. For a brief moment, he considered giving up his quest. But the low, demanding growl of his stomach spurred him on. His breeks and boots and a freshly washed tunic lay over a nearby stool.

Carefully, he pulled on his garments, leaving the tunic unlaced at the throat and walked out of the room to the landing. Night had fallen, and the only light came from the evil-smelling torches mounted on the wall. Slowly, so as not to jar his wound, he descended the stairs and followed the light into the hall. His eyes widened at the picture before him.

Reclining on a wolfskin rug before an enormous fire, a look of rapt adoration on his face, was his squire, Thomas Droune. Mairi sat across from him, her hands fingering a small wooden instrument that resembled a lute. Edward waited, hidden by shadows, as the sweet, piercing notes filled the room. His guess had been accurate. It was a lute but unlike any that he'd heard before. The music quivered, trembled, and rose, exquisitely clear, heartbreakingly pure, until the very walls vibrated with the aching sadness of the border ballad. Horrified, Edward felt his eyes sting. Blinking rapidly, he forced back the suspicious wetness gathering at the corners. By God, the woman was a witch. She could charm the spirits from their netherworld haunts.

When the last of the notes died away, he moved out of the shadows and made his way to the fire. Thomas noticed him first. Jumping to his feet, the boy stammered a garbled apology. "My lord," he gasped. "I—you—"

Edward ignored him. His mind was completely occupied with the woman before him. Slowly, as if in a dream, she stood and faced him. The fire threw an arc of light against the blackened walls, highlighting her face in its golden glow.

She stared back at him, saying nothing, her eyes noting the pulse in his brown throat, the golden hair straying from the laces of his shirt, and the tightly clenched hands that gave away more, much more, than she knew he wanted her to know.

Thomas backed away. The once comfortable room welcomed him no longer. The two had not even touched, but he felt as if he were an intruder in a moment of such intimacy that the scorching heat between them would consume anyone caught in its path. Holy God. He had never seen such a look on the king's face. This development could be dangerous for the both of them. Mairi of Shiels was the daughter of the late laird of Clan Maxwell. An insult of this nature would not bode well for England. If the Maxwells sent the cross throughout Scotland, not a clan in the entire country would support Edward. Doubt clouded his boyish features as he slipped, unnoticed, from the room.

A log snapped in the fire. Sheets of driving rain found their way down the long chimney. The flames hissed and curled around the life-giving drops, shriveling them into smoke. Edward spoke first. "Will you play for me?"

Mairi shook her head. The music had left her. There was room for only this man, lean and predatory, standing like a golden lion in the firelight. She swallowed.

"Do you want me to leave you, lass?" His voice was thick and rough in his throat.

Again she shook her head.

He knelt before her on the wolfskin and held out his hand.

Mairi allowed him to pull her down beside him, her eyes intent on his face.

"You should not have left your bed," she whispered. "The wound needs rest to heal."

He shrugged off her concern. "It will heal." Her hair pooled like silk on the floor around her. He could not resist fingering the shining strands. "I wish you would sing. 'Tis a lovely voice you have, Mairi of Shiels."

She tilted her head, considering his words as if to gauge whether they were flattery or truth. Finally, she smiled. "I can sing no more tonight, my lord, but if you like I'll tell you a kelpie tale of the Highlands."

He stretched out on the rug, his sound arm behind his head. "I should like it above all things."

"Very well then." She leaned back on her hands and began to speak. "Once, the land beyond the Grampians was occupied by Celts, small, dark people with wisdom in their eyes and purity in their hearts. Some say they dealt in magic, but others insist their power lay in the earth goddess they worshipped above all others."

Her voice had a hushed, mystical quality that Edward had heard in only the most skilled bards. He listened carefully, caught in the web of her words.

"A young girl was born into one of the northern tribes. From the beginning, all who knew her saw that she was different. She spoke to the wind and rain and the animals and all growing things, and they answered her. The earth goddess was growing old, and there were those who believed that Ceilith, the young girl, was destined to take her place."

Mairi stared into the sputtering flames. Edward watched, enchanted, as the firelight played across her face, shadowing the hollows of her cheeks, highlighting the thin nose, the elegant bones of her face, and the faint dusting of freckles on her skin.

"One spring day," she continued, "when Ceilith was gathering herbs on the moors, a stranger came to the Highlands. He was tall and fair and rode a dark stallion. Caught by Ceilith's beauty, he captured her and took her far away, beyond the sea. There he made her his bride. She was very unhappy. She could not eat nor drink, and her song that called up the sun each day dried in her throat. Ceilith's people mourned her. In the Highlands that year, the spring and summer were short. In the land beyond the sea, darkness descended, and the people were afraid. Finally, Ceilith's husband realized that she would die. Although his heart was sore, he brought her home to her beloved Highlands and, there on the moor where he found her, bid her good-bye. At first Ceilith was happy. Flowers bloomed, grain grew plentiful, and brightness covered the land. But soon, Ceilith was sad again. She hated the frozen north, but she loved a man. She longed for the man who was her husband. She loved the Highlands and the people of her tribe, but she was lonely."

Mairi was silent for a long time. Finally, Edward prodded her. "What happened? Did she leave her people and return to him?"

"No." She wet her lips. "He was a king, you see, and a king needs an heir. When Ceilith's husband left her, he returned home and married a woman of the north. Ceilith died of a broken heart."

Edward's heart stopped. Had she found him out or was Mairi's tale an incredible coincidence? The silence lengthened. He could bear it no longer. Gently, his hands slipped beneath her chin to her throat, turning her head so that she looked directly at him. Those shining gray eyes were incapable of deception. Her face was inches from his own. He could smell the rose-petal scent of her hair. Her breath caught in a quick, sharp intake, and he was lost. The flickering heat in his loins blazed into a roaring inferno. Involuntarily, his hand clenched as he fought his desire.

"Edward," she choked, "you're hurting me."

Cursing himself and his newly found strength of character, he released her and stood up. There were fingermarks on her neck. Tomorrow they would be bruises. "Forgive me, lass," he muttered, "I forgot myself. You are a gifted weaver of tales, but I fear you were right. My wound needs resting."

Mairi watched him leave the room, a thoughtful expression on her face. He did not look at all like a man who needed rest, more like a lion kept too long at the end of a leash.

✳25✳

Edward belted his tunic and looked around for his scabbard. It was nowhere to be found. He grinned and tucked a small dirk inside his sash. The lass was too intelligent to allow a stranger free use of his sword. Mairi of Shiels was an unusual woman. An astute mind lay beneath her lovely face. He opened the door and walked down the hall to the stairs. No one was about. The air was cold, and he drew a deep cleansing breath into his lungs. He'd never quite grown accustomed to the foul-smelling herbs that were inevitably strewn across all sickroom floors.

He walked down the stairs to the great hall. The door to the entry was open. God's blood! Where was everyone? Didn't the woman have servants? He opened his mouth to call for Thomas, then remembered he'd sent him back to London bearing the message that the king still lived. Hunger and the tempting smell of spice propelled him out the door and across the yard to a small dwelling he was sure would be the kitchen.

Edward pushed open the door and stepped inside. A rush of pleasure caught him by surprise. She was here, overseeing the preparation of apple tarts. Her black hair, held away from her face by a strip of velvet, hung down her back. Her cheeks were red from the heat and a smudge of flour marked her nose. His mouth watered. He wasn't sure whether it was the smell of food or the incredibly appealing sight of Mairi of Shiels dressed in the simple clothes of country maid.

"You shouldn't be out of bed," she chastised him.

He grinned. "I had nothing to occupy my time. You haven't been to visit me in two days."

"There is more to running an estate than dalliance," she said.

His grin broadened. "'Tis glad I am to hear it. I was afraid you'd been avoiding me."

She lifted her chin and looked directly at him. "Don't be absurd. Why would I do that?"

Edward promised himself he would leave the lass pure, but his time was growing short. A bit of flirtation wouldn't harm her. "Perhaps because I was ungracious enough to refuse your proposal," he said.

The cooks' ladles stopped in midair as they turned to look at their mistress in astonishment.

"Of course not," Mairi said hastily. "You must know I wasn't serious."

"I'm sorry to hear it," replied Edward. "If you don't wish to marry me, perhaps you'll agree to feed me instead."

Her hand flew to her mouth. "Sweet Mary, 'tis past time for the noon meal. I forgot." She turned to the cooks. "Why did no one remind me?"

"Pardon me, mistress," a plump, apple-cheeked girl spoke up. "But often times you have no appetite in the middle of the day."

"I'm afraid 'tis so," Mairi confessed.

Edward folded his arms across his chest and leaned against the door jamb. He was so tall his head brushed against the ceiling. "I know how to bring back your appetite," he said. "We shall have a picnic."

She frowned. "A picnic?"

"A meal out of doors," he explained. "Surely you've done it before."

Mairi shook her head. "I don't think—"

His smile was brilliant. "You needn't think, lass. Just pack up some bread, a bit of cheese, and a flask of wine, and we'll be on our way."

Who could argue with such enthusiasm? Certainly not Mairi. She knew, with a sinking feeling in her chest, that he was not a man to accept refusal refusal easily.

He watched her efficient movements with fascinated interest as she gathered the food, stuffing it into a flour sack and knotting it firmly at the top. This was a lady of the manor that he had no experience with. Her capable hands had the slender fine-boned lines of an aristocrat, but her nails were clipped short and he'd felt the callouses on her palm when she'd touched his chest. Mairi of Shiels was not afraid of hard work. For some reason, the knowledge pleased him. Manual labor was something Edward was unfamiliar with. The idea that this border lady with the light-touched eyes was proficient in areas he was not challenged him.

Mairi untied the linen cloth from around her waist. "Shall we go?" she asked, embarrassed at the obvious interest of her servants.

"Aye." Edward pushed away from the door and held out his hand for the sack.

She gave it to him and waited until he stepped outside before she followed. They walked for several minutes in silence. He spoke first. "You didn't want to come with me, did you?"

A smile played across her lips. If he could be direct, so could she. "On the contrary, I wanted to very much."

"I don't believe you."

The wind tugged at her hair, tangling the fine strands into tiny knots. She brushed it back away from her face so that the pure line of her jaw was exposed to his gaze. "Believe what you wish. We both know the truth."

Intrigued and yet slightly annoyed, Edward reached for her hand. She stopped and faced him, her back very straight. She was tall for a woman, but nothing compared to his great height. Her head came up to his shoulder. "What is the truth, lass?" he asked gruffly.

Edward knew she would not dissemble. He was not disappointed. She looked him straight in the eye and spared nothing. "I know you want me, Edward of Durbridge," she said softly, "and I know that you do not intend marriage. You are also a knight, and English knights do not seduce virgins."

He had asked for plain speaking, but he was not prepared for the effect of her words. Like a boy with his first maid, he stared down at her, tongue-tied and red faced, unable to defend himself. No one had ever read his character as clearly as this leggy, half-grown girl he had known less than one week. The air caught in his throat. Holy God, she was lovely beyond belief. But it was more than her beauty that drew him. It was the uncompromising honesty in her gaze, the regal set of her head, the straight dignity of her back, the graceful play of her hands, and the glorious, heart-shattering purity of her smile.

Edward had never considered marrying for love. His marriage to Eleanor had been a political match, debated for hours in the chilly halls of Westminster and the Tower. It had never occurred to him to wonder how his wife's mind worked. God's wounds! He could barely remember what she looked like. What he wouldn't give to be free at this moment, to offer everything he had to this woman who intrigued him more than any other had before her.

The blood burned like fire through his veins. A tic twitched at the corner of his mouth, a sign of the effort it took to control his emotions. Dropping her hand, Edward walked on. He could offer her nothing, not even the truth, and it shamed him.

She caught up with him near the black oak overlooking the burn. "A surly companion is not what I'd expected when you suggested a picnic, m'lord," she teased him.

Her smile was sweet and beguiling, like wild honey. Happiness flooded through him, warming the chill around his heart. He took her hand and drew her down beside him. "'Tis as good a place as any for a picnic."

"Aye." Mairi looked around her at the green-gold beauty of the hills. The sky was a deep, piercing blue, and the clouds hung so low she felt as if she could pluck one with her fingers. At her feet, the burn rushed clear and cold. The water flowed gold colored from the sun and the brown peat stones it crossed on its way to the sea. She sighed. The day was perfect. She was grateful she'd allowed him to persuade her out of doors.

"I had no idea your country could be as lovely as this," he said.

She looked at him, surprised. "Surely you've been to Scotland before this?"

He nodded. "Aye, but only to take part in battle. My mind was not on the landscape."

There was much she wanted to say but decided against it. Their time together was too short for recriminations. She did not want this Englishman's last memory of her to be that of a woman with a shrewish temper. "Is your home very different?" she asked instead.

He leaned back on his hands, his eyes closed, his face turned toward the sun. The carven beauty of his mouth made her throat go dry.

"Aye," he said carefully. "I live in London most of the year, but even in the south of England, the land is dryer with fewer trees." He opened his eyes, and his voice dropped. It was lower, more intimate, caressing. "I would show it to you if I could."

"Why can't you?" Deliberately, she kept her question light.

A sound, almost a groan but more muffled, came from within his chest. "Lass, have you learned nothing of maidenly decorum?"

"I am Mairi of Shiels," she said with quiet dignity. "I have no need for decorum."

Her hand on his cheek undid him. He turned toward her touch to find her gaze upon him. Searching her face for the smallest sign of regret, he found none. "God help you, my heart," he murmured. "May He forgive me for the sin I would willingly commit."

"I'll warrant it will not be your first," she teased him.

He did not smile. "Lass," he whispered hoarsely, "you cannot do this."

Her expression grew serious and the cool, light-struck eyes widened until they seemed to fill her entire face. "I know not what brought you here, m'lord, but from the first I knew how it would be between us."

"Sweet Jesu." He damned the emotions within him that demanded honesty at such a price. "I am not who you think."

"Hush." She laid her finger across his lips, down his chin and throat into the crisply curling hair escaping from the top of his shirt. "It doesn't matter."

"Mairi," he groaned, throwing out his final and most damning argument. "I have never known another woman like you. I would wed you if I could, but I am not free."

Her exploring fingers had unlaced his shirt and were making shockingly intimate forays down his chest. Her question was a whisper against his ear. "You are be-trothed?"

"Nay, lass," he confessed, cursing the hunger surging through him. "I am married."

Her hand was on his rib cage, her touch more sensuous than any courtesan he had ever known. She could not have heard him for she did not draw away.

"Mairi," he began and stopped. Her face was close to his own. Her hair smelled like roses and her skin, bathed in afternoon sunlight, was flawless. Her lips parted ever so slightly, and he heard his own harsh intake of breath. Of their own volition, his hands reached out to caress her throat, her cheeks, and finally to thread the silken strands of her hair between his fingers while he gently cradled her head. She closed her eyes. Her lashes rested like dark half-moons against her cheeks. Her mouth quivered in silent invitation.

"I am a man, not a saint," he murmured. "By all that is holy, I swear you shall not regret this." With that he lowered his head and touched his mouth to hers.

Whatever Mairi had expected, it wasn't this piercing sweetness, this exquisite, aching fire that started in the pit of her stomach and traveled through every nerve until she hummed like a branch struck by lightning. Who would have guessed that a man as tall and hard as a mountain had lips softer than angel's wings, whose sheltering arms held magic in their touch, whose words of love muffled against her throat could heat her blood to fevered heights? Her hands slid up his back, reveling in the hard strength and hot male flesh stretched so tightly across the bunched muscles. She raked him lightly with her nails.

"My God, Mairi," he groaned, lifting his head to look down at her passion-flushed face. "Tell me you want this. Let me hear your words before 'tis too late to stop."

Something deep and elemental blazed to life in her eyes. When she spoke, her voice sounded nothing like herself. "I shan't stop you, Edward. I want it too, more than any-thing."

His hands trembled as he molded them over the sweet rise of her breasts and stroked their tips with his thumbs. When he felt her response, he untied her kirtle and pushed aside the bodice of her tightly fitting tunic. Her arms were bare and the thin linen of her shift revealed the outline of her nipples and the darkness between her thighs. Edward's breathing altered. He was no longer in control. Even if she wanted him to stop, he couldn't. She was too lovely and he'd thought of nothing but burying himself inside her warmth for a seemingly endless length of days and nights.

He tore his gaze from the enticing roundness of her breasts to look at her face. She was staring at him, unembarrassed and unafraid. There was hunger in her eyes and something else, something that reached out and touched him with a longing that left him shaken and wanting. When his mouth took hers in a searing kiss, her lips opened, and her tongue eagerly sought his. White heat flamed through him. He moved over her, pressing himself into the triangle of her thighs. He had never been so hard. He feared he would hurt her, but there was no help for it. Mairi of Shiels lay beneath him, open and welcoming. Only God Himself had the power to stop this coupling.

Mairi did not feel the coolness of the air or the pebbles rubbing against her skin as her shift was lifted over her head and thrown aside. She did not hear the squirrels chattering and scolding one another in the trunk of the great black oak that sheltered them. She did not see the single whaup circling overhead or hear the shrillness of its lonely cry. She felt only a firm mouth on her lips and a man's hands on her skin. She heard only the wild singing of her blood that promised her this first long-dreamed-of taste of passion.

Again and again Edward moved against her with all the skill of a man familiar with the secrets of a woman's body. He stirred the dormant embers of her need into leaping flames of desire. Her skin ached and her nerves throbbed against the insistent coaxing of his hands and mouth. When he parted her thighs with his leg, she was more than ready.

He moved over her, breathing heavily. The turgid length of his sex probed at her. Mairi looked up through her lashes. His eyes were open, their blue-green color more brilliant than the sky that framed his head. He stared down at her with a look of such yearning hunger that she could not bear it. Reaching up, she touched his face.

With a harsh cry, he surged into her, forgetting his resolve to go slowly, to exercise control, to bring her the greatest pleasure she had ever known. The cords on the side of his neck swelled. He buried his face against her throat. Taking in deep gulping breaths, he willed his raging heart to slow its beat.

Mairi concentrated on the sensations she was feeling. It was not an unpleasant feeling exactly, just different. She felt stretched and full. Edward was a large man, and she was slender. The sharp end of a pebble stabbed into her hip. Experimentally, she shifted her hips. He stiffened.

"Don't move lass," he muttered hoarsely, "or it will be over before 'tis even begun."

"Edward, I—" She gasped as his mouth closed over the sensitive peak of her breast.

The tiny sound was his undoing. His entire body tensed, and then, with an inarticulate moan, he thrust deeply over and over until she caught his rhythm and the tension she felt when his seeking fingers first touched her rose again. Before she could reach her own crescendo, an incredible warmth spread through her belly and she felt him slump, full weight, on top of her.

Mairi frowned. He was heavy, and she was cold. The exquisite sensations she'd felt in the beginning had disappeared, leaving a burning ache between her legs. She twisted her hips and felt him slip out of her.

"I'm sorry lass," he murmured, "but I couldn't wait." He lifted his head and grinned sheepishly. "Say you'll forgive me."

She said the first thing that came into her mind. "Is more supposed to happen?"

His expression didn't change, but his eyes darkened, the pupils blotting out the color. "If you'll give me another chance, I'll show you," he said at last.

Holding his gaze with her own, Mairi nodded. When his mouth slowly descended to find the pulse point in her neck, she closed her eyes, and when his hands moved down her body, she held her breath, but when he finally entered her and the slow, sensuous mating dance began once again, her blood warmed and her hands clenched, and when at last the dizzying whirl of passion reached its peak, she exploded in a vision of light and heat and fire. Mairi dug her nails into his back and buried her face against his chest, inhaling his smell, tasting his skin, crying out his name in one endless, heartstopping cry of need.

Later, much later, she lay still, her eyes closed, her cheeks burning with embarrassment. Never in her life had she felt so vulnerable, so exposed. Never would she have believed her body could respond in such a way. At that moment, she would have given all she had on earth and much of what heaven held in store to know what the man who held her so tightly against his chest was thinking. As if in answer to her silent prayer, he spoke.

"I love you, Mairi Maxwell of Shiels. Believe what you will, but I've never said that to another woman."

"Not even your wife?" Before the words were out, she wished she could call them back.

He took a deep breath. Eleanor was his wife, and he would not speak ill of her, but neither could he lie to this woman with whom he had found something he hadn't known existed. "No," he said simply.

Mairi slid out from beneath him and rested her head on her elbow. "How long do we have?"

He thought of the message sent with Thomas and the days already past. Again he refused to lie. "Only tonight."

There were no recriminations in Mairi's eyes, only a quiet acceptance. She nodded. "Shall we make the most of it then?"

Edward I of England rode out of the gates of Traquair House the following morning a humbled man. For the first time in his life, he understood the meaning of courage. He had known many men and seen many battles during his reign, but courage, he now knew, was not to be found in the midst of war. Courage was not the death-defying charges of men in full mail, their horses foaming at the mouth, their swords dripping with the blood of their enemies. Courage was the dry eyes and straight back of a gray-eyed girl who had given a stranger all that was hers to give only to watch him ride away forever. He would never seek out Mairi of Shiels again. The cost was too great for the both of them.

❧26❧

Traquair House
1993

It was nearly midnight. Morning was hours away, but I needed food desperately. I managed the darkened stairs and pushed open the door of the kitchen, confident that I would be alone. The brilliantly lit room startled me. After the darkness of the hall, it took several stunned seconds for my eyes to adjust to the brightness. I didn't actually see Kate replacing the circle of keys on their nail, but from her position in the room and the fleeting expression of guilt on her face, I was sure that she had recently done just that. Her presence unnerved me. I hadn't expected her. There had been no time to rehearse the carefully chosen words I wanted her to remember when I fired her.

"Good evening, Miss Murray," she said. "I had no idea you would be home tonight. Your mother told me not to expect you."

Without speaking, I brushed past her and opened the refrigerator. The remains of a roast beef, bread, and two large hunks of cheese would do. Kate watched me as I sliced the meat and bread. I didn't bother with a plate or silverware but stuffed several pieces into my mouth, chewed, and swallowed quickly. Pouring myself a large glass of juice, I sliced two pieces of cheese. Again, using the palm of my hand as a plate, I carried the food over to the fire that perpetually burned in the kitchen hearth and sat down in a chair.

"Would you like me to make you some tea, Miss Murray?"

Rage consumed me. "You'd like that wouldn't you?"

"I beg your pardon?"

"I can't believe that Ian hasn't told you."

"Told me what?"

I studied her face carefully. There was nothing in her expression to indicate that she lied. It disconcerted me. Why hadn't Ian warned her that I knew everything? It occurred to me that I had a tremendous advantage if the two of them had not yet compared stories. I decided to begin again. "I know who you are, Kate, and it won't do you any good at all. If you had approached me fairly when I first came, things might have been different. As it is, you're fired. I want you out of here first thing in the morning."

Her face looked pale, but her eyes were hot and black with hate. "We have labor laws in Scotland. It won't be easy to dismiss me."

"You may do as you please, Mrs. Ferguson. But unless you have a very good excuse for drugging me, I wouldn't take this any farther than it's already gone."

"Are you threatening me?" Her voice died to a whisper.

"Not at all. I would rather put this whole thing behind us."

She didn't argue. Lifting her head, she threw me one last scathing glance and left the room.

I ate several more slices of meat and washed it down with another glass of juice before climbing the stairs to my room. I felt incredibly satisfied, almost light-headed. Kate's shadowy presence and thinly veiled disapproval would no longer haunt me. Tomorrow when I woke, she would be gone. The idea of choosing my own housekeeper was appealing. I had no idea how to go about it, but I was sure someone in town would help me. I could always ask Ian—No. Pain squeezed my heart. Ian was gone. I couldn't ask him anything again. Curled into a fetal position, I fell asleep.

London, England
1292

"May I congratulate you on the new prince, Your Grace?" The nobleman smirked ingratiatingly and bowed over the queen's hand.

Eleanor, queen of England, smiled. "You may indeed, m'lord. He is a lusty babe." She withdrew her hand and looked up at him curiously. "'Tis been an age since we have seen you at court. Have you come for his christening?"

"Of course, Your Grace." Northumberland had no idea that the christening of England's new heir would fall during his visit to London. It had been two years since he'd put in an appearance at Edward's court. If necessity hadn't demanded it, he would never have made the uncomfortable journey. The filth and overflowing gutters of London disgusted him. He much preferred the pristine beauty of the north country. But there was no help for it. Border raids had increased at an alarming rate, and if the king did not take action soon, he would lose every horse and cow he owned to the Scots reivers. Edward had not traveled to the borders in a long time. Long enough to have forgotten his rash promise of aid made after that frightening interlude two years before when he'd disappeared and the entire country believed him dead.

The queen had spoken and was waiting for an answer. Northumberland hadn't heard a word of it. He flushed. It was hardly a fortuitous beginning.

Fortunately Eleanor hadn't noticed. She was diverted by the appearance of a large, fair-haired man bearing down upon them. "Ah, here he is." She held out her hand to her husband. "Edward, 'tis Northumberland, come all the way from the borders to witness the christening."

Edward lifted his wife's hand to his lips. "How fortunate we are, my dear, to have such a loyal subject. How are you, Northumberland? We haven't seen you at court in years."

"Only two, Your Grace." Northumberland was quick to remind him. "'Tis not wise to leave a stronghold unattended when one lives in the borders."

Edward had already lost interest. His eyes flickered past his guest to the dancers at the far end of the banquet hall. "Indeed. Have you supped, m'lord? Our cooks have surpassed themselves tonight."

"Not yet. I've only just arrived."

"We won't keep you." Edward nodded and waved the man toward the groaning tables of food.

Eleanor smiled as Northumberland backed away. She

turned to her husband and spoke through set teeth. "That was rude of you, m'lord."

"Was it?" He sounded amused. "I hadn't noticed."

"Extremely." Her slippered foot tapped sharply on the wooden floor. "What has he done that you must treat him so shabbily?"

Anger blazed to life in Edward's eyes and then died again. He sighed. "I need no reason, my love. I am king of England."

"'Tis hardly an excuse."

"On the contrary. I find it an excellent one. Just as your rank excuses your waspish tongue, mine excuses me of rudeness."

Quick tears sprang to her eyes. "Edward," she pleaded, "must it always be this way between us?"

He frowned. "What in heaven are you talking about, Eleanor?"

"Must you be cruel to me as well?" she whispered.

"I?" He looked genuinely surprised. "How am I cruel? Do I shout at you, starve you, beat you? How can a woman who has everything complain of cruelty?"

"Everything but affection," she shot back. "Isn't a wife entitled to her husband's love?"

Edward beckoned to a servant carrying huge goblets of wine. Lifting one from the tray, he drained it quickly, replaced the goblet, and took another. These encounters with Eleanor were becoming tedious. "I do love you, Eleanor. How can you think otherwise?"

Her lips trembled as she fought for control. Nothing would be worse than public humiliation. "My women tell me otherwise."

"What do they tell you?"

Eleanor lifted her head and acknowledged the couple gesturing from across the room. "They say you've a mistress in every township in England and that your bastards litter the countryside."

"Is that all?"

Eleanor forgot her dignity. A deep flush rose from the low-cut bodice of her dress and stopped at her cheeks. "Isn't that enough, Edward? How can you say you love me when your behavior proves otherwise?"

He shifted uncomfortably under the scrutiny of his wife's accusing eyes. How did one tell a woman that she wasn't his choice, that a political union was a matter of state for the purposes of breeding heirs? Why hadn't she been told from the beginning?

Edward was not a cruel man. He spared her as much as he could, but he had no intention of changing his behavior. "I am no different than any other man, Eleanor. You have nothing to fear. You are my wife and I care for you deeply. I admit I've not been faithful, but the others mean nothing to me." He set the goblet on the mantel and took her hands in his. "Rest assured, my love, there is no one in my kingdom who has a greater claim on this heart than my wife."

"What about outside your kingdom?"

Edward looked startled. Where had she come by that bit of information? Certainly not Thomas. He was the soul of discretion. "Don't be absurd, Eleanor. I haven't been outside of England for two years. Acquit me of that, at least."

She managed a watery smile. "You are right, of course. Forgive me, my darling. Shall we join the dancers?"

He smiled down at her, grateful that the crisis was over. "By all means," he said, tucking her hand under his arm. "The music is especially fine tonight."

"Will you dance with me?" she asked pleadingly.

Edward sighed. He despised dancing but no more than he hated the wounded expression on Eleanor's face.

"Of course," he said, drawing her across the room, into the circle just forming. He took his position in the outer ring and turned to face her. Her cheeks were flushed. She looked youthful, almost girlish. Edward grinned and waited for the music to begin. As custom ordained, Eleanor inclined her head in a brief curtsey.

The slight movement was enough for Edward to catch a glimpse of a slender, black-haired figure on the other side of the circle. She faced away from him, toward her partner. From the back he could see that the woman was tall but fine boned. She wore a scarlet gown and carried herself with the dignity of a queen. A memory, long repressed but never forgotten, awakened inside him. A tingling sensation started in his toes and traveled upward. His heart thundered in the prison of its chest. Unconsciously, he rubbed his perspiring hands on the soft fur of his mantle. Sweet Jesu, it couldn't be, and yet he knew of no woman at court with hair of such color and thickness.

By their own volition, his feet moved to the music. With an intricate flip of the wrist, he moved Eleanor to her next partner and bowed low before his own. Again and again, he bowed and circled, bowed and circled, until he stood next in line to the black-haired beauty.

A boneless sensation weakened his legs. His feet still moved in their mindless rhythm, but the hands he held out to her were blocks of ice. He stood before her, the woman he had tried for so long to forget. She looked directly at him. There could be no more doubt. The light-filled eyes that had haunted his dreams for two long years looked at him now with such naked joy that his blood sang. Happiness filled him. He was a boy again with the world at his feet. "Mairi," he whispered.

She smiled, and his breathing altered. Perhaps there had been other women in Edward's life who were as lovely as Mairi of Shiels, but all memory of them vanished. There was room only for this woman, standing before him in a crimson gown, her head held high, her heart in her eyes. Too soon she moved on, he to the left, she to the right. His gaze followed her as she smiled and held out her hand, curtseyed, and circled and turned about in her partner's arms. The scent of roses wafted through the air. His stomach clenched. He could barely curb his impatience. When would this infernal dance end? He ached to be alone with her, to hold her, to taste her, to run his hands—

Awareness, like the blast of winter wind, stopped him in midstride. He stumbled, apologized to the woman whose toe he had crushed, and found his step again. He was Edward, king of England, and for the first time in his life, the very thought of what that meant made his blood run cold.

The music ended. He looked around for Mairi. She stood near the banquet table with a lean, dark-haired man he recognized as David Murray. Edward was no coward. She would learn his identity soon enough, and he preferred that she hear it from him. Drawing a deep breath, he started across the room. A hand on his sleeve stopped him.

"Don't, Edward." Eleanor's face was very pale. "Don't humiliate me tonight."

Gently, he disengaged her clutching fingers. "It isn't like that, Eleanor. You must believe me. This has nothing to do with you."

"It never does." She nodded toward Mairi. "She is uncommonly lovely but not, I think, in your usual style."

The bitterness in her voice surprised him. He did not dream that she cared so much. "I am truly sorry for your pain, my dear."

She looked up at him, surprised and touched by his apology. "Does that mean—?" Eleanor left the rest of the question unsaid.

His handsome face reflected regret, but she was wise enough to know that contempt followed swiftly on the heels of pity. Lifting her head, she nodded toward the dancing tumblers concealed behind the doors. "They await your signal," she reminded him. "Surely, the woman would not want you to shirk your duty."

Mairi had already disappeared from sight with young Murray. "Very well, my dear," he said, impatience flitting across his features. "You've won this time. I'll not spoil your game. We shall signal the dancers."

Eleanor walked beside her husband to the dais. Climbing the three steps leading to the royal banquet table, she seated herself beside him. Edward lifted his hand, and the entertainment began. Out of the corner of his eye, he could see Mairi, directly across from him at another table, sharing a trencher with David Murray. It was obvious to anyone with eyes that the two were close friends. Edward watched as Murray speared an oyster with his knife and held it to her lips, laughing at her grimace of distaste. Irrational jealously flooded through him. "Damn him to hell," he swore under his breath. He would not watch another man paw his woman.

Deliberately, he tore his eyes away from the handsome pair and concentrated on the dancers. A woman, clad in a diaphanous garment, bent over backward, lifted her legs into the air, and walked on her hands. The audience roared with approval and banged their mugs on the oaken tables.

Edward's head ached. The noise and wine coupled with his own guilt was too much. Something must be done.

Suddenly, the performance was over, and the dancers disappeared behind the doors. Lord Northumberland stood and raised his goblet. "A toast," he cried, loudly enough to still the merrymaking guests. "A toast to Edward, king of England."

The cry was picked up and carried throughout the hall. One by one the nobility of England leaped to their feet and raised their mugs to honor their king. In the entire room, only two were still seated. Edward's jaw tightened. There would be no mercy for Northumberland, that weasel from the borders. But now, he must face her. There was no help for it. The die was cast. Slowly, painfully, his gaze settled on the pale, shocked features of the woman he had lied to, loved, and abandoned.

From across the room, Mairi could see the startling color of Edward's eyes. There was regret and something else in the ice-blue depths. Something that her mind refused to identify. Sweet Jesu, the king of England!

Why couldn't she feel? She should be outraged, humiliated, shocked, anything but this dull, vacuous ache filling her chest. The knife she clutched in her hand slid out of her numb fingers and clattered loudly on the oak table. People were beginning to stare. Besides the king, she was the only one still seated. Dear God. Could it be true? Her brain began to work again. Edward wasn't Lord Durbridge from the south of England. He was the king. The nobleman who had fallen in a bloody heap at her feet, the teasing companion who sat with her in front of the fire demanding a border ballad, the man who had shared her bed and cut his teeth on her heart, was none other than the king of England.

David stared at her, a troubled expression on his face. Blood rose in her cheeks. It seemed as if the eyes of the entire world were upon her. Rage and shame warred with each other in her breast. Carefully, she stood, her knees threatening to buckle beneath her. For a long moment her eyes met and held the anguished gaze of the king. Then, with a glittering smile and a murmured apology to David, she turned and walked down the long hall, through the suffocating silence, and out the door.

Eleanor looked out over the sea of pale, curious faces. Her color was high, but she had been bred from birth to maintain composure at all costs. Raising her glass in salute, her voice rang out in a clear command. "Northumberland has proposed a toast. Drink, everyone."

Dutifully, goblets were tilted. Everyone sat down, and conversation resumed. The queen spoke to the lord high chamberlain on her left and then turned toward her husband. "Find her, Edward," she said through smiling lips. "Find that woman and take her away. I care not how long you dally, but never allow her to set foot in London again."

Edward heard his wife's voice through a fog of guilt. The look on Mairi's face haunted him. By his enormous conceit, he had betrayed the one woman who had valued him as a man without the trappings of wealth and power. His actions were not honorable and the knowledge left a bitter taste in his mouth.

"Have you nothing to say, Edward?" Eleanor's grating words interrupted his thoughts. "No apologies, no remorse?"

His lips thinned. "Aye, my lady. I have much to say but none of it to you. However, I am most grateful for your understanding." He stood and looked down at her, his eyes a distant, wintry blue. "I know you will forgive me for retiring early."

Her face whitened. "You cannot be serious. Where are you going? What of the christening?"

"I shall return for the ceremony. Nothing else need concern you."

"Don't be a fool," she began.

The stark rage in his expression stopped her. "I beg your pardon, Edward," she whispered. "Godspeed."

With a curt nod, he shouldered his way through the crowd, beckoning David Murray to follow him. Outside the hall, in the torch-lit darkness, he spoke directly, wasting no time on explanations. "Where can I find Mairi Maxwell?"

David frowned. "In her south tower apartments, Your Grace, but surely you know she meant no offense. She was taken ill," he lied. "Mairi is a loyal subject, devoted to Your Grace."

Edward grinned. "Is she now? She must have changed a great deal since I saw her last."

"How do you know my betrothed?" David asked, surprised into rudeness. Immediately he realized his mistake. "I beg your pardon, Your Grace," he stammered.

"Your betrothed?" Edward's voice was dangerously soft. "I think not."

"Indeed, 'tis true," David assured him. "Mairi has finally agreed to our marriage. We came to London to request your permission."

Edward's expression would have frozen the fires of hell. From his superior height, he looked down at the earnest young man who dared lay claim to the woman he wanted. "I'm sorry, lad," he said at last. "You are too late. Permission denied."

Struck dumb with shock and confusion, David watched the king climb the stairs to the south tower.

❋27❋

Edward didn't bother to knock before throwing open the door. He heard her outraged gasp and from across the chamber saw the blazing fury in her eyes.

"Get out," she ordered, pointing back to the hall from where he came.

"Lass." He spread his hands in a gesture of supplication. "I did not intend for it to be this way."

Without answering, she turned toward the window and folded her arms protectively against her chest. Edward swallowed and looked around the scented chamber. He needed whiskey, and there was none to be had. A servant cowered on her knees. He dismissed her, and she backed out of the room.

"Mairi," he began and stopped. He had no words with which to defend himself. Nothing to save him but the truth. He could demand that she return to Scotland, of course. His peace of mind would be restored and his wife's suspicions calmed. Tomorrow would dawn just as today had, without embarrassing complications. But was that really what he wanted?

Until an hour ago, Edward had believed that to be true. His tryst in the borders was his alone, a pleasant indiscretion to be brought out and savored late at night when the embers burned low and sleep wouldn't come. If the truth were told, he had remained faithful in heart if not in deed to Mairi's memory. He had taken other women to his bed, but when the candles were doused and the room blanketed in darkness, it was black hair that slid through his fingers and dark, feathery lashes that tickled his chest and framed light, cloud-colored eyes. It was Mairi's mouth that opened to the demand of his questing tongue and it was her voice crying out her pleasure that brought his own release.

Edward watched her silently, a pale, still figure outlined against the wine-colored tapestry. His memory dimmed before the flesh-and-blood woman. She was here and so much more than any memory he could possibly evoke. He would not give her up again.

"You will hear me out," he demanded, breaking the tension in the overheated room.

"Will I then have a choice?" she countered, turning to look at him.

"Aye." He nodded. "I would not spoil what we had by taking you against your will."

"Very well. Explain." It was a mistake. Mairi knew it the moment she said it. She should never have agreed to hear him. He stood before her, just as he had in the beginning, in the courtyard of Traquair House, proud and vulnerable, the golden hawklike ferocity of his gaze melting her anger. Firelight touched the planes of his cheeks and the silvery crown of his head. His eyes were bluer than she remembered and filled with troubled uncertainty. It was strange to think that the king of England had once told her that he loved her. Stranger still to realize that she had the power to refuse him. Mairi chewed the inside of her cheek and waited.

"My men and I were set upon by border reivers. I was wounded," he began. "It would have been the height of foolishness to reveal my identity to anyone." His voice was low and humble, the words haltingly forced from his lips. "Later, I was afraid."

"Afraid? The mighty Hammer of the Scots afraid of a woman?"

He winced at the scorn in her words. How could he make her understand? Wetting his lips, he crossed the room to stand before her. "'Twas not fear for my person, Mairi. I was afraid you would deny me."

"It was you who denied me," she reminded him. "Aye, more than once."

"I did it for you," he burst out in frustration.

"I don't believe you."

"'Tis true." His voice gentled. "God knows I am no monk. I will not lie, Mairi. You are not the only woman I've bedded outside of my marriage, but I swear, you are the only one I have loved."

She didn't speak, but she was listening. Her mouth had softened, and her arms were at her sides. She was so lovely. Edward ached to touch her.

"Why did you not tell me later?" she whispered.

The blood rushed to his cheeks, turning the sun-darkened skin even darker. "I am the king," he said gruffly. "Sometimes a king forgets what it is to be a man."

She stared at him for a long time, judging his words, weighing the truth in his soul. Then she smiled, the brilliant wide-toothed smile immortalized by the bards. "No one could ever doubt that you are a man, Your Grace."

Stunned and speechless, he stared at her. Had he imagined her words? Could she possibly be so generous, so quick to forgive? "Mairi," he asked in wonder, "can you trust me?"

She held out her hand, and he took it in both his own. "I made a scene tonight," she said. "I'm dreadfully sorry."

He grinned, lighthearted as a boy. "No matter. 'Tis a small price to pay to have you here with me."

Her eyes widened. "But I am not with you, Edward. I came with David to ask the king's"—she corrected herself—"*your* permission to marry. David Murray has waited an ungodly length of time for my answer. I can put him off no longer, nor would I even if it were possible. I am two and twenty, nearly past the age for childbearing. I want children of my own."

"I'll give you children." He had not intended to say it, but there it was, out in the open between them. He would not take it back.

She stared at him in amazement. "Is that how you think of me?"

" 'Tis not such a bad life, to be mistress to the king. I will take care of you, Mairi. You'll have gold and jewels beyond your wildest dreams."

"Our children would be bastards, tainted by our deed, condemned by holy church."

"A royal bastard is not the same. I shall bestow titles and lands—"

"Stop." She pressed her hand against his chest. "You say that you love me. 'Tis a poor sort of love you offer, Your Grace."

"Once you didn't think so." His voice was low and intimate, evoking the memory of a night filled with warmth and magic.

Mairi closed her eyes against the pain of it. She had put that time behind her, content that because of one man and one night she would go to her grave knowing that bit of life all women long for and too few experience. The man she wanted was unattainable. David loved her. He would ask no questions, and she would be a good wife to him. What cruel act of fate had brought Edward back into her life now when she was reconciled to her future? Why had she come to London? No good could come of this.

Her hand moved to her throat. "You said you wouldn't force me," she whispered.

"Nor will I." He stepped forward and placed his hands against the wall, imprisoning her against the tapestried panels.

He was very close. Mairi could smell the clean smell of soaproot on his skin. His golden beauty overwhelmed her. In an effort to avoid his eyes, she focused on his mouth and too late realized her mistake. He lowered his head to within a fraction of her lips and stopped. Her breathing altered. Unconsciously, she tilted her head and wet her lips with her tongue.

With an inarticulate groan, Edward set his mouth against hers, hard. The kiss that he intended to be exploratory and tender was nothing of the sort. It was bruising and sensual, with all the power and yearning of his need. She answered with her own.

Their teeth scraped and tongues mated. Limbs entwined and bodies joined as frantic hands searched and stroked in their quest for the heated silk and steely muscle of bared flesh. Neither knew how their clothing came to be removed or how they found their way to the feather mattress beneath the bedcovers.

Edward lost the restraint for which he was renowned. Gone was the desire to caress and bring pleasure. Every inch of him was on fire. His body cried out for possession. Without releasing her mouth, he moved between her legs and thrust deeply. He felt her tense beneath him and heard her swift intake of breath.

Grateful for the lighted room, Edward lifted his head and looked down at her face. He'd hurt her. Her lip was caught between her teeth and she was holding back tears. Cursing himself for a clumsy fool, he stopped moving and kissed her forehead, her eyelids, and the tip of her nose.

Mairi stared at him with solemn eyes. After a two-year abstinence, she had been unprepared for the sudden invasion of turgid flesh inside her body. Edward had changed. Her memory of their coupling did not include pain nor this raging tide of emotion that consumed him. He had been a passionate, but skilled lover. Now he seemed driven, almost desperate, as if he hadn't had a woman in a very long time.

"I'm sorry, lass," he murmured as his lips skimmed the smooth column of her throat. "You are so lovely, and I came so close to losing you."

Willing herself to relax, Mairi stroked the winter-bright hair. She would tell him now and be done with it. Tomorrow she would break David Murray's heart, an ugly thought, but the alternative was worse. Edward needed her, and if the passion awakening in her bruised body was a sign, she needed him as well. Cradling his head in her hands, she brushed her lips against his ear and felt him shudder deep inside her. "You will not lose me, my love," she whispered. "I could not leave you even if you commanded me."

Something inside Edward came alive, piercing his heart with its brilliance. Folding her in his arms, he held her tightly against his chest, moving gently, rhythmically, until her desire matched his own. Only then, when he saw the look of wonder in her eyes, did his control break. For the first time in two years, he stayed the entire night with a woman.

Traquair House
1993

It was an hour before dawn when I peeked into the guestroom where my parents slept. The two dark shapes huddled close together in the four-poster bed looked peaceful and familiar.

I closed the door, careful not to wake them. They would know I was home when they saw the car in the port. I'd break the news about Kate later, after I'd found what I was looking for.

The priests' chamber was my destination. I didn't really expect to find anything momentous, but I couldn't sleep and I had a feeling, call it a premonition, about that room. Every one of my ancestors who came close to finding the stone had started there. I had nothing to lose.

By now I knew that I could do nothing to expedite the process of events unfolding inside my mind. Janet Murray's diary and the Bible where I'd found the entry of Jeanne's twins were nothing more than mediums by which I entered the lives of people who had lived before me. It was there, in my visions of the past, that I'd learned everything I knew. It was there that I would find the stone. Mairi would show me, just as she had the others. She would come when she wanted, but there was no harm in being ready. My chances were good. I'd figured out more than either Jeanne or Katrine. Unlike those poor doomed women, I knew who my enemy was.

From the darkened hallway, I turned the knob and pushed open the door. The first uncertain fingers of dawn filtered through the window, lighting the room and its contents to varying shades of gray. The mysterious silvery essence reassured me. Steeped in foggy shadows, the moldings, the paintings, and the ornate, ancient furnishings whispered in the language of another lifetime, persuading me to stay awhile, to rest my mind, to gather myself before beginning the final lap of my journey. I followed my instincts and sat down on a sheet-covered chair to wait for further inspiration. It seemed right somehow that this hazy, half-toned world should match my mood.

I must have drifted into that place between waking and sleeping when I heard a noise. It was the sound of footsteps in the hall. They were tentative, coming on slippered feet to an unfamiliar place. The doorknob turned, and I tensed. When I saw whose head peeked around the doorframe, I relaxed.

"Hi, Mom," I said. My meticulous parent hadn't bothered to pull a robe over her plaid flannels, and her blond hair was disheveled.

"Christina. You scared the life out of me. What on earth are you doing up at this hour?"

I looked at her in amazement. "You're up early yourself."

She stepped all the way into the room. "Something woke me. I don't really know whether it was a noise or not. I can't remember now." She dismissed the thought as if the reason for her waking and finding her way to the most remote part of the house was of no importance. "Kate usually has coffee brewing in the kitchen, but I was just there and nothing's started." She looked around the room and rubbed her arms. "It's cold. What are you doing here?"

Something in the misty light and soft worried expression in her eyes made me tell her. If I couldn't trust my own mother, the woman whose blood and bones I shared, the woman whose Maxwell genes had given me life, there was nothing left. "Sit down, Mom," I began. "It's a long story."

She sat, and I told her. Beginning with the letter from Ellen Maxwell and the terrible horror in her face when she first saw me to my meeting with Ian and the step-by-step unraveling of the curse. I told her of the diary and my dreams and the Bible and Professor MacCleod. I told her of Ellen and Ian's father and of her link and my own to Kate Ferguson, housekeeper of Traquair. There was a long silence when I'd finished.

"It's over then, you and Ian?" she asked after a long time. I nodded.

Mother stood up, crossed the space between us, and knelt before me, taking my hands in her own. She wet her lips. "Your father and I were concerned when you left us the note the other day. We did some investigating on our own, beginning with Ellen Maxwell's lawyer. He told us about Kate. I won't say that I'm over the shock of learning who my father was and that I have a half sister, but at least I'm reconciled to it. It really has nothing to do with my life. It does have something to do with yours, Chris. That is, if you intend to stay here in Scotland and raise your child. Surely you can see what motivated Kate. As for Ian, I don't believe he's done anything so terrible. For the sake of the baby, I'd give him another chance."

I stared at her in amazement. How could she have lived with me for eighteen years without really knowing me?

"The rest of this is impossible," she continued. "I can't believe that you've allowed it to go this far without seeking out some sort of professional help. Why haven't you spoken with your father? You've confided in him since you were a little girl. He could have helped you."

"I don't need professional help," I said through set teeth.

"You certainly need something." Her voice was sharp with worry. "Your imagination has always been an active one, but these delusions are harmful. I'm seriously worried about you." She stood up. "I want you to come with me now. We'll wake your father and have a rational discussion."

I sat, stone-faced, on my chair and didn't move.

She wilted. "Please, Chris," she pleaded. "Just come with me to see Dad. That's all I ask."

The rebellion drained out me. What had I expected? This was my mother, Susan Donnally Murray, a woman who read nothing but the newspaper and fitness magazines. A more practical, rational person didn't exist. Nothing would be gained by opposing her. "All right, Mother. If you think I should talk to Dad, I will. Why don't you go wake him. I'd like to stay here for a while."

"Promise me you won't go anywhere." She hovered anxiously by the door.

I smiled reassuringly. "I'm not crazy, Mom. I promise I won't leave Traquair House without telling you."

With an encouraging smile that did not completely erase the worry lines etched in her forehead, she disappeared behind the door. I waited for several minutes. When the sound of her footsteps had faded completely away, I stood and walked to the rosewood mantel. The panel was there, exactly where I'd expected it to be. As if I'd done it everyday of my life, I pressed first in the center and then on the far left petal of the rose. On creaking hinges, the door swung open. I took the flashlight from my pocket, flicked it on, and pulled the panel shut behind me.

I was winded before I reached the top of the stairs. The attic room where I'd found the picture of Jeanne Maxwell was exactly as I'd left it. This time, as if someone were whispering instructions to me, I knew what to do.

Setting the flashlight face up on the floor, I pulled Jeanne's cloth-covered portrait aside. In the semidarkness, the small doorway looked like nothing more than a crack in the wall. I leaned into the right side and pushed with my shoulder. The door opened. Leaving it ajar, I picked up the flashlight and stepped inside. The stairs, narrow and damp, twisted spiral fashion below me. Tentatively, I took one step down and then another and another until I lost track of time. Instinctively I knew that I was below ground level.

Even with the flashlight, the darkness was absolute. My eyes were useless. Senses, instinctive but long subdued by modern efficiency, rose to the occasion. I could smell the dank, mineral-wet essence of the earth. Water dripped from an ancient spring. I felt the cold, roughly hewn walls narrowing on either side of me. Something alive and fur-covered rubbed against my ankle, its whiskers furtively twitching, before scurrying past.

I lost track of time, but still I continued. It was so familiar, this never-ending descent into absolute darkness. Somehow I knew when the missing step was imminent. I stepped over it. I couldn't see my own feet, but I knew when the ceiling lowered and the tunnel narrowed.

The twisting passageway had been straight for some time now. Was it my imagination or was there a glow in the distance? Heart hammering, I switched off the flashlight. Darkness engulfed me. I waited. There was nothing. Dis-couraged, I switched on the flashlight. Nothing. I switched it off and then on again. Still nothing. Panic rose in my throat. Whimpering, I leaned against the wall and slapped the metal wand several times against my palm. The darkness pressed in on me.

With trembling fingers I unscrewed the top and lifted out the batteries. Someone once told me that rolling dead batteries in your palm revived them. My perspiration-slick hands shook uncontrollably, but I managed to replace the first battery. Then the unthinkable happened. I lost my grip on the second one. It landed with a dull thud. Frozen with shock, I stood and listened for a long time as it rolled away from me down the gradual descent. There was no possibility of finding it in this suffocating darkness.

Defeated, I turned around to go back the way I came. Icy fingers closed around my shoulders. The breath left my lungs. Paralyzed with fear, I could no more have struggled out of that persistent grasp than I could have sprouted wings and flown up the stairs and out into the light.

Visions swam before my eyes. Mairi's body crushed and bloodless, David Murray's face twisted with pain and hate. "No!" I screamed. "Go away. I don't want you now." Sobbing, I tore at the terrible weight holding me motionless in the dark corridor. There was nothing to feel, nothing to fight.

Bursts of color flashed through my mind. My head

exploded with intensity. I twisted and turned and fought, but there was nothing to hold on to, nothing but the terrible weight pressing down on me. Shock and the accompanying rush of adrenalin were too much for me. I felt the familiar lightness that all diabetics instantly recognize. I craved insulin, and there was none to be had. Sagging against the wall, I slipped into merciful unconsciousness.

❊28❊

The Tower of London
1293

Mairi looked down at the newborn infant suckling at her breast. The child was the image of Edward. Not an ounce of Maxwell blood was evident in her golden skin and piercing blue eyes. Even her hair, wisps of silvery fuzz, reminded Mairi of a Viking baby.

Edward had visited her the day before. He was delighted with his infant daughter. Eleanor had given him sons enough for the succession. This wee bairn was his to indulge. He had already bestowed a duchy upon her.

The child had eaten her fill. Her eyes were closed. Mairi shifted her to one shoulder and rubbed the delicate back. Within seconds a tiny belch exploded against her ear. A fierce surge of protectiveness flooded through her. This was her daughter, her firstborn.

The door opened, and her servant stepped inside. "There is someone to see you, m'lady," she said tentatively.

Mairi frowned. Anne was more friend than servant. It wasn't like her to be so nervous. "Who is it?" she asked.

Anne looked down at her feet and shook her head. "I dare not say."

"Very well." Mairi's eyes were the gray of tempered steel. "I shall refuse to see him."

"Oh no, m'lady," Anne gasped. "Please do not ask me to take back such a message."

Mairi laid the sleeping baby beside her on the bed and tucked the blanket around her. The task took over a minute. Finally, she folded her hands across her flattened stomach and looked across the room at the cowering woman. "Close the door," she said quietly.

Anne obeyed.

"Are you afraid of me, Anne?" Mairi asked gently.

Anne flushed, refusing to meet her mistress's eyes. "No."

"Are you afraid of my visitor?"

"Aye," the woman admitted.

"Whom do you serve?"

"You, m'lady."

Mairi inspected the fringe on her bedcover. "You are not serving me now. Perhaps I have been too lenient with you."

Anne lifted miserable eyes to Mairi's face. "Please do not turn me off, m'lady. I would serve you until I die, but this time I cannot. A higher authority commands me. I dare not disobey."

Mairi was no longer listening. There were only two people in all of England with authority over Mairi of Shiels. "Thank you, Anne," she said quietly. "You may tell the queen to come in."

With a frightened moan, Anne curtseyed and disappeared behind the door.

Careful not to disturb the child, Mairi straightened her pillows. She did not want to face Edward's wife lying flat on her back.

Eleanor did not keep her waiting. Before Mairi could begin to wonder at the reason for this unprecedented visit, the queen had already entered the room and closed the door behind her.

The two women took each other's measure. They had never before engaged in conversation. Mairi waited for Eleanor to speak. "I come from my father's estate in Nottingham to see the child," she said at last.

Mairi gasped. "Why?"

"My own daughter did not live past a se'enight."

Mairi's heart ached for her. "I'm truly sorry, Your Grace."

The queen glanced at her curiously. "I believe you mean that." She walked over to the bed and looked down at Mairi's daughter. A look of relief crossed her face. "It is just as I thought. She is all Edward."

Mairi's arm curled protectively around her child. "What do you want of me, Your Grace?"

Eleanor frowned. "Are your countrymen always so blunt, Mairi of Shiels, or is it only you who is lacking in manners?"

"My manners are my concern," retorted Mairi. "Tell me the reason for your visit."

The queen's hands clenched into fists, but her tone remained unchanged. "I had hoped to strike a bargain with you."

"I don't think so."

"Be careful, Mairi. I can be a formidable enemy when I choose."

Mairi nodded. "I'm sure you can, but there is still Edward."

The queen smiled contemptuously. "Despite your years, you really are a child, my dear. Edward will tire of you. He is a man, after all. Where will your child be then when he has found someone younger and the sight of you is an embarrassment?"

It was a question Mairi had asked herself more than once. Bitter tears had wet her pillow for many a night when she learned that Eleanor was again with child. The queen had already given her lord three healthy sons. There was no excuse for Edward to return to his wife's bed, no excuse except lust. Looking at her rival's pale, gilt-colored beauty was like a knife thrust deep into Mairi's heart. "What is the nature of your bargain?" she asked.

Eleanor pulled a stool close to the bed and sat down. "Your daughter is beautiful," she began. "She should be a princess. I have only sons. Give me your daughter, Mairi, and return to Scotland. Wed with a man of your own race and give him sons and daughters of his line. I shall raise Edward's daughter as my own. No one will know she is bastard born."

Mairi's face paled to the color of polished marble. "You would take my child?" she whispered. The horror of such a possibility had not yet become clear to her. "How could you manage such a deception? Everyone will know."

Eleanor shook her head. "No one, not even Edward, knows of my child's death. The midwife is discreet. She will tell no tales."

"Dear God," Mairi moaned. "You actually mean to do this."

Leaning closer, Eleanor spoke clearly and carefully. "Think on it, Mairi. Your daughter will be raised in the royal house of England's king. I shall betroth her to France or Spain. She will be a queen. What would she have with you but the shame of her birth? Where will she find a husband? Mark my words. Edward will not always be king. One day my son will reign." She ran a gentle finger down the baby's rose-petal cheek. "With me she will have everything."

"What of love?" Mairi's voice cracked with the memory of her own motherless years. "What of a mother's love?"

Eleanor's lip trembled. Her eyes were overly bright. Her gaze moved over the beautiful, thin-boned face of the woman her husband loved. "Never fear, Mairi of Shiels. She will have a mother's love. I was prepared to take her even if she resembled you. It is almost as if God Himself had a hand in this. Why else would he give you a child who is the image of Edward?"

Mairi opened her mouth to speak, but Eleanor held up her hand. "Do not decide before you see Edward. He leaves for Falkirk within the week to fight the Wallace. I'm sure he will visit you before he undertakes the journey."

Bile rose in Mairi's throat. The news had shocked her into silence. William Wallace was the hope of Scotland, her country's last desperate cry for independence. She stared at Eleanor with wide, accusing eyes.

Slowly Eleanor nodded. "You are not stupid after all," she said. "There is no reward for you, Mairi, no matter who is the victor at Falkirk. Do not condemn your daughter to such a life."

Mairi found her voice. "Edward will know. He has already seen the child."

Eleanor laughed bitterly. Edward had not yet bothered to visit his legitimate daughter. "You little fool," she whispered. "How innocent you are. Surely you know that Edward's bastards litter the countryside. Tell him the child died. He'll not recognize her when I return to London and present her as his legitimate daughter. Think carefully, Mairi. Timing is most important." She took one last look at the baby before leaving the room.

"I'll not do it," whispered Mairi to the walls. "No matter that she is the queen. She cannot make me give up my daughter." Leaning back against the pillows, she closed her eyes and thought.

If Edward died, she would return to Traquair and raise the bairn alone. No, that wouldn't do. The daughter of Edward the Hammer would not be safe in Scotland. Why not remain here and live quietly on the estates Edward had given his daughter? Perhaps they would be safe there. Mairi's heart sank as she thought it through. Eleanor would rule as regent. There would be no peace in England for her husband's mistress. With growing desperation, Mairi discarded one flawed solution after another. Was there no help for her? Had she brought forth life only to have it taken away before it was truly hers? Of course, Edward might be victorious. He had never before known defeat. But for Mairi, the risk was too great. If he died in battle, her life and the life of her child would be forfeit. For three tormented hours, she wept and prayed and argued with herself. When, at last, she came to her decision, there was no more room for tears.

Tenderly, she picked up the bairn and cradled her against her heart. "You will have a good life, *m'eudail*," she murmured, buring her face in the baby's neck and inhaling the sweet milky smell of her. Slowly, so as not to wake her, Mairi lay the child across her lap and unwrapped the swaddling blanket. She was so small, so delicate. Lovingly, she caressed the tiny arms, the rounded belly, the dimpled knees. She worked her finger into the center of the tightly clenched fist. The child's grip was strong. Mairi smiled. "You are a bonny lass, my love. Someday, perhaps when you are grown, our paths will cross again."

There was a knock on the door. "Enter," she called out.

Anne brought a tray of food. Mairi waved it away. "Bring me paper and ink," she ordered. "I wish to send two messages, one to the king and the other to the queen."

He found her on the knoll, watching the sunset, a slight, solitary figure outlined against the brilliant sky.

"I'm so sorry, lass." Edward's eyes were dark with misery. "I came as soon as I heard." His large hands reached out to clasp her shoulders. "Sometimes it happens. There will be other bairns."

"No, there will not." Mairi's voice was low and filled with something he had never heard before. "I am going home, Edward, to Traquair House. I can no longer live like this."

"I've no objection to your visiting Traquair," said Edward reasonably. "When this business with Wallace is over, I'll join you."

"It won't be a visit. I wish to go home . . . permanently."

Edward frowned. "Mairi," he began and stopped. She was upset over the child. He would not cause her further pain. "You may go wherever you wish, my love," he said gently. "But I ask you to wait until Wallace has been defeated. 'Tis too dangerous for a woman."

She turned to face him, and he was shocked at the anger in her eyes. "I am a Scot, Edward. Have you forgotten that? How should I behave when you speak of skewering the hero of my country?"

"You know nothing of it. William Wallace is a traitor."

"No, Your Grace. Wallace is a patriot. John Balliol was the traitor until he was convinced otherwise. You'll not hold Wallace in your dungeon. He'll die before he submits and half the clans in Scotland will die with him."

Edward's eyes were as cold and hard as splintered glass. "You are overset. I'll not listen to this." He turned to leave her.

Her words stopped him. "I leave on the morrow, Edward. Whatever was between us is over. David Murray rides with Wallace as do the Maxwells of Shiels and Traquair. My heart is with them."

Slowly, he turned around and came toward her, his face a carved bronze mask beneath the winter-gold hair. One hand reached behind her neck, the blunt fingers tangling in her hair. The other closed over her throat, holding her immobile. He spoke through set teeth. "You are mine, Mairi of Shiels. No man will claim you but me." His mouth was close to her own. "Tell me you no longer love me."

She remained silent.

He laughed triumphantly. "You cannot lie, my love. There is no one else for you."

"How fortunate that I do not demand the same from you, my lord."

"Explain yourself," he demanded.

Tears of shame prevented Mairi from answering.

All at once Edward understood. "I cannot ignore her completely, Mairi," he said gently. "She is my wife. The insult would be too great."

"I, too, wish to be a wife."

Edward dropped his hands, shaken at the anguish in her plea. This was a Mairi he had never seen before. His Mairi was strong and proud, without the needs of ordinary women. "You ask for something I cannot give. God knows I would do it differently if I could begin again. Please believe that."

Mairi lifted her head and looked directly at him. "I do believe you, Edward. But you must also believe me. At first light, I leave for Traquair. David Murray wishes to marry me. I've decided to accept him."

Shock rendered him speechless. There were few men who would risk crossing words with Edward I of England. For a woman to set herself against him was unthinkable. He recognized the roaring in his ears. It was the sound that came to him with the first exhilirating rush into battle, when swords engaged and the raging blood lust against the enemy filled his soul with hate and fury.

His hands snaked out across the distance that separated them and caught both of her arms in a punishing grip. The rage in his heart consumed all rational thought. He stood over her, dominating her, bending her back over his arm. It no longer mattered that she'd given birth less than a week before. The memories disappeared, the nights they'd shared, the slow sweet burn of her touch, the softness of her lips, the heartbreaking glory of her smile, they were gone, replaced by a fever of red so complete and so dangerous that time and place meant nothing.

His hands closed around her throat. Mairi refused to close her eyes. "Kill me," she whispered, "and be done with it. My life is worth little enough. End it now."

He stared down at her face. Slowly, the rage receded. His fingers around her throat relaxed. "I shall kill you, Mairi." His voice wasn't entirely steady. "The day you climb into David Murray's bed your fate is sealed." Abruptly he released her and, without looking back, strode down the knoll.

Mairi walked back to her chamber on shaking legs. Anne's gasp of horror confused her until she looked into the glass. Fiery red welts, the shape of fingers, marked her throat.

She touched the bruises. "Bring water and salve or else they'll show purple in the morning."

"But, my lady," Anne protested, "who did this to you?"

Mairi ignored her. "I leave for Scotland on the morrow, Anne. Is there another in the castle you would willingly serve?"

The woman's eyes widened. "Surely you will return."

Mairi did not answer. Her eyes were fixed on the darkening skin of her neck. Edward had marked much more than her body. From the first, he had claimed her, wooed her, taught her the power of passion. Mairi of Shiels had been loved by a man she would use to judge all others. Tomorrow she would leave England and never return. But she would not wish away the circumstances that had allowed them to meet. She would never regret the soul-shaking love that would burn in her heart for all of the life that was left her.

David Murray watched her ride to the top of the knoll to meet him. She was still beautiful but far too thin. The bones of her cheeks were very pronounced and the hollows deep beneath them. There was a sadness about her mouth that had not been there before. She reined in her mount several feet from where he waited.

His stallion danced on nervous legs. David took a moment to gentle him. He welcomed the diversion. It had been over a year since he'd last seen Mairi. "So, you are back," he said, his expression unreadable.

"Yes."

He surveyed the entourage behind her. "Where is the bairn?"

Mairi's eyes met his, and she read in his dark-eyed gaze everything that he was unable to say. In that moment filled with words unsaid, she knew she could not lie to him, her dearest friend, the soulmate of her childhood. "She is lost to me, David. We'll not speak of her again."

Her look undid him. He could not bear to see such pain on Mairi's face. Instinct took over. Urging his mount alongside hers, he lifted her from her saddle and held her against his chest. The words he spoke into her ear were soothing and filled with the longing of a lifetime. "Don't, my love," he whispered. "I'll take care of you. I promise I will. Nothing will ever hurt you again."

❋29❋

Traquair House
1298

"My lady," a tentative voice spoke from the shadows, "they come."

"Aye." Mairi raised tormented eyes to her servant. "And God's will be done." Swiftly, she left the room and ran down the stairs. Surefooted as a cat, she descended the narrow steps, carrying no candle. She needed none. She was Mairi of Shiels, wife to the earl of Murray, and she knew every twist and turn, every knot and hold, every miss and shortened length of the slippery stone under her feet. Around and around she flew, faster and faster, until at last her slippered foot touched the rush-strewn floor of the great hall.

"Knaves," she cried, centuries of command in her voice. "Bring it quickly. He comes."

Moving with alacrity, footmen wearing the crest of the Murrays emblazoned on their tunics hurried to do her bidding. Within moments they returned, their muscles straining under the weight of a large, irregular boulder.

"Place it there," she ordered, "on the banquet table. Scotland's Stone of Destiny should not rest on the ground with the dogs."

The men looked at one another, their faces a combination of fear and surly defiance. Only one had the temerity to question his orders. "M'lady." Sweat beaded his upper lip and formed large wet circles under his arms.

"What is it?"

"I dinna' wish to burn in hell," he ventured tentatively. "If there be another way—"

"Art you a fool?" snapped Mairi. "If there were another way, I would have thought of it first. Do as you are told."

Fear made him brave. "But, m'lady, what o' the prophecy?"

"Words, knave, only words." She whirled on him in savage fury. "I do this for all of us. For your life and the life of Murray's heir. How dare you question me? Leave at once."

Chastened but unconvinced, he backed out of the room.

Mairi tore the coif from her head and unpinned her hair. Braids, thicker than a man's wrist, fell to her knees. With frantic fingers she loosened the plaits until the heavy mane fell all about her, silky fine and black as a crow's wing. Her hair was beautiful as was the gown she had chosen. She would need all of her beauty this night. Once, not so very long ago, Edward of England had been very much a man. Mairi hoped it was still true. She had staked the life of her child on it.

Horses' hooves clattered in the cobble-stoned courtyard. The Bear Gates stood open. There was no guardtower, no portcullis, no drawbridge to lower, no castle wall to storm. A symbol of grace and beauty nestled in a sheltered valley, Traquair was a home, not a fortress.

The wooden doors burst open, and men on horses, in full battle armor, filled the room. Mairi lifted her chin in a gesture of defiance, her eyes fixed on the circle of swords mounted above the entrance. No hated enemy would see her fear.

The line of horses parted, circling to the left and then to the right, until every inch of wall was guarded. No one spoke. She waited in trembling silence, her nails digging into her palms, for the encounter she knew was inevitable.

He came on foot, in full mail, holding his helmet under his arm. Moving with sure, impatient steps, he stopped directly before her. She would have known him anywhere. Tall, strong, incredibly handsome, magnificently royal, a man beloved by his subjects and feared by his enemies. Edward I of England was exactly as she remembered, every inch a king.

For a long time they took each other's measure. She was the first to look away. Issuing a low, brief command, he relinquished his helmet to a horseman, who stepped forward. The knights, lined up in glittering rows, looked on impassively as he reached for Mairi's hands.

"Please." Unbidden, the single plea escaped her lips. She had not intended to beg. Maxwells never begged. He lifted a hand to caress her cheek. Mairi turned away but not before she felt the large knuckles graze her skin. Tears stung her eyelids. In all of her imaginings of this meeting, she had not expected gentleness. It was very unlike him. Edward, Hammer of the Scots, was not a man given to gentleness.

The hand that touched her face so sweetly was the hand of his sword arm. The same hand had severed the head of Llywylyn of Wales and carried it to London, where it sat skewered on a pike above the city gates until scavengers picked it clean. It was that hand, wielding a sword and targe, that defeated Wallace, the hope of Scotland, at the Battle of Falkirk. Ignoring his pleas for mercy, Edward ordered him strung up, drawn, and quartered, his body left, carrion for scavengers.

It was the very same hand that had closed over her throat, threatening to choke out the very breath of her life if she went through with her marriage to David of Murray. It was the hand of a builder, a statesman, a warrior . . . a butcher.

Never, for one moment, would Mairi forget who he was and what he had become. But neither could she forget what he had been. It made her deception so much harder to bear.

"There was a time when you begged for my touch." His voice, low, intimate, and amused was pitched for her ears alone.

"That was a long time ago."

He moved closer. "Was it, Mairi? Have you forgotten everything we had?"

She stared at the sun-darkened line of his jaw, refusing to answer such a question.

Edward frowned. Holy God, the woman was stubborn! He gazed at her face, surprised at the awakening hunger he felt at the mere sight of her. He thought it was finished, that the years had cured him of his impossible obsession. But now, standing within arms' reach of her again, he realized the passage of time meant nothing. He would never be finished with Mairi of Shiels.

Eight years had passed since he'd fallen to the ground at her feet. She stood before him now, as she was then, the woman he would move heaven and earth to possess, the woman he was cursed to love and never call his own.

Mairi was done with silence. She lifted her eyes to meet his. "Take it," she said, pointing toward the table where the large boulder rested. "'Tis our stone."

"Aye." Edward looked thoughtfully at the stone.

Mairi dared not breathe. Was there something beyond curiosity in his gaze? Edward was no fool. He would wonder why she had surrendered so easily.

He walked to the table and placed his hand on the granite. This was Jacob's Pillar, the Royal Stone of the Belgic Kings brought from Dunstaffnage in A.D. 838. Scotland's Stone of Destiny for five hundred years would now rest in Westminster Abbey. Edward's voice was rough with emotion. "I, Edward, king of England and overlord of Scotland, claim this Coronation Stone as my right."

Mairi turned and walked toward the stairs.

Edward's steely voice stopped her. "You have not asked permission of your king to leave."

She stared straight ahead, her back to him, and spoke through clenched teeth. "You will never be my king."

He cursed under his breath and started forward. Instinctively, Mairi lifted her skirts and ran. Before she reached the stairs, his hands circled her waist, and she was flung over his shoulder. He climbed the stairs, two at a time, caring nothing for the extra weight. Mairi was not so foolish as to struggle. One slip meant instant death for the both of them. With bitter resignation she realized that Edward knew Traquair House as well as any castle of his own. She knew exactly where he was taking her.

He kicked open the door of her bedchamber and set Mairi on her feet. "Leave us," he growled at the cowering servant. With one terrified backward glance at her mistress, the woman hurried to do his bidding.

Mairi braced herself on the back of a chair and pushed the hair away from her face. From deep within the core of her being, she summoned the courage to challenge him. "What do you want of me, Edward?"

He raked her slim, high-breasted figure with a burning glance. "Need you ask?"

"I am married," she announced.

"Did you really believe I wouldn't know that?" He walked to a small table near the hearth and poured a goblet of wine, grimacing as he swallowed it. " 'Tis sour stuff. I prefer ale."

"I beg your pardon, Your Grace." Her voice was thick with sarcasm. "If I had known you intended to invade my bedchamber, I would have prepared more carefully."

He drank off the last of the wine and removed his breastplate and pavis. "You should have expected it," he replied calmly. Sitting on the bed, he pulled off his boots and leggings, peeled off the garters, and rolled down his hose. At last he stood before her, barefoot, in a saffron tunic and woolen breeches.

Her eyes were wide with fear and something else that made Edward's heart beat faster. He hadn't intended this, but perhaps it was inevitable. She inflamed him beyond rational thought. No longer counting the cost, he would carry the memory of this coupling through all the years without her. Tonight, her hair and eyes, the thin discriminating nose, the curve of her cheek, the shadow above her lip, the graceful, elegant way she moved, would be his alone. He would make her forget there had ever been another in her bed.

She made one last futile attempt to stop him. "I am wife to the earl of Murray. Would you take me in the very room I share with my husband?"

"Aye." He leaned toward her, brushing her lips with his. "In his very bed if I must."

"I despise you," she cried desperately. "Would you stoop to rape?"

His calloused hands cradled her face and brushed away the tears that collected in the corners of her eyes. "It will not be rape, Mairi. I promise you that."

She sobbed and cursed him as his mouth moved from her eyelids to her throat and then to her breast. When he removed her gown and lifted her to the bed, she was strangely submissive. He wooed her with memories, with soft words, firm lips, and skilled, careful hands. The driving force of his kiss broke her reserve. With a last despairing moan, she threaded her fingers through his hair and pulled him inside of her.

Later, much later, when her naked, sweat-dampened body lay curled against his, he spoke. "Did you think I wouldn't know?"

She turned her head, her eyes meeting his in the shadowy darkness. "Know what?"

"The child. Did you think I wouldn't know she was ours?"

Mairi closed her eyes. Even if she'd wanted to lie, she could not have forced the words from her throat. The time for dissembling was over. "What did you name her?"

"Margaret. I call her Maggie."

"Maggie." She tested the name on her tongue. "Maggie. Does it suit her?"

Edward grinned. "It does."

"Eleanor said you wouldn't know."

"Eleanor is a fool," he said emphatically. "But for the color of her hair, the lass could be you."

Mairi's eyes widened. "The bairn was the image of you, Edward. How can she be like me?"

"'Tis more a similarity of temperament than feature," he explained. "She is fair, but not so fair as an English lass, and her temper is wondrous to behold."

"Are you sure it isn't you she takes after?" Mairi retorted.

"She is tall for a lass and slim with eyes as gray and clear as rainwater. No one who knows you as I have would believe Eleanor is her mother."

"Does Eleanor know your thoughts?"

"Aye," said Edward shortly. "She knows."

Mairi bit her lip. "Then it was all for nothing."

His arms tightened around her. "How could you do it, lass? Why did you lie? I would not have thought it possible for you to leave a child of your blood to be raised by another."

"I had no choice. You were leaving for Falkirk. What future was there for us if you never returned?"

"But I did return," he reminded her, "and you were gone. I was in the devil's own temper, Mairi. I would have come for you immediately, but I learned of your marriage to Murray." He tilted her chin up and looked down at her face. "Have you any idea what you did to me? For an entire year, I fell asleep dreaming of painful ways to murder David Murray."

She drew a deep sobbing breath and buried her face against his chest. "Oh, Edward. I am so sorry. What have we done to each other?"

His breath was warm and soft against her ear. "I love you, Mairi. Whatever pain I've brought you, know that at least. You hold my heart still as surely as you did the first moment I saw you."

Tears slipped from beneath her eyelids and rolled down her cheeks. She wiped her nose on the back of her hand. There were words to be said, and the saying of them would be difficult. "You must leave in the morning and never come back again," she whispered. "Please, Edward. I cannot bear it if you do not."

His lips were on the curve of her throat. Her skin burned where he touched her.

"Never fear, love," he murmured. "I shall leave in the morning, but I'll be back. Until the day I die, I'll come back to you."

Three weeks later

Mairi slipped out of bed and pulled on a robe over her nakedness. With a quick glance, reassuring herself that her husband still slept, she walked out of the room and closed the door quietly behind her. David Murray needed his rest. He had been with Wallace at Falkirk and now rode with Robert the Bruce. His stay would be brief, his purpose to assure himself that his wife and son remained unharmed after Edward's visit. Tomorrow he would ride out at the head of the Bruce's army.

Making her way to her son's room, Mairi chewed at her bottom lip and fervently prayed that her husband would soon be on his way. She loved David Murray as dearly as she had every day of her life since she was eight years old. They had grown up together. He had been her childhood champion, her friend, her cousin, and finally, her love. He knew of her misguided passion for England's king. He knew that he would not take a virgin bride to his marriage bed and that there was a part of her heart he would never have. Still, in the entire time they'd been wed, he had never doubted her. She was a Maxwell of Shiels, his wife, the mother of his son. He trusted her, and for all that, she'd betrayed him.

The betrayal was even more heinous than the breaking of her marriage vows. Mairi had looked directly into David's trusting brown eyes and lied. She had lied about Edward and she'd lied about the stone. She did not tell him that Edward had carried her into the room she shared with her husband, that she had found such pleasure under his rough, large English hands that she had begged him to take her, not once, but three times throughout that endless, forbidden night. And she would never speak of the stone. For the child's sake, David would forgive her for Edward. But he would never forgive her for Scotland's Stone of Destiny.

Bending over the bed, she scooped the babe into her arms and buried her face in his chubby neck. He laughed, showing two perfect front teeth. "There, my love," Mairi crooned, tickling his stomach. "You've waited long enough. I'll feed you." Baring her breast, she brought the baby's lips to her engorged nipple and sat down in a chair. The slight clenching of her stomach and the eager pulling of the bairn's mouth restored her calm. David need never know about Edward. The servants were discreet. This was Traquair House, home to the Maxwells. Mairi Maxwell, a daughter of the house, would command more loyalty than David Murray. Eventually he would learn about the stone. Everyone would. But perhaps Robert would be victorious, and the truth could be told.

"M'lady." A servant stepped into the nursery. "There are soldiers and townspeople at the gates. The Bruce leads them."

Fear, as great as any she had ever known, froze the milk in her breasts. The baby suckled to no avail. Whimpering, he stared up at his mother, confusion in his eyes. Mairi stood and handed him to the maid. "I'll dress and find out what they want."

A long look passed between the two women. Mairi reached out and clutched the servant's arm. "Take care of the bairn," she whispered. "If I know he is safe, I can bear anything."

"Shall I wake Lord Murray?" the woman asked.

Mairi shook her head. "Say nothing. He'll waken soon enough."

Robert the Bruce looked down from the height of his stallion on David Murray's wife. They were in the courtyard of Traquair House, surrounded by his soldiers and a mob of angry citizens from Selkirk and Galashiels.

"Where is Lord Murray?" the Bruce asked coldly.

Mairi lifted her chin, meeting the biting anger in his green eyes without fear. "He sleeps, m'lord."

"Send a servant to wake him. I want him here when I accuse his wife."

"He'll know soon enough," she replied calmly. "Of what am I accused?"

"Sedition." He flung the word at her feet, expecting her to grovel and plead for mercy.

Mairi of Shiels did neither. She smiled as if the entire scene amused her. Turning to a lackey who stood by the door, she spoke. "Wake my husband, knave. Tell him his" she hesitated over the word—"his king desires speech with him."

Robert flushed and set his teeth, waiting for the man to do her bidding. He knew that Mairi of Shiels had held him up to measure and found him wanting. Grudging admiration dimmed the anger threatening to explode in Robert's chest. Holy God, she was magnificent. How had Murray won such a woman? He could see why she had taken Edward of England to her bed, but why had she wed David Murray? There was a time, before her marriage, when Robert had wanted her for himself. In terms it still pained him to remember, she had refused him. There wasn't another woman in all of Scotland who wouldn't succumb to the silver-tongued charms of red-haired, green-eyed Robert the Bruce, not even when he'd been the landless earl of Carrick. By the blood of Christ, he was more than ready to bestow royal mercy on such a lass if only she could be persuaded to look upon him with favor.

Moments later, David Murray came through the doors of Traquair, rubbing his eyes. He blinked in amazement at the entourage surrounding his king. "What is the meaning of this, Robert?" he asked quietly.

"Your wife knows better than I," replied the Bruce.

"Mairi?" David's dark eyes smiled at her across the courtyard.

It would do no good to spare him. "I am accused of sedition," she said, making no attempt to soften the blunt words.

"That's impossible," replied David flatly.

"How do you know?" demanded the Bruce.

"I know my wife."

"A woman who beds down with Edward of England is not a woman a man can know."

David's jaw clamped down angrily. "You lie, Robert of Carrick. My wife is true."

A smile of triumph crossed Robert's face. "Ask her."

"I shall do so." David crossed the courtyard and took Mairi's hands in his own. From his trembling grasp, she knew how much this cost him. "You've never lied to me, Mairi. Speak the truth now."

Despair tore at her heart. She wet her lips, forcing the ugly words past them. "I took Edward to my bed. But I did not betray my king or country."

"That depends of which king you are speaking," Robert broke in. "The charge for sedition is death."

David turned on him. "If every woman guilty of adultery is accused of sedition, why are not the heads of your mistresses mounted on pikes throughout Scotland?"

"How dare you?" Robert growled.

"She is my wife," David reminded him.

A burly lackey dressed in the livery of the Maxwells stepped forward. Mairi recognized him immediately. "What of the stone?" he shouted. "Ask her about the stone."

"What of the stone, Mairi of Shiels?" Robert asked. "Scotland's Stone of Destiny no longer rests on Moot Hill."

Mairi stared at him, saying nothing. She had known it would come to this, but she had hoped for more time.

"Speak, Mairi," Robert commanded her. "Speak or you sign your own death warrant."

"Think what you will," she cried. "I did not betray my country."

"Mairi," David pleaded. "Tell them the truth. Where is the Stone of Scone?"

"It is safe," she whispered. "Ask me no more."

His fingers dug into her shoulders. "They are going to kill you," he whispered.

Her back stiffened. She lifted her head, her eyes flashing silver fire at the man who called himself king. "I am a Scot," she said, centuries of dynastic pride revealed in her haughty voice. "Descended from Macus, king of the Isle of Man. My family has ruled the borders since the Picts of Dalriada. You are of Norman blood, Robert the Bruce of Carrick. I have a greater stake in this land of my ancestors than you shall ever have. Hear me now and leave me in peace. I did not betray my country."

Robert stared down at her for a long time, ignoring the murmuring of peasant voices at his back. David held his breath. Suddenly, the crowd parted, and a tall woman, richly dressed, strode forward to stand before Mairi.

"Mother." David's bewilderment was obvious. "What are you doing here?"

Robert spoke first. "I asked her to come. Lady Douglas is Mairi's accuser." He nodded at the woman. "Tell your son what you saw."

David gasped, and the color left his face. His mother was famous throughout Scotland for her second sight. There were some who called Grizelle Murray Douglas a witch. She had known of Mairi's affair with Edward and had tried to dissuade her son from marrying her. Since Grizelle's own marriage to the third earl of Douglas, she made no secret of her hatred for her son's wife.

"I saw her," she said, pointing at Mairi. "She took the stone from Moot Hill."

"A woman, alone in the darkness, couldn't possibly carry away a stone of that size," David argued.

"She wasn't alone," Grizelle countered. "There were men and horses with her."

The woman lied. Mairi knew it was a lie just as she knew her fate was sealed. There had been only one horse and one wagon that night. Everyone else was on foot. She stepped closer to Grizelle, gray eyes staring into brown. Her voice was pitched low so that only the two of them heard her words. "Why do you do this, Grizelle? If you truly have the sight, you know that I speak the truth."

Mairi was so close that Grizelle could breathe her fear. The fear she would never show. She was a stone's throw from death, and still she would not plead for mercy. She stood as she always had, proud and tall, with a regal poise unusual in a woman. For a moment there was a flicker of regret in Grizelle's dark, witchlike eyes, and then it was gone. She hardened her heart. "I've waited a long time for this, Mairi of Shiels," she whispered. "You will die accursed for your deed."

"Which deed, m'lady?"

Grizelle's eyes narrowed, and she stepped back. Pointing a shaking finger, she screamed, "I curse you, Mairi of Shiels and Traquair and all the daughters of your line. For your treachery they will never rest. Cursed to pay for your deed, their sleep will be haunted by the dead until they die of foul and tragic means. Only when Scotland's Stone of Destiny is found, will the curse be lifted."

"'Tis your own flesh and blood you condemn," cried Mairi.

An angry murmuring swelled through the crowd. Dogs growled and barked. A baby cried.

Robert held up his hand. Again, there was silence. "Bring out the stones," he ordered, confident Mairi would confess once she saw the instrument of her death. Four men in yokes, straining against thick ropes tied to their shoulders, dragged an enormous slab of granite into the courtyard.

"No," gasped David. "I won't allow it."

"Restrain him," ordered the Bruce.

Two soldiers stepped forward and gripped David's arms. His face haunted, he began to struggle. "Robert, I beg of you. Do not do this," he shouted, twisting against the arms that held him like bands of steel. "Please." Panic caused his voice to crack. "Spare my wife."

Mairi was pale as a ghost, but her back was straight and her eyes, gray and icy as a mountain tarn, stared at the man who would be king.

"Your end is near, Mairi," Robert said. "Speak now or stand before your God with a lie on your lips."

The flashing scorn in her eyes withered him. He could scarcely form the words. "Kill her."

Two guards stepped forward. Each took one arm. Mairi looked at one and then the other. Chastened, they released her and stepped back. Quickly, with graceful, catlike steps, she walked to the slab and lay down upon it.

Six more men carried a second slab, equal in size to the first, to where Mairi lay.

"Noooo . . . ," moaned David. The tears ran freely down his face.

With Herculean effort, the men lifted the granite slab above their heads and heaved. Mairi folded her arms across

her chest and turned her head. "Hail Mary, full of grace—"
Her lips moved in prayer, but her eyes never left her
husband's face. Not even when the stone landed, full force,
crushing the life and breath from her body.

30

Traquair House
1993

A sting in my thigh woke me. Groggily, I tried to open my
eyes but couldn't quite manage it. The sensations of damp
and cold penetrated my sweatshirt and leggings. I was still
on the ground, my body twisted into an unnatural position
on the stairs. Someone crouched beside me. It was a
woman. I could tell from the cloying floral scent of her
perfume.

"I know you're coming around, Christina," Kate Ferguson said in a voice that wasn't the least bit servile. "There is
no use pretending. I've brought you some orange juice. I
want you completely alert when I tell you what I've
planned."

The insulin traveling through my veins renewed me. With
only minimal effort, I opened my eyes. It was no longer
dark. Kate stared down at me, holding an empty syringe in
one hand and a thermos in the other. A flashlight sat on the
step beside her, its circle of light reflecting off the ceiling
and capturing the two of us in its artificial glow.

I wet my lips. "What are you doing here?"

She smiled contemptuously. "Do you really believe that
I'd take orders from someone like you? Traquair belongs to
me. I've no intention of ever leaving it."

I sat up and reached for the thermos. She surrendered it

immediately. Twisting off the top, I drank directly from the container, gulping the liquid down in huge restoring mouthfuls. The sweet juice cooled my parched throat and cleared away the remaining cobwebs from my brain. I wiped my mouth with the back of my hand and replaced the cap.

"How did you know where to give me my shot?"

"I took care of Ellen Maxwell for years. This isn't the first time I've administered an injection."

I needed time to think. Grasping at the first words that entered my mind, I spoke. "Maybe I was rather unfair," I said, setting the thermos on the step. "Why don't we see if we can come to some kind of arrangement."

"I don't think so."

I looked up quickly, surprising a look of pure hatred on Kate's face. The hair lifted on my arms and the back of my neck. "What do you mean?"

"Your time is up, Christina Murray." She laughed, but the sound was humorless. "Did you think to escape your fate? I knew it was you the moment I saw your face."

"How?" I whispered.

"The portrait of Jeanne Maxwell."

"You hid it from me, didn't you?"

She shrugged. "I needed more time before you learned of the connection between yourself and the others. But I misjudged you, Christina. You were such a shy, rabbity little thing when you first came. I didn't believe that you'd take charge as soon as you did. It took me until now to plan a way to be rid of you."

"You can't mean that. Why would you bring me medication and juice if you planned to kill me all along?"

"I'm no murderer. I have no intention of killing you. That will be taken care of for me."

I stared at her in fascinated horror, a germ of awareness growing inside my brain.

Her dark eyes glowed with a fanatical light. "You'll never find it," she crowed. "You're doomed just like they were."

Suddenly, I realized who she reminded me of. "You're insane," I whispered.

"I'm not the one searching for a stone to end a curse that began over seven hundred years ago." Her gloating face was painful to look at. "When they find you in here, you'll have died of natural causes. What does three days without insulin do to a diabetic, Christina?"

Desperately, I searched the stairs for a way out. Kate stood above, blocking the only escape route. There was only one way to go and that was down. I considered pushing her aside but discarded the idea. Although Kate was older than I and not nearly as tall, she outweighed me by twenty pounds. One slip on the damp stairs would leave someone injured. The odds were against me. I decided to stall for time, hoping for an inspiration. Maybe there was some way I could get around her.

I stood and leaned against the wall, crossing my arms in what I hoped was a nonthreatening posture. "What exactly do you want from me, Kate?"

She opened her mouth and then closed it again without speaking. Her brows drew together, and a look of confusion crossed her face. "What did you say?"

"I asked what you wanted from me," I repeated. "There should be some way to work this out. After all, we are related."

"Don't be ridiculous. There is no blood tie between us."

Now it was my turn to be perplexed. "Of course there is," I argued. "My mother is your half sister. Your father and my grandfather was James Maxwell. I know everything, Kate. I found the documents in the Hall of Records in Edinburgh."

"What did you call me?" Her voice had changed. The consonants were softer, the brogue stronger. Something was definitely wrong.

"Are you all right?" I asked, reaching out to touch her arm.

"Whore," she said, deliberately stepping backward. "You dishonor me with your touch."

The blood rose in my face. I took a deep breath, consciously dredging up what remained of my self-control. "In the name of fairness, I'm willing to overlook a great deal," I said reasonably. "However, it would be wise to remember who is the legal owner of Traquair House. You won't get anywhere by insulting me."

"I need nothing from you." She spat contemptuously.

"Lord Douglas's estates are vast. What would I want with Maxwell leavings?"

The tight bun she normally wore had loosened. Wisps of dark hair framed her face, emphasizing the pale skin and oddly slanted dark eyes. There was no longer any doubt. The woman was truly insane. Kate Ferguson, housekeeper of Traquair, had disappeared. It was Grizelle Douglas, her witchlike eyes filled with hatred, who stared back at me.

Words, questions, half-formed responses, crowded together in my mind, tangled in my throat, and froze on my lips. I was speechless.

"What is it, Mairi?" the strange voice continued. "Did you think I wouldn't find you? Did you hope to succeed this time?"

"Stop it! Stop it!" I shouted, finding my voice at last. "Don't do this. We've got to get out of here." Responding to a primitive instinct, I reached out and clutched her shoulders in a desperate effort to shake the madness from her.

With surprising strength, she pushed me back against the wall, blocking my chance for escape. "You're not going anywhere. This is your fate, Mairi of Shiels. This is where you'll spend eternity."

Hysteria began to close in. Forcing myself to concentrate, I sat down on the step and took several deep, even breaths.

I expected her to turn, walk back up the stairs, and leave me behind, locked away forever in the ancient burial vault of Traquair House. But she didn't. She waited, watching me with a silent, empty expression while my breathing and my terror stabilized.

"Why?" I whispered. "Why do you hate me so much?"

"You betrayed Scotland."

I looked up quickly. Perhaps there was a way out of this after all. If it meant playing out the drama, so be it. Wetting my lips, I assumed the identity she'd given me. "You know I didn't, Grizelle. If you have the sight, you know I did nothing to betray my country."

"You were the English king's whore. You bore him a child and then came back to my son. Your actions soiled the House of Murray. At court they laughed at David behind his back."

What now? Could this really be happening? I'd read about schizophrenia, of course, but never before had I heard of anyone so skillfully concealing multiple personalities. Or was it something else? For how long had Kate believed she was Grizelle Douglas?

Again, I attempted to reason with her. "David didn't agree. He married me of his own free will. We had a child, your grandson."

She smiled triumphantly. "The child was better off without you. I raised him myself. Your name was never spoken. The taint of his Maxwell blood disappeared."

Despite my fear, I was fascinated. How much did this woman who thought she was her seven-hundred-year-old ancestor really know? I couldn't help myself. I had to find out. "What happened to David, Grizelle? Did he marry again?"

"He died at Bannockburn, fighting with the English against the Bruce."

"Dear God."

She nodded, and her mouth hardened. "That was your fault as well. He could not forgive Robert for your death."

"You had a part in that," I reminded her. "Did he forgive you?"

She brushed the question aside. "The hour grows late." Picking up the flashlight, she turned to walk up the stairs. As an afterthought, she looked back at me. "I'll not be seeing you again, Mairi Maxwell. 'Tis over between us."

"But why?" I couldn't let her go, not yet, not with the only available light. "You won, didn't you? You wiped my name from the face of the earth. I've paid the price. Why must I die again?"

She turned back and stared at me as if I were a demented child. "Because of Ian Douglas, of course. You've bewitched another of my blood, Mairi. You carry his child. Your line must end forever."

"No, please," I begged. "Don't take the light. At least leave the light."

She considered my request and then shook her head. "You won't need it."

Heart hammering, I scrambled to my feet and followed her, staying just out of reach. I felt light-headed, but I knew that as long as I had strength there was no choice except to continue. If I reached the top of the stairs at the same time she did, I had a chance of overpowering her and pushing my way out of the door.

There was enough light to recognize the landmark short step. Kate was just ahead, around the next bend. Suddenly, I heard a voice too low to be Kate Ferguson's.

Hurrying, I followed the curving stairs and stopped short, almost dropping with relief. Ian Douglas, a flashlight in one hand, a jacket and paper bag in the other, was staring at Kate with a look of disbelief on his face. Whatever else I knew of Ian, I was confident that he meant me no harm.

"What in the name of bloody hell are you doing here?" he asked Kate.

"I might ask the same of you," she replied. Apparently she was herself again, slipping into her present-day personality as easily as she had left it.

"Ian," I cried out, stumbling in my hurry to reach the safety of his side.

Kate blocked my way. "There is no other way, Ian. She is the one who carries the curse. Without her, there will be no more of Mairi's line. The Murrays will be avenged."

"Don't be ridiculous." Ian's face was ashen in the pale glow of the flashlight. "This isn't about a curse, and you know it. You've allowed this inheritance business to cloud your thinking. We've had enough." He reached out his hand to me. "Come, Christina."

"No." Kate's voice was shrill. "She stays here."

Disregarding her completely, Ian shouldered his way past her and pulled me into his arms. "Are you all right?" he asked, relief evident in his voice. "Your mother told me about your conversation this morning. I assumed you'd be here. Thank God I was right."

"I'm fine," I mumbled into his shirt, "and very glad to see you. Did you bring something to eat?"

He laughed. "Of course. But it wasn't my idea. Your mother deserves the credit." He pulled away to look down at me. "I want no more half-truths between us."

Neither of us noticed Kate coming down the stairs toward us. I was rummaging through the bag when her voice stopped me.

"Stay with her if you must," she shrieked, brandishing a kitchen knife with a pointed blade. "The two of you shall meet your fate together."

With a curse, Ian stepped in front of me just as she lunged forward. The knife caught his forearm in a deep gash. Blood soaked his sleeve and dripped down over the stairs. His knees gave way, and he doubled over. I screamed and cradled him in my arms, trying to pull him away from her.

Kate laughed and lifted the knife again. I closed my eyes, fully expecting that moment to be my last. One second passed, then two. Nothing happened. Cautiously I lifted my lids, a fraction at first and then completely. She had focused on something behind us. The glee on her face had been replaced by fear. For a full minute she stared, seeing something in the darkened space that I, no matter how hard I strained, could not. After what seemed an eternity, she snarled and turned away from us to climb the stairs.

Ian struggled to his feet. His left hand was clamped down tightly over his wound. "I'm going after her," he said. "She's obviously mad, and your mother is waiting for us at the top. With that knife, I don't know what Kate will do to her."

Ian handed me the light and started up the stairs after her. She was already far enough ahead of him to make my heart stand still. If she got to the top before he did—"Hurry, Ian," I shouted. "Hurry."

My head swam, and I sat down again, overcome by weakness. I couldn't begin to think of following them until I'd eaten. It was a long way to the top. An endless climb of narrow passages and slippery steps, requiring complete concentration. I simply wasn't up to it.

Positioning the flashlight on the step below, I reached into the bag and took out an apple. Blessing my mother's foresight, I stared into the inky blackness outside my circle of light and ate down to the core. It wasn't until I'd replaced the remains in the bag that I noticed the light. It came from somewere below me, soft and comforting, nothing like the dim, murky battery light surrounding me.

Slowly I stood, forgetting the food and the flashlight, forgetting everything but the mesmerizing pull of the glow before me. As I continued downward, the stairs ended and leveled out until I stood before a wall illuminated by white light. There was a narrow opening on one end. Turning sideways, I squeezed through into a room so bright I was momentarily blinded. When my eyes adjusted, I saw exactly what I'd expected.

It was the burial vault of my dream, complete with death masks and shadows and thousands of flickering candles. Beneath a small altar on a raised dais was Scotland's Stone of Destiny. Behind it, her hands resting at her sides, her eyes steady on mine, was Mairi of Shiels.

This time she did not look tormented. In fact, she looked pleased. I smiled tentatively. She smiled back and beckoned me to join her. I crossed the distance between us and looked down at the stone. This was Jacob's Pillar, the Royal Stone of the Belgic Kings brought from Dunstaffnage in A.D. 838, Scotland's Stone of Destiny. Mine were the first human eyes to rest on it for over seven hundred years. "Thank you," I whispered. "Thank you for helping me find it."

She nodded, and we looked at one another, communing in silence for what seemed to be a long time.

"Christina," Ian's voice called out to me. "Christina, where are you?"

Alarmed, I looked at Mairi, a question hovering on my lips. Her eyes were kind and filled with understanding. Words were unnecessary. She knew my mind as well as I knew hers. The candles were the first to disappear, throwing the death masks and the ancient altar into deep shadow. The brilliant rainbow quality of light emanating from the stone faded until only a pale reddish glow remained. Mairi was gone for good this time.

I drew a deep breath. "I'm here, Ian," I shouted, "behind the wall."

Within moments he walked toward me, bandage around his arm, flashlight in hand. "Your parents have Kate," he said.

"Is everyone all right?" I asked.

He nodded. "Everyone except Kate. She's ill, Christina, really ill. She belongs in a hospital. I can't believe that I didn't see it before this." He held out his hand. "Let's go."

Without a word, I pointed to the stone. He aimed his flashlight and stared. Disbelief on his face changed to awe.

Reverently, he circled the dais, his flashlight moving over every inch of the glowing granite. "This is incredible," he said at last. "There must be some kind of radiation coming from the rock, maybe uranium."

"I don't think so."

"I'm not a geologist, but what other explanation could there be?"

"You still don't believe in the supernatural, do you, Ian? Even after all we've been through."

He waved the flashlight in the air. "It doesn't matter what I believe. The point is, you've done it. You've proven that Scotland's stone has been here at Traquair House all the time. You'll be famous."

I shook my head. "That isn't what she would want."

"What are you saying?"

I walked to where he stood and looked up at his face with eyes that finally recognized the truth. Without the blinders, I noticed the resemblance at once. The same thick, light hair and fair skin, the bluer than blue eyes, the masculine cut of nose and chin, the arrogant flair of nostrils. He was so very like him, a Saxon warrior thinly disguised by the clipped hair and civilized clothing of the twentieth century. Our lives had been linked as Mairi and Edward's had been.

Gently, I reached up to touch his face and attempted to explain. "We were brought here and allowed to see this for a reason. Me, because of who I am, the last descendent of the Maxwell of Traquair. You, because you are a Douglas of Grizelle's line. Don't ask me to explain how I know that. It's enough to tell you that without the two of us seeing this together, the curse wouldn't be over."

"You're beginning to sound like Kate." He sounded exasperated, as if his patience had finally worn to the breaking point. "Come now, Christina. You're an educated woman. You can't really believe in an ancient curse."

"That isn't important. You know as well as I do what will happen once we break it to the world that the stone in Westminster Abbey is a fraud. Teams of archaeologists and geologists and everyone else you can think of will park themselves on our doorstep and dissect our lives and our stories until neither one of us will be able to step outside again."

"It doesn't matter," he countered stubbornly. "This is too valuable an artifact to be covered up and dismissed. It belongs in a museum."

"What about your work? Do you really want your name to be a household word?"

"Don't be ridiculous. This is Scotland, not Hollywood."

I gave up. There was nothing more I could say. "Have it your way," I muttered. "I'm going home to Boston."

"Christina." He reached out to touch my arm. "You can't mean that. What about the baby?"

He said something else, but I no longer heard. I was looking at the stone. The red glow had disappeared. Except for the flashlight, the room was shrouded in darkness. I reached out, groping for the warm granite. There was nothing. I turned back to Ian.

Slowly, he aimed the flashlight in the direction where the stone had been. It was gone. Even the dais had disappeared. Moments passed with the two of us staring at each other in frozen silence. Finally, as if some wordless message had passed between us, we left the way we had come, climbing the stairs to light and life.

❧ EPILOGUE ❧

Traquair House
January 1995

Everything fell into place after that. I never did go back to Boston. Kate Ferguson was committed to a psychiatric hospital. My parents stayed until after the birth of my children and then left for home. Ian was reconciled to my decision to have the babies alone. Out of consideration for me, he had spent much of the last year in Edinburgh with the exception of a short period after the twins were born. His visits were brief but regular, and I had to admit, for a man who knew nothing about babies, he looked very natural holding his black-haired children close to his heart.

Then there are Eileen and John, my children. Twin miracles. It was still hard to believe that I'd given birth to them. Eileen was six months old before I noticed her resemblance to me and even then I probably wouldn't have recognized it if Mother hadn't sent my baby pictures. The likeness between us was uncanny and I suspected that, like her ancestress so many years before, she saw what her brother couldn't.

For hours she would sit in her carrier and watch light play against the shadows, laughing and cooing for no apparent reason. Occasionally, and only for an instant, I thought I saw what she did. A woman with long braided hair and a red gown walking through the heather, creating shapes with her fingers, tickling bare baby toes, and smiling with love. Sometimes, before the children were mobile, I would fall asleep in the garden, stretched out on the grass, the babies beside me, bees droning overhead, knowing that an unseen presence watched over us, guarding us from harm. It was

Mairi's gift to us, the only one she had to give. But it was more than enough. Because of her, we would go on.

If there was an emptiness in my life, if my heart stopped for the briefest of seconds whenever I spotted a tall blond man on the streets of Peebles, I never spoke of it. After all, I had chosen the path I'd taken.

Most of the time, I ignored the ringing door chimes at Traquair House. Curious tourists were always pulling the bell, saying they didn't mean to be a bother but could they please look around. Usually, I instructed the housekeeper to say no. My privacy had become very important to me in the past year. The house was open in the spring and summer for tourists, but the blazing beauty of autumn and the bleak stillness of winter belonged only to me and my children.

Today, however, I anticipated the bell-like sound. The Maxwell family solicitor was due any time. After nearly two years, probate on Ellen Maxwell's estate was over. Although seeing the title in my name was only a formality, it made me feel more official somehow, as if I could move forward with certainty knowing that the house and I belonged together.

I dressed carefully for the occasion in a short, slim-fitting skirt of heather blue with matching tights and pumps, a feminine white blouse, and blue sweater. Waving Mrs. Aames, the housekeeper, back to the kitchen, I smoothed my skirt, walked to the door, and opened it.

Ian Douglas, in all his blond magnificence, stood on the threshold looking down on me. "I hope I'm not intruding," he said formally.

"I am expecting someone." I looked past him to the small compact coming through the gate. "Is anything wrong?" It wasn't like Ian to stop by without calling first.

"There is something I'd like to discuss with you," he admitted, "but it can wait." He hesitated. "May I see the children?"

"Of course." I moved back to allow him inside. "They're in the nursery."

He climbed the stairs, stopping at the landing to call down. "Will you be long?"

"Are you in a hurry?"

Ian watched the lean, athletic-looking figure of the solicitor climb out of his car. "No. Take your time." His voice sounded strangely hollow.

I held the door open. The lawyer was tall and narrow hipped, a man of about forty with black hair and horn-rimmed glasses. He held out his hand. "I'm James Murray, with MacDougall and Finney of Edinburgh." His handshake lasted longer than was normal for mere courtesy.

I led the way into the sitting room. He sat on a long sofa in front of the coffee table. I took the arm chair across from him. "Where is Mr. MacDougall?" I asked.

The man raised one eyebrow in a quizzical arc. "He retired three months ago for medical reasons. I hope that isn't a problem."

"Not at all," I replied, leaning back in the chair. "What did you say your name was?"

"James Murray."

"Are you related to me, Mr. Murray?"

A shock of black hair fell over his forehead. He was busy pulling papers from his briefcase and replied without looking up. "Not that I know of. Murray is a common name in Scotland."

"I suppose so."

He organized the papers into two stacks. "These will need your signature," he said, pointing to one of the piles. "The others are your copies to keep. Take your time reading. If you don't mind, I'll just wander around and look at your magnificent portraits." He nodded toward the painting of Jeanne Maxwell above the mantel. "That one is incredible. Fifteenth century, isn't it?"

"Early sixteenth," I corrected him. "I wouldn't have expected a lawyer to know art."

He turned to look at me, surprise etched into the lines around his mouth. "Barristers aren't cretins, Miss Murray, and I know what I like." He looked at my legs, very visible beneath the brevity of my skirt.

The blood rose in my face. It had been a long time since a man had noticed that I was attractive.

"I apologize if I sounded patronizing," I said hurriedly.

"The portrait is a likeness of my ancestor, Jeanne Maxwell. She married her distant cousin and was mistress of Traquair House in the early sixteenth century." I placed the pen beside the unsigned papers. "Would you like some tea, Mr. Murray?"

"Yes, please." He had a charming smile. "I'd like that very much."

I could have asked Mrs. Aames for the tea, but I needed an excuse to leave the room. My composure was nearly gone. There was something about James Murray that disturbed me. It wasn't an unpleasant disturbance exactly. It was something else, a kind of tension that I'd felt before but couldn't remember the circumstances.

Armed with tea and biscuits, I took a deep breath and walked back into the sitting room. He was standing by the mantel, looking up at Jeanne Maxwell. His coat was off, his tie loosened and shirt rolled up to expose strong wrists and forearms. He turned to look at me. His glasses lay on the table, and from across the room I saw the color of his eyes. They were midnight dark, framed with thick black lashes— legacy of David Murray.

My legs felt like jelly. I was close to losing my grip on the tea tray. Quickly, he crossed the room and rescued the tray from my hands. "Are you unwell, Miss Murray? You look pale."

I stared at him, unable to speak. Without the glasses and formal coat, the likeness was very pronounced. I wondered if he'd ever heard of David Murray. It didn't matter. Nothing mattered except that he was here, and because of him, I knew what it was that I'd been waiting for.

I wet my lips. "Will you excuse me, Mr. Murray? I'd like to look over the papers before I sign. I'll drive them back to your office in the morning."

He frowned. "Is anything wrong?"

My heart was pounding so loudly I could barely hear him. "No, nothing. At least, I don't really know yet. Please. Drink your tea. There is something I need to do immediately."

Leaving the barrister alone and confused, I hurried up the stairs. A peel of low masculine laughter came from the nursery. I hesitated. It was one thing to reach a conclusion in one's own mind but quite another to act on it. Bracing myself, I opened the door and stepped inside.

Ian sat on the floor with a baby on each arm. A musical jack-in-the-box lay on the rug in front of him. He looked up. "Finished already?"

What is it, I wonder, *that makes a woman recognize one man as different from all the others? What is it that allows the two of them to travel a thousand dusty roads before they pass each other, and for a single moment, time is suspended while they glance first and then smile and touch and finally one changes direction and falls in step with the other?*

It was that way with Ian and me. James Murray knew nothing of his heritage, but his presence had awakened something lying dormant within me for over a year. Like Mairi of Shiels, I had been given a choice. I had seen it in the eyes of the man downstairs and again in the one staring at me from across the room with my children in his arms. But I would choose differently than Mairi, for I knew now that Ian was my destiny.

He must have seen what I did for his face changed. "Christina?" There was reverence and awe and more than a little hope in the question that came out as my name.

I smiled and heard the quick, involuntary catch of his breath. Confidence surged through me as I watched him stand and walk across the room to stand before me, the babies still in his arms. I reached out to him and was clasped tightly against a chest that was deep and strong enough to hold the three of us.

When he spoke, his voice wasn't entirely steady. "This last year has been hell for me, Christina. Marry me. Marry me now, please."

I thought of my parents and what they would say if I married without them. I thought of a gray-eyed woman, dead for seven hundred years, who would never hear those words from the man she loved and the regret in the heart of a flaxen-haired man because he could never say them. "Thank you, Mairi," I whispered, "for making this possible for me."

I looked into Ian's eyes. Enough time had been wasted already. "Is tomorrow soon enough?"

The expression on his face was answer enough. There would be questions, of course, and the need for explanations. But that would come later. For now, it was enough just to know that the Maxwell–Murrays had come full circle and that everything would be well.